"I hope you will forgive me," she added suddenly, turning back to him, "if I ask you to kiss me." Then wrapping her arms around his neck, she lifted her face and plastered her mouth to his.

In his dozen years working for the Crown, Rayne had rarely been caught so off guard. But the press of her full lips against his was an utter surprise, one that sent a jolt of pure pleasure rocketing through him.

Her mouth was ripe and warm, as was her body, so once more he reacted on sheer instinct: He returned her kiss with an involuntary hunger.

Her taste was keenly arousing and unexpectedly sweet. Without thought, Rayne increased the pleasure by parting her lips with his thrusting tongue.

At first she stiffened in response, as if startled herself by the novelty of his action. Yet she opened to his exploration, perhaps because she was too stunned to do otherwise.

He might have gone on kissing her for some time if not for the gruff male voice intruding on the intimate moment.

"What the devil is the meaning of this!"

By Nicole Jordan

The Courtship Wars
TO PLEASURE A LADY
TO BED A BEAUTY
TO SEDUCE A BRIDE
TO ROMANCE A CHARMING ROGUE
TO TAME A DANGEROUS LORD

Paradise Series
MASTER OF TEMPTATION
LORD OF SEDUCTION
WICKED FANTASY
FEVER DREAMS

Notorious Series
THE SEDUCTION
THE PASSION
DESIRE
ECSTASY
THE PRINCE OF PLEASURE

Other Novels
THE LOVER
THE WARRIOR
TOUCH ME WITH FIRE

TO TAME A DANGEROUS LORD

A NOVEL

Nicole Jordan

BALLANTINE BOOKS • NEW YORK

Copyright © 2010 by Anne Bushyhead

Excerpt from *To Desire a Wicked Duke* © 2010 by Anne Bushyhead

Published in the United States by Ballantine Books, an imprint of The Random House Publishing Group, a division of Random House, Inc., New York.

BALLANTINE and colophon are registered trademarks of Random House, Inc.

This book contains an excerpt from the forthcoming book *To Desire a Wicked Duke* by Nicole Jordan. This excerpt has been set for this edition only and may not reflect the final content in the forthcoming edition.

ISBN-13: 978-1-61523-929-0

Cover art: Hankins & Tagenberg

Printed in the United States of America

To all my wonderful pals at

TheGoddessBlogs.com

You've made these past few years very special.

Chapter One

I wish you were still here to counsel me, Maman. You never warned me that a man's kiss could be so thrilling, or that a simple embrace could shatter a woman's senses. It was a most startling revelation!

Near London, September 1817

"Of all the dratted ill luck," Madeline Ellis muttered as she peered out the inn's bedchamber window at the dimly lit stableyard below. "First the stage and now Lord Ackerby."

Her heart sank at her worsening predicament. It was vexing enough that the stagecoach carrying her to London had lost a wheel in the middle of a torrential rainstorm this afternoon, stranding her an hour short of her destination, which meant depleting her meager funds on a night's lodging at a posting inn. But now the lecherous Baron Ackerby had somehow found her trail.

Madeline had just retired for bed when she was alerted by the commotion of the baron's traveling chaise arriving in the cobbled yard of The Drake. She could see his lordship's elegantly garbed figure below in the lamplight, could hear his imperious voice giving orders to change his team while he inquired inside.

When his gaze swept upward, Madeline ducked behind the window curtain to avoid being seen.

"This is beyond maddening," she said through gritted teeth.

For years Lord Ackerby had merely hinted at his desire to have her for his mistress, but recently his unwanted advances had become disgustingly overt, and eluding him was proving an exercise in futility.

Madeline winced at the thought of the persistent libertine finding her here. She couldn't believe Ackerby was actually licentious enough to try to ravish her to force her compliance, but even so, she was far too vulnerable in her nightdress and bare feet. Regrettably, though, she had no dressing gown with her, since her trunk was still strapped to the back of the stagecoach. And her cloak was clammy and damp from traipsing down the road in a pouring rain after the wheel mishap. She likely had no time, either, to pull on her muddy half boots. Doubtless the baron would inquire of the innkeep if a lady of her description—medium brown hair, average height, drab attire—had passed this way today. And he would be directed to her bedchamber upstairs, where the flimsy door latch would provide scant deterrence. *Heaven forbid.*

In determination Madeline squared her shoulders. With her employer's recent demise and her brother's untimely departure, she had no one to depend on but herself. *So you might as well take action instead of standing here frozen like a halfwit,* she scolded herself. Besides, she was a soldier's daughter who had learned to be strong and self-sufficient.

"He thinks me defenseless, *Maman,* but he will discover differently," Madeline added as she searched her reticule in the darkness.

She had the admittedly eccentric habit of talking to her late French mother, seeking her unspoken counsel. Jacqueline Ellis was long in her grave, much to the grief of her husband and two children, having been carried off by a deadly ague the winter when Madeline was thirteen. It had been the saddest day of her life. But carrying on imaginary conversations with her dear departed mother made her feel as if *Maman* were still with her.

To Madeline's further sorrow, her father had been killed in the war five years later. And her only remaining family—her younger brother Gerard—had left the district this week, having secretly eloped to Scotland with his childhood sweetheart.

Madeline felt a trifle better when she located her small, single-shot pistol in her reticule. Yet she didn't relish waiting here like a helpless mouse being hunted by a bird of prey.

"And soldier's daughter or not, there is no shame in retreating when the odds are against you," Madeline reminded herself. Papa would have said it wasn't cowardly to flee under such circumstance, merely wise.

After checking that the pistol was primed and loaded, she opened her bedchamber door and peered out. The corridor was empty, she saw in the dim light of a wall sconce.

Slipping from her room, she shut the door quietly and crept down the hall, heading toward the rear of the inn. She could hear laughter and raucous masculine camaraderie from the taproom below as she rounded the corner searching for a place to hide.

To her relief, she saw an open door to what was obviously a parlor rather than a bedchamber. A welcoming fire crackled in the grate, while a low-burning lamp illuminated the near side of the room.

Hearing an ominous tread of footsteps on the staircase behind her, Madeline slipped inside the parlor and took up a defensive position behind the door.

Dismayingly, Baron Ackerby's persistence had only been emboldened three weeks ago when her longtime position as a lady's companion ended with the passing of her elderly employer, a crabby but dear noblewoman. At the moment Madeline was heading to London to seek work at an employment agency, since it was even more imperative now that she find the means to support herself. In championing the course of true love, she'd helped her brother elope to Scotland and had given him all her remaining savings.

Madeline loathed being in such a vulnerable situation, virtually penniless and at the mercy of a powerful, wealthy lord who thought he ruled everything and everyone in proximity to Chelmsford, Essex. She was convinced that Baron Ackerby wanted her chiefly because she had always resisted him. Why else would he pursue a spinster of somewhat plain looks and outspoken wit if not for the challenge of vanquishing her?

Apparently, her stubborn defiance only roused his determination to have her for his mistress. Even so, Madeline could scarcely believe Ackerby's gall when he'd voiced his humiliating proposition outright not two hours after her employer was laid in her grave!

Madeline's bloodlines, too, were a strike against her. The French émigrés in their community were generally poor and had little defense against the whims of the nobility and gentry. Madeline was only half French—her father had been a captain in the British Army and a brilliant intelligence officer serving under General Lord Wellington—but even so, she had little protection now against a lascivious nobleman bent on owning her.

Standing there in the parlor, barefoot and scantily dressed, Madeline shivered. Perhaps she should have wrapped a bed quilt around her to stave off the chill. Even holding her pistol at the ready, she felt vulnerable. She *despised* this feeling of powerlessness. She could feel her heart beating much too rapidly as she wondered what excuse the baron would have given to the innkeep for following her—

Just then the hair on the back of her neck stood up. Evidently she was mistaken about the parlor being empty, for she sensed a threatening presence behind her.

Her heart practically stopped when a man's strong fingers suddenly closed around her wrist like a manacle. Gasping, Madeline whirled to face him, but the next instant he claimed her pistol and hauled her against him. She was jolted by the impact as arms of steel clamped around her body, holding her immobile.

Stunned, she gazed up at her raven-haired captor. He was tall, powerfully built, with a sense of danger about him that was unmistakable. But it was his physical masculine beauty that took her breath away: strong, chiseled features, winged black brows, and dark fringed blue eyes.

Eyes that were pinning her with a deadly look at the moment.

Dear heavens, Maman . . . what have I done? Madeline wondered before silently answering her own question.

Evidently she had jumped from the proverbial frying pan into the fire.

She swallowed hard, wondering if it would benefit her to scream.

Rayne Kenyon, Earl of Haviland, had seen a good deal in his illustrious career with British Intelligence, but it was not every day he encountered a woman garbed only in a nightdress brandishing a pistol.

And to think he was just lamenting again how dull his life had been of late, Rayne reflected as he tightened his hold on the intruder.

He didn't take kindly to the threat of weapons when he was unarmed himself. Besides, the last female to brandish a pistol at him had been a French spy out for his blood. Therefore, when this scantily dressed interloper had barged into the private parlor where he was awaiting the arrival of a relative, his survival instincts had taken over, along with his highly trained reflexes.

But now that he'd disarmed her, a different set of impulses swiftly gained control. His senses registered the lush warmth of her body, the sweet scent of her skin, the luminous shock in her wide gray eyes.

Bloody hell, Rayne thought wryly, clamping down on his urges. It was damned foolish to be lusting after a strange female who might be bent on assassination. Although it was unlikely anyone wanted to kill him just now. His days as a spymaster were long over.

And she looked startled enough that he doubted his assassination was her chief aim.

"I b-beg your pardon," she stammered, her voice

shaken and breathless. "I d-didn't realize this parlor was occupied."

He relaxed his hold a measure, although he kept one arm around her waist while he examined her pistol.

When he saw her eyeing the weapon longingly, Rayne shook his head and lowered the pistol to his side. "I'll keep this, if you please."

"I would not have used it on *you*."

"Then why were you carrying it?"

She went rigid upon hearing footsteps out in the corridor. "Please," she whispered urgently, peering over her shoulder toward the door. "Don't give me away."

She was clearly concerned about whomever was out in the corridor.

"I hope you will forgive me," she added suddenly, turning back to him, "if I ask you to kiss me." Then wrapping her arms around his neck, she lifted her face and plastered her mouth to his.

In his dozen years working for the Crown, Rayne had rarely been caught so off guard. But the press of her full lips against his was an utter surprise, one that sent a jolt of pure pleasure rocketing through him.

Her mouth was ripe and warm, as was her body, so once more he reacted on sheer instinct: He returned her kiss with an involuntary hunger.

Her taste was keenly arousing and unexpectedly sweet. Without thought, Rayne increased the pleasure by parting her lips with his thrusting tongue.

At first she stiffened in response, as if startled herself by the novelty of his action. Yet she opened to his exploration, perhaps because she was too stunned to do otherwise.

He might have gone on kissing her for some time if

not for the gruff male voice intruding on the intimate moment.

"What the devil is the meaning of this!"

To Rayne's regret, the woman in his arms gave a jerk and pulled her mouth away. She was flushed and trembling when she turned to face the newcomer, but under the circumstances her poise was admirable when she said coolly, "Lord Ackerby, what brings you here?"

She obviously knew the tall, auburn-haired gentleman who was pinning her with an intense stare.

"Why, you, of course, Madeline. I heard that you had left Chelmsford to look for employment, so I thought to convey you to London myself."

"That is kind of you, my lord, but I have no need of your assistance."

"Certainly you do. You currently have no income, and no means of transportation."

Her chin raised at a slight angle of defiance. "I can manage on my own. And as you see, I am busy at the moment. I should think even you would realize it is rag-mannered to interrupt a tryst."

The nobleman looked taken aback before his eyes narrowed with skepticism. "You intend me to believe you came here to meet your lover?"

"You may believe what you choose, my lord," she replied sweetly.

It had taken Rayne little time to realize she was pretending a liaison with him in order to thwart her pursuer. Deciding to go along with the charade for the moment and play the part of her lover, he tightened his arm around her waist possessively and drew her closer to him.

"Ackerby, is it? You should heed the lady's wishes. She has no desire for your company."

His face darkening, the nobleman swung his gaze to Rayne. "Just who the devil are you?"

"I am Haviland."

"The Earl of Haviland?" the man asked in apparent recognition.

"Yes."

Rayne's illustrious title gave Ackerby pause. Evidently it was one thing to pursue a defenseless, unemployed woman. It was quite another to challenge a wealthy earl who could clearly take care of himself and her as well.

"You have no business interfering, sir," Ackerby finally retorted.

"But he does," Madeline countered smoothly. "It is *you* who have no claim to me, my lord."

Ackerby's tone turned conciliatory. "I traveled a great distance on your account, Madeline. I am concerned for your welfare."

"Indeed?" Her tone had gone dry. "I hardly think my welfare was your chief motive in following me. But I have told you numerous times, I am not interested in your proposition. Now perhaps you understand why. I already have a protector."

She was more than holding her own, Rayne observed, yet he thought it time to intervene. "I suggest you take your leave, Ackerby, before I am compelled to assist you."

The nobleman was clearly disbelieving about being dismissed—and furious as well. His gaze skewered first Rayne, then the woman.

"You have not heard the last from me," Ackerby warned her before spinning on his heel and stalking out.

She had been holding her breath, but after a long moment, she shuddered in relief.

"Thank you for not giving me away," she murmured, turning her head to gaze up at Rayne. "Truly, I did not mean to trouble you."

"It was no trouble," he replied lightly. "I daresay it flattered my vanity to play your paramour."

Her cheeks warmed to a becoming pink. "I do not usually kiss perfect strangers—or anyone else for that matter." Her attention shifted to the weapon he still held at his side. "May I have my pistol back, please?"

"It depends on how you mean to use it. You'll understand my discomfort at the threat you presented when you suddenly appeared."

Her mouth quirked. "You were never in any real danger from me. I only armed myself in case he tried to accost me. Baron Ackerby has . . . less than honorable designs upon my person."

"So I deduced," Rayne said. "Would you have shot him?"

"I don't imagine so, but I thought it better to be prepared."

"I take it he offered you a position in his bed and you refused?"

She wrinkled her nose. "Certainly I refused. I won't be any man's mistress. Particularly one whose arrogant manner drives me half mad. His conceit will not permit him to accept my refusal. But obviously I underestimated him. I did not expect him to follow me to London." She glanced worriedly at the door again. "I believe I will wait here for a while longer, if you don't mind the intrusion."

"Not in the least, but I should think you would dislike. being alone with a stranger."

That brought her considering gaze back to Rayne. "I will take my chances with you. You appear to be a gentleman."

Rayne returned her regard while drawing his own conclusions about her. She was well-spoken, a lady by the sound of it. Her bearing, too, suggested gentility.

He understood why the baron would want her in his bed. She was not a beauty; in truth, she was rather plain, with square, somewhat masculine features and a sallow complexion. And her hair was a mousy, nondescript brown, which she wore scraped back from her face in a serviceable plait. But her body was another matter altogether. He'd felt her ripe curves hidden by the folds of her practical, unflattering nightdress.

She was a lush armful that he found extremely appealing—

"You may release me now," she said rather breathlessly, interrupting Rayne's lustful thoughts and reminding him that his arm was still draped around her waist.

Strangely he didn't want to let her go, although he did so. "At least tell me your full name." When she hesitated, he added, "I should like to know whom I rescued."

Her mouth curved. "You did not *rescue* me precisely. I believe I can claim the larger credit."

"I see. You're ungrateful now that the danger has passed."

Amusement flashed in her expressive gray eyes, and

Rayne found himself unaccountably intrigued. Since Napoleon's final defeat at Waterloo two years ago, his days of excitement and danger were over, much to his regret. The need for spies to thwart a French tyrant bent on world domination was a relic of the past. And even though Rayne had stretched out his career as long as possible, through the Congress of Vienna when the triumphant powers had divided up Europe and redistributed Boney's territorial claims, he'd been forced to return to England the previous year when he inherited the earldom at his father's passing.

He was utterly bored by the tameness of his current life and the necessity of hunting for a bride. He'd spent the past interminable week at a house party in Brighton as a favor to his grandmother, the dowager Countess Haviland. He'd accompanied Lady Haviland there and intended to escort her back to London at the conclusion, but it had been a relief to escape early because of a desperate summons by his distant cousin, Freddie Lunsford. Rayne was awaiting Freddie now, but this particular lady was also proving a welcome respite.

He had no excuse for not returning her pistol, though. When he handed the weapon to her, she stepped back from him with an expression of relief. "Thank you. I won't inconvenience you further, Lord Haviland."

"You needn't go just yet," Rayne said, laying a hand on her arm when she started to turn away. "A bounder like Ackerby may still be waiting to pounce on you."

"He has left the inn by now . . . I hope." She didn't sound convinced, however. Putting her arms around her thinly clad form, she shivered.

"You are chilled," he noted. "Come stand by the fire."

Apparently she recognized the wisdom of his suggestion, for after another moment's hesitation, she nodded.

Taking her elbow, Rayne guided her into the parlor toward the hearth. On the way, he collected his caped greatcoat, which he'd laid over the end of the sofa, and draped it around her shoulders.

"Thank you," Madeline murmured once more, snuggling into the depths of the fabric and then holding out her hands to the blaze.

When his greatcoat began to slip, Rayne caught it and moved to stand in front of her. Reaching up, he started to close the lapels across her bosom. But then she looked up at him and his altruistic gesture arrested.

The firelight lent a golden glow to her skin and brought out the shining, honey-bright highlights of her hair, Rayne saw. But it was her mouth that most attracted his attention. Red and ripe, it beckoned to him.

Rayne went utterly still, recognizing the primitive sensations streaking through him: possessiveness, hunger, lust. Sexual awareness was suddenly rife between them.

She felt it also, he knew. The tension in her body had returned with a new, sharp-edged tautness he could actually sense.

Madeline shivered again, but not with cold, he suspected. When her lips parted in a wordless inhalation, Rayne couldn't resist, despite his assertions of being a gentleman.

He lowered his head to claim another kiss from her.

She gave a faint gasp at the first potent contact of their mouths, while his own breath quickened at the enticing taste and feel of her. Her lips trembled under his . . . soft, resilient, lush, the texture of silk, although she seemed too stunned to participate in her seduction.

Therefore, he changed the slant of his mouth and took her mouth more thoroughly, insistently coaxing her surrender.

He felt a measure of triumph when her tongue met his almost willingly this time. Raising a hand to cradle her jaw, Rayne angled his head even further and deepened the pressure, the better to drink her in.

Her breath softened to a sigh as their tongues tangled, mated. The tantalizing promise of her response stirred heat and need in Rayne's loins. It didn't help either to know she was naked beneath her nightdress. He could feel his hunger rise the longer he went on kissing her. He felt primed and more than ready to strip off her nightdress and explore the ripe curves of her oh-so-feminine body.

Hearing a warning voice clamoring in his head, Rayne fought the urge to pull her closer. Even so, his hand shifted to her throat, caressing the fine skin above her nightshift's high neckline. He found her pulse thrumming wildly, and when she moaned, the soft sound only sharpened his desire. His greatest longing just now was to cup her full breasts and kindle her pleasure even further, but he wouldn't permit himself to go so far. Instead he allowed his imagination to flourish.

He could picture himself baring the luscious mounds of her breasts. Savoring her taste when he sucked her peaked nipples into his mouth. Stroking his hands down her back to her rounded buttocks. Raising the hem of her nightdress and sliding his fingers between her parted thighs.

She would be hot and wet and ready for him, he knew. A fierce shaft of need arrowed through Rayne as he envisaged lifting her up and plunging into her welcoming heat, locking her legs around his hips as he took her.

He settled instead for embracing her while claiming her mouth, all of his senses focused on the vibrant woman in his arms. Like him, she had become lost in the powerful sensuality flowing between them.

Of her own accord, she moved closer, pressing her breasts flush against his chest, her belly tight against his erection. When she arched against Rayne, his hands went to her hips, holding her supple figure even tighter, molding her softness to his much harder frame. He wanted to seize her, to ravish her, to sink into her—

At last acknowledging the danger of losing his control, Rayne determinedly shackled his need and forced himself to stop. Breaking off his passionate embrace, he lifted his head. Her eyes were closed, he saw, and when he eased back, Madeline swayed weakly.

He caught her shoulders to support her, and her eyes fluttered open. She looked dazed, shaken even.

Staring up at him, she raised her fingers to her lips, as if feeling the burn there. "W-why did you kiss me again?" she whispered, her voice a mere hoarse thread.

He gazed down at her, admiring the alluring picture she made—her cheeks flushed, her lovely eyes wide with shocked arousal, her lips swollen and damp and parted to accommodate her uneven breaths.

The fierce ache in his loins actually increased.

Muttering a silent oath, Rayne shook himself. He couldn't remember the last time a mere kiss had affected him so powerfully, or when his possessive male instincts had been so sharply aroused.

And her question was not one he could answer readily. Why *had* he kissed her? He sure as hell knew better than to take advantage of a defenseless woman's plight, but his honor had escaped him for the moment.

"What if I said I got carried away, playing the role of your lover?" he asked, his voice thicker than he would have liked.

She blinked, as if struggling to come to her senses. Then her eyes narrowed. "But you are *not* my lover."

She was recovering from her daze, he noted, discomfited when she squared her shoulders and tightened her grip on her pistol, although not aiming it directly at him.

Rayne's mouth curved involuntarily. It would serve him right if she decided to pull the trigger, for his raging male impulses had been every bit as licentious as her baron's.

"You needn't fear," he said, attempting to keep his voice light. "I won't touch you again. If I do, you have my leave to shoot me."

He meant what he said, Rayne reflected. Deciding it wiser to remove himself from temptation, though, he retreated to the sofa and settled there, crossing one leg over the other, the better to hide the swollen bulge in his pantaloons.

"Allow me to introduce myself. I am Rayne Kenyon, Earl of Haviland."

She gave a start of recognition. "Kenyon?" she repeated as if surprised by his surname.

"Do you know me?"

"No . . . but I believe you knew my father. Captain David Ellis."

It was Rayne's turn to start. "*You* are his daughter Madeline?"

"Yes."

Rayne stared. Her revelation gave matters an entirely different perspective, since Captain David Ellis was the friend and fellow spy who had once saved his life.

Now he damned well knew he should never have kissed her.

Chapter Two

I never expected aid to come from such a quarter, Maman, and certainly I am grateful. But I am discovering that Lord Haviland can be quite exasperating.

Still half dazed, Madeline regarded Lord Haviland in surprise. She had difficulty focusing her mind on his identity, though, since he'd abducted her wits along with her senses. Her lips throbbed, while heat ribboned throughout her body.

Deplorably, Haviland's sensual assault had bewitched her. For the first time in her life, she understood the joy of being kissed by an expert lover. She'd been thoroughly jolted, shaken down to her toes by this ruggedly beautiful nobleman.

Yet that was not the sole source of her inner turmoil, Madeline knew. It was that she had never imagined feeling such . . . *passion* with a man. Indeed, she found it shocking that she could be so aroused and enchanted.

Even so, that is no excuse to stand here like a tongue-tied moon-calf, she scolded herself.

Attempting to recover her wits, Madeline cleared her throat. "I did not realize you had gained the rank of earl," she said finally, striving for the appearance of composure.

"I came into the title last year." Haviland paused, his features softening as he studied her. "I was terribly saddened by your father's passing. He was a good man and a good friend."

At least the mention of her late father took her mind off that amazing, heart-stopping kiss. Madeline managed a brief smile, despite the sudden lump in her throat. Her father had been her idol, and she'd grieved immensely at his untimely death.

"You were clearly a good friend to him as well, Lord Haviland. Thank you for sending his effects home to us along with his last letter. I cherish those final remembrances of him."

"It was the least I could do. Your father saved my life once, did you know?"

"No, he never mentioned it."

Haviland smiled. "He wouldn't. David Ellis was never one for self-aggrandizement. He often spoke glowingly of you and your brother, however."

"He spoke of you also. He respected you greatly."

Madeline had heard about Rayne Kenyon from other sources in the close-knit émigré community as well. Indeed, he was practically a legend, for he had saved countless lives in service to his country. But he had worked in the diplomatic corps of the Foreign Office, not the military. Her father had reported directly to Wellington and was occupied chiefly with enemy troop movements and supply transports. Haviland, on the other hand, had controlled a network of agents involved in political intrigues—a shadowy world of secrets, betrayals, treachery, and greed. His had been a dangerous business in the battle against French might.

Yet he shrugged off her compliment while his expression turned rueful. "I regret my behavior toward you just now. I never would have kissed you had I known you were Captain Ellis's daughter."

She was glad Haviland hadn't known her identity, for then she would have missed out on his shattering kiss. She doubted she would ever again experience anything so magical. Unconsciously, Madeline found herself gazing at his mouth—the wicked, sensual mouth that had made her breathless and weak-kneed and all too eager to surrender to forbidden passion.

Remembering, she swallowed. "Well . . . thank you for coming to my aid, Lord Haviland. But I should take my leave now."

"Not so quickly, Miss Ellis," he responded, rising from the sofa. "I first want to know how you came to be in such a predicament."

His great height was a trifle intimidating, Madeline thought, resisting the urge to back away as he approached her. Every instinct she possessed screamed that he was dangerous. She stood her ground, however, vexed at herself for feeling so vulnerable. "You needn't involve yourself any further in my affairs."

"But I wish to. I feel some responsibility toward you after what your father did for me."

His implication made Madeline frown. "You most certainly are not responsible for me."

"Then indulge me. I am agog with curiosity. Come, let us sit while you relate your story."

She hesitated, suddenly aware again of her bare feet and scanty attire. "I am not dressed to entertain an interview with a gentleman," she hedged, pulling his greatcoat more tightly around her.

Haviland flashed her a grin. "After our kissing so

thoroughly, I think we may dispense with the usual proprieties, don't you?"

She liked the gleam of humor in his blue eyes but not the determination she saw there, as if he would brook no further protest from her. Suspecting he wouldn't let her go until she explained, though, Madeline sat on the far end of the sofa, while Haviland settled on the other.

Since she didn't want his pity, she didn't linger on the details, merely recounted the most important events of late.

"Until three weeks ago, I earned my living as a lady's companion to an elderly noblewoman, but my employer passed away before writing me a character reference. And without one, it is better to apply in person when seeking work. I meant to visit an employment agency as soon as I reached London, but then the stage broke down and stranded me here for the night."

"Which allowed Lord Ackerby to catch up to you," Haviland concluded.

"Yes." Madeline wrinkled her nose. "To my great regret."

He was studying her again with that same intrigued expression. "You seem to be making light of what could have been a dangerous situation."

She managed a wry smile. "It was only dangerous if I could not handle his lordship. But I was armed, and I am accounted an excellent shot, thanks to my father." Recalling the primed pistol she still held, Madeline set the weapon carefully on the sofa. "I admit I've had a spell of exceedingly bad luck recently, but hopefully it will not last."

"What of your brother?" Haviland asked. "Isn't he old enough by now to protect you?"

The hardening of his tone took her aback. "In age, I suppose he is. Gerard is twenty now, four years younger than I. But he is occupied with more important matters at the moment."

"What could be more important than protecting his sister when she is in dire straits?"

Madeline debated how much to say about her brother's elopement with Lynette Dubonet two days ago. It was not her secret to share, especially since the girl's parents—the Vicomte and Vicomtesse de Vasse—were not even aware of the marriage yet. The aristocratic émigrés were staunchly set against their only child's union to an untitled Englishman whose chief wealth consisted of a modest farm. But Gerard was madly in love with Lynette, and Madeline wanted her brother's happiness more than anything in the world. Thus, she had helped to fund their dash to Gretna Green in Scotland so they could be married over the anvil.

"Gerard is traveling just now," Madeline responded to Haviland's query. "And in his defense, he had no notion that Lord Ackerby would pursue me once I left Chelmsford for London. Neither of us did. I am not dependent on my brother to find genteel employment, however."

"What sort of employment are you seeking?"

She answered readily enough. "I would prefer another post as a companion . . . although I acted more nurse to Lady Talwin this past year. She was frequently in pain, so much of my responsibility consisted of cajoling her to take her medicines and allow a breath of fresh air into her stuffy sickroom. I refused to let her sink into despair. We sparred far more than is usual for a lady and her servant. But our rows seemed to bolster her spirits, if not her failing health."

Madeline smiled sadly at the memory of the dear, crotchety noblewoman. She missed the elderly Lady Talwin and doubted she would find another employer so well matched to her own temperament and mind.

Haviland's heavy brows had lowered as his expression grew thoughtful. "Are there other positions you would consider taking?"

She eyed him curiously, wondering at his persistence. "Perhaps a governess would suit. I am fairly adept with children. I raised my brother from the time I was thirteen, after *Maman* died, since my father was away for much of the year." Her lips twisted with dry humor. "But I may not be acceptable to certain employers. I am known for speaking my mind. Lady Talwin appreciated my tart tongue, for it 'kept her wits sharp,' she was fond of saying. But not all employers are agreeable to having outspoken underlings in their households, particularly noble households."

"And you have no marital expectations at present?"

She gazed at Haviland blankly now, startled by the bluntness of his question. "I beg your pardon?"

"You could marry and solve your financial problems."

"That presumes that I have any reasonable prospects. But gentlemen are not in the habit of proposing to penniless spinsters."

His brows drew together. "Are you penniless then? I should have thought your father would have provided for you."

Madeline stirred uncomfortably on the sofa. "The direction of this conversation has grown rather personal, has it not, my lord?"

Haviland smiled a bit ruefully at her pointed remark. "Forgive me, Miss Ellis. These past dozen years I've spent less time in polite company than most peers. My social manners are not the best. In truth, I am only concerned for your welfare. But rest assured, you needn't worry about Ackerby any further. I will see you safely to London as soon as I conclude my business here at The Drake."

At his disarming apology, her resistance had begun to ease, but Madeline's eyebrows shot up when he added his calm announcement about conveying her to London. "*You* will take me?"

"Yes. My carriage is in the stableyard."

"I cannot travel to London with you, Lord Haviland. For all that you were close to my father, you are a perfect stranger to me."

"No," Haviland countered easily. "Even though we have never met until now, we are certainly not strangers. Come now." His tone lightened, becoming more charming and persuasive than commanding. "You claimed me as your protector a few moments ago. You should allow me to fulfill the role for a while longer."

Madeline flushed in remembrance of her own boldness. "You know I did not mean it. I only wished to dampen Baron Ackerby's ardor."

"Which you did admirably. But I am not in the same league as that lecher. You may trust me, Miss Ellis. There is nothing untoward in my offer. And there is no question about my helping you, either. Your father saved my life. I owe him a debt I can never repay."

Madeline's speechlessness returned as she realized Lord Haviland was truly serious about taking responsibility for her welfare.

When she remained uncustomarily silent, he continued as if musing aloud. "I would invite you to reside with me until you find employment. I have several homes . . . a town house in London, a family seat in Kent, a country villa near Chiswick, and other properties as well. But that obviously won't do, since a single lady cannot properly live with a bachelor. However, there is a quiet hotel in London that is appropriate for gentlewomen," Haviland added before Madeline could respond.

"I'm afraid I could not afford a hotel. I mean to take a room at an inexpensive lodging house."

"I would be happy to fund your stay."

Madeline shook her head firmly. "I will not accept your charity, Lord Haviland."

"It isn't charity in the least. Think of it as my belatedly fulfilling an obligation to a friend."

"Lord Haviland," she said with growing exasperation. "I have always fended for myself, and I mean to do so now."

"Perhaps you have, but these are unusual circumstances."

Straightening her spine, Madeline enunciated slowly, as if he might be hard of hearing. "I assure you, I can manage on my own."

"I have no trouble believing that, but my conscience would give me no peace if I left you to your own devices."

"Your peace of mind is of no great import to me."

Haviland smiled and cocked his head at her. "Has anyone ever suggested that you are too independent for your own good, Miss Ellis?"

She was independent because she'd had to be, yet he gave her no time to say so.

"I admire your determination to be self-sufficient, but it is foolhardy to refuse my help when I am more than willing to give it."

Unexpectedly, Madeline was at a loss for words. Perhaps she *was* being foolhardy in turning down Haviland's offer of assistance. In truth, his kindness brought another unwanted lump to her throat. She was fully accustomed to caring for others, not having someone care for *her,* particularly a near stranger. And she was sorely tempted to rely on the strength that radiated from him.

Despite the temptation, however, she couldn't accept. Not only because of the impropriety, but because she didn't wish to be in his debt. "Thank you, but I cannot accept your largesse."

"Well, I am not letting you go to London on your own." Then Haviland suddenly changed the subject again. "What about teaching?"

Madeline blinked. "What about it?"

"My closest neighbors in Chiswick are three genteel sisters who have recently married. They are looking for suitable replacements to teach at their academy for young ladies. It could be an ideal solution for you. In fact, I can take you to stay tonight with the eldest sister, Arabella, Lady Danvers. I just saw her and Danvers at a house party in Brighton, but they left early, even before I did, to return home to Chiswick. Before that, they were away on their wedding trip for some weeks and needed to see to their obligations."

"I could not possibly allow you to do any such thing."

That gave him pause. "Are you saying you don't want to teach?"

"No, I am not saying that at all. I might like teaching very well. But I cannot just show up on her doorstep un-invited."

"Of course you can. I will vouch for you, so you needn't worry about being turned away. I promise you will be doing Lady Danvers a kindness if you can teach adolescent girls how to become ladies." He held up a hand to forestall her continuing protest. "I am not inviting debate, Miss Ellis."

Madeline's spine stiffened again. "Are you always this overbearing?"

"Are you always this stubborn?"

"Yes!"

His smile moved from his lips to his beautiful eyes. "At least you gave me fair warning. You do indeed speak your mind."

She couldn't help but laugh—although why she should find it amusing to have a nobleman running roughshod over her, she couldn't imagine.

As if sensing that she was wavering, Haviland prod-ded her further. "At least consider my idea, Miss Ellis. I sincerely want to repay my debt to your father, and this will allow me to in some small measure. Besides, you were correct earlier when you said I am a gentleman, and it would not be at all gentlemanly to leave you to the mercy of a bounder when I could easily prevent it."

When Madeline continued to debate with herself, he added provokingly, "Surely you won't refuse just to spare your pride? It is not charity to help find you gain-ful employment."

Pride was indeed a major flaw of hers, Madeline con-ceded. *Maman* had frequently lamented her failing. And admittedly, she was prickly about the need to accept charity. She bit her lower lip, wondering what her *maman* would do in this situation.

"So are we agreed?" Haviland asked, watching her expression.

Madeline raised a hand to her temple. Her head was spinning at the speed with which this man was directing her life. Yet if he merely gave her an introduction to Lady Danvers and secured her an interview for a position as a teacher . . . well, that would not be so bad—

She gave a start when another male voice interrupted her thoughts.

"I say, old chap, I did not realize you were occupied."

At the unexpected arrival of the newcomer, Madeline jumped to her feet, and in the process, Haviland's greatcoat slipped from one shoulder to expose her nightdress.

The rather gangly blond-haired gentleman who had just entered the parlor stopped abruptly to give her an admiring perusal. "Leave it to you to find a willing female to comfort you on a foul night like this, Rayne," he said with a touch of envy in his tone.

Madeline flushed pink as she righted the garment to cover her exposure, while Haviland rose and spoke to the blond man rather sharply. "Stubble your wicked misconjectures, cawker. Miss Ellis is a lady. You merely find her under unfortunate circumstances."

His tone softened as he addressed Madeline. "I beg your pardon, Miss Ellis. This sorry bleater is a distant cousin of mine—the Honorable Mr. Freddie Lunsford."

Mr. Lunsford eyed her skeptically for another moment, then executed a gallant bow and flashed a charming grin. "Do forgive me, Miss Ellis. I frequently eat both of my feet at once. But you can see how I could have misconstrued events."

He seemed sincere, Madeline decided, judging from his earnest tone. So she returned a faint smile. "Yes, indeed, Mr. Lunsford, I quite understand. And it is I who should ask your forgiveness for intruding on your meeting with Lord Haviland."

When she picked up her pistol from the sofa seat, however, Lunsford's blue eyes widened, and it was Haviland's turn to smother a grin. "You will learn it is wise not to provoke Miss Ellis, Freddie."

Lunsford swallowed, and his voice seemed a trifle high when he asked, "You don't mean to shoot anyone, do you, ma'am?"

Madeline gave Haviland a repressive glance before saying sweetly, "I hope the need for shooting has passed, Mr. Lunsford."

There was still a gleam of amusement in Haviland's eyes when he spoke again to his relative. "I know we meant to discuss your situation, Freddie, but I fear our plans will have to change. I must convey Miss Ellis to Chiswick tonight, and it would be best not to arrive too late."

"But time is growing devilish tight, Rayne," Lunsford protested even before Madeline could make her own objection to the scheme.

Haviland held up a hand. "My apologies, old fellow, but Miss Ellis's welfare takes precedence over yours just now since her case is more immediate. I can return here in a few hours—or you may follow us in your carriage and stay the night at Riverwood, which will allow ample time for you to tell me your tale. In any event, it will be morning before I can act, so we will not actually lose any time. Moreover, I'm certain you don't wish to air your grievances in a lady's hearing."

Freddie opened his mouth to speak, then evidently thought better of saying too much in front of Madeline and sighed in resignation. "Very well, I will follow you. But if I cannot deliver within a week, my goose will be well and truly cooked."

"I understand. But it will not come to that, I promise you. Your goose will be quite safe."

Haviland turned to Madeline. "You should return to your chamber and dress, Miss Ellis, while I pay your shot with the innkeep."

She lifted an eyebrow. "I thought I explained my feelings on the subject of charity quite clearly."

"And I thought we agreed not to argue. Do you have any luggage to stow in my carriage?"

Madeline stared at Haviland in disbelief, but he regarded her evenly.

"Have you any luggage to take with you?" he repeated with the cool assurance of a man who inevitably got his way.

"Merely a bandbox. My trunk was still on the stage the last I knew."

"I will have innkeep fetch your trunk and arrange for its delivery to Chiswick."

"Lord Haviland—" she began before his deep voice interrupted in a silken tone.

"Do you need me to escort you to your room, Miss Ellis?"

He was clearly single-minded of purpose, leaving her with the feeling of being swept along in his wake. It was exasperating in the extreme. . . . But still, throwing her lot in with Lord Haviland seemed the best alternative, given her circumstances. She felt safer with him than stranded on her own at a strange inn, although that was not saying much.

Before making her decision, Madeline looked to his cousin. The congenial Mr. Lunsford seemed harmless enough. In fact, his charming manner reminded her somewhat of her brother, Gerard. She was marginally comforted to know Mr. Lunsford would be following them to Chiswick. Yet she didn't relish the prospect of being alone with Lord Haviland in his carriage. Such close proximity would remind her too keenly of his devastating kisses. On the other hand, he was a trusted friend of her father's, so surely she could trust him also.

Madeline found herself giving the same sigh of resignation that his cousin had given. "No, my lord, I do *not* require an escort."

Haviland smiled then, a slow, spellbinding, approving smile that took her breath away. "Good. We will await you here and depart as soon as you are dressed."

Forcing herself to exhale inaudibly, Madeline gave a curt nod to Haviland and a polite curtsy to his relative, then hurried toward the door.

The last thing she heard as she left the parlor was Mr. Lunsford complaining in a half-amused voice. "I suppose you cannot help playing the white knight, Rayne, but need you rescue a distressed damsel just when I need you the most?"

Haviland's response, when it came, was in a similar amused vein. "No, I cannot help myself—and you should be grateful for my compulsion, since you will benefit from it."

"Oh, I am, I am. . . ."

She was grateful to Lord Haviland as well, Madeline decided as she quickly made her way down the corridor to her bedchamber. Yet she couldn't help but worry that by putting her fate in the hands of a nobleman of Haviland's stamp—a dangerous lord whom she found overwhelming and nearly irresistible—she was truly leaping from the frying pan into the flames.

After apologizing once more to a disappointed Freddie for the change in plans, Rayne pulled the bell rope, which brought the innkeeper scurrying to do his bidding. He paid the bills and arranged for Miss Ellis's trunk to be delivered to Riverwood near Chiswick and for his own coach to be readied, then compensated the proprietor handsomely to stifle any urge he might have to gossip. Finally, Rayne settled on the sofa to hear Freddie's tale of woe.

What he learned about his scapegrace relative did not surprise him: Freddie, lamentably, had indulged in a torrid affair with a French widow named Solange Sauville and was now being blackmailed with the love letters he foolishly wrote to her.

"She wants two thousand pounds, devil take her," Freddie lamented. "If I cannot come up with the blunt, she's threatened to go to my father. You must save me, Rayne. Not only will my quarterly allowance be cut off, I'll be banished to the wilds of *Yorkshire*."

It was not an idle threat, Rayne suspected, knowing Freddie's high-stickler sire. If Lord Wainwright learned of his son's rakish escapades with the Frenchwoman, he would doubtless cut him off without a penny.

Thus when Freddie had written and implored him for help, Rayne had willingly extricated himself from the house party in Brighton where he was dancing attendance on his grandmother.

Since their early school days together at Eaton, he'd shielded Freddie from bullies and the sly cruelties that boys perpetrate on one another. It was a habit that continued through Oxford and long into their adulthood— in part because Rayne had always had an outsized protective streak from the time he was a mere youth, but also because he felt obligated by Freddie's connection to his late mother's family. And in truth, Freddie was charming, good-natured, fiercely loyal, and often entertaining, if not overly bright. Furthermore, his cheerful optimism was the perfect antidote to the darkness and death Rayne saw far too frequently in his career.

However, he barely had time to reassure Freddie of his intention to save him from the widow's attempt at blackmail before Madeline Ellis reappeared in the doorway. She had spent little time dressing—doubtless in an effort to be prompt, Rayne suspected.

Scanning her drab attire, however, made him frown. She wore a plain brown cloak and black bonnet that did nothing to enhance her pale complexion, while her black-gloved hands carried a small bandbox in addition to the greatcoat he'd loaned her.

Inexplicably, Rayne couldn't help feeling a measure of guilt that she had fallen on hard times, even though he was certainly not responsible. But his protective streak had asserted itself powerfully in her case. Honor, too, would not permit him to abandon the daughter of the army officer who'd once saved his life. At the very least he intended to shield her from the Baron Ackerbys of the world.

"I am ready, Lord Haviland," she murmured a little breathlessly.

"Then we should be on our way," he answered, rising along with Freddie.

After donning the greatcoat she returned to him, Rayne escorted Miss Ellis down to his waiting carriage. When she stepped out into the chill, foggy night, she shivered—and when he put a hand at her back to guide her to his waiting coach, he realized the likely reason.

"Your cloak is wet through," he commented, his tone holding disapproval.

"Yes. I was caught in a rainstorm this afternoon."

Rayne immediately called to his coachman to stow her bandbox and provide her with a carriage lap robe, then handed her inside. After speaking briefly to Freddie to ensure he would follow them, Rayne settled on the seat opposite her.

She had removed her cloak and bonnet, he saw in the light of the interior lamp, and had wrapped the woolen blanket snugly around her shoulders.

"Thank you," she murmured as the coach began to move. "That was kind of you."

"You needn't keep thanking me, Miss Ellis," Rayne said more sharply than he intended, disliking her gratitude as much as she disliked having to accept it.

She stiffened almost imperceptibly before saying rather tartly, "Very well, I won't."

At her retort, Rayne reminded himself that she was not precisely a damsel in distress. Madeline Ellis was no meek, submissive miss. Indeed, she was feisty and brave and, apparently, every inch her father's daughter.

It was almost amusing that she looked so staid and unassuming, he decided.

"Why the black garb?" he asked about her unbecoming bombazine gown as the well-sprung coach settled into a gently rocking rhythm.

"I am wearing mourning in honor of my late employer," she replied.

Her attire was appropriate to a governess or a companion, he supposed. Additionally, she now wore her hair pulled tightly back from her face in a coiled braid, with no curls to soften the angular lines of her features. The severe effect was rather unbecoming, yet her large gray eyes saved her from being completely plain. And her full, red-ripe lips were sin itself.

Rayne shifted uncomfortably in his seat, remembering the taste of those sensual lips and her ardent response. From outward appearances he never would have guessed such a colorless-looking creature would have such a passionate nature.

He regretted his own lustful physical response to her, however. In the interest of distracting his mind, Rayne decided he might as well occupy the hour-long journey learning more about her.

"Your mother was French, I understand?"

A soft smile curved her lips. "Yes. *Maman*'s parents fled the Revolution and settled near Chelmsford in Essex, a district that is heavily populated with émigrés. She met my father there when he was on leave from the Army, and they were married a fortnight later. It was a case of love at first sight, yet the haste was also necessary since he had to return to his post."

"I thought your father owned a farm."

"He did . . . an inheritance from his late uncle, which was passed down to my brother. But it is neither very large nor very profitable. I lived there until I was eighteen, when my father died, but with Gerard to support and his schooling to fund, I decided to seek outside employment in order to make ends meet. And Lady Talwin's estate was only three miles away."

"Can you not return now to your farm to live?"

"I could, but Gerard has—" She paused suddenly, as if reconsidering what she was about to say.

"He has what?" Rayne prodded.

Miss Ellis shrugged. "He has his own future to see to. And I don't want to burden him when I am perfectly capable of earning my own living."

"Ah, yes," Rayne said lightly. "Your vaunted independence." When she gave him a quelling glance, he added, "It cannot be easy for a lady to make her way in the world alone, which is why I assumed marriage would seem a preferable alternative for you."

That amused gleam returned to her eyes. "How singular that a bachelor such as yourself would be so interested in my marital prospects, Lord Haviland."

In point of fact, he had indeed been thinking of matrimony a great deal of late, since he'd promised his grandmother he would settle down and produce heirs. "Most women of your age are interested in marriage," Rayne replied, keeping the focus of the conversation on her.

"In my position as companion, I had little opportunity to meet any eligible gentlemen. At least not any I would want for my husband. And a good marriage is not readily made if you have neither rank nor fortune to recommend you. It is even more difficult if you lack beauty."

She seemed to hold a pragmatic attitude about her looks and her fortune as well. Miss Ellis ran her gloved hand admiringly over the plush velvet squabs. "I confess I am not accustomed to such luxury. Lady Talwin's carriage was nearly an antique, since she rarely left the house during her last years."

His mouth curved wryly. "It is one advantage of having a wealthy family. My grandmother was an heiress."

Her brow furrowed. "If I may ask, how did a wealthy nobleman's son end up serving in the Foreign Office?"

"I suppose you could say I was the black sheep of my family."

He neglected to mention the boyhood incident that had utterly changed his life, when he'd saved a young thief from arrest and probable hanging. As a consequence, Rayne had received a unique education in the lower classes and the London stews—including the squalor and the criminal elements who resided there—and thus had developed any manner of skills that had served him well later in his chosen profession.

"Did your family approve of your avocation?" she asked when he was silent.

Rayne's mouth twisted with humor. "Not in the least. Spying is not a particularly honorable profession."

"I know. Papa was barely considered a gentleman, even though he was an officer."

"My family preferred to pretend I was off traveling the world, sowing my wild oats. That was how my grandmother in particular explained my frequent absences from England."

"Then why did you choose such a career?"

"The truth is," he replied honestly, "I wanted to make a difference in the world."

She nodded. "That was Papa's sentiment exactly." Madeline's gaze searched his face. "And now? I should think you would miss it after so many years of dedication to a cause."

Rayne felt surprise that she seemed to understand why he found himself at loose ends. It was not that he regretted the war's end. On the contrary, he was infinitely glad to see the last of death, destruction, and deception. Yet he missed his fulfilling life as a spymaster—saving lives, righting injustices, championing the weak, and experiencing daring adventures.

For most of his adult life, he'd been driven by one single overriding purpose—to win the bitter, bloody struggle against Napoleon Bonaparte—and he had yet to find a suitable replacement to fill the emptiness of his days. He still had not grown entirely accustomed, either, to the stark changes he'd faced upon his return to civilian life. Nor had he adapted well to the meaningless social expectations of the ton.

"I do indeed miss it," he said finally, "but my familial obligations take precedence for now. My own father died last year, far earlier than I could have wished. I never wanted to inherit the earldom, but it was my lot since I am an only son."

She smiled. "I suspect there are very few gentlemen who would feel as you do."

"Perhaps so," he agreed congenially.

"I would have preferred to be born a man," she said rather wistfully. "When I was a child I wanted to march off to war and fight evil and tyranny. It was only when I grew older that I realized how terrible war can be." Her voice turned quiet. "My father rarely spoke of his experiences, but the haunted look in his eyes. . . ."

"Your father was an incredibly courageous man," Rayne said softly.

"How did he save your life?"

"He had gained intelligence about a scouting party in

the area where we were traveling and so was more alert than usual when we came upon an ambush. When we were attacked, he startled my horse to one side just as one of the enemy soldiers fired at me. The bullet lodged harmlessly in the tree behind me instead of my head or my chest."

"I am glad you were spared," she said quietly.

She fell silent then, apparently lost in thought, while Rayne's reflections shifted from his past to his future.

He planned to marry to fulfill his duty to his new title but more to appease his persistent grandmother, since the family seat was entailed and would go to Rayne's uncle if he failed to produce an heir.

He wasn't eager to forfeit his bachelorhood or his freedom, but he bore his aging grandmother great affection. Mary Kenyon, the dowager Countess of Haviland, had practically raised him after his mother died in childbirth and so thought of him as her own child. She'd claimed to be on her deathbed and wrung a promise out of him to marry and give the title an heir before she expired of a heart condition, which she'd severely exaggerated.

Rayne was well aware he was being manipulated, but this was the only significant thing his grandmother had ever asked of him. And at three and thirty, it was time he settled down.

And so he had agreed to diligently search for a bride. In fact, he had already interviewed numerous possible candidates, although thus far he'd found none who appealed to him.

He was more than willing to make a marriage of convenience. Indeed, he wanted nothing more intimate, since his one hapless experience with love had cured him of the sentiment entirely.

Abruptly cutting off that line of thought, Rayne glanced over at his companion, aware that the silence between them had drawn out.

Yet it was not uncomfortable in the least. In fact, Rayne greatly appreciated a female who knew how to hold her tongue instead of chattering on and on to fill a gap in the conversation. For all Madeline Ellis's claim to be outspoken, she seemed keen-witted and eminently sensible. Come to think of it, she reminded him of a favorite governess he'd once had who was also inclined to speak her mind and who wasn't afraid to discipline him when he sorely needed it.

Except that never once had he ever entertained thoughts of bedding his former governess the way he did Madeline Ellis.

Remembering her suppleness and womanly warmth, Rayne shifted his position to relieve the pressure at his groin. She might not be a beauty, but her lush figure and kissable mouth had unquestionably stirred his blood.

Her appeal was out of character for him, he acknowledged. Like most men, he was drawn to beautiful women. In the past year since returning from the Continent, he'd indulged his physical needs with temporary liaisons among the demimonde, never frequenting any one Cyprian for more than a few months at a time. He wouldn't risk becoming more intimate, for intimacy invited betrayal.

Perhaps he could be forgiven for mistakenly thinking Miss Ellis a lightskirt when she'd sought refuge in his hired parlor this evening, given that she'd been barely dressed. He knew better now, but deplorably, the urge to have her still teased at his loins.

He wanted her. A dangerous sentiment, considering that she was forbidden to him. He had no business lusting after the spinster daughter of the friend who'd once saved his life when he should be helping and protecting her.

He would not touch her again, Rayne promised himself, forcibly tamping down his carnal desires.

Even so, the temptation would be there. Which was another excellent reason to billet her at Danvers Hall rather than allow her to spend the night in his own home.

He could perhaps have taken her to stay at his grandmother's London residence, but he knew Lady Haviland would not readily welcome a servant into her home as a guest—even an upper-class servant—or relish being reminded of his former indecorous career. Nor, likely, would his elder sister. And his younger sister was in Kent at present, which was too great a distance from Chiswick.

He hadn't realized the passage of time until the carriage slowed to make a turn. Glancing out the window, Rayne recognized the large stone pillars that guarded the entrance to the Danvers estate.

"We are nearly there," he observed.

Miss Ellis gave a start and sat up, looking embarrassed that the rocking motion of the carriage had lulled her into relaxing her straight posture. Reaching for her bonnet, she donned it and began tying the ribbons.

"I believe you called your home in Chiswick 'Riverwood'?" she remarked, peering out the window into the dark night.

"Yes. The property abuts the River Thames, as does Danvers Hall. I only came to the neighborhood this past year, since I wanted a place of my own. My grand-mother resides at Haviland Park in Kent much of the year, and my sisters live nearby. That is too much family for my tastes."

"You have sisters?"

"Two in fact, one older and one younger. They each have two sons of their own, ranging from ages four to twelve. I enjoy my nephews, but they are still rather young and their mothers fear my influence."

Miss Ellis raised an eyebrow, and he could hear the humor in her tone when she responded. "Are you so very dangerous then? Or are your sisters merely inclined to coddle their sons?"

"The latter."

"My brother worshiped my father," she admitted. "If your nephews are anything like Gerard, they adore you as well."

Rayne couldn't deny that the boys seemed extremely fond of him, and he returned their affection. His nephews were one of the brightest spots in his regret-tably dull life these days.

When the carriage finally drew to a halt before the Danvers Hall manor, Rayne handed Miss Ellis down and escorted her up the front entrance steps. She wore her bonnet but carried her damp cloak, and the black bombazine gown did not appear to provide much pro-tection against the chill night air. Rayne had to stifle the urge to wrap her in his greatcoat again. She would have warmth and shelter soon enough.

Once he'd applied the knocker, however, it was some time before an aging butler dressed in a nightcap and dressing robe opened the door and held his candle high to inspect the newcomers. Obviously, the household had already retired for the night.

"My Lord Haviland," the butler greeted Rayne calmly before admitting them to the vast entrance hall.

"Good evening, Simpkin. I should like to speak to Lord and Lady Danvers, if I may."

"Regrettably they are away at present—in London. But they are expected to return sometime tomorrow morning."

"Then I must ask you to do me a service. This is Miss Madeline Ellis, a family friend. She needs lodging for the night, but naturally she cannot reside with me. So I would be obliged if you would put Miss Ellis up for tonight."

"Certainly, my lord," Simpkin replied without batting an eyelash at the uncommon request. "Welcome to Danvers Hall, Miss Ellis," he added with a polite bow. "I will call for Mrs. Simpkin to show you to your room. May I take your cloak and bonnet?"

Miss Ellis, however, held on to her garments, looking chagrined. "I should like a word with you, my lord," she said in an urgent undertone.

When Rayne obliged by drawing her aside a short distance, Madeline gazed up at him in disbelief. "You do not mean to simply leave me here?" she whispered in dismay.

"You have some objection to remaining?"

"Of course I have an objection! I cannot impose myself on people I have never met when they are not even at home."

"You know propriety will be better served if you remain here. And Danvers Hall has ample guest rooms."

"That is hardly the point."

"Do you wish to go home with me?"

She hesitated. "No," she said with obvious reluctance.

"Then I will see you in the morning. As soon as Lady Danvers returns, we will sort out your future employment at her academy."

When Madeline remained there, eyeing him in mingled exasperation and frustration, Rayne smiled, wanting to reassure her. "I am not abandoning you entirely, Miss Ellis. I only live next door, a scant half mile away as the crow flies. If you find you need my protection, you may send a footman to fetch me. But I doubt the daughter of a war hero will need rescuing."

At his deliberate challenge, her gaze narrowed in recognition that he'd used her father against her and impugned her courage in the same breath.

The next instant her spine straightened, just as Rayne had expected it would. Then Madeline shook her head in exasperation, while a reluctant smile twitched at her lips. "Do you always employ your persuasive brand of logic to get your way, Lord Haviland?"

"Frequently. But Mr. and Mrs. Simpkin will take good care of you. Won't you, Simpkin?" he asked in a louder voice.

"Indeed, we will, my lord."

"There, you see, Miss Ellis? Simpkin, don't concern yourself with me. I will see myself out."

He heard Madeline murmur something under her breath as he turned away but didn't pause to investigate. Instead, Rayne returned to his carriage, satisfied that he had made the right decision by stepping in to alter the course of her life.

The drive to Riverwood took little time, yet Freddie

Lunsford was already awaiting him when he arrived. Freddie had always run tame in Rayne's various homes and made free with his liquor, so it was not surprising to find his relative ensconced in his study, sprawled on a sofa, staring morosely into a generous glass of brandy.

"Why the long face?" Rayne asked as he poured his own glass. "I said I would help you."

Freddie barely glanced up. "This is not a long face. This is the depths of despair. You would be despairing, too, if your entire future depended on securing two thousand pounds to pay off a blackmailer."

"You won't be paying off the Widow Sauville."

"No?"

"No. We will get your letters back instead so you may burn them. Otherwise there will be no end to her extortion. She will keep bleeding you dry."

His expression arrested, Freddie sat upright. "Just how do you mean to accomplish the retrieval of my letters?"

"I haven't had time to consider a plan, but I will. Cease fretting, man, and leave me to deal with Madame Sauville."

"By Jove, Rayne, you are a Corinthian. I knew you would not let me down."

Looking more cheerful, Freddie downed the expensive liquor in one long swallow, then shuddered at the effect.

"Sorry, old chap, for doubting you. It is just that I have been at my wits' end ever since learning of that viper's demands. And you were off in Brighton, wooing genteel young ladies at your grandmother's behest. And then, when at last I manage to get word to you and you agree to meet me, I find you playing Sir Galahad."

Freddie shuddered again. Rising to replenish his glass,

he gave Rayne a penetrating glance. "I can scarcely credit that you saddled yourself with a spinster. I should think it the last thing you would want, given that you will soon be leg-shackled to a wife."

"On the contrary, I am looking forward to the diversion," Rayne said in all sincerity.

He was glad to finally have some excitement in his life. He'd been restless and on edge of late, but in the course of an evening, he had acquired two unexpected challenges to deal with.

A spark of anticipation surged through him. He thrived on action, and solving Freddie's dilemma and seeing to Miss Madeline Ellis's welfare was precisely what he needed to harness his restless energy and fill the emptiness in his life.

Furthermore, it would allow him to postpone his search for a bride for a time, and to forget that he had sworn to surrender his much-cherished freedom in order to settle down in matrimony and sire an heir.

Chapter Three

You know I have rarely fretted over my circumstances, Maman, but learning of Lord Haviland's search for a bride makes me wish I had more to offer him.

Madeline woke reluctantly the next morning, enveloped in the remnants of a delicious dream. For much of the night she'd been held spellbound by Rayne Haviland's kisses. Loath to leave the delightful fantasy behind, she raised her fingers to her lips, recalling the stunning sensuality, the simmering heat, the ardent tenderness in his touch. . . .

The lovely sensations suddenly burst as Madeline opened her eyes to the cold light of day.

It took a moment, however, for her to recognize her surroundings: a luxurious guest bedchamber at Danvers Hall. Lord Haviland had abandoned her there unceremoniously last night, to her chagrin. But apparently her subconscious had forgiven him in favor of reveling in his sinful kisses.

Vexed at herself for indulging in fruitless dreams, Madeline sighed and shook off the tantalizing memories, then rose to wash and dress. She was foolish to fantasize about Haviland kissing her. Last evening he had simply mistaken her for a lightskirt and had acted with sheer male lust, taking bold advantage of her presumed availability.

And you responded with unabashed ardor, passionately returning his embrace like any wanton.

Madeline blushed in acknowledgment of her wicked behavior, and yet she couldn't help feeling wistful, knowing she would never again experience anything so enthralling. Haviland had promised it would never happen again, and he was a man of his word . . . to her immense regret.

Muttering a rebuke beneath her breath, she donned her undergarments and then reached for her gown. She wished she had something to wear other than ugly black bombazine—

Immediately Madeline quelled the thought as a pang of conscience struck her.

"I know, *Maman.* I should not be lamenting my lack of pretty clothes when some poor souls have only rags to wear."

She should not be thinking ill of Lord Haviland either, even if his domineering, take-charge manner was more than a little aggravating. And indeed, she *was* grateful for his generosity in rescuing her. She had needed his help last evening. And because of him, her prospects were looking up.

The possibility of changing her occupation from companion to teacher at a young ladies' academy held serious appeal. It would be pleasant to no longer be at the beck and call of a cantankerous elderly mistress, Madeline conceded.

Still, it surprised her that Haviland had put off his own pressing affairs in order to escort her here. Based on her admittedly limited experience with noblemen, she had a rather low opinion of the breed. Quite often, members of the British aristocracy were indolent care-for-nothings.

"But I confess I was impressed with Haviland, *Maman*. Compared to Lord Ackerby, he could not be more different."

Not only was Haviland more honorable, he had worked his entire life—at a dangerous occupation, no less—even though he certainly had not needed to, given his noble bloodlines and family's wealth. And he hadn't seemed to look down his nose at her for working, either. And while she didn't want to feel obliged to him, it was imperative that she find employment soon so she needn't rely on her brother to support her. Gerard should begin his married life unburdened by a spinster sister.

Madeline felt a surge of affection at the thought of her younger brother. Marrying his sweetheart was Gerard's best opportunity for happiness, and she wouldn't deprive him of this chance. Her great hopes for him stemmed in part because she felt responsible for him. Growing up motherless—and for much of each year, fatherless—she and Gerard had only had each other.

It was Madeline's most profound regret that their mother had died so young. But their sadness had only been compounded because afterward, Papa had wrapped himself in his work out of grief.

Their parents had been so deeply in love, and now Gerard was over the moon as well. Madeline couldn't help but envy her brother a little. She had always wanted someone to love, a husband to cherish and grow old with, a tender lover who would give her the children she longed for.

In her wildest dreams she'd envisioned being swept up

into passion and romance. Yet she had never even had a beau. The trouble was, with her rather plain appearance and lack of dowry combined with the demands of her reclusive employer, she had failed to attract any eligible suitors—although infuriatingly enough, she had managed to rouse the unwanted attentions of her lecherous neighbor, Baron Ackerby.

Even so, she yearned for love. Sometimes the feeling was so strong it was a physical ache.

But there was no use dwelling on what she was missing in her life, Madeline sternly reminded herself as she pinned up her brown hair into a simple knot. Moreover, she had more important worries at the moment. The Danvers Hall butler and his housekeeper wife, Mrs. Simpkin, had been unfailingly kind, but Madeline felt exceedingly uncomfortable staying at a noble estate without the owners present.

She intended to call upon Lord Haviland as soon as she finished dressing. Perhaps her trunk had arrived by now, and she needed a change of clothing more suitable to a teacher if she was to have an interview with Lady Danvers later today.

"Otherwise she will think me an old crow, *Maman,* and I will need to impress her if I wish her to hire me for her academy."

Madeline frowned as she surveyed herself in the small oval mirror on the dressing table, aware that her desire to be more attractive was based in large part on another motive altogether.

She wanted to impress Lord Haviland as well as Lady Danvers.

Which was patently absurd. A man of his stamp could have no romantic interest in her—and she had no business fostering any romantic interest in him, for she would be doomed to disappointment.

In truth, though, Haviland was someone she could easily come to love. His kindness, his sharp mind, his sense of humor, and even more, his sense of honor, stirred her admiration every bit as much as his devastating kisses had awed her. The thought of facing him again set butterflies leaping in her stomach.

Madeline took a deep breath, striving for composure. Surely in the light of day the Earl of Haviland would not be as overwhelmingly captivating as she had found him last night.

And even if he was, she should be better able to hold her own with him now that she'd had time to regain her emotional footing and recover her usual practical common sense.

With that hopeful reflection, Madeline turned away from the mirror to go in search of Mr. and Mrs. Simpkin.

"I still worry," Freddie Lunsford complained as he piled his breakfast plate high from the sideboard, "that you underestimate the urgency of my quandary, Rayne. I have very little time left to thwart Mrs. Sauville and prevent her from revealing my transgressions to my father."

"I understand the urgency quite well," Rayne replied absently, his attention more focused on perusing the morning papers.

Freddie settled beside him at the breakfast table but did not appear convinced. "How can you possibly retrieve my letters in time?"

Looking up, Rayne eyed his impatient cousin. Deciding he might better allay Freddie's fears by sharing details of the plan that had started to take shape in his mind, Rayne folded his newspaper and set it aside. "I mean to gain access to the Widow Sauville's London home by attending one of her famous soirées Tuesday evening."

"But Tuesday is four days from now."

"And her deadline is Wednesday. I promise you, the letters will be safely in your possession before then."

"How will you manage it?" Freddie asked, shoveling a forkful of soft-boiled egg into his mouth, followed by a bite of kipper. Evidently the threat of impending disaster had not impaired his appetite much.

"You said Mrs. Sauville claimed to have your letters locked away in her jewel case."

"Yes, in her bedchamber."

"So I will see that she is occupied while I search her bedchamber for her jewel case."

Freddie frowned. "It will not be easy to simply waltz into her boudoir undetected and then waltz out again with my letters. Precisely how do you mean to do it?"

"Why don't you leave the particulars to me—"

Rayne abruptly cut off his reply upon realizing that his majordomo, Bramsley, had appeared at the open door to the breakfast parlor. Directly behind the distinguished servant stood Miss Madeline Ellis.

Rayne was immediately struck by his unexpected pleasure at seeing her again, although he managed to repress the sentiment. Wondering how much she had overheard, he rose politely in welcome as Bramsley announced her.

Freddie leapt to his feet also and finished swallowing

before blurting out, "Miss Ellis, what the devil are you doing here?"

Rayne sent his relative a quelling glance. "Won't you come in, Miss Ellis?"

She hesitated on the threshold, evidently aware that the conversation had instantly stopped at her arrival.

"Have you breakfasted yet?" Rayne asked.

"No, not yet," she replied. "I disliked putting the Danvers staff to the trouble of preparing a meal solely for me."

"Then will you join us?"

Glancing between the two gentlemen, she nodded slowly. "Yes, thank you, Lord Haviland. I believe I will."

"Bramsley, please serve Miss Ellis," Rayne said as he seated her on his left, across from Freddie, then resumed his place at the head of the table.

Looking rueful, Freddie hurried to wipe his mouth with his napkin and sat down again, his fair complexion showing his embarrassment as he fell all over himself to apologize. "I sincerely beg your pardon, Miss Ellis. This is the second time I have chewed my feet upon meeting you. You must think me a clunch."

She smiled gently. "A charming clunch, perhaps. But truthfully, Mr. Lunsford, it is refreshing to encounter a gentleman who doesn't mince words. In fact, you remind me favorably of my younger brother, Gerard. He seems to have a taste for feet as well."

Freddie grinned and looked relieved. "Did you walk all this way from Danvers Hall?" he asked while the majordomo poured her coffee and brought various dishes from the sideboard for her to choose from.

"It was not so far—barely a half mile. I enjoy walking,

and the Danvers housekeeper advised me how to access the path between the two estates. The view of the river is lovely with the autumn colors beginning to show."

Then speaking directly to Rayne, she lowered her voice enough so that Bramsley could not overhear. "I have a serious bone to pick with you, my lord."

Rayne dismissed the majordomo as soon as her plate was served. Bramsley had been with him for many years and could be trusted implicitly, but there was no point in having an audience if Miss Ellis wanted to have it out with him.

As Rayne expected, she waited until the servant was gone before taking him to task. "Mr. Lunsford seems to have developed a knack for apologizing. You could learn from him, my lord."

"Oh?" He observed her over his coffee cup. "Do I owe you an apology, Miss Ellis?"

"You know you do—for abandoning me at Danvers Hall. Granted, you said your social manners are lacking, but even you should realize it is exceedingly gauche to impose on a hostess with no warning."

Her tone was light, her expression quite pleasant, yet Freddie Lunsford's eyebrows shot up. He was not accustomed to seeing the Earl of Haviland subjected to a scolding.

Nor was the earl himself.

Rayne drank a swallow of coffee before replying in a casual drawl, "By now Lady Danvers likely knows to expect less than civilized behavior from me. You can always lay the blame at my door."

Miss Ellis had a ready reply. "But she will expect high standards from me if I am to teach at her academy. I will have to prove myself worthy from the very start. So you see why I would rather not be tarred by your same brush before I even meet her?"

"Indeed, I do see. But will you give me no credit for attempting to protect your reputation?"

She smiled sweetly. "Certainly I will. But for a brilliant spymaster, I expected better from you. You are clever enough to have thought your way out of my dilemma."

"In my own defense, I had to decide on the spur of the moment."

"A rather weak defense, is that not?" she replied, fixing him with her candid gaze. "I confess disappointment that you failed to live up to your vaunted reputation, Lord Haviland."

Rayne had to wonder if Miss Ellis was purposely baiting him. At least her bright eyes suggested she was enjoying putting him on the defensive.

And she continued in that same light vein when she added, "I will contrive to forgive you, my lord. But naturally I could not remain at the Hall this morning. After Lady Danvers arrives home, I would be obliged if you would escort me there and perform the introductions. Until then, I mean to batten myself on you. You *did* make yourself responsible for me, after all."

Rayne inclined his head. "So I did," he agreed with growing amusement. "You are welcome to take refuge here for as long as you like."

"Thank you." Miss Ellis turned back to Freddie as she buttered a scone. "I believe it is I who owes you an apology this time, Mr. Lunsford. I did not mean to overset your plans last evening or to interrupt your conversation with Lord Haviland this morning. Please feel free to continue. I believe you were discussing searching for some letters in a particular lady's boudoir?"

Freddie nearly choked on his eggs, while Rayne had to bite back a laugh. He was certain now that Miss Ellis meant to be provoking, perhaps as retribution for abandoning her last night. And evidently she had overheard his plan to steal Freddie's letters back and drawn her own conclusions.

When Freddie gazed at her in dismay, Miss Ellis smiled in sympathy. "It was clear last evening that you are in a predicament, Mr. Lunsford."

"You could say so," he replied morosely.

"I assume this was an affair of the heart?"

"Well . . . not precisely."

"Then what was it?"

Rayne broke in before Freddie mired himself any deeper. "I suggest you stow it, old son. You always have been too loose-lipped for your own good."

Miss Ellis, however, ignored Rayne's suggestion. "Certainly I don't wish to pry, Mr. Lunsford, but is there any way I may help? I should like to repay Lord Haviland for arranging an employment interview for me, even if I cannot like his high-handed methods."

"Well," Freddie answered, "the thing is . . . this particular female—I cannot call her a lady—is in possession of several letters I wrote to her some months ago. And my father will have my head on a platter if I don't get them back. He would never understand how a chap can get seduced by a pretty face, particularly a pretty *French* face—the old cod's head," he muttered in addition.

Miss Ellis sent Freddie a mock look of reproach. " 'Cod's head'? Surely you do not mean to label your father that disrespectful way?"

Freddie frowned, then narrowed his eyes at her. "Oh,

I say, you are not one of those managing females, are you, Miss Ellis?"

A warm laugh bubbled past her throat. "My brother would say I am—chiefly because it fell to me to run our affairs for many years. If it is any consolation, I can sympathize with your plight, Mr. Lunsford. Gerard is always getting into such scrapes himself . . . and I have often been able to extricate him."

Freddie turned to Rayne. "By jove, I like her!"

"I like you too, sir," Miss Ellis said good-naturedly. "And I am eager to aid you any way I can."

His face lit up. "I am desperate enough to take any help I can get—"

Rayne intervened again, not wanting to involve her in any shady dealings with a blackmailing French widow. "Your aid won't be necessary, Miss Ellis."

His firm tone sent her eyebrow arching upward. "You mean to say that I should not put my nose where it does not belong?"

Rayne's mouth curved. "Your acumen is admirable."

"Very well, but if you change your mind. . . ."

He wouldn't change his mind, Rayne knew, but he was struck by Madeline Ellis's keen intelligence. Freddie had said very little last evening about his circumstances, but she had deduced his predicament with little effort. Some of Rayne's best female agents had possessed her same alert powers of observation. And yet she seemed to be motivated by simple kindness with her offer of help.

Freddie apparently thought she deserved a less harsh rebuff, however, for he hastened to add, "Thank you, Miss Ellis, but Haviland is no doubt correct. He can manage exceedingly well on his own. I have great faith in his abilities to save me from my folly. It is why I turned to him in the first place."

Her lively gaze shifted to survey Rayne. "Lord Haviland seems to make quite a habit of saving people. I suppose that explains why he was so determined to come to my aid last evening?"

"Oh, yes," Freddie answered. "He has been known to rescue any manner of waifs and strays. He cannot help being a hero."

"Is that so?" Her luminous gray eyes were dancing. "How fascinating."

It was clear to Rayne that Madeline and Freddie were finding pleasure in ribbing him.

"Indeed," Freddie continued. "I have always thought Rayne was born in the wrong century. He would have made an admirable knight at King Arthur's Round Table."

"I can imagine him riding on a white charger," she agreed.

Rayne couldn't dispute his cousin's contention. From the time he was a small boy, he'd always been committed to righting wrongs, to defending the weak and vulnerable. He couldn't bear to see injustice and do nothing about it. Doubtless that was what left him so restless now. He was searching for a new mission in life, of course, but thus far he'd found nothing remotely satisfying to occupy his time or talents.

"Yet his derring-do is not all pretense," Freddie declared in an evident attempt at fairness. "He has risked his life countless times over."

Miss Ellis immediately sobered and shot Rayne a rueful look. "So I understand. I should not have made game of you, my lord."

He preferred her laughing at him than looking contrite. "I am hardly a saint."

"I never imagined you were. But still you are to be commended, not ridiculed."

"Pray, remember that the next time you want to take issue with my lack of manners. Now, eat your breakfast, Miss Ellis. Your eggs are growing cold."

His command was a deliberate provocation on his part, and he received the desired response. Her gray eyes sparked before glimmering with humor once more.

"Yes, my lord," she murmured meekly—and then surprisingly did as she was bid.

Her submissiveness was an act that hid her true nature, Rayne knew as he applied himself to his own breakfast. Madeline Ellis was impertinent and tart-tongued and fearless when it came to knowing her place in the ton's social order. And yet he had to admit her lively spirit appealed to him.

Indeed, he found a number of things appealing about Madeline. Her eyes were even lovelier in the morning light, clear and deep and lustrous. And her mouth . . . Rayne found himself watching that sinful mouth as she bit down on a crumpet.

He regretted having a taste of her last evening, though. If he didn't know how pleasurable kissing her could be, he wouldn't be having these unwanted carnal thoughts now.

In truth, his lust surprised him. The glow of firelight was gone now, but he continued to have visions of bedding Madeline. For a moment Rayne's gaze lowered to her full breasts. He could imagine stripping off that ugly black gown and wrapping her luscious body in something softer and more inviting, a rose-hue silk, perhaps.

Or a deep lavender to bring out the depths of those re-markable eyes. . . .

Rayne felt his loins stir with a renewed ache. He would have to keep severe control of himself and his body's forbidden urges in the future.

Even so, he was glad for Madeline's presence in his life. Although he'd rescued her last evening out of a sense of obligation to her late father, he was now set on helping her for his own sake—because his ennui magically disappeared whenever she was present. Therefore, he meant to use his best powers of persuasion to convince Arabella, Lady Danvers, to employ her as a teacher.

He wanted Madeline to remain in the neighborhood so she would continue to enliven his tame existence.

Since Madeline very much wanted to be hired for the academy, it seemed only natural that her nerves were sorely on edge when she finally had the opportunity to interview later that morning. Fortunately, her trunk had arrived at Riverwood so she was able to change into a more suitable gown of dark blue kerseymere.

At Madeline's urging, Lord Haviland properly wrote to Lady Danvers to request an appointment, then drove her to Danvers Hall in his carriage to pay a formal call, an approach far more appropriate than traipsing over the countryside between the two estates.

Upon receiving them in the drawing room, Lady Danvers not only welcomed Madeline with surprising warmth but brushed off any thanks for lodging her for the night. Haviland had been correct on that point as well, Madeline soon realized. Lady Danvers was actively searching for teachers and expressed pleasure that Madeline was interested in a position.

The countess appeared to be about her same age but was quite a beauty—tall and elegant with fair hair that was a pale reddish-gold color, a lady to the core. And yet she seemed quite passionate about the Freemantle Academy for Young Ladies as she discussed the premise.

"I and my two sisters started the academy several years ago with the help of our patroness, Lady Freemantle," Lady Danvers explained. "But we are more a finishing school than a typical boarding school. We teach the daughters of the wealthy working class how to fit into the drawing rooms and ballrooms of the Beau Monde."

"What subjects do you offer?" Madeline asked curiously.

"Most of our pupils have been educated by private governesses, so by the time they come to us, they are usually proficient in the typical subjects, but they lack the polish and grace expected of a lady. So for the final years before they make their comeouts, we instruct them in deportment, manners, speech, conversation, and also genteel accomplishments such as riding and driving, dancing, archery, and how to give musical performances with ease. Our goal is to expose them to the kind of culture and refinement they will find if they marry into the gentility."

Madeline hid a frown, realizing that the curriculum Lady Danvers described was quite different from what she'd expected. But she made no comment as Lady Danvers continued.

"In the past, my sisters and I usually taught at least one class a day, but since we all three married this year, we were required to revise our instruction schedule. Moreover"—the countess smiled softly to herself—"I am in the family way, and after the baby comes next spring, I expect I will have even less time to devote to our academy. We have a headmistress who manages the daily operations of the school. And I recently hired another full-time teacher to oversee most of the classes, plus a close friend of mine also teaches there frequently. But with twenty-seven pupils, we could use someone of your qualifications to supplement our instruction, Miss Ellis."

Madeline decided it was time to speak up. "I am not certain my qualifications match what you need for your academy, Lady Danvers. Growing up, I was privileged to have an excellent governess, so I am well versed in such subjects as drawing, embroidery, history, geography, and even a smattering of accounting, since we owned a farm and I managed the books. But I am not musical in the least, and my knowledge of culture and refinement is severely lacking. I have certainly never moved in your elite circles. The closest I have come to the haute ton is my late employer, Lady Talwin, and during her final years, she was confined to her sickbed."

Lady Danvers smiled. "Miss Ellis, I think you may have a mistaken impression of my own social qualifications. Until this past year, my sisters and I lived under the cloud of a family scandal, so we were utterly shunned by the ton. And since we were virtually penniless, we had to work for our livings. Fortunately, the academy provided us livelihoods and a measure of independence so we were not compelled to wed unless we chose to."

"I see," Madeline said, surprised and relieved by the

countess's confessions of her former modest circumstances. And by her desire for independence as well. Madeline herself had always gnashed at the limiting boundaries that genteel ladies had to face, and she had never wanted to marry simply to survive.

"You are obviously well-spoken and reportedly extremely well-mannered," Lady Danvers added, casting a lively glance at Lord Haviland, who was seated in a wing chair across from them. Their unspoken communication made Madeline surmise that in his message requesting an interview, Haviland had mentioned her insistence on observing proper etiquette. "And if you dealt well with your ill employer, you can likely handle our pupils."

"What would be my responsibilities, do you expect?"

"Haviland says you are fluent in French, so I would like to make the most of your particular skills. Your primary duties would be to teach French and therefore English. In my experience, learning a foreign language improves one's English speech and grammar, which will be vitally important to our students' success in life. And as a teacher, the more enjoyable you can make the process, the more readily your instruction will sink in. Your area of expertise will actually give you a certain cachet with our girls, Miss Ellis. They are wild about French fashions, so if you could somehow procure a handful of magazines from Paris—the equivalent of our *La Belle Ensemble*—they will no doubt worship you."

Her amusement stirred by the countess's wry tone, Madeline finally allowed herself to smile in return. "I believe I can comply, Lady Danvers, since I have numerous connections in the émigré community, many of whom were aristocrats in their own country before the Revolution deprived them of their lands and titles."

"All the better," Lady Danvers replied. "Very well, then. I would like to offer you a position at our academy, Miss Ellis—one class per day to begin with. I can promise you a generous salary, although your employment would be temporary for now. Haviland will vouch for you, but since your late employer failed to supply you a character reference, I'm sure you understand that I would be wise to investigate your background more thoroughly. If you could suggest a list of your former neighbors or other acquaintances, I will write to them immediately. We will make the position permanent once I have had the chance to confirm my initial instincts about you. And of course, you will want to be certain that you enjoy teaching enough to continue."

It was indeed wise, Madeline thought, and only fair. She would be in charge of shaping the lives of over two dozen young women, and Lady Danvers had a responsibility to ensure that their teachers were highly qualified.

Madeline was confident, however, that she would take well to teaching. After serving as a lady's companion for so many years, she was eager for the mental stimulation and social interaction that working at the academy would provide her. And her deficiencies in pretending subservience would not be as great a drawback. Indeed, teaching should suit her best of the few genteel occupations open to her.

"Thank you, my lady," she said sincerely. "I would very much like to accept your offer."

"Excellent. But please, call me Arabella. If you are agreeable, I will take you to visit the academy tomorrow. Our classes on Saturdays are only for half days, so that will be an opportune time to introduce you to your fellow teachers and pupils. I would do so this afternoon, but I am holding a ball here this evening and I need time to prepare."

"That is entirely agreeable," Madeline said, appreciating even more that her new employer had taken time out of her busy schedule to conduct their interview when she had a ball to plan.

"Oh, and you must stay here at Danvers Hall until we get all the details of your employment sorted out and you can find suitable lodging of your own."

Madeline started to refuse the countess's remarkable offer of hospitality, not wanting to impose, but Lord Haviland spoke for the first time in several minutes.

"You can count your lodging here as part of your salary, Miss Ellis," he pointed out, as if knowing exactly what was on her mind. "And you will be doing her ladyship a favor, beginning your duties on such short notice."

"Indeed, you will," the countess agreed.

Not wanting to appear ungrateful, Madeline amended her reply. "You are very generous, Lady Danvers."

"Arabella, please . . . and I hope I may call you Madeline."

"Yes, of course . . . Arabella."

"Ah," Arabella said suddenly, "I should have thought of it. You must attend our ball this evening, Madeline. You may meet our headmistress and other teachers then—except for my youngest sister, Lily, who is traveling in the Mediterranean just now. But my middle sister, Roslyn, has recently returned from her wedding journey and will be there. In fact, Roslyn will be eager to see *you*, Lord Haviland." Arabella glanced at him directly again, this time with unmistakable amusement. "This courtship business can be highly awkward, my lord, can it not?"

"Indeed," he answered dryly.

Not understanding the undercurrents between them, Madeline was surprised to see him shift in his seat, as if uncomfortable with the change of subject.

She was uncomfortable herself, although she was well aware of the reason. Arabella's invitation to the ball was much less welcome than her offer of employment. Madeline had no desire to attend this evening's fête. She knew she could hold her own in society, even though she was accustomed to being considered an upper servant. Yet she lacked the appropriate attire for a ball. Moreover, she had never learned to dance very well and didn't wish to advertise her shortcomings.

"You are quite generous, Arabella, but I feel I must decline. I am not quite ready to appear in society."

"Very well, as you wish. But you will come, Haviland, won't you?" the countess asked.

His hesitation was obvious. "I have a houseguest staying with me at the moment, Lady Danvers, and I shouldn't like to leave Lunsford to his own devices."

"Mr. Frederick Lunsford? We would be pleased to have him as well."

"Then I accept on his behalf." Haviland winced, as if girding himself for an unpleasant task. "I suppose I should look at it as an opportunity."

"Yes. Roslyn will make good use of the occasion." Arabella turned back to Madeline, seeking to explain. "At Haviland's request, I and my sisters have banded together to find him a suitable bride, although Roslyn is chiefly in charge. We have suggested several marital candidates for him, but thus far no one seems to suit him."

Madeline managed a faint smile to hide her dismay, which was absurd. Why in heaven's name should she be dismayed to learn that the Loring sisters were helping the Earl of Haviland search for a bride?

Because you have become foolishly attracted to him yourself, came the unbidden thought.

Of course she had little hope of attaching him, but for one fleeting moment she imagined how wonderful it would be to have Haviland see her as his prospective bride. To be courted by him at the ball tonight. To be kissed by him and enveloped in his stunning passion. . . .

If she were a dreamer, she could let herself indulge in such impossible fantasies. Fortunately, though, Madeline had no time to dwell on her foolish reflections because Arabella rose.

"Now, if you will please excuse me, I must see to the preparations for this evening. My husband had business in London regarding his sister Eleanor's upcoming nuptials, so we were late returning here to the Hall. Haviland, pray make yourself at home," she added as both he and Madeline stood politely. "When you are ready, Madeline, Mrs. Simpkin will help you settle into your rooms. And you will be very welcome at the ball this evening if you change your mind."

Madeline started to thank Arabella again, but Haviland spoke before she could. "I will do my utmost to persuade her to attend."

Realizing that he didn't mean to take his leave just yet, Madeline eyed him warily. She didn't want to be alone with him just now, for she suspected his "persuasion" would be difficult to resist.

Her wariness was justified. As soon as Arabella had gone, he took up the issue again. "Why don't you wish to attend the ball?"

Madeline settled for honesty. "I dislike ostentatious events, for one thing, particularly when I know I will be held under close scrutiny and judged by total strangers who may find me wanting. And I haven't a ball gown, for another."

"I imagine Lady Danvers would readily loan you one of hers."

Madeline gave him a look of reproach. "It is simply not done. And even if it were, we are not the same size."

She felt his masculine gaze appraise her. She was not quite as tall or as slender as Arabella, and she was definitely more buxom, but she couldn't tell from his enigmatic expression what he was thinking.

"You can always have a gown altered," was Haviland's unexpected suggestion.

"Not on such short notice."

"For a price, it can be done."

"A price I cannot afford."

"I could advance you the funds. You can repay me from your first salary."

Madeline stared at him. "You know I will not accept financial support from you, Lord Haviland."

"Ah, yes, your pride rears its head again."

She bit back a retort. Perhaps she *was* a touch oversensitive about accepting charity, yet her feelings were only natural. Of course a man as wealthy and blue-blooded as Haviland would not understand why she would be embarrassed to borrow another lady's gown.

She doubted, however, that his response was solely because he was uncaring and insensitive. More likely it was because he had scant concept of social inferiority since he himself cared little for society.

"It is not only pride," Madeline insisted. "I am not about to accept the loan of a gown from my new employer only to cut it up."

"Well, regardless of how you are dressed, I should like it very much if you would attend tonight."

His tone had suddenly softened, and when he gave Madeline a lazy smile, an unaccountable surge of pleasure warmed her, despite her certainty that Haviland was attempting again to use his charm as a weapon. She couldn't help noting the small laugh lines around his eyes, either. Those lines had been less visible in the dimmer light last evening.

"Your wishes are *not* at issue here, my lord," she retorted, her tone more prickly than he deserved because of her effort to remain indifferent to his appeal.

"I know, but you ought to attend for your own sake—to meet your fellow teachers as well as your new neighbors, since you plan to live here. And I would count it as a favor. I need an ally tonight."

"An ally?"

"I have a decided aversion to debutantes, but I expect to be swarmed by them since word is out that I am in the market for a bride."

Haviland wanted *her* to protect him against the marriageable young ladies who were sure to hound him during the ball?

Madeline had no ready answer. "Do you expect to marry soon?" she asked more weakly than she would have liked.

"If my grandmother has her way, I will." His faint smile was wry. "She was resigned to my 'scapegrace ways,' as she calls them, while my country needed me. But she puts great store in carrying on the family lineage and expects me to produce an heir."

Madeline would be hard-pressed to explain the sinking feeling that revelation aroused. She had no reason to be concerned about Haviland's matrimonial prospects, and no reason to be jealous of the other candidates, either. Yet she stood there tongue-tied for a moment, considering him.

He would have no trouble finding a bride of his choosing, she knew. With his fascinating allure, the most dazzling beauties of the ton would pursue him. That hint of danger about him, combined with that easy, seductive smile, was sure to win female hearts. He would be the object of every woman's most secret dreams . . . or at least *her* secret dreams. And when Haviland gazed at her so intently with those vivid blue eyes, as he was doing now, she wanted to melt.

It was deplorable to think she was developing an infatuation for him, Madeline reflected. She had no desire to do his bidding like any foolish romantic.

Yet she *did* owe him a measure of gratitude for his generosity toward her. And perhaps he would indeed need an ally at the ball this evening. Furthermore, she very much wanted to meet her fellow teachers and the gentry who would be her neighbors in the foreseeable future.

"So will you attend the ball after all, Miss Ellis?"

She could make do, Madeline decided, with her lavender crepe evening gown, the nicest gown she owned.

"Yes," she agreed, hoping she wouldn't regret her acceptance—or further compound her ridiculous attraction to Haviland at an event where she would be out of her element.

"Excellent," he said briskly as if he'd known all along how she would decide, obviously confident in his powers of persuasion. "I look forward to seeing you this evening. Meanwhile, I will have your trunk delivered here to the Hall. But don't hesitate to send a message to Riverwood if you require anything else of me."

With a brief bow, he was gone, leaving Madeline to stand there gazing after him, feeling a profound sense of disappointment. Haviland intended to marry very soon, and she was not a candidate for his bride.

She raised a hand to her temple, wondering at her foolishness. How could she possibly have dashed hopes when she hadn't even been aware such hopes existed? She was nothing like the debutantes he would want for his countess.

Madeline bit her lip hard, acknowledging her despondency. She had rarely allowed herself to regret her plain appearance. Indeed, she had always believed that brains and character were more important than looks. Yet now that she had met the handsome, magnetic Rayne Haviland, she suddenly found herself wishing she were beautiful and stylish and accomplished the way Lady Danvers was.

A sizable dowry wouldn't hurt either. Beauty and fortune might have made her eligible to be on Haviland's list of possible brides.

Turning toward the drawing room door, Madeline tried to quell that ridiculous thought. She wasn't one to view fate through rose-colored glasses. She was pragmatic, practical, sensible, dispassionate. She kept her emotions well-disciplined, locking them down deep inside where they could never hurt.

If she ever felt envious of other women her age who led fulfilling lives with husbands and children and love, well, she always crushed her envy instantly. There was no use pining for what one couldn't have. It would only make her bitter.

And pining after Lord Haviland could only lead to bitterness. She knew very well that he was far beyond her reach.

But still, she couldn't entirely quell her yearning as she forced herself to leave the drawing room with the intention of settling into her temporary lodgings.

Chapter Four

It is fascinating to watch so many beauties attempt to attract Lord Haviland's notice, Maman. I would never behave so shamelessly, yet I cannot help wishing he would look at me as he does the stunning Duchess of Arden.

The ballroom at Danvers Hall glowed with lights from myriad chandeliers, while the extravagant attire of more than a hundred guests heightened the glittering splendor.

Yet for Madeline, the ball was just as uncomfortable as she'd feared it would be. Not only did she feel out of place in this illustrious crowd, but seeing Lord Haviland dance with one beauty after another was entirely too disheartening.

She had watched him for the past half hour without making her presence known to him. She was *not* hiding precisely, Madeline firmly told herself, even though she remained largely concealed from his view by a bank of potted palms. She merely didn't want Haviland to see her looking so dowdy compared to every other lady present. Her high-waisted, puff-sleeved gown of lavender crepe was suitable enough for a country ball, but not for a blue-blooded affair such as this.

The cream of society seemed to be here tonight, perhaps because Danvers Hall was only a half dozen miles from London's wealthy Mayfair district where much of the ton resided when not at their country estates. Haviland himself looked as handsome as sin in a tailored black coat, elaborately tied white cravat, silver embroidered waistcoat, and white satin knee breeches. Indeed, his rugged masculine beauty made every female head turn. Even from across the ballroom, his enormous charisma was apparent. And he appeared to be pouring on the charm with each of his dance partners, although his smile was almost gentle. Madeline suspected he was holding back so as not to frighten any innocent young belles with the dangerous edge of his appeal.

A wolf in sheep's clothing, Maman, she thought as he escorted yet another fawning miss back to her chaperone. Haviland was powerful, cunning, even deadly under certain circumstances, Madeline suspected; in his former profession he would have needed to be.

He was also exciting, tantalizing, and fascinating. And evidently, nearly every woman in the room thought so, too.

The shameless way various beauties were throwing themselves at him made Madeline grind her teeth. Much worse, she herself was not immune to his lordship's appeal. Possibly because she had led a somewhat sheltered life in Essex. Certainly she had never met a man like him before now.

Madeline clenched her jaw, deploring her physical attraction to Haviland. The fact that all those unattached ladies longed to be his countess was yet another reason to crush her infatuation for him. She didn't want to behave like the gushing, giddy debutantes who were bent on pursuing him.

Just then Haviland began a quadrille with Arabella's sister Roslyn, who was now the Duchess of Arden. The duchess was a rare beauty—tall, slender, serenely elegant, with exquisitely delicate features and pale gold hair. She was also very clever and well-educated, according to the Danvers housekeeper, Mrs. Simpkin.

As the beautiful duchess danced with the Earl of Haviland, Madeline couldn't control the stab of envy that assaulted her. They were laughing together as if they were old friends . . . or something even more intimate. And yet from what she had gleaned from Mrs. Simpkin this afternoon, Roslyn was very happy in her recent marriage to her duke and deeply in love.

No doubt the duchess would arrange a dazzling match for Haviland. *But you,* Madeline reminded herself, *will not be on the list of candidates.*

Her heart sank at the thought, even as her conscience scolded her for her foolishness. She would *not* start feeling sorry for herself!

In truth, she didn't consider herself inadequate or inferior to the present company. Yet it was difficult to avoid such natural sentiments, Madeline acknowledged. She looked exactly what she was—a spinster who was required to work for her living, whose shabby gentility stood out among the resplendent guests.

She was an outsider to this world, not only in terms of wealth and bloodlines, but in inclination as well. She'd always chaffed at the pretensions and dictates of society. And on the rare occasions that she did mingle with the ton, she found herself biting her tongue all too frequently. Moreover, to her mind, balls were a frivolous waste of time. She felt a bit useless now with nothing to do and no tasks to occupy her.

And honestly, there was no reason for her to be here. Haviland obviously didn't need her protection as he'd requested. He was handling all his conquests quite well on his own. And Arabella appeared too busy at the moment to introduce her to her fellow teachers.

Madeline had just turned toward the entrance door, intending to retreat from the ballroom, when her name was hailed by a friendly male voice.

Her spirits rose at the sight of Mr. Freddie Lunsford, even though he always seemed to blurt out the first thought that came into his head. "I say, Miss Ellis, what the devil are you doing here, hiding behind the palms? Rayne and I both have been searching for you."

"I am not very fond of balls," she answered frankly, while her heart skipped a beat at the claim that the earl was searching for her. She couldn't credit it, for if that were so, his lordship could have easily found her.

"I don't care much for 'em either," Freddie agreed, tugging slightly at his cravat as he moved to stand beside her. "Too demmed hot and tedious. A fellow has to be on his best behavior at a ball. And I am so flat-footed that I endanger a lady's toes every time I take to the floor. I am better off not dancing, and what fun is a ball if you can't dance?"

"Indeed," she murmured in agreement. "Haviland seems to be enjoying himself, however," Madeline couldn't help saying, glancing at him as he danced with the duchess.

"Oh, no, his enjoyment is only an act," Freddie declared. "He would rather shun balls altogether, with all the grasping young chits fighting over his favor. But he is more eager to get his grandmother off his back by marrying."

"He and the Duchess of Arden seem to be on good terms," Madeline prodded.

"Well, of course. They were neighbors for much of last year. And he courted her before she decided to marry Arden. Nearly dueled over her, in fact."

Madeline felt an inexplicable pressure squeeze her chest. Haviland had lost Roslyn Loring to the Duke of Arden? "When was that?" she asked, her voice holding a deplorable weakness.

"Why, last summer . . . barely a few months ago. I think Rayne proposed to her, too—or so rumor says. But it obviously came to naught."

Madeline wondered if Haviland still pined after the lovely duchess. Probably so, if he'd harbored strong enough feelings for her to propose marriage.

"At least he is finally doing something his grand-mother approves of," Freddie added. "His spy career was a blot on the family ledger, don't you know."

"I can imagine." Madeline hesitated before making a deliberately leading comment. "Haviland said his grandmother expects him to marry and produce an heir."

"Oh, yes. The dowager Countess of Haviland wants him to carry on the title something fierce. And she will likely get her way. She keeps insisting that she is near her last breath. If you ask me, it's blackmail, pure and simple."

"Lord Haviland doesn't really wish to marry?"

"Not precisely. It's not the shackles of matrimony he wants to avoid so much as the chains of the ton. He detests the superficiality of society. But his grandmama is a high-stickler—like my Papa, only a generation older— and believes she can make a proper nobleman out of

Rayne if he marries well. Lady Haviland is badly mistaken, if you want my opinion. Rayne won't change his entire character just to please his grandmama, even if he bends to her wishes regarding marriage."

Freddie gave Madeline no time to reply. Instead he grimaced and launched into another complaint. "But I would not like to be in his boots. If I were he, I would be dragging my heels, trying to make my final moments of freedom last. But not Rayne. For example, there was no need for him to come here tonight. He had a few days' respite from his grandmother's hounding, since she is still at a house party in Brighton given by Lady Beldon. Lady Haviland is a bosom friend of Lady Beldon's, who is Lord Danvers's maternal aunt."

Madeline frowned, trying to follow the tangled relationship, while Freddie gave a mock shudder. " 'Tis utterly frightening, how matrimony seems to be in the air."

"What do you mean?"

"Well, the three Loring sisters all recently wed, you see. And Danvers's younger sister, Lady Eleanor, became betrothed to Viscount Wrexham just this past week. Now Rayne is very likely to be next."

Madeline felt her spirits sink again. "Does he have someone in mind for his bride?" she asked, although not really wanting to know the answer.

She was unaccountably relieved when Freddie shook his head. "Thus far he has only searched among the kind of young ladies his grandmother would find acceptable. But I think he needs to look farther afield, and so I told him just today."

Freddie suddenly gave Madeline a penetrating look, but she was still dwelling on the depressing possibility of

Haviland's marrying soon, as well as wondering about the kind of ladies his grandmother would approve.

She didn't have the requisite beauty and fortune to compete, of course. She was not particularly elegant or ladylike, either, even though she was a gentleman's daughter. Her mother had died much too young, and her father had treated her more as a son than a daughter. Thus, she'd learned a number of masculine skills, which admittedly appealed to her more than the tame diversions young ladies were allowed, but which served her poorly in a ballroom.

Why that thought should dishearten her, Madeline had no idea. A bare three days ago, she had been content with her lot in life. All this talk of Haviland's marriage prospects had evidently unearthed hidden longings she had resolutely repressed.

To hide her dissatisfaction—as well as to distract herself—Madeline turned the conversation to Freddie's predicament. "It seems you are having your own difficult experience with blackmail, Mr. Lunsford."

His face drooped. "Yes, Solange Sauville. She is a French widow who holds a certain cachet in literary circles. I mistakenly let myself be dazzled by her beauty. My father would be appalled to know I have sunk so low, not only because he doesn't condone licentiousness, but also because he particularly dislikes the French."

Madeline's mouth curved faintly; it was a common sentiment among the English aristocracy, disdaining a people who had beheaded their king and queen along with innumerable other nobles merely for the crime of their blue blood. "I am half French myself, actually."

"At least it isn't obvious with you," Freddie said bluntly. "Madame Sauville looks and sounds French. I should never have become involved with her, I know that now. But my father will never believe that I have learned my lesson."

"Do you know yet how you will extricate yourself?"

"On Tuesday evening Rayne means to attend *La Sauville*'s soirée in London in order to steal my letters back."

Madeline gave him a puzzled look. "I overheard you say that the letters are in her bedchamber."

"So she claimed. Rayne hopes to find them there, at any rate."

"Then I wonder if I could be of use after all," she said thoughtfully.

Freddie's eyebrow rose. "How so, Miss Ellis?"

Her gaze fixed on him. "Perhaps I could accompany Lord Haviland to the soirée on Tuesday night—as his guest or perhaps a family friend. He could keep Mrs. Sauville occupied while I search her rooms. I am less likely to be noticed, since I am a woman."

Freddie stared at her a beat before his expression brightened. "Your idea is bang-up clever, Miss Ellis. Rayne could doubtless use a female to help him. He may be a master of disguise, but even he can't look as if he belongs in a strange lady's boudoir. And if you are half French, you will readily fit in at Madame Sauville's elite gathering, since many of her usual guests are émigrés." Freddie paused. "Yet Rayne may not be willing to take you along. He likes to do things his own way."

"You should ask him to allow me to," Madeline remarked. "I would very much like to help you in any way I can."

"By jove, you are a capital sort, Miss Ellis," Freddie exclaimed, beaming.

Madeline found herself returning his smile, but Freddie's next remark took her aback.

"If you succeed in helping Rayne, then you should be rewarded for your efforts."

"Rewarded?" she repeated cautiously.

"You know . . . a monetary remuneration."

Heaven knew her finances were in a sad state, since she'd spent all her savings on her brother's elopement. But she was not about to take Mr. Lunsford's money.

"I do not want a reward," Madeline replied. "I merely want to help ward off your father's retribution, and in some small measure repay Haviland for coming to my rescue."

Freddie looked quizzical, but then he shrugged. "As you wish, Miss Ellis. *I* simply want to retrieve my letters from that she-devil."

He bowed then, and strode off with a jaunty step, looking far more cheerful than he had this morning, but leaving Madeline feeling quite alone again in the crowded ballroom.

She cast another glance at Lord Haviland as he finished the quadrille with the Duchess of Arden. A fresh surge of envy washed through her, along with an inexplicable pain in the vicinity of her heart.

There is no point in my remaining here, Maman, just so I can be miserable, Madeline thought, turning toward the ballroom doors to make a retreat.

Perhaps she would retire to her bedchamber—or better yet, find a pleasant nook in this enormous manor where she could indulge in a bout of melancholy in private.

* * *

"I know that none of the candidates I put forth last month interested you," the lovely Roslyn, Duchess of Arden, told Rayne as their quadrille concluded, "but I have high hopes for this evening. There are at least seven young ladies here you should meet."

"I have danced with three of them," Rayne acknowledged.

"But none of them suit your fancy?"

Rayne managed an apologetic smile. "I am afraid not, your grace. But I appreciate your efforts on my behalf."

The duchess gave him a congenial smile in return. "They may improve upon further acquaintance, but if not, you needn't despair. I am determined to find the ideal bride for you."

Roslyn herself would have made him the ideal wife, Rayne thought as he guided her toward the sidelines. She was well-bred, gracious, and thoroughly versed in the social niceties. She would have made an admirable hostess for balls such as this, and would have pleased his grandmother as well. But Roslyn had rejected his proposal this past summer in favor of her duke.

She wanted love in her marriage, she'd claimed, and Rayne would never have given her love. He'd been physically attracted to her, certainly—what red-blooded man would not? But he hadn't harbored any deeper feelings for Roslyn than admiration and respect, while Arden was head over Hessians in love with her.

Unfortunately, she was vastly superior to every other possibility Rayne had considered over the summer. He couldn't imagine spending the rest of his life with any of the proper, insipid young ladies he had interviewed thus far. Their fawning attempts to impress him only made him want to send them scurrying back to their schoolrooms, where they could spend a few more years maturing from girls into women.

Rayne turned Roslyn over to her new husband and stood conversing a moment with his former rival. Surprisingly enough, there was no lingering hostility between them. He quite liked Drew Moncrief, Duke of Arden, for his keen intelligence and ironic sense of humor. That and his aristocratic demeanor made him a perfect match for his beautiful bride, Roslyn.

Speaking of keen intelligence . . . Rayne glanced around the crowded ballroom, searching for Madeline Ellis. He wondered if he would have to make a foray up to her bedchamber and physically compel her to come down to attend the ball. He didn't care for fêtes such as this any more than she did, but he wanted to help pave her entrance into local society and introduce her to the gentry who would be her new neighbors.

He was looking forward to seeing Madeline for his own sake also. Her company would enliven this dull affair, Rayne knew, feeling a surge of pleasant anticipation.

Just then Freddie Lunsford strolled through the throng, looking highly pleased with himself.

"What has you grinning like a moonling?" Rayne asked when Freddie reached him.

"Miss Ellis. She's a game one. She knows how to put a fellow at ease."

Rayne cocked his head, wondering just how she had won his cousin over. "Only this morning you were calling her a managing female."

"Oh, she is—but in a kind way. I told her about the Widow Sauville's blackmail attempt."

Rayne thought he understood. "She wormed the details out of you, did she?"

"Well, yes. Miss Ellis is rather clever."

"Indeed," Rayne agreed dryly, amused in spite of himself.

"She has volunteered to help you retrieve my letters."

"Is that so?"

"She said you need a female to navigate the widow's lair—and I agree."

Frowning, Rayne shook his head. "You'll recall, she already offered her help this morning and I refused."

"Yes, but that was before she pointed out that being a woman has its benefits. She is more likely than you to get into Madame Sauville's bedchamber undetected. You should let her help, Rayne. Besides, she could use the funds."

"Funds?"

"I offered her a reward if she participates. As a gentleman, I cannot welsh now."

Rayne felt a decided twinge of exasperation. "I told you to let me deal with Mrs. Sauville, Freddie."

"I know, but I thought Miss Ellis raised a good point," his cousin said stubbornly.

"Even so, I don't want to put her at risk if something goes wrong."

That argument at least made Freddie hesitate. "Well, perhaps you are right."

Rayne refrained from replying that of course he was right. Freddie was not entirely witless, merely thoughtless. He often failed to think things through, as opposed to Rayne, who had spent the past decade analyzing possible outcomes of various actions, usually regarding issues of life and death.

Freddie gave a soft, self-deprecating laugh. "I suppose I let Miss Ellis sway me too readily, but she has an easy way about her. . . . When she talks to a chap, she sounds perfectly logical, as reasonable as any man."

"That she does," Rayne agreed.

" 'Tis a pity you cannot choose her," Freddie added almost to himself.

"Choose her for what?"

He angled his head, gazing at Rayne thoughtfully. "For your bride. Since you must marry, Miss Ellis might be a good choice for you."

"I beg your pardon?" Rayne's gaze sharpened on his cousin. "Are you foxed, Freddie?"

"Not a bit of it. Miss Ellis is a comfortable sort, and courageous besides—" He broke off, shaking his head. "Never mind. It was a damn fool notion."

Rayne had gone very still, hiding the range of emotions his relative's offhand suggestion had stirred in him. The chief one was startlement, followed swiftly by intrigue. "No, I want to hear your thoughts on the matter."

Freddie's expression turned sheepish. "You will only laugh."

"I assure you, I won't."

"Well, in truth, Miss Ellis is much too plain to be your countess. On the other hand . . . her lack of looks could be an advantage. She will likely be grateful that you are willing to wed her and solve her financial difficulties. It isn't as if she will have many offers at her age. Spinsters cannot be choosers, you know."

Rayne had no chance to respond since Freddie was evidently warming to his theme. "She likely won't complain of neglect if you seek your pleasures outside the marriage bed. And with her womanly hips, she should be able to bear children easily and thus give you the heir you need to satisfy your grandmother."

Although Rayne disliked his cousin making such intimate observations about Madeline Ellis, he was definitely struck by the idea of wedding her.

"Moreover," Freddie was saying, "she doesn't seem to be the romantic sort, so you needn't worry about her going all daft with love for you."

That was a significant point in her favor, Rayne acknowledged silently, since he was determined that love would play no role in his marriage. He would allow himself no emotional ties with a wife—and wanted none from her either.

"Where is Miss Ellis now?"

Freddie's eyebrows shot up. "Do you mean you might seriously consider my idea?"

"I might. Where can I find her?"

Freddie pointed toward the far end of the ballroom. "A moment ago she had secreted herself over there by those palms, but I don't see her now."

Had she escaped the ballroom? Rayne wondered. If so, he would go in search of her. "A proposal is certainly worth contemplating, but I should first like to speak to her."

Rayne turned toward the row of palms, leaving Freddie to stare after him in incredulous wonder.

His cousin had catalogued the advantages of wedding Madeline Ellis quite accurately, Rayne decided as he traversed the length and breadth of the ballroom in search of her. A marriage between them would achieve several goals: He would fulfill his duty to his title and his promise to his grandmother, in addition to satisfying the personal obligation he still felt toward Madeline's late father for saving his life. As his countess, she would no longer have to scrabble for her living, or be vulnerable to lechers such as Baron Ackerby. And naturally, he would provide financial support for her younger brother.

Of course, judging by his grandmother's standards, Madeline was not the ideal wife for him. She would never move in elite circles the way Roslyn Loring could, for instance. Yet the qualities he sought in a wife were different from those his grandmother wished for him.

Rayne agreed that Madeline's plain appearance was not necessarily a drawback, since beauty was often accompanied by cruelty or vapidness. He prized intelligence and wit far more than appearance, attributes that Madeline had in abundance. And she was spirited enough to keep him challenged.

That, perhaps, was the chief reason the idea was so amenable to him, Rayne realized. Because he'd been looking for a woman who challenged him. With her refreshingly frank manner and provocative wit, Madeline would keep him on his toes. He enjoyed sparring with her, despite her outsized pride and prickly independence—or even because of them.

Another point in her favor was that he could be fairly honest with her, Rayne conceded, since she knew of his past occupation. He wouldn't have to mince words around her, or pretend to be anything but what and who he was.

Her genuine warmth attracted him as well, and he even liked that she was stubbornly self-sufficient. In short, he found Madeline Ellis more interesting and appealing than any of the other obsequious matrimonial candidates he'd been exposed to thus far, and he enjoyed her company significantly more. Moreover, the male fantasies he'd had about bedding her were certainly hotter than any he'd had for other prospective brides.

The thought of taking Madeline to their nuptial bed stirred a distinct surge of pleasure in Rayne's loins. He wanted to see her lovely eyes soft and hazy with passion. He had little doubt that she would welcome his lovemaking with an earthy ardor or that she would make a fiery lover once he taught her whatever skills she currently lacked.

Yet their relationship would be purely physical, he would see to it. There was little danger of his falling in love with Madeline, since she was far from the alluring femme fatale who had once betrayed him.

Betrayal had a way of making a man wary, while having his heart cut out had made Rayne determined to shun love. He was older and wiser now, though, and he was not about to suffer that pain again.

In truth, he was glad that Madeline was no beauty, as Camille Juzet had been, since she was less likely to have another lover waiting in the wings.

A decade ago, during his early career with British Intelligence, Rayne had fallen in love with an alluring French aristocrat who needed his fortune and associations to save her family from danger and bring them all safely from France to England. Camille had used his seduction for her own ends, and afterward, sorrowfully confessed that she was in love with another man, that she'd had no choice but to use Rayne to protect her family.

He no longer felt much anger or bitterness at letting

himself be duped like a callow youth, Rayne acknowledged. But he had no desire ever to repeat his folly or risk his heart again. Therefore, he hadn't balked when his grandmother had pressed him to wed and sire an heir. He was perfectly willing to make a union of convenience with a genteel bride as long as *he* chose the lady he would be shackled to for life.

But do you want to wear those shackles with Madeline Ellis?

Rayne tried to imagine himself wed to her, testing the idea in his mind like a tongue probing a sore tooth. She was certainly the best alternative thus far. And if he settled on her, he could immediately cease looking for a bride.

But could you live with that irrevocable decision?

Concluding that he could, Rayne left the ballroom, intent on finding Madeline Ellis and making her a proposal of marriage.

Chapter Five

I do not know what is more shocking, Maman. Haviland's pursuit of me . . . or my yearning to surrender to his seduction.

Madeline found refuge from her bout of melancholy in an unusual place: the children's nursery.

The largest room was obviously used for teaching, judging by the small desks and the smattering of books and primers for young readers on the shelves, while next door were bedchambers, including one for an adult—probably a nanny or governess or nursemaid. The rooms all were freshly renovated and one had a new wooden cradle, Madeline saw, recalling that Arabella had said she was expecting her first child next spring.

Returning to the schoolroom, Madeline set her candle on a table and went to the window, cracking it open to let in a whiff of fresh air. The room was rather chilly but stuffy from disuse.

Even so, this nursery brought back wistful memories of her own childhood when her mother was still alive. They'd had so many wonderful times together . . . *Maman* teaching her and Gerard to read and do sums and locate on the globe the latest countries where Papa was serving.

Now, however, both her parents were gone, and her brother had married and moved on to a brand-new life without her. She had to make her own future now, all on her own.

Sinking onto the cushioned window seat, Madeline gazed out at the moonlit night. The Thames was down there beyond the terraced gardens, she knew. The scents reminded her of home as well, since their farm was situated on the Chelmer River. However, she could hear faint strains of music from the musicians in the ballroom below, which was strikingly different from home.

Attending the ball had been a mistake, Madeline reflected, since it had only made her feel dispirited. She was better off here, away from the gaiety below, where she could pretend to ignore the certainty that the prime of her life was passing her by. She would never be part of that glittering world—the Beau Monde with its beautiful, wealthy gentility.

And in truth, she didn't want to be. Nor did she want to envy the flirtatious young ladies in their fashionable, expensive gowns and stylish coiffures.

And yet if she were one of their numbers, then Haviland might look at her in a different light. If she could afford flattering gowns to wear and a lady's maid to dress her hair differently—

Stop that at once, Madeline scolded herself angrily. She knew it was futile to let herself dwell on her straitened circumstances.

Just as there was no point in longing for her own children to fill a nursery like this, since she would never marry without love, and finding a husband whom she loved and who loved her in return seemed highly unlikely at this juncture in her life.

"I know, *Maman,* if wishes were horses, then beggars would have mounts to ride. And I can be perfectly content without a horse."

"So this is where you have hidden yourself."

Madeline started at the sound of Haviland's deep male voice. Jumping to her feet, she whirled to face him and inhaled a quick breath at the sight.

The schoolroom suddenly seemed much smaller with him in it, she thought, seeing his tall, muscular form in all its formal glory. He was carrying his own lamp, and in the golden glow, he looked stunningly handsome with his pristine white cravat that contrasted so starkly with his tanned features and raven hair.

He glanced around, then fixed his blue gaze on her as he moved farther into the room. "Were you speaking to someone?"

She flushed, not wanting to admit that she regularly conversed with her late mother. "I sometimes voice my thoughts aloud," she murmured, compromising with a variation of the truth.

He seemed to accept her explanation, or at least he didn't press her further. After leaving his lamp on the same table as her candle, Haviland came to stand before her.

Madeline suddenly felt breathless as she looked up at him.

"You disappoint me, Miss Ellis. I specifically tasked you with rescuing me from a horde of grasping debutantes, but you abandoned me to their tender mercies."

His tone was light, even teasing, yet she couldn't respond in kind. Her wits had gone begging with his close proximity.

"You did not appear to be in need of rescue," she finally managed.

"But I was." He inclined his head toward the school desks. "The nursery? You chose a curious place to hide."

His casual remark pricked her, possibly because he had hit so close to the mark. "I am not *hiding*."

"No? Then why are you here? Because you are not attired in the latest fashion?" His measuring gaze raked slowly down her lavender gown. "You look perfectly acceptable to me."

Madeline's breath faltered altogether at his perusal, but she forced herself to reply. "I told you, I do not care much for balls."

"Nor do I. I dislike the trappings and pretensions of society in general. So much idle pleasure seems frivolous after decades of conflict across the Continent. It has always amazed me that the good denizens of the haute ton seemed insensible to the bloody carnage occurring just across the Channel."

Madeline felt a surge of sympathy at the reminder of how much war and death Haviland must have seen. "True. And I am accustomed to being occupied."

"So am I. But you are not a servant in this household, Miss Ellis. You are a guest, and as such you are entitled to enjoy yourself tonight."

"I know."

He offered no reply but continued regarding her in that searching way, as if he were seeking something in her expression.

As time stretched between them, Madeline began to grow uncomfortable. She wondered how Haviland had managed to find her. But then she remembered; he was a master spy, after all.

"Why are *you* here, my lord? You should be courting your future bride."

He hesitated, then gave a mock wince. "Must you remind me?"

"You are the one who said you planned to use the evening to further your search."

"I thought I deserved a respite. But you disappeared before I could solicit your hand for a waltz."

That took her aback. "You wished to waltz with me?"

"Why does that surprise you? You would make a far more interesting partner than any of the young ladies I danced with tonight."

Madeline stared at him warily. "I do not waltz, my lord."

His expression turned curious. "Why not?"

"I never learned."

"Your education is sorely lacking then."

His observation struck a nerve. "No doubt, but just when would I have had the opportunity to learn to waltz?" she asked. "I have been employed as a companion since it was imported from the Continent two years ago, and in no position to engage a dancing master."

Realizing how peevish she sounded, Madeline softened her tone and managed a wry smile. "Besides, Lady Talwin considered the waltz a vulgar display of hedonism."

Haviland cocked his head, considering her. "You could always play whist. There are two card rooms set up for those who don't care to dance."

She shook her head. "That would not be advisable. I am a sharp at whist."

His mouth curved in amusement, but his response seemed to question her claim. "Indeed?"

"I am not boasting. Lady Talwin and I played many a hand for imaginary pennies, and she loathed it when I failed to give my all. If I were to play here, I would surely win, and I don't wish to fleece Lady Danvers's guests. That is no way to repay her kindness to me."

"I expect not," he agreed, his lips twitching. "Very well, then. Since you cannot play cards, allow me to show you how to waltz."

"*Here?*" she asked, startled.

"What better time? Listen. We even have music."

The lilting sounds of a waltz were indeed filtering through the partially open window, Madeline noted.

"Come," Haviland murmured. "Let me show you."

Her heart leapt as he took a step closer. When he reached for her gloved hands, she stiffened as if afraid of his touch.

Yet she was not afraid of *him* precisely, Madeline vowed silently, allowing him to position her right hand on his shoulder and her left hand in his warm, larger one. She feared her *response* to him.

She was unnerved by the powerful effect Haviland had on her. He merely touched her, and she lost the power to think. She could feel heat radiating off his body as he placed his left palm at her waist and drew her closer.

Yet strangely, he made no move to teach her the proper dance steps. Instead, he simply held her in his light embrace, staring down at her.

Madeline waited, frozen in place, her heart lurching in her chest. She felt as if she were drowning in the depths of his sapphire eyes. His sheer physical presence over-whelmed her senses, while his warmth enveloped her.

Her gaze slid lower to his mouth, that firm, sensual mouth that had given her such pleasure last evening. . . . Heavens, was it only last evening that Haviland had kissed her at the inn?

A fierce longing rose up in Madeline, a craving for him to repeat his stunning assault of her lips. The feeling was so intense, her fingers curled into his shoulder, gripping the superfine of his coat.

"No," she whispered in protest of her own need. "I cannot. . . ."

In a desperate effort to maintain control, she pulled back from his embrace. "I don't care to learn the waltz or any other dance, my lord."

Her action thankfully made him release her, breaking the spell he had cast over her. But when she backed away from him, Madeline forgot that the window seat was directly behind her. As her skirts came up against the wooden panel, her knees literally gave out on her and she sank down onto the cushion.

The impact jarred her, but not as much as what Haviland's gaze was doing to her.

She inhaled a deep breath, striving for composure. Her pulse had yet to quit racing, but she managed to say in an uneven voice, "As it happens, I am glad to have the chance to speak to you, Lord Haviland. I wished to ask you about Freddie Lunsford's missing letters."

He gave her a long look, then moved to sit beside her on the window seat. "I suspected you might."

Madeline tensed but resisted the urge to stand up and flee across the room. She was not *that* much of a weakling.

"Pray proceed, Miss Ellis. I am all attention." His tone quite clearly indicated he was being ironic. He was not at all eager to hear her out.

Madeline forged ahead anyway. "I want to offer my help in retrieving Freddie's letters. Did he not mention my suggestion to you?"

"Regrettably, he did," Haviland answered dryly.

"Then you will allow me to accompany you to Mrs. Sauville's soirée Tuesday evening?"

"Tell me, just how would that help?"

"It should be obvious. As a woman, I will be less noticeable than you would be, sneaking around a widow's house and slipping into bedchambers."

"You might, but I don't want you involved."

"Why not?"

"For one thing, if you were caught, you might find yourself charged with theft and wind up in prison."

He was trying to frighten her away, Madeline surmised. She was certain Haviland would never allow her to be sent to prison. "Then I will take care not to be caught. And even if I were, you will be there to intervene."

"You might be recognized later by one of the widow's guests, have you considered that? If so, your teaching career might suffer."

She hadn't thought of that possible outcome. Teachers needed to conduct themselves with circumspection, and she particularly had to take care, since she was only assured of a temporary position at the Freemantle Academy. And yet she had been tasked with teaching French to her pupils in novel ways in order to engage their interest more effectively.

"But I have a legitimate reason for attending," Madeline mused aloud. "One that Lady Danvers will likely support. Freddie said that a number of Madame Sauville's exiled countrymen will be present at her salon. I can claim that I want to meet some of my mother's people, to interview them about France and Paris and to learn about French fashions for my students, just as Arabella directed."

The suggestion gave Haviland pause, although only briefly. "Perhaps you could, but that is beside the point."

"So you intend to go alone?" she asked skeptically.

"At present that is my plan."

"Have you ever attended one of Mrs. Sauville's soirées before? Won't she be suspicious if you suddenly appear just when she is attempting to blackmail your cousin?"

"She may not be aware of our relationship."

"But what if she is? You don't want to alert her and give her time to hide the letters."

"I will not give her time." When Madeline opened her mouth to argue, Haviland reached up to press his fingers against her lips. "Trust me, I can deal with Mrs. Sauville. And if I judge that I need assistance, I can call on any number of people who are expert at that sort of thing."

She drew back at the physical contact. Despite knowing he expected her to be intimidated by his intimate gesture, she didn't dare risk letting him touch her so brazenly.

"I have no doubt," Madeline said in a dry voice of her own. "You probably know a great many shady characters from your previous occupation."

"That I do."

"Even so, my attendance would provide a good excuse for you to be there, one that Mrs. Sauville could readily accept. I don't see why you will not let me help."

"Because I don't want you endangered in any way. Your father would have my head if he were still alive."

"My father has nothing to do with this."

"He would want me to protect you."

Madeline's chin came up. "I don't relish being treated like a fragile, helpless female, Lord Haviland. I am not made of china."

"I never thought that for one moment."

Giving a doubtful huff, she crossed her arms over her chest, which had the unexpected result of making Haviland glance down at her bosom.

His gaze lingered there for a heartbeat or two before returning to her face. "Why are you so damned insistent on accompanying me?"

Madeline was silent for a moment, not wanting to reveal how badly she wanted to be on more equal footing with Haviland. It was rather humiliating, always having him take care of her. She wanted to help him for a change.

"Because I like to earn my way. And you did me a generous service by helping me to secure a teaching position with Lady Danvers. I would like to repay the favor."

"You will be doing me a service if you stay well out of it." He held up a forbidding hand. "That is enough about Freddie's letters, love. I have another subject I wish to discuss with you."

It exasperated Madeline that he refused even to listen, but she swallowed her protest. She would not give up so easily, yet for the time being, she thought it wiser to allow Haviland to have his way. "Very well, what do you wish to discuss?"

"I want to ask for your hand in marriage."

Madeline stared at him with incomprehension. Surely she had not heard him correctly.

"Will you do me the honor of marrying me, Miss Ellis?" Haviland said more plainly.

A dozen chaotic thoughts streaked through her mind, while a riot of feelings flooded her—disbelief, confusion, elation, suspicion. . . .

She narrowed her eyes. "Are you roasting me, Lord Haviland?"

"Certainly not."

"You cannot possibly be serious," she insisted, her voice rising in pitch. "You want to *marry* me?"

His expression sobered. "I assure you, I am entirely serious, Madeline. I would like to have you for my wife and countess."

He honestly was not jesting, she realized, dumbfounded with astonishment. He could not have shocked her more if he had suddenly offered her the moon on a silver platter.

She parted her lips in an effort at speech, but then shut them again when she realized she had nothing to say. She felt as if the very breath had been knocked out of her.

"Pray contain your enthusiasm," Haviland said dryly.

In response, Madeline scrutinized his face. Was she dreaming? Only moments ago she'd been lamenting the fact that Haviland would never look twice at her, and now he was proposing *marriage*?

She swallowed hard, striving to regain her wits. "You must admit your proposal is extremely far-fetched," she finally rasped.

"It isn't far-fetched in the least. I am in need of a well-bred wife to give me an heir. You need someone to support and protect you. By marrying we can kill two birds with one stone, so to speak."

Her heart sank. So *that* was his motivation. She should have realized his astounding proposal had nothing to do with any growing attachment he felt for her.

"I am not fond of killing birds," Madeline replied distractedly. "Why would anyone wish to harm innocent creatures?"

He laughed softly. "You know that is a figure of speech. And you are evading my question. Will you marry me, Madeline?"

Evading his question even further, she responded with one of her own. "Why ever would you offer for *me*? You could take your pick from half the female population of England."

"I don't want half the female population. I want you."

"*Why?*"

"You have any number of qualities I want in a wife."

"Name a single one."

"I can name several. I feel comfortable around you, for a start."

The joy Madeline had momentarily experienced was swiftly dissolving. "Comfort is a lackluster basis for wedlock."

"It is a good beginning. I cannot say the same for any of the young chits I have considered thus far. And you are not bent on flattering me or attempting to impress me. Believe me, I find that extremely refreshing."

Thankfully, Madeline was recovering from her initial shock. The more Haviland explained his rationale, the less inclined she was to accept.

"I don't believe you are enthralled by my qualities,"

she said flatly. "You are only proposing to fulfill a perceived obligation to my father. But you have already repaid any debt—if indeed there was one—by helping me to find employment."

Haviland hesitated. "It is true that I still feel an obligation toward your father. He saved my life, and that is a debt I can never repay. But I would never let obligation alone determine so serious a decision."

"Well, I won't marry anyone who is proposing from a misplaced sense of guilt."

"And you should not refuse because of a misplaced sense of pride."

Conceding the point, Madeline bit her lower lip. "I doubt my pride is misplaced," she said with an edge of stubbornness. "You consider me an object of charity."

"You are willfully misunderstanding me."

"I believe I understand you perfectly. You want me for a broodmare."

His expression showed a faint trace of exasperation. "You would be my *countess*, Madeline, as well as the mother of my children. With all the advantages of wealth and privilege the title entails."

He made a good point, she admitted, suddenly questioning her wisdom in refusing the Earl of Haviland. This was her very first proposal by the man of her dreams. Why on earth was she not leaping to accept?

Because he had said nothing about love, Madeline reminded herself. Only that he wanted an heir. And he had made his offer in a dispassionate, businesslike manner that had indeed stung her womanly pride.

On the other hand, Haviland could give her the children she longed for. Could she turn down such a tempting proposition? Just a few short days ago she would doubtless have been ecstatic at the chance to have children, but now, unfathomably, she wanted more for her future than a loveless union for the sake of procreating.

Am I mad to want more, Maman?

Perhaps she shouldn't reject Haviland out of hand, though. Perhaps she should give herself more time to consider his tantalizing proposal. . . .

Madeline shook her head, corralling her unruly thoughts. She had come solidly down to earth and meant to remain there.

"I have never sought a title, Lord Haviland. And I don't require a life of leisure. In fact, I would probably loathe it. I am accustomed to working for my living."

"As am I. It is another reason I think we would suit."

"But there are numerous reasons we would *not* suit. We may frequently be at loggerheads."

"That does not concern me. Some men want a dutiful and obedient wife, but I am not one of them." He sent her a soft, persuasive smile. "Think of it as a bargain. You provide me with children in exchange for financial security."

Her frown, Madeline suspected, held all the dismay she was feeling. "That is certainly a cold-blooded way of looking at marriage."

Haviland gave a shrug of his broad shoulders. "We would be making a simple union of convenience. It is done all the time."

"Perhaps in *your* family, but not in mine." Without giving him time to reply, Madeline pressed on. "You could choose any number of ladies to give you an heir, my lord. Indeed, I hear you already have. Freddie Lunsford told me that you wanted to wed Roslyn Loring this past summer."

"Freddie has a loose tongue," Haviland said, grimacing slightly.

"True, but he said only that you courted her, that it was *rumored* you proposed to her. Did you?"

"Yes."

"But she refused your offer? Why?"

"Because there was no love between us. In fact, she was madly in love with Arden." Haviland's gaze suddenly became intent as he observed Madeline. "That is one advantage you have over her. You are not madly in love with another man—are you?"

His tone was surprisingly hard, almost a demand, and Madeline was taken aback. Yet she answered evenly. "No, I am not."

"Then I don't see the difficulty."

She raised her eyes to the ceiling. "The *difficulty,* my lord, is that I don't care to enter into a loveless marriage, either."

When he failed to reply, she glanced up at him. "I still don't believe you truly wish to marry me. If it is not charity, then you are simply acting on impulse."

"Perhaps. I am following my instincts, and my instincts have served me well these past many years."

"They are mistaken in this instance. Come, admit it. You don't *want* to wed me."

His mouth curved. "I admit that you would be doing me an immense kindness if you accept my offer. I could call off my search for a bride and wouldn't have to endure any more vapid debutantes."

She gave a humorless laugh. "Ah, now we get to the heart of the matter."

"I was jesting."

"But I am not."

"Tell me why you don't wish to marry me," he challenged.

Madeline shivered. It was *not* that she didn't want to marry Haviland. On the contrary. He was offering her a future she could only imagine in her wildest dreams. Yet she would be taking an enormous risk by accepting him. So uneven a match—a plain, penniless spinster wedding a handsome, charismatic lord who had no interest in love—would likely lead to unhappiness and even heartache for her.

She was already far too enamored of Haviland. She had never met a man who could fire her passion and inspire her as he did. If she were freely offered any husband in the world, she would choose him without a doubt. He was heroic, compassionate, intelligent, generous, alluring. . . . From the very first he had bowled over her wits and her senses.

And therein lay the trouble. She was much too susceptible to falling in love with him, while her ardor would remain unrequited.

Haviland must have seen her shiver, since he reached back to close and latch the window while he waited for her to gather her thoughts. Madeline was grateful for his consideration, even though the chill seeping into her heart had nothing to do with the night air wafting into the nursery.

When she spoke, however, she tried to keep her response light. "I am idealistic enough to want love in my marriage."

His expression turned enigmatic, his tone cool. "Love is vastly overrated in my experience."

Searching his face, Madeline knew that she had read his sentiments correctly. He obviously did not care about such maudlin emotions as love. Yet she did. Fervently.

Granted, she had never really expected to find the wonderful love her parents had known. And she was prepared to be stoic about her loss. Yet if she wed Haviland now, she would likely be cutting off any hope of true love—and she couldn't bring herself to destroy her dreams just yet.

Madeline had no intention, however, of revealing her deepest yearnings and fears to him.

"You have yet to mention any of my faults," she said instead. "I am far too outspoken, to begin with."

He seemed prepared for that argument. "I can deal with outspokenness. In truth, I find your frankness as refreshing as your honesty."

She had always felt free to speak her mind with Haviland because she'd thought he would never look twice at her. Now, however, she was feeling highly self-conscious.

"But I am much too plain for someone like you, my lord. The fact that you proposed to the Duchess of Arden before you offered for me only proves my point. You are a man. You want beauty in your wife."

"Not necessarily. Beauty like hers can be cause for jealousy and strife. I value loyalty over beauty any day."

Madeline winced, even though she didn't think he meant his remark as a slight. Averting her gaze, she murmured in an offhand way, "If you want loyalty, you should purchase a dog."

He didn't laugh or even smile as she expected. Instead, surprisingly, Haviland placed a finger under her chin and compelled her to look at him. "You have little faith in your feminine appeal, don't you?"

It was unnerving, the way he seemed to know her thoughts. "I see no reason to delude myself."

Haviland's gaze softened. "You may not be considered a ravishing beauty, Madeline, but you are not plain in the least. A liveliness of spirit can make up for any number of physical imperfections."

It was absurd how his words stung when he was only trying to reassure her. And he spoke no less than the truth. She had never been beautiful and never would be.

Hiding her chagrin, Madeline responded with a careless retort, although she was not feeling at all careless. "*Now* who is offering false flattery?"

His reply held a note of seriousness. "I would not insult you by offering you lies. Especially knowing you would not welcome them any more than I do."

She gave a sigh. "It is pointless to continue this discussion, Lord Haviland. I understand that the proper response is to first thank you for your kind offer, but I must refuse."

That made him pause. "You won't even consider it?"

"No." She wouldn't let herself hope, for she would only be cruelly disappointed.

"Still, I would like you to think on it. You needn't make your decision just now. My offer will remain open for a time."

"Until you find another candidate who entices you more than I do," she muttered, unable to keep the bitterness from her tone.

Haviland's gaze fixed intently on her. "I'll have you know, you *do* entice me."

"*Indeed?*" Her tone was not only skeptical but edged with sarcasm.

"Yes, indeed," he said calmly. "You are overlooking one of your prime advantages."

"What advantage?"

"You have a marvelous body."

Suddenly her heart was jumping like mad. Involuntarily, Madeline's gaze locked with his. "How could you know?"

"I have seen you in your nightdress, remember?"

"My nightdress is too concealing for you to have seen much."

"Let me rephrase. I have *felt* you in your nightdress."

Madeline didn't know if she could credit the compliment, yet she couldn't deny that Haviland *seemed* sincere. "I would rather be appreciated for my mind," she finally muttered.

He smiled the beautiful, lazy smile that never failed to hold her spellbound. "I appreciate your mind also, believe me."

She couldn't fool herself that he wanted her, though. Deliberately, Madeline stiffened her spine, determined to resist that seductive smile.

"I see the problem, Lord Haviland," she declared airily. "You cannot credit that I would refuse a wealthy, handsome earl. You are accustomed to having women swoon at your feet. But I am not in the habit of swooning."

"I would be amazed if you were. And you should call me by my given name . . . Rayne."

She tensed when he reached for her gloved hand. "I don't wish to be on such intimate terms with you."

"But I do. And I usually get my way, sweet Madeline."

His eyes had softened with laughter and something else she couldn't name. It looked almost like . . . desire.

She had to be mistaken. Or perhaps it was real and he had manufactured that look to weaken her defenses. If so, it was *extremely* effective.

It was even more effective when he took her gloved hand and brought it to his lips to press a kiss against her knuckles. She could feel the heat even through the fine kidskin.

"I find you to be a most singular woman," he murmured, "and I want you very much."

Madeline herself wanted desperately to snatch her hand away, and yet she couldn't find the strength; he had robbed her of willpower with the slightest touch. And when he slid his other arm around her shoulders, her already racing pulse went wild.

"You do *not* want me, Lord Haviland," she accused in a high, breathless voice. "You are merely trying to persuade me to accept your offer."

"Of course I am trying to persuade you." Abandoning her hand, he reached up to brush her cheek lightly with the backs of his fingers. "As for wanting you . . . I see I will just have to convince you of that also."

She strained away from him, to no avail. Haviland bent his head, letting his mouth hover over hers, heating her lips. When she sucked in a breath of anticipation, he took full advantage and claimed her mouth.

Madeline quivered at the enchanting feel of his kiss . . . the warm, tempting friction, the slow thrust of his tongue. As it tangled with hers, stroking, desire shimmered through her.

His intoxicating mouth was arousing her just as he'd planned. Alarmed by his success, she made one last effort to resist, pressing her palm against his chest, feeling the hard muscles there beneath the rich layers of fabric.

Unexpectedly, her protest resulted in Haviland breaking off his kiss and lifting his head.

"K-kissing me," she rasped in a shaken voice, "will only prove that you are an expert at throwing females into flutters."

"*Am* I throwing you into flutters, sweetheart?"

"You know you are . . . devil take you."

"But I have barely begun."

His voice was teasing but his eyes were hot.

"Lord Haviland . . . you cannot seduce me—"

"I can, love." His hand shifted to her nape, his fingers splaying against her sensitive skin. "Now hush and let me kiss you properly."

He bent and took her lips more forcefully this time, angling his head so that he could go even deeper. Madeline forgot to breathe altogether as a searing rush of heat flooded her. His taste was hot and heady as he drank her in, his mouth coaxing, teasing, possessing.

His devastating kiss went on for an eternity. Her head swimming with pleasure, Madeline was only vaguely aware that both his arms had closed around her, and that she was clinging to him in return. Her fingers clutched at his powerful shoulders to keep her from drowning in the wonderful sensations he stirred in her.

She was even less aware that he had unfastened the hooks at the back of her gown until at last he gave her one final, heart-stealing kiss and raised his head.

"Ah, my sweet Madeline, how can you doubt your delightful charms?"

She opened her eyes, dazed, panting for air.

"You have such lovely eyes," he murmured in a husky rasp, gazing down at her.

His own eyes had grown heavy-lidded and dark with

passion, she realized as his gaze swept lower, over her face.

"And you have the most luscious lips. . . ."

His head dipped so that he could nibble on her lips.

"And your breasts . . ."

He slid the lavender crepe of her bodice down over her shoulders so that her undergarments were exposed. Before she could protest his brazen action, he dealt with the modest neckline of her shift and pulled the edge of her corset down so that the full mounds of her breasts burst free, exposing her bare nipples.

Her skin fairly burned as his heated gaze drank in the sight of her.

"Your breasts are magnificent," he whispered before letting his hand follow his gaze.

She felt the caress of his fingers down her throat and over one ripe swell—and a shameful thrill raced through her when she understood his intent.

Then he cupped her fullness, his touch blatantly possessive, shockingly intimate. She gasped at the sharp sensation spearing through her. His thumb swirled in scorching circles over her nipple, prodding it to a tingling erection. Then bending her back over his arm, he lowered his head again to capture the taut peak in his mouth.

Madeline whimpered and arched against him as he coaxed the pebbled tip with his tongue, laving, stroking, teasing. He was lighting sparks in every nerve ending in her body, kindling hot embers low in her feminine center, deep between her thighs.

After a moment, though, he left off the one breast to attend the other, first scattering hot, open kisses over her flesh, then claiming the nipple. His tongue and lips softly abraded the sensitive bud, alternately suckling and soothing.

The tender, ruthless seduction of his erotic mouth soon had Madeline shuddering with need. She was no longer fighting the ache he roused in her. Instead she gave herself up to the fiery delight of his caresses, straining weakly toward his seeking mouth, her hands caught in his hair, pulling his head closer as she tried hopelessly to ease the longing that welled so fiercely inside her. . . .

Unaccountably, Haviland paused with his mouth hot on her breast. A long heartbeat passed before he left off suckling her.

"Damnation," he muttered thickly under his breath. "What the devil am I about?"

He eased away, staring down at her as if suddenly realizing he had half undressed her—although Madeline was trembling so badly that he had to continue to support her with his arm.

Her fevered senses had difficulty registering that he had halted his wicked attentions, yet she suddenly had no trouble realizing that she was on wanton display for him, sprawled there on the window seat with her clothing in shameful disarray, her naked breasts rising and falling with her uneven breaths.

Her cheeks flushed hotly even before he added almost to himself, "I let myself get carried away by your charms."

He sounded rueful, as if he truly regretted having to control himself. "I had best stop before I forget that I am a gentleman and take you here and now."

Inexplicably, a flood of disappointment washed over Madeline—which left her furious at herself. How in heaven's name could she be disappointed that Haviland had taken his lovemaking no further?

She sat up, shaken, and fumbled with her corset. When she had covered her breasts, she jerked her gown up over her shoulders to make herself decent. But when she would have risen from the window seat, Haviland put a hand on her arm to stay her.

"Allow me to help you dress."

Since he could reach the back of her gown more easily than she, Madeline waited restlessly while he turned her and refastened the hooks. The moment he finished, though, she jumped up and moved away, putting a safer distance between them. She stood there halfway across the room, breathing hard, her chest still rising and falling rapidly as she strove to regain some semblance of composure.

Haviland didn't follow her, thankfully. Instead he remained where he was on the window seat.

When he was silent, Madeline glanced back to find him adjusting the front opening of his breeches. When he smoothed the satin fabric over the swollen bulge at his groin, he grimaced as if he were in pain.

His half smile was definitely rueful when he caught her watching him. "If you doubted your effect on me, darling, you have your proof."

She had obviously aroused him, she realized, her face growing even warmer.

"So, are you ready to accept my proposal yet?" he asked casually.

Was he jesting? Madeline wondered, turning fully to stare at him. Did he honestly expect her to surrender so easily? Haviland had tried to tempt her into agreeing to wed him, exploiting her weakness for him, but she was not quite such a gullible mark.

"You had best return to the ball, my lord, before you are missed," she suggested in a terse voice.

"My name is Rayne."

"Rayne, then. Will you please go?"

"Yes, on one condition."

She eyed him warily. "What condition?"

"That you agree at least to consider my proposal of marriage."

A surge of rebellious defiance swept through her. Haviland was clearly a master of manipulation, determined to have his way. She suspected he wouldn't give up trying to seduce her until he won . . . unless she gave the appearance of yielding.

Attempting to hide her vexation, Madeline tilted her head and regarded him thoughtfully. "I might be willing to *consider* your proposal. At least I won't reject it out of hand. But I have a condition of my own. You will let me accompany you to Mrs. Sauville's soirée Tuesday evening and aid you in retrieving Freddie's letters."

Haviland's gaze narrowed on her. "Freddie was right. You *are* a managing female."

"I never denied it," she pointed out sweetly.

Amusement tugged at his mouth. "You are your father's daughter also, Madeline. You drive a hard bargain."

"I will take that as a compliment, Lord Haviland. But you may address me as *Miss Ellis*."

He still seemed reluctant to let her participate, so she summarized their respective conditions. "You will take me along Tuesday evening and give me a role to play. Who knows? I might actually make you a good accomplice. If nothing else, I can keep Mrs. Sauville occupied while you search for the letters in her rooms. And in exchange, I will give serious deliberation to your offer of marriage."

"Very well," he responded finally.

"Then we are agreed on the terms?"

"Yes." Haviland stood and strode slowly toward her. "But I want another kiss to seal our bargain."

"No!" Madeline exclaimed, holding up her hands and backing away until he halted. "Absolutely not." She couldn't let him touch her again. Her lips still felt the fire of his kisses; her breasts still throbbed with sensation from his brazen caresses.

"Lord Haviland, will you please *go*?" she repeated with more urgency. "Your adoring debutantes will be pining for your attention."

His mouth curved. "No doubt you are right."

He seemed satisfied with his victory for the moment, Madeline thought with relief. His gaze swept over her one last time before he went to the table to fetch his lamp. Then he turned toward the door.

She held her breath, watching his graceful, muscular body until he was gone. Renewed dismay filling her, Madeline brought her fingers up to touch her aching lips. Haviland's seduction had left her aroused and reeling. Worse, she'd just made it easier for his sensual assault to continue by letting him believe she might eventually accept his proposal.

Doubtless she was unwise to leave the matter unresolved. She was probably also unwise to press him to let her help in recovering the letters. The less she had to do with Haviland the better, for she clearly had no willpower where he was concerned.

She couldn't let herself yield to him, though, no matter how stunning his caresses, Madeline warned herself. She couldn't give in to her yearning for him, regardless of how powerfully all her instincts and emotions were protesting.

Surrender would leave her heart much too vulnerable to hurt.

Even now, she realized with a sinking feeling in her stomach, her resolution might be too late, for she was very much afraid she was already falling in love with him.

Chapter Six

Simply being with Haviland is exhilarating, Maman,
which bodes ill for my resolve to refuse his proposal.

"You are *not* in love," Madeline repeatedly told herself over the course of the next few days. "It is impossible to fall in love so abruptly, with a man you scarcely
know."

It is indeed possible, dearest, Maman insisted on arguing. *I did so with your Papa within a few short days of*
meeting him.

Madeline strove to ignore her mother's dissenting
voice. Whatever her feelings for Haviland, she was certain she would be wise to turn down his shocking proposal of marriage.

Yet that didn't mean she could stop dwelling on his
offer during her waking hours or entirely quell the secret
yearnings of her heart. When she slept, her preoccupa-
tion with him was even worse, to her immense frustration. If Haviland had filled her dreams before, his erotic
caresses the night of the ball made her vivid dreams
about him even more potent.

Except in her wildest fantasies, however, Madeline

knew he was not the husband for her. Not when all he wanted was a cold-hearted contractual alliance.

On the other hand, she admitted, he was right on one score: Such an enormous, life-changing decision should be made with careful consideration and not rejected completely out of hand.

Thankfully, she had her immediate future to distract her. Madeline tried her utmost to concentrate on her new employment as she established a routine at Danvers Hall—her temporary lodgings until her situation was completely settled—and learned her duties as a teacher at the Freemantle Academy for Young Ladies.

Arabella was kindness itself on Saturday morning when she took Madeline on a tour of the grounds and buildings. They stopped first at the office to meet Miss Jane Caruthers, the elegant spinster who ran the day-to-day operations of the academy, and the newest teacher, a lively older widow, Mrs. Penelope Melford.

Both ladies were friendly and welcoming, to Madeline's relief, and Arabella promised that the other part-time teacher would be just as pleased to have her on the staff.

"My good friend, Tess Blanchard, is away at a house party just now," Arabella remarked, "but I will have the pleasure of introducing you once she returns. You will like Tess, I am certain."

Arabella went on to explain the school's design as they toured the premises. "Our academy was actually converted from a former country estate so as to prepare our pupils for the varied experiences they will encounter in high society. The majority of classes are held here in the main manor, but we have a smaller, more formal mansion that is representative of a Mayfair residence, complete with a large drawing room and ballroom. We also have our own stable and park to practice outdoor skills, and a dormitory to lodge the students who board here full-time—which includes most of them. And we are fortunate to be close enough to London that we can attend plays and operas so our young ladies can practice their social graces in authentic settings."

"Didn't you say that your sister Lily is away on her wedding journey?" Madeline asked.

"Yes, and she will be gone for several more weeks, so Penelope Melford has taken over teaching Lily's outdoor activities. You will primarily be assuming Roslyn's role, Madeline. I believe she expressed her gratitude to you at the ball last evening. Roslyn is the real scholar among us, although you would not know it to look at her. She hated to abandon her pupils, but Arden's responsibilities with the government require that he remain in London much of the year, so Roslyn will be unable to maintain her normal duties as she would have liked."

Madeline was highly impressed with everything she saw, and by the time they returned to the main manor, the students had finished breakfasting and had begun Mrs. Melford's class on conversation.

The widow had a natural charm that made her instruction extremely enjoyable. Thus, at the conclusion of the class, Madeline tried to adopt that same pleasant demeanor when Arabella introduced her.

The young ladies showed only polite interest until Madeline's French origins were revealed, and then they paid avid attention to every word she spoke, eagerly peppering her with questions—which not only boded well for her reception but gave her some ideas about how she might approach her own classes that were to begin on Monday morning.

Upon returning to Danvers Hall, Madeline devoted the afternoon to preparing her lesson on French grammar and vocabulary, an exercise that made her lament the poor references she had at her disposal.

On Sunday, she attended service at the village church and accepted an invitation afterward to take luncheon with Miss Caruthers and Mrs. Melford, where they discussed the importance of Madeline's classes and how to increase their effectiveness.

"You see, Miss Ellis," Jane Caruthers explained, "we believe that learning correct pronunciation of a foreign language will give our young ladies better command of their own native tongue, and speaking English with proper accents will help them go much further in society—or at the very least, help them avoid automatically being labeled as coming from the lower classes."

"I understand," Madeline replied, recognizing Arabella's theory, "and I completely agree. But I hope to find a better French primer than the one our pupils now use."

Miss Caruthers nodded in approval. "An excellent idea. You might try Hatchard's bookshop in London. They have the largest selection of books anywhere. And of course, the academy will fund any purchases you make on our pupils' behalf."

Madeline greatly enjoyed getting to know her fellow teachers, but she had the rest of the day to herself, since Lord and Lady Danvers had left that morning for London. Before taking tea alone, Madeline started a letter to her brother to tell him of her unexpected change in fortune and her new employment.

Yet no matter her occupation, the Earl of Haviland was never far from her thoughts. Madeline didn't know whether she was relieved or disappointed to have seen no sign of him or Freddie Lunsford the entire weekend.

She did, however, receive a short missive from Haviland shortly after dinner that confirmed their agreement to attend Mrs. Sauville's salon together on Tuesday evening. While his messenger waited, Madeline wrote the earl a quick reply, asking if they might visit Hatchard's bookshop beforehand in order to investigate reference materials for her French classes.

Madeline couldn't help but view the upcoming trip to London with eager anticipation. Thus far she'd lived an utterly tame life, growing up on a country farm and then serving as a lady's companion for so many years. Purloining letters from under the nose of a blackmailing widow might be the most exciting adventure she had ever experienced. Moreover, sharing that adventure with a former spymaster of Haviland's vaunted reputation would likely prove fascinating.

The novelty of going to London at least helped ameliorate her nervousness at the prospect of conducting her first class on the morrow. Perhaps that was why, Madeline realized once she had passed the test at the academy with flying colors, her initiation into the world of teaching went so well.

However, when both missing gentlemen called on her at Danvers Hall on Monday afternoon, her nerves returned full force. Madeline deplored the way her heart leapt when Lord Haviland entered the library where she was poring over a map of Paris in preparation for her next class.

Even so, she couldn't stop herself from drinking in the

sight of him, or dismiss the feeling that she had just been passing time until his reappearance in her life.

I am suffering from a sad case of infatuation, Maman, Madeline lamented inwardly as she invited the gentlemen to be seated in wing chairs near the fire and asked Simpkin to bring refreshments for her distinguished callers.

Despite her determination to conquer her idiocy, she listened with only half an ear as Freddie Lunsford rambled on with an apology for neglecting her these past few days, claiming that he had been in London.

When Haviland offered the same excuse, she found herself looking at his mouth, remembering the taste of him, and eyeing his strong, capable hands, recalling their sensual touch on her skin the night in the Danvers nursery. How thoroughly he had overwhelmed and enchanted her that evening—

"I say, Miss Ellis," Freddie interjected, "didn't you begin teaching today?"

"Yes," Haviland seconded. "How did your first French class go?"

Flushing, Madeline jerked her errant thoughts back to the present. "It seemed successful. I centered my vocabulary lesson around French fashions and had my young ladies pretend we were in Paris, patronizing various modistes and milliners. Tomorrow I mean to expand our environs to historical sites."

Haviland raised an eyebrow. "Have you been to Paris?"

"No, but many of my mother's compatriots returned there once the royalists were reinstated after Napoleon's defeat, so I think I've heard enough tales and descriptions to convey the flavor of the city. And as you know, much of the British aristocracy flocked to Paris after the war's end. As a result, our English fashion magazines show a decided French influence. I plan to capitalize on that to spark our pupils' interest in proper grammar and pronunciation."

Just then, Simpkin entered, carrying a large tea tray. When he had left Madeline alone with her visitors again, she turned to the topic that was foremost on her mind.

"I admit I was relieved to receive your missive yesterday, Lord Haviland. I feared you might change your mind about letting me accompany you."

"No, I decided your ideas were good ones. You have a legitimate interest in attending Madame Sauville's gathering and conversing with her countrymen so you can better teach your pupils. And my escorting you there provides me a reasonable excuse to attend without raising her suspicions." A half smile touched Haviland's mouth. "Furthermore, we had a bargain, Miss Ellis. I mean to uphold my end of it, and I expect you to do the same."

Reminded of her promise to consider his proposal, Madeline wrinkled her nose. "I fully intend to."

Freddie was looking between them with puzzlement, but Haviland ignored him and proceeded to explain that setting his plans in place was the chief reason for his recent trip to London. "I managed a chance meeting with a friend of Mrs. Sauville's to confirm the program for Tuesday evening. She has planned a poetry reading for seven o'clock, with a supper afterward."

"Will we attend without an invitation?"

"Yes, to avoid giving her any advance warning. If for some reason she does suspect me of plotting to regain the letters, I don't want to allow her time to move them to another hiding place."

Impressed by his foresight, Madeline voiced her next question. "When should I be ready tomorrow?"

"I will call for you at three o'clock to convey you to London. That should allow us ample time to visit the bookshop you mentioned. We'll discuss the details of the plan during our drive."

Realizing she would have to be content until then, Madeline nodded slowly, just as Freddie piped up:

"There will be an ample reward for you, Miss Ellis, if you succeed."

"A reward won't be necessary," she replied.

The opportunity to repay Haviland's generosity a small measure, and the satisfaction of helping extricate his cousin from a plot to blackmail him, would be reward enough, Madeline knew. And so would the chance to enliven her admittedly rather dull existence.

Despite her concern about spending so much time alone with the irresistible Lord Haviland, she would be eagerly waiting for three o'clock tomorrow.

Rayne arrived exactly on time late the following afternoon, and he complimented Madeline on her own punctuality as he handed her into his coach.

"I feared you might leave without me if I was tardy," she replied, settling back against the comfortable squabs.

"That is another reason we would be compatible in marriage," he pointed out as the vehicle moved off. "We both value promptness."

He saw her bite back a wry smile. "I expected you to

take this opportunity to press your suit, my lord. Just not as the opening salvo."

"My name is Rayne, remember?"

"Very well . . . Rayne. Your requirements in a wife are rather curious. If you esteem promptness so highly, you would do better to hire a secretary. You can demand that he follow your schedule to the minute."

"I already have a secretary to handle my affairs in the Lords. Unfortunately he cannot present me with offspring."

A soft laugh escaped Madeline. "That indeed is a drawback when you are seeking an heir."

Rayne surveyed her with interest. "What about you, sweeting? During my proposal I neglected to ask your opinion about children."

Her look turned uncertain. "What do you mean?"

"Do you want children of your own?"

She answered with no hesitation. "Yes, I want children. *Provided* I have the right husband."

"I suspected you would," he said seriously, ignoring her pointed exception, "since you had the patience to act as companion to an invalid, and since you seem to have taken to teaching adolescent girls so readily."

Madeline shifted in her seat, as if uncomfortable with the direction of their conversation. "Didn't you say you would share the details of your plan with me during our drive to London?"

Rayne's mouth curved as he recognized her diversionary tactic. Even so, he complied. "The basic plan is simple. As soon as possible after we arrive at the salon, I will make my way upstairs to Madame Sauville's rooms and search for the letters."

"I still think I would be better able to slip into her boudoir undetected."

"Perhaps, but I want you well out of it."

Madeline eyed him quizzically. "Are you reluctant to use me because I am a woman?"

"Not necessarily," Rayne replied. He didn't mind employing female agents if they were skilled and suitable for the task at hand. The ones he'd known had all been experts at espionage. They could be cold and deadly when necessary, and could take care of themselves. "I don't like using civilians."

"Civilians?"

"Amateurs."

Madeline made a face. "You are afraid that I am not brave enough."

"No." That wasn't the case at all. She was brave enough for any ten women. "I don't question your courage, love. In fact, I admired the way you dealt with Baron Ackerby. But you don't have the necessary training or experience for this task."

Madeline's expression held a touch of skepticism. "You aren't being overprotective simply because you knew my father so well?"

That was partly true. He wanted to keep her safe, more so because he felt responsible for her. "You cannot claim your father would approve of my putting you at risk," Rayne countered.

Her retort was sweetly spirited. "Oh, I think he would. Papa taught his children to fend for themselves. He would be more disappointed if we needed to be sheltered. Besides, the danger is not all that great, is it?"

Her life would not be in jeopardy, Rayne acknowledged. If that were so, he would never chance letting

Madeline accompany him. He'd lost more than a few agents in his time, deaths he could not have prevented, yet he still bore the guilt. And his guilt would be magnified a thousandfold if he let harm come to David Ellis's daughter. "I told you, I don't want to chance you being taken for a thief."

"Even so, I truly would like to help. I've had little opportunity to make any meaningful difference in anyone's life, as you have."

Rayne had difficulty resisting that imploring gaze, especially when Madeline added in a softer voice, "Won't you allow me any role at all?"

"You *will* have a significant role, love. You will keep Mrs. Sauville in sight at all times. If you see her break away from her guests and attempt to leave her salon, you will distract her. The same goes for any suspicious activity among her servants. And if I require more time to search her apartments upstairs, you may have to create a disturbance of some kind."

"What sort of disturbance?"

He gave a light shrug. "It depends on the circumstances. You could fall down in a swoon, or spill wine on one of the guests, or tip over a candle. . . . You'll have to rely upon your wits to decide the most effective course and then improvise."

Madeline's features held both intrigue and disappointment. "So I am only to serve as a distraction if one is needed?"

"Yes. Nothing more."

"Very well," she said reluctantly.

Rayne fixed her with a level gaze. "I want you to promise that you will follow my commands to the letter, sweetheart. Otherwise we will call the whole thing off."

Madeline hesitated before a glimmer of amusement entered her lovely eyes. "Certainly I will, O master."

When Rayne's glance sharpened, her look turned innocent. "You won't let me address you as 'my lord.' I thought you might prefer 'master.'"

Laughter and exasperation battled within him. "Simply Rayne will do."

Pulling a leather pouch from a side pocket of the carriage door, he handed Madeline a folded paper. "Freddie has drawn up a floor plan of the widow's house from memory. I want you to study it in the remote event it becomes necessary for you to go anywhere but the drawing room."

"Do you prepare this much for every operation?" she asked curiously.

"More or less. When your life depends upon the smallest detail, you learn the wisdom of careful planning. But there are always unknown factors that can upend your best-laid plans, including simple ill luck, so you develop contingencies in case of trouble. Now apply yourself to learning the layout, love, starting with the widow's bedchamber."

"I won't ask how Freddie learned so much about *that* particular room," Madeline murmured impishly before turning her attention to the drawing.

Rayne watched her for several minutes as she frowned in concentration. When she began worrying her luscious lower lip, he recalled doing the same thing to her mouth the night of the ball. In truth, he'd almost lost control of himself that night. Even though he'd merely planned on kissing Madeline, he couldn't resist the vibrant woman in his arms—her eyes soft and hazy, like silver smoke, her magnificent breasts bared for his pleasure. He re-

membered plucking those taut nipples, rolling them between his fingers, pulling them into his mouth, hungry
to taste his fill of her. . . .

He'd somehow resisted the urgent impulse to carry
Madeline into the nearest bedchamber and take his persuasion all the way, but it had been a close thing. Even
now an image of her spread wild and wanton before him
made Rayne stir uncomfortably in his seat.

Her response to his passion, however, had only increased his desire to have Madeline in his nuptial bed,
while her reaction to his proposal had confirmed his decision to wed her.

Admittedly, Rayne was mildly astonished that she'd
refused him with such conviction. Yet after considering
it, he was rather glad she hadn't leapt to accept his offer.
He valued a challenge, and Madeline would be a challenge worth striving for.

Meanwhile, he would have to suffer the pain of unful-
filled need. It was another reason he didn't want her
working with him on this operation. She was too much
of a distraction.

Even so, he was glad to have Madeline with him.
Spending an afternoon and evening together gave him
the opportunity to woo her subtly without raising her
resistance further. He could show her his home in London and give her a taste of the advantages and pleasures
she could expect as his countess. God knew, Madeline
had enjoyed few pleasures in her life thus far.

And once they had safely retrieved the letters, Rayne
reflected, he could turn his full attention to convincing
her to become his wife.

*   *   *

Watching Madeline that afternoon brought its own pleasure, Rayne decided two hours later. He first escorted her to Hatchard's, where she seemed enraptured to find so many varied tomes available for her perusal. To her additional delight, the proprietor had an excellent French primer in stock, and agreed to write the publisher and order three dozen copies for the Freemantle Academy.

Madeline sighed upon leaving the bookshop. "How wonderful it would be to have so many books to choose from. One could read a different volume every day for years and still not come to the end."

"I have a fair library of my own," Rayne informed her. "You are welcome to read them all."

She gave him a knowing glance. "Is dangling such a treat before me meant to advance your matrimonial plans?"

Rayne smiled. "In part."

"Your offer is indeed tempting, but with the salary I will earn from my new position, I can afford to subscribe to a lending library."

"Then let us see if I can conceive of a better way to influence you. . . ."

Continuing his plan to woo her, Rayne escorted Madeline to a nearby tea shop, where he bought her three different flavors of ices over her objections, as well as one for himself.

"This is truly decadent," she murmured when they were seated at a table by the window overlooking the busy street. "I haven't tasted an ice in years, and now I have an overabundance."

Her enjoyment of the sweets, however, seemed to match her enjoyment of watching the passersby outside the shop window, Rayne noted. Under that spinsterish exterior, Madeline Ellis had a hunger for living that was palpable.

Rayne waited until she had finished every last spoonful of her ices before standing and holding out his hand to her.

"Come, we should go. I don't want to be late to the soirée."

Madeline looked puzzled as he helped her to rise. "I thought we had more than an hour before it begins."

"We won't be going there directly. We need to make a stop at my London home first to collect a few accessories."

"What accessories?"

"I want to replace your cloak, for one thing, and dress up your gown a bit."

"What is wrong with my gown?" Madeline asked, her chin lifting in a position of pride.

His gaze dropped to the lavender crepe dress she wore under her drab brown cloak. "Nothing is wrong with it," Rayne said, keeping his tone mild. "But for you to be welcomed by Madame Sauville's guests, you need to look the part. The aristocrats there put great store in dressing well—I suspect because they cling to the grandeur they once knew before the Revolution, or would have known had they not been exiled and stripped of their lands and fortunes. Additionally, I need to change my own attire for something more appropriate to carrying a packet of concealed letters."

"Oh," Madeline said, seemingly mollified.

She willingly accompanied Rayne back to his coach, and, while driving to his house on Bedford Avenue, she commented on his choice of professions.

"It is curious that the heir to an earldom would become an agent for British Intelligence. How did you become involved in spying in the first place?"

Rayne's mouth curved in remembrance. "Would you believe a stolen loaf of bread inspired my career?"

"Truly? I should like to hear *that* story."

Deciding there was no harm in Madeline knowing how he had gotten his start as a spy, he told her the truth.

"I had a great deal of restless energy as a boy, for which I could find adequate outlets in the country, at Haviland Park. But when my parents came to London for the Season, I frequently escaped my tutors and spent numerous hours prowling parts of the city far from Mayfair. One day when I was eleven, I happened upon a ragged lad about my same age who had been apprehended by a baker for stealing a loaf of bread. The thief likely would have hanged or wasted his life away in prison, and since I didn't think that fair for so minor a crime, I created a diversion and helped him escape from the baker. We became fast friends after that."

Madeline's eyes were bright and eager as she prodded him for more details. "I would imagine your parents were not happy about your new acquaintance."

Smiling wryly, Rayne nodded. "My parents cared little about how I spent my time, but they would have been horrified to know I was associating with such riffraff. My thieving friend came from the London stews. With no home or family, he was living in alleys, scrounging for scraps to survive. *I* was horrified by his circumstance, so I gave him the funds for food and decent lodgings, but while he was grateful to have enough to eat, he refused to be confined to civilized surroundings. After living on the streets for so long, he was a bit savage, like a feral fox."

"So how did that lead to you becoming a spy?"

"To satisfy my curiosity and my longing for adventure, my new friend introduced me to the sordid but fascinating London underworld and taught me some rather unique skills that were critical to his way of life—such as how to pilfer and to slip in and out of places undetected. And in exchange, I taught him how to pass for a gentleman . . . how to speak properly, to read, to ride, to shoot and fence. I thought it a great lark at the time, but years later we put our skills to good use. We both joined the Foreign Office and then worked our way up the ranks."

"So you saved a stranger's life, and in turn, he changed yours," Madeline said softly, admiration clear in her eyes.

"A fate for which I will always be grateful," Rayne acknowledged. "Otherwise I might have ended up a reckless care-for-nothing buck with too much time on my hands, getting into the kinds of scrapes Freddie regularly lands himself in, or worse."

"I doubt that would ever be possible," Madeline murmured. "You were meant to be a knight in shining armor."

Perhaps so, Rayne silently agreed. His experience with Will Stokes was his first encounter with the heartbreaking misery and poverty that afflicted much of London's citizenry and the injustices they bore because of their less-than-genteel origins. It had made him keenly aware how fortunate he was to be a member of the privileged upper class. But even at age eleven, he'd realized it was his duty to help those in need.

In response to Madeline's observation, however, Rayne merely shrugged.

"What happened to your friend?" she asked, then added when she noticed his fond smile, "What is so amusing?"

"The irony is that now he works as a thief-*taker* for Bow Street."

"He is a Runner?"

"Yes, and quite a good one, since he knows all the tricks of the trade. Even more amusing is that he married a baker's daughter and has two sons similar in age to my youngest nephews."

Madeline digested that information in silence for the remainder of the drive. And upon arriving at his house on Bedford Avenue, she held her tongue when they were met in the entrance hall by his chief aide, Walters, who acted as part butler, secretary, valet, and henchman.

Madeline remained wide-eyed and curious, absorbing everything she saw, as Rayne escorted her through the large house, passing rooms adorned with furnishings designed more for masculine comfort than a display of wealth.

Her eyebrows rose, however, when he led her down the back servants' stairs. Beyond the kitchens was a door to the wine cellar, and beyond that was a large chamber that resembled part storeroom and part dressing room such as the lead actors at Drury Lane commanded.

"I never considered it before," Madeline murmured, "but I suppose spies need disguises when they play different roles."

"Occasionally," Rayne replied. "This room rarely gets

used anymore. Now it mainly houses equipment I've needed at one time or another."

As expected, Walters had carried out his orders to his exact specifications.

"The accoutrements for your role tonight are on that table," Rayne said, pointing to one side of the room.

He watched as Madeline inspected the items laid out for her—a shawl of delicate silver lace, a bandeau with white ostrich plumes, and a pair of silver combs for her hair.

Moving behind her, Rayne helped her remove her cloak so she could don the shawl, then had her sit at a dressing table so he could arrange her hair and head-dresses to his liking.

"How did you learn to devise disguises?" Madeline asked, peering at herself in an oval hand mirror as he worked.

"Various thespians taught me here and there."

He didn't add that one of the actresses in question had been a former mistress.

Reminded of their upcoming task, Rayne related some background information about their target to Madeline, the better to prepare her for what to expect. "Madame Sauville is not considered a courtesan in the usual sense, in that she doesn't sell her wares overtly. But she has been the mistress of a number of notable figures in the government and elsewhere. I was surprised that she stooped to try her blackmail schemes on Freddie—and that he didn't have the sense to steer clear of her. She must be getting desperate for funds to support her extravagant lifestyle."

"What will you do if you are caught searching her private rooms?" Madeline asked.

"I won't be caught."

She hesitated but didn't question his assertion. "Her bedchamber is where you will start searching?"

"Yes. There is always a chance she deceived Freddie when she boasted that she 'slept with his letters,' but odds are she was being truthful while taunting him. She wanted his peccadillo to sound even more scandalous to increase his fear of his father's wrath."

"I thought she told Freddie the letters were in her jewel case."

Rayne smiled to himself, impressed with Madeline's powers of recollection. "She did that also. Most likely she keeps the case in her bedchamber."

"And if you find her jewel case locked, what will you do?"

"I will pick the lock." Rayne directed her attention to the small leather bag lying on the dressing table in front of her. "That bag contains various-sized metal picks and special keys whose vanes turn on the shaft. You may see for yourself."

Looking intrigued, Madeline opened the bag to examine the contents. "What happens when you do find the letters?"

"I will confiscate them and replace them with forgeries."

"Forgeries? Why?"

"I don't want Mrs. Sauville to know they are gone in the event I have to return to search for more of them."

"Is that likely?"

"Perhaps not. I won't know until Freddie inspects the entire lot to make sure none are missing." Again Rayne gestured at the dressing table, this time indicating a satin pouch that was filled with newly forged letters. "He composed some quite innocuous missives this time, with no mention of his passion for the lovely French widow. If La Sauville does feel compelled to show these to his father, she will be made a laughingstock."

Picking up the satin pouch, Madeline eyed the stack of letters inside as if estimating their size. "It is unfortunate that Freddie was so prolific," she said with amusement.

"True, but he fancied himself in love."

Madeline evidently caught the note of derision in his tone. "You don't believe he is capable of love?"

Rayne exhaled a humorless laugh. "Oh, I suspect he is capable, but he was a fool to let himself be taken in by Sauville's allurements."

After studying Rayne's face for a moment, Madeline returned to the subject. "How will you smuggle so many letters in and out without being obvious about it?"

"I have a special coat equipped with slots in the lining."

"Interesting." She pursed her lips thoughtfully. "How would *I* carry the letters if I were the one sneaking into her boudoir?"

Rayne found his gaze dropping to that ripe mouth of Madeline's. "You would put them in your reticule, or hide them under your skirts."

Her glance shot up to his. "Indeed?"

"That pouch you are holding can be strapped to your thigh by means of a special clip that attaches to your stocking garter."

Madeline slanted her head at him, her expressive eyes suddenly dancing again. "I *told* you I would be better suited to stealing the letters back," she pointed out. "You may have difficulty hiding so many in your coat because of the bulk, whereas I could easily conceal them under my skirts."

Rayne grinned at her. "I'll take my chances, love. However, if it will console you, you can wear the pouch tonight. There is always the possibility I might need to pass the letters on to you to avoid detection."

"Perhaps I will."

Her luminous eyes remained amused as he finished arranging the combs and feathered bandeau in her hair. Upon observing his handiwork in the mirror, Madeline murmured in surprise, "I do look as if I belong at a literary salon." She glanced up at him in admiration. "You really are quite good at this, aren't you?"

"This was my profession for a long while," Rayne replied, brushing off her compliment.

He wasn't about to let her praise go to his head. Tonight's task was merely business, and he'd learned the hard way not to mix emotions with business.

With that pointed self-reminder, Rayne took the letters from Madeline and stepped back, intending to fetch his special coat before he was tempted to claim that kissable mouth of hers again.

Chapter Seven

It is difficult to resist a force of nature, Maman. His seduction is like having all my senses struck by bolts of lightning.

After such a lovely afternoon spent with Haviland, Madeline wondered if she might have misjudged his feelings about love and matrimony—until his disdainful remarks about his cousin's failings only confirmed her misgivings.

Madeline had little chance to contemplate his marriage proposal during the drive to the soirée, however, since all her nerves were exasperatingly on edge. Haviland, on the other hand, lounged nonchalantly in the seat across from her, looking perfectly at ease.

Yet why should he not be calm? Madeline reminded herself. He was daring, fearless, accustomed to confronting danger and death. Whereas *she* had never faced anything more dangerous than a rogue cow who'd trampled a fence to graze in the herb garden. Unless she counted Baron Ackerby, that is—

"You are worrying needlessly," Haviland said, breaking into her anxious thoughts.

It was disconcerting, how he seemed to be so attuned to what she was thinking and feeling.

"Aren't you just the least bit nervous?" Madeline asked.

His half smile made her heart flutter in a way that had nothing to do with her concern about the evening ahead. "Enough experience with danger can make you inured to fear."

"You are never afraid?" she said in surprise.

"Certainly I am, but I've learned to control it. It's a matter of training and willpower. Take a deep breath, love, and try to relax. You don't want to alert the Widow Sauville by appearing agitated."

Of course he was right, Madeline acknowledged. They had a logical strategy to outsmart the widow and had prepared several contingencies in the event the initial plan went awry, including strapping the empty satin pouch to her stocking garter.

Still, Madeline couldn't help the way her heart rate sped up when the carriage came to a halt five minutes later.

They had arrived at the soirée.

At least the first part of their scheme went according to plan. Upon being admitted, Madeline saw upward of thirty genteel guests mingling in the salon. Most were men, but there was a smattering of women among the crowd as well. Mrs. Sauville, Rayne had said, lived on the fringe of society, so holding intellectual gatherings of poets and artists and politicians afforded her a sense of importance.

The widow was an exotic beauty, stunning in a jaded sort of way, with raven hair and a milk-white complexion that only hinted at her clever use of cosmetics. Her ripe figure was garbed in a low-cut gown that had obviously been dampened to cling to her curves and display her generous bosom to alluring advantage.

It is no wonder Freddie fell for such a femme fatale, Madeline thought as Rayne introduced her to their hostess and apologized for their unexpected intrusion.

Mrs. Sauville appeared surprised but pleased that Lord Haviland had deigned to patronize her salon.

"*Mais non,* it is no intrusion in the least, milord," she exclaimed in a somewhat breathless voice, her accent proclaiming her French origins. "You find me excessively honored."

She was decidedly less welcoming toward his companion, however, surveying Madeline with a calculating eye that left her feeling dowdy, despite wearing her best gown and the elegant accessories Rayne had loaned her.

Thankfully, the widow seemed to accept their reason for attending—that Miss Ellis desired to meet some of her late mother's countrymen and garner material for her French classes.

"But of course, milord," Mrs. Sauville murmured. "I would be pleased to make your little friend known to my guests directly after the poetry reading. And you must sit beside me during the presentation, I insist."

Taking his arm, she guided Haviland toward the front row of chairs, ignoring everyone else in the room. When the widow drew him down, Madeline followed and sat at Rayne's other side. Absurdly, it stung her to be dismissed as no competition by the beautiful Frenchwoman, even though she knew she was only there to play a supporting role.

Rayne was certainly playing *his* part to the hilt, Madeline observed. He commanded the widow's complete attention, smiling down at her with that charming, masculine smile that made feminine hearts quicken.

The sight made Madeline grit her teeth. It was *not* that she was jealous, she told herself firmly. It was only that if the alluring widow remained latched on to him for the duration of the reading, their entire plan would be threatened.

Resolved to allay any suspicions their hostess might have about their attendance at her salon, Rayne hid his boredom well as he flattered and charmed the Widow Sauville. He'd had ample practice at using seduction to gain his ends in his career; it was one of the tools of his former trade, and he was highly skilled at it.

The beautiful Madame Sauville was equally skilled, Rayne conceded, as she let the delicate silk shawl she wore "accidently" slide to the floor between their chairs. Giving a murmur of feigned dismay, she brought her hand to her heart, drawing his attention to the smooth expanse of bare skin at her bosom.

"*Comment gauche de moi.* Will you kindly assist me, milord?" she entreated, gazing up at him coquettishly through her long, kohl-darkened eyelashes.

Rayne responded with equally feigned gallantry. "It would be my pleasure, madame."

As he draped the shawl around her shoulders, she canted her head to one side, making certain he had an enticing view of her lush cleavage. She even managed to press her fingers over his for a moment, encouraging his hand to move closer to her breast.

But this was a duel for which Rayne well knew the rules. Obliging her, he bent down slightly, letting his warm breath caress her bare neck, eliciting a delicate shiver from her.

"It is a shame to conceal such beauty," he murmured, although he had to quell a grimace at the cloying heaviness of the fragrance she wore.

The widow gave a little trill of laughter and slowly smiled up at him. The artful gesture was meant to tempt and arouse, but Rayne found it intensely unappealing.

The truth was, he didn't trust beautiful, seductive women. He'd learned that bitter lesson with Camille Juzet many years ago. As a result, this Frenchwoman's obvious attempt to attract him only set his instincts on savage alert.

Rayne's mouth curled sardonically when he recognized the sentiment. Even if he found little pleasure in the company of *this* beautiful woman, he should at least be enjoying the challenge of the game and the chance to once again match wits with a worthy opponent.

Therefore, when Madame Sauville offered him a husky murmur of thanks, Rayne masked his distaste and smiled back at her while asking her to comment about the poets she had engaged for the evening.

An hour later, at the conclusion of the reading, the guests all rose from their chairs and began to mingle. The widow, however, still clung to him. Rayne was debating how to extricate himself from her irritating possessiveness when Madeline spoke up to provide him a suitable excuse.

"I am so very parched, Lord Haviland. Would you be so kind as to fetch me some refreshment?"

His eyes glinted in appreciation as he met Madeline's innocent glance. "Why, certainly, Miss Ellis."

The widow, however, immediately raised an objection. "I have servants to perform such tasks, Mademoiselle Ellis. Moreover, a buffet supper will be served in a short while."

"Oh, I doubt Lord Haviland minds," Madeline said airily, stepping in front of him. "And it will give me a chance to speak to you alone, Madame Sauville. I should dearly love to know about the modiste you patronize, so that I may tell my pupils. Your gown is so lovely, and with such a tasteful sense of fashion. Also, you promised to introduce me to your guests, did you not?"

Looping her arm through their hostess's, Madeline purposefully led the widow away from Rayne. "I should like to meet your poets as well. My brother has tried his hand at poetry once or twice, but I fear his efforts were rather sad. . . ."

Rayne's mouth curved as Madeline's voice trailed off. He had needed her to distract the widow after all, he admitted as he left the salon in order to hunt for the letters.

As time dragged on, Madeline could see Madame Sauville becoming more and more frustrated by her unwanted attachment, but she refused to budge from the scheming Frenchwoman's side. She kept one eye on the mantel clock, however, trying to hide her worry while wishing Rayne would hurry.

When at last he returned to the salon with glasses of wine for both her and Madame Sauville, Madeline breathed a bit more easily. Yet only when, in response to her quizzical glance, Rayne gave her a slight nod to indicate that he'd found the letters, could she begin to relax.

"My apologies for my tardiness, madame," Rayne

said smoothly. "I delayed to speak to an old acquaintance."

Madeline's relief was so great that she almost didn't mind when he turned his attention again to charming the widow.

The three of them took supper together, but when Rayne expressed their intentions of leaving the soirée directly afterward, the widow looked extremely disappointed. "Must you leave so soon, milord?"

"I'm afraid so. Since Miss Ellis has a school lesson to conduct on the morrow, I must return her to Chiswick tonight, and we have a lengthy drive ahead of us."

Mrs. Sauville shot a look of vexation at Madeline before smiling at the earl once more. "I hope that you will call upon me anytime you wish, Lord Haviland. You would be very welcome."

With a bow, Rayne pressed a kiss to the widow's proffered hand. "Thank you, madame. I look forward to it."

So saying, he took Madeline's arm and steered her toward the salon door and out to his waiting carriage.

Madeline waited to speak until Rayne was settled in the opposite seat. "I gather you found the letters?"

"Yes, but it took me longer than expected," he answered as the coach pulled away from the house. "They were indeed locked in her jewel case, which was hidden among her lingerie." Madeline thought his expression looked approving as he surveyed her in the dim glow of the interior carriage lamp. "You did extremely well keeping the widow occupied while I conducted my search."

She flushed at his praise. "I am just relieved it is over.

I fear I'm not cut out for spying. My nerves were rioting the entire time you were gone."

She saw Rayne smile. "I had every confidence in you, love."

"Now that is a falsehood if I ever heard one," Madeline responded with good humor. "You never believed that I could help you. You didn't even want me to accompany you tonight."

"True, but I didn't doubt your courage. I worried for you, which is not the same thing as doubt."

She couldn't help her own smile. "I would like to see Madame Sauville's face when she discovers the exchange."

Rayne's tone turned dry. "Trust me, you don't want to be within range of her rage when she does. She would likely try to claw your eyes out."

"I expect you are right."

"Now let us hope we retrieved them all," he said, drawing the curtains across the coach windows to afford them privacy from the London streets.

Madeline watched as Rayne shrugged out of his coat and carefully removed the letters concealed in the lining, then examined each one briefly.

"Freddie will have to read these himself, but from his account, I believe this is the entire lot."

Bending, Rayne opened the large leather satchel at his feet. After safely tucking the batch of letters inside, he pulled out Madeline's brown cloak, which Walters had packed away earlier.

"You will want to remove your evening attire before we arrive home."

Madeline was strangely reluctant for the night to be over, and even more reluctant to exchange the lovely silver shawl and matching accessories for her own drab cloak. And yet she didn't want to return to Danvers Hall wearing Rayne's plumed bandeau and hair combs, either.

When she reached up to remove the bandeau, however, she had difficulty finding the hairpins that held the headdress in place.

Seeing her struggle, Rayne said casually, "Come sit beside me, love, so that I may help make you presentable."

She hesitated a moment, then obeyed.

"I confess relief that you haven't taken to wearing caps yet," he murmured as his fingers searched for the pins. "Your hair is too lovely to keep it covered."

Madeline shifted uneasily in her seat, certain he was offering her false flattery again. The mention of caps made her uncomfortable as well. She hadn't yet resorted to donning the lace caps that signified spinsterhood, since it would be too final an admission of her passing years and her waning hopes for love and marriage.

Thankfully, Rayne dropped the subject and worked in silence. Madeline was keenly aware of his gentle touch, though. Stiffening her spine, she braced herself against the beguiling effect, but her task was made more difficult by the rocking of the coach.

It was several minutes before he removed the bandeau and combs from her hair and pronounced her fit to be seen by the Danvers staff.

"You will do," Rayne said, surveying her.

"Thank you," Madeline murmured, easing away from him.

He smiled slightly, as if understanding the reason for her defensiveness. "We aren't quite finished, love. Let me take your shawl."

When she held out her arms, he lifted the garment from around her shoulders and tucked it inside the satchel along with the combs and bandeau.

Without the added layer of fabric, Madeline was hard-pressed to explain why she was suddenly overly warm. No doubt it was Rayne's close proximity that affected her temperature so profoundly, along with the contemplative way he was looking at her.

When she started to return to her own seat, however, he stopped her by lightly touching her arm. "You still have the letter pouch attached to your garter, remember?"

"I can manage to remove it on my own," she said in a breathless voice.

"A pity," was his mild reply.

Reaching down, Madeline fumbled beneath her skirts for the clip that hooked to her stocking garter. Retrieving the pouch, she slipped it into the satchel and smoothed her gown down again. But even then Rayne would not let her return to her former seat.

Instead, he drew her back against the squabs and made her look at him.

Madeline caught her breath, wondering if he had decided to take advantage of their enforced intimacy to spur her surrender, and if he would use his potent masculine appeal and devastating charm to do it.

Her suspicion was confirmed with his next words.

"We still are not finished, sweetheart," Rayne murmured. "I want to show you why you should give my marriage proposal serious consideration."

Weakly, Madeline shook her head. "I already agreed to give it serious consideration."

"But I doubt you truly meant it."

He lifted his hand to run a finger over her lips in a sensual caress, sending a spark of heat rippling through her. Then he leaned toward her, until he was so close she could feel the warmth of his breath.

The air was abruptly charged with electric currents as Madeline comprehended that he meant to kiss her. She tried to steady her racing heartbeat and pull back from him, yet she couldn't seem to move as he lowered his head the final distance.

Without haste, he licked her bottom lip, making her open for him. Then he slid his tongue inside, a hot, leisurely stroke that stole her willpower even further. His mouth moving slowly over hers, he kissed her with lingering thoroughness—until she finally found the strength to press her hands against his chest.

"I know what you are about," she complained in a shaky voice. "You are bent on lowering my defenses."

He flashed her an easy smile, the one that was so effective at winning female hearts. "Certainly I am. And I give you fair warning, lovely Madeline. I am not a man to give up easily."

She most definitely did not need any warning. She already knew how dangerous Rayne was. Dear heaven, he was lethal with his beautiful face so close to hers, with his seductive mouth a mere breath away. His nearness was even more hazardous with her body still vibrating with aftershocks from his kisses and her traitorous senses urging her to give in.

Yet she made another effort to foil his intentions. "I thought you were a white knight who put great store in chivalry. It is not the least chivalrous of you to try to seduce me."

"Ah, but I have your best interests at heart, darling. I

intend to bring out all that hidden passion you have inside you."

Madeline swallowed. "What hidden passion?"

"You know very well what I mean. The hunger you feel is bursting to be free just now. It's only to be expected, since danger can be an aphrodisiac."

It was true, Madeline conceded. His potent kisses combined with the excitement of the evening had set her body humming with desire for him. She was aware of the giddy welling of her senses, even before Rayne dazzled her with another lazy smile. "Let me give you a taste of the passion you will know as my wife, love."

She was *not* his love. It was merely a figure of speech . . . his attempt at manipulating her into submission before devastating her defenses. But the seductive way Rayne was looking at her made her heart pound harder. And there was no denying that she wanted him to kiss her again—fervently.

When he obliged her unspoken desire, Madeline froze, bracing herself for the impact as his lips moved to take hers. To her dismay, this caress was even more powerful than the last. His mouth claimed hers forcefully this time—bold, hot, devouring.

Her breath seized as his tender assault went on endlessly while her blood heated. She had no notion of time until she felt the glide of his fingertips along her inner thigh. . . .

What scant breath Madeline had left strangled in her throat when she realized Rayne had lifted the hems of her gown and her shift beneath.

Dragging herself up from the spellbinding daze, Madeline grasped his hand to stay it and pulled her mouth away from his.

"What are you *doing*?" she gasped.

His gaze locked with hers. "I mean to take up where we left off the night of the ball, Madeline. I have much more to show you about pleasure."

The provocative promise in his tone combined with the dark glimmer of desire in his eyes rendered Madeline's protest stillborn.

Nor could she make a sound when Rayne left his seat to kneel before her and draw down her garters and stockings. It was unbelievable that she would allow him to take such liberties, yet she didn't stop him when he bent down to her and kissed the sensitive bare skin at the inside of her right knee, or when his lips moved further upward, caressing every exposed inch along the way.

He paused in his journey to soothe the mark the clip had made on her inner thigh, nibbling softly, stroking tenderly with his tongue. At the erotic gesture, Madeline groaned, a faint, hoarse rasp, but Rayne never ceased his purposeful ministrations. It was outrageous, scandalous, wanton, what he was doing, yet she fell back against the seat cushions, feeling too faint to resist.

When he pushed her skirts all the way to her waist, baring all her feminine secrets, her thighs opened involuntarily.

Rayne murmured a husky sound of approval as he bent down to her and breathed in the scent of her desire.

Then, as if he knew her own body better than she did, he unerringly found her most sensitive feminine flesh hidden beneath the dark curls at her woman's mound and began to tease her with slow, delicate laps of his tongue.

The shock of it made Madeline go rigid. With a gasping moan, she gripped his raven hair with clutching fingers, yet she didn't know if she wanted to push Rayne away or hold his magical mouth in place.

To her regret, he took the choice from her by drawing back enough to command in a husky whisper, "Be still, love. Let me enjoy pleasuring you."

Trembling, Madeline obeyed. She sank back even farther when he went on flicking light brushstrokes over and over the taut nub of her sex in time with the rhythmic rocking of the coach. And when he delved deeper into her intimate folds with his tongue, she gave a soft cry at the incredible heat he was arousing inside her. The bright flare of sensation that had begun low at her core was swelling to a burning need throughout her whole body.

Urging her on, Rayne parted her thighs even wider and filled his hands with her bare buttocks. Then lifting her to gain better access, he increased his searing caresses, laving her with the flat of his tongue, gently abrading, then soothing her with kisses from his warm, wet lips.

Madeline was almost sobbing by now as she arched helplessly beneath him, straining against the wicked mouth possessing her, yearning for Rayne to assuage the fierce ache inside her. The need built and built . . . until finally erupting in an explosion that flooded her with shuddering heat and rocked her entire body.

The stunning force left Madeline's breath rasping in harsh gasps and her limbs trembling with a wonderful aching weakness.

Without speaking, Rayne replaced her stockings and drew her gown down to cover her naked thighs, then resumed his seat as casually as before, as if he hadn't just given her the most shattering pleasure she had ever known in her life.

For a long moment, Madeline lay sprawled there on the seat, boneless, languid, frightened at the intensity of her response to him. Yet she knew he was watching her as he brushed a strand of her hair away from her damp temple.

"Don't you have anything to say?" Rayne asked, his tone both curious and tender.

She squeezed her eyes shut and moaned in dismay.

"Is there a problem, sweeting?"

Yes, indeed. Yet again he had made her abandon all her good sense.

"I think *you* are my problem," she rasped as she struggled to sit up.

His smile was infinitely sensual. "And at the moment, you are *mine.* I want you badly, Madeline."

"You just want to have your way."

"That, too. But you have a powerful effect on me." He caught her hand and brought it down to cover the front of his breeches, over his bulging groin. "It is remarkable how aroused I become by merely kissing you. And hearing your cries of pleasure only compounds my ache."

The knowledge that she had aroused him so thoroughly both thrilled and alarmed her.

Drawing her trembling hand away, Madeline strove to keep her voice even. "What is remarkable is how you refuse to listen to me. I have no desire to marry you."

"Regardless of your desire, I think you have just compromised me far beyond what is proper, so you might as well accept my proposal."

"I . . . compromised *you*?" She gave a strangled laugh. "I won't be coerced, Lord Haviland."

"Of course not." Placing a finger under her chin, Rayne made her look at him as he fixed her with that brilliant blue gaze. "But I intend to claim you for my wife, sweetheart. So you might as well give in gracefully and spare us the trouble of a lengthy courtship."

She shivered. Rayne was a man who pursued what he wanted, and in this case, he wanted *her*. But that didn't mean she had to oblige him.

As if reading her mind, he shook his head. "You are not allowed to refuse me just yet. I upheld my end of our bargain by letting you accompany me tonight, so you owe me at least a week to consider your answer."

Madeline paused for a long moment, wondering how on earth she would be able to resist him for so long. But really, it was only fair that she fulfill her side of their bargain. "Very well, one week."

Her answer would still be no, however, Madeline vowed shakily, even if her refusal filled her with regret and sadness. She was too emotionally vulnerable to Rayne. If they wed, she would surely lose her heart to him and he would never reciprocate.

Not looking at him, Madeline snatched up her cloak from the seat beside her. And since her only safety lay in putting a great distance between them, she moved across the coach to the far corner of the opposite seat.

"I'll thank you to keep on your side, Lord Haviland," she muttered as she struggled to don her cloak.

"As you wish, love," he said easily. "I am satisfied that I made my point tonight."

He had indeed made his point, Madeline reflected in dismay. Now that she'd had a taste of the excitement and passion Rayne could give her, she only wanted more.

And despite her determination to keep far, far away from him from now on, as she finished fastening the hooks of her drab cloak and prepared to resume her normal dull life, she had the sinking conviction that after tonight, she would never, ever be the same again.

Chapter Eight

It is the height of irony, Maman, to have two noble-men fight a duel over me—a plain, penniless spinster. I can scarcely credit it.

Madeline failed miserably in her attempt to forget the intimate interlude in Rayne's carriage, in part because she had no early duties at the academy Wednesday morning and thus faced several hours to herself, alone with her chaotic thoughts.

To banish her unwanted memories—and to expend some of her fitful energy—Madeline escaped to the formal gardens at the rear of the manor, where she proceeded to cut fresh flowers for half the rooms in Danvers Hall.

She was not quite finished with her task when Freddie Lunsford hailed her as he strolled down the gravel path toward her.

"A very good morning to you, Miss Ellis," Freddie said cheerfully. "Simpkin told me I could find you here."

Dropping her gardening sheers into the flower-filled basket at her feet, Madeline turned to greet him with a smile as she drew off her gloves. "Good morning to you also, Mr. Lunsford."

"I called early in hopes of catching you before your class begins."

"My class is actually not scheduled until later this morning. My pupils and I plan to take luncheon together so we can pretend we are dining at a Paris hotel."

"I see. In any event, I wished to give you this."

Accepting the paper he offered, Madeline realized that Freddie had given her a bank draft, but her eyes widened at the large sum. One hundred pounds was twice the yearly salary she had earned as companion to Lady Talwin.

"It is the reward I promised you," he explained when she raised her surprised gaze to his.

"But I told you, I do not want a reward."

"I insist, Miss Blanchard. You helped save me from utter disaster, and I must show you proper gratitude."

"Your thanks is gratitude enough," Madeline began, trying to return the draft to him. But Freddie stepped back, holding up his hands with a grin.

"Rayne warned me you would likely refuse, but he agrees that you earned it. I am to hound you until you accept it, and to summon him if I need reinforcements."

Realizing that she was outnumbered, Madeline graciously acknowledged her defeat with a laugh. "Very well, then, thank you. I will send this to my brother since he could use the funds just now."

"So could you, I'll warrant," Freddie stated in his usual tactless fashion, his gaze raking her nondescript gray morning gown and black spencer. "You should buy yourself a nice dress or two, Miss Ellis."

Madeline felt her face flush at his evident condemnation of her wardrobe, but rather than argue, she slipped the draft into her skirt pocket and changed the subject.

"So, has Mrs. Sauville's attempt at blackmail completely ended?"

Freddie grimaced. "Lord, I hope so . . . or at least I trust it will all be over in a few days. I mean to write her this morning, telling her I won't pay her extortionist demands and that she ought to reread those letters of mine." He grinned again. "She will be in for a rude shock when she discovers that her leverage over me has mysteriously disappeared."

"I expect so," Madeline agreed, smiling back.

"And now, I will take my leave of you, Miss Ellis. There is an enormous breakfast awaiting me back at Riverwood, and Rayne would not permit me to eat until I had called on you. I vow, I am famished. I have scarcely been able to swallow a bite this entire week past— Oh, would you care to join us, Miss Ellis?" Freddie asked, interrupting his own soliloquy.

Wanting urgently to avoid facing Rayne at the moment, Madeline hastened to decline. "Thank you, but I have already breakfasted."

"Very well, then. . . . But if I may ever repay the favor you did for me, you have only to ask."

"I will, Mr. Lunsford," she assured him, although she couldn't imagine ever needing to be rescued from a blackmailer.

With a gallant bow, Freddie doffed his hat to her, then spun jauntily and took himself off. He was whistling loudly when he disappeared from her view.

Still smiling to herself, Madeline returned to her gardening. Yet she was surprised when a short while later, Simpkin appeared to inform her that she had another caller, this time a Lord Ackerby, and was she "at home" to him?

Madeline felt her stomach clench at the mention of her noble nemesis and former neighbor.

Before she could reply that she most certainly was not at home, she saw the auburn-haired baron himself striding down the garden path. Even from a distance she recognized Ackerby's tall, well-dressed form by his imperious bearing. Evidently he hadn't trusted that she would receive him and so decided to give her no choice by following the butler to her location in the garden.

The elderly Simpkin frowned at this deliberate violation of proper etiquette, but Madeline hid her own grimace of distaste. "Thank you, Simpkin. I will speak to his lordship alone."

"As you wish, Miss Ellis."

Wondering what had brought her unwanted visitor here, Madeline waited until the butler had gone before asking Ackerby that very question.

"Why you, of course, my dear," he responded in an easy tone. "Imagine my surprise to discover that you had landed here. You are like a cat with nine lives."

She regarded him with an arch look. "Did you drive all the way from Chelmsford to discuss cats, my lord?"

"No, I came from London, where I have been staying these past several days." Ackerby glanced around at the luxurious terraced gardens. "Haviland has set you up in fine style, I see."

Madeline stiffened at the offensive insinuation that she'd become Rayne's mistress. "You are greatly mistaken, sir—and you insult Lord Haviland by impugning him with your own lecherous motives. He is merely a friend of my late father and so did me a kindness by helping me find employment here in Chiswick at a young ladies' academy owned by Lady Danvers."

Ackerby raised a dubious eyebrow. "Indeed? That relieves my mind then," he drawled as if disbelieving her.

She longed to wipe that smirk off his dissipated face. "The state of your mind matters little to me, Lord Ackerby."

He held up a hand as if to ward off another tart retort. "I don't wish to quarrel with you, my dear."

Madeline pressed her lips together, striving to keep her temper. "Then what *do* you want?"

"Restitution, merely that."

"Restitution?" she echoed. "Whatever do you mean?"

"Your brother is a thief and a scoundrel, Madeline. He stole a precious heirloom from me, and I want it back at once."

"I beg your pardon?" she said, staring. Gerard could be a scamp at times, playing pranks on friends and foes alike, but there was no real harm in him. And he most certainly would not steal so valuable an object from their wealthy neighbor.

And yet when she searched the baron's face, hoping to find some sign that he was jesting, his expression remained entirely serious.

"I trust you will explain your absurd accusation," she said finally.

"There is nothing absurd about it. Your brother left town last week shortly before you did. It wasn't until the day after I saw you at the inn that I discovered the de Vasse Necklace missing."

Madeline had heard of the priceless diamond and ruby necklace, which had formerly belonged to the Vicomte and Vicomtesse de Vasse, the parents of Gerard's new bride, Lynette.

"Whatever gave you the idea Gerard stole it?"

"One of his accomplices confessed," Ackerby replied. "Upon realizing the jewels were gone, I naturally questioned all of my servants. Under duress, a chambermaid revealed that your brother had seduced her to gain access to my home so that he might locate my safe and break the lock to steal the necklace."

"I don't believe it," Madeline declared flatly. Gerard was madly in love with Lynette. He would be the last person to dally with a serving maid.

"You should. Where can I find your brother?"

Madeline refused to answer. She could have told the baron that Gerard had eloped to Scotland with his sweetheart, but it was not common knowledge yet, and she intended to keep her sibling's secret as long as he needed her to. "I am not certain where he is at just this moment."

Which was mostly true. Upon returning from Scotland, Gerard and Lynette had planned to take refuge in Kent at the cottage of one of her French cousins, where they were to write Lynette's parents and present them with a *fait accompli*. But Madeline did not know for a fact that the newlyweds had arrived there. And even if she *had* known, she wouldn't reveal their location to Baron Ackerby so that he could pursue them there.

"Then I suggest you find him," Ackerby said tersely, watching her face to judge her truthfulness. "It will go harder for Ellis if he puts me to the trouble of searching for him." He paused. "If he returns the jewels to me immediately, however, I might consent to be lenient. He will only face prison instead of hanging."

Dismay filled Madeline as she considered the baron's threat. Was it possible he was right? That Gerard had actually taken the necklace and then gone into hiding to escape the nobleman's retribution? The jewels were worth a fortune, but Gerard might have wanted them more for their sentimental value, since they'd originally been stolen from the Vicomte and Vicomtesse when they fled the French Revolution to avoid losing their heads.

Madeline shivered. Such chivalry sounded precisely like something her quixotic brother would champion. In Gerard's mind, justice could seem a good reason to purloin the necklace and return it to the true owners' family.

Determined to present a loyal front, however, she manufactured a scoffing sound as she gazed scornfully at Ackerby. "You have no real proof of his guilt, my lord. Only a chambermaid's claim, which you yourself said was obtained under duress."

"I will have all the proof I need when I find the necklace in your brother's possession. I promise you I will search tirelessly for Ellis, and when I locate him, he will hang for his crime."

Dismay turned to fear inside Madeline at the thought of her brother hanging. If Gerard *did* have the necklace, he had to return it, no matter how noble his motives might have been in taking it. Which meant she would have to find him before the baron did and convince him of the madness of his actions—

Madeline winced inwardly, realizing that she was no longer adamantly refuting the baron's allegations. Ackerby might be a libertine, but he would not have come all this way to make baseless charges. The unyielding conviction in his expression, too, lent credence to his claim and sent chills through Madeline.

As she silently debated how to respond, a sly look crept over the baron's features. "I'll wager you would not care to have your new friends"—he waved a hand toward the Hall—"learn that your brother is a common criminal. It will not reflect well on you, Madeline, and might even cost you your teaching position."

"And I suppose you mean to tell them?" she asked warily.

"That depends."

"On what?"

"Your selflessness. Are you willing to sacrifice for your brother's sake?"

"You are speaking in riddles, Lord Ackerby," Madeline retorted, tired of his evasion.

"Then let me be more plain. I would be willing to overlook your brother's crime in exchange for . . . certain concessions on your part."

She knew *exactly* what concessions he meant. Madeline's hackles rose as she comprehended Ackerby's real purpose in hunting her down here at Danvers Hall. *He was still bent on having her in his bed!* Even more certain, he was determined to conquer her, to bend her to his will in retaliation for her continued rejection of him—and this time he had leverage over her.

Her teeth clenched. She now knew how Freddie had felt at being blackmailed by an unscrupulous widow. Ackerby knew very well she would never let Gerard hang. But neither would she simply bow to his extortion. "I have told you before, I will *not* become your mistress."

"Not even to save your brother?"

"You cannot be certain that he is even guilty!"

"Oh, he is guilty. And I will eventually prove it. Meanwhile, you don't want me to alert your new employer to your brother's misdeeds."

"Pray, go ahead and do your worst," she bluffed.

Ackerby pressed his lips together, obviously displeased with their standoff. As his complexion reddened with growing anger, Madeline decided that perhaps she was mishandling the situation. Even if Gerard was completely innocent, Ackerby could harm her reputation by making his accusations public. She had no desire to lose her new position at the academy because her family was tainted by scandal.

Nor did she want Rayne to discover that Gerard might be a thief. Rayne could understand—and even condone—filching a loaf of bread in order to survive the cruel ravages of starvation, but he would never countenance stealing a valuable heirloom.

In any case, she needed to buy time with Baron Ackerby to prevent him from going directly to the authorities. Then she had to make certain Gerard truly was guilty. If so, she would have to knock some sense into her brother's witless head and make him return the stolen property before he was found with it and arrested.

Unlocking her clenched jaw, Madeline forced herself to adopt a more conciliatory tone. "There is no reason to share your suspicions with anyone here in Chiswick, my lord. You could be mistaken about Gerard, and if so, making false accusations would reflect poorly on *you*. And if my brother does indeed have the necklace, I promise you, I will persuade him to return it."

"I am afraid that is not good enough."

The gleam in Ackerby's eyes told her clearly that he was enjoying making her squirm. Surprisingly, then, he seemed to back down. "Perhaps we can reach a compromise, my dear."

"What sort of compromise?" she asked warily.

"I will settle for a kiss."

Renewed anger and indignation streaked through Madeline at his gall. Ackerby was taking advantage of her vulnerability again, just as he'd done barely a month after her elderly employer's passing when he'd made his shameless proposition that she become his mistress.

Her gaze dropping to his lips, Madeline shuddered at the thought of kissing the lecherous baron. When he took a step toward her, she tensed, reminding herself that her gardening shears were at hand if she needed to defend herself.

And yet he had her at a severe disadvantage and they both very well knew it.

"Let me see if I understand you correctly," she said, striving to hide her disgust. "If I kiss you now, then you will allow me time to speak with my brother and persuade him to return the necklace to you—presuming he even has it? And in the meantime you will say nothing to anyone about the missing necklace or Gerard's possible role in its disappearance?"

"Yes. It will be our little secret. Do we have a bargain?"

She wasn't sure she could bring herself to say yes, no matter how much she loved her brother. Madeline muttered a silent oath as she stood there feeling trapped. She intended to save Gerard from his own folly, but when she found her incorrigible brother, she would throttle him for putting her in this untenable position.

At her hesitation, however, the baron closed the distance between them and grasped her shoulders, evidently taking her silence as acquiescence. Madeline barely had time to raise her hands between them before he bent his head to claim her lips.

His kiss was every bit as repugnant as she anticipated. Then Ackerby made it worse by thrusting his tongue forcefully inside her mouth. Madeline tried not to gag as she pushed her hands against his chest in an effort to make him release her, but his left arm wrapped around her waist to embrace her and draw her even closer.

When his right hand shifted from her shoulder to grope her breast, though, Madeline had had enough. Utterly repulsed, she gave a muted cry of protest as she struggled to shove him away.

At the same instant, she heard a fierce masculine growl that sounded like a curse. To Madeline's startlement, the baron suddenly freed her, making her stumble backward. By the time she regained her balance, she realized that Rayne had grabbed Ackerby by his coat collar and hauled him away from her.

Before she could utter a word, Rayne spun the other man around and drew back his fist, contacting the baron's jowl with a powerful blow that sent him flying to the ground with a decided thud.

Madeline was alarmed to glimpse the fury on Rayne's face before he lunged after the fallen man, clearly set on dragging Ackerby to his feet so he could pummel him again.

With another, more vocal cry this time, Madeline grasped Rayne's arm and held on for dear life.

"Stop, please—don't hit him again!" she exclaimed breathlessly, trying to keep the two of them separated.

"Why not?"

"You might kill him."

"That is *precisely* my intention."

Looking deadly, he advanced another step, despite Madeline's effort at restraining him.

"*Please,* Rayne," she repeated more urgently.

She was very glad he'd interrupted that revolting kiss. But while it touched her to have his protective fury aroused on her behalf, she could not very well explain why Ackerby had been kissing her, not without revealing her brother's likely criminal misdeeds, which she was loath to do. Besides, Rayne might be even more enraged if he learned of Ackerby's attempt to blackmail her into becoming his mistress. While it would give her satisfaction to see the baron punished for his humiliating insults, he didn't deserve to *die* for them.

Ackerby, however, was clearly enraged by the affront to his person. He lay sprawled there amid the rosebushes, holding his bruised jaw and glaring up at Rayne, the picture of wrath.

"How dare you strike me, you . . . you . . . cretin. I demand an apology at once!"

"You will have a long wait," Rayne gritted out. "You owe Miss Ellis an apology for mauling her."

"The devil I do!" Ackerby began before Rayne cut him off.

"You will beg her pardon or name your seconds."

"Then I will name my seconds," he snapped.

"Pistols or swords?"

"Pistols. It will be my pleasure to put a bullet through you."

"It will be *my* pleasure to teach you a lesson in appropriate behavior toward women."

Madeline felt her jaw drop as she stood there, rendered speechless with shock. Rayne had just challenged the baron to a duel and the baron had accepted!

"No!" she exclaimed in a high, weak voice. But neither nobleman was listening to her.

"Tomorrow at dawn?" Rayne demanded.

"Agreed," Ackerby snarled back.

"Here or London?"

"London. It will inconvenience me less. We can meet at the usual location."

Rayne gave a brusque nod. "My second will call upon yours to finalize the particulars about weapons and such."

The baron hesitated then, as if suddenly realizing what he had gotten himself into.

Madeline glanced up at Rayne, who still looked deadly as he stared down at his opponent. The baron must have thought so too, but he couldn't back down without losing face.

"Very well," Ackerby muttered as he struggled to his feet. "My home in London is located at Number Seven Portman Square."

He was evidently having second thoughts, Madeline conjectured, but he was too irate or too proud to withdraw his acceptance.

She was not too proud to ask him to reconsider, though. She had to calm Ackerby's fury so that he wouldn't act against her brother before she could convince him to return the priceless necklace.

"Lord Ackerby," she said in a pleading tone. "I am exceedingly sorry about this misunderstanding, but surely you don't wish to fight a duel?"

The baron merely gave her a savage glance as he brushed the dirt off the back of his coat. "Good day to you, Miss Ellis. You will hear from me when this is over, I *assure* you."

Without another word, he snatched up his hat that had tumbled into the flower bed and then stalked off.

Utterly dismayed, Madeline stared after him until he was out of sight before turning on Rayne to voice her distress. "What the devil do you mean, calling him out? Are you *mad*?"

"Not in the least. It's time someone taught that lecher manners." A muscle in Rayne's jaw clenched. "I suspected the worst when Freddie told me he saw Ackerby arrive here at the Hall, so I came at once. It was fortunate that I did."

In a distracted corner of her mind, Madeline realized that Rayne had not entered the gardens from the Hall, but from a side gate that led from Riverwood. Crossing the grounds separating the two estates instead of taking the long way around the park would explain why he had arrived so quickly.

"There was nothing *fortunate* about it," she exclaimed. "Not if your confrontation leads to one of you dying." She took a deep breath, struggling to hold on to her composure. "I did not need you to play the white knight, Rayne. I could have handled Ackerby myself."

"A fine job you were doing of it," he retorted sardonically.

Madeline bit back her own retort. She was mortified that Rayne had seen the baron pawing her, but she was appalled to think of what might happen if they actually dueled. Rayne might be hurt or even killed. Even if he escaped unharmed, there could still be devastating consequences.

"Did you ever consider that you might *lose* a confrontation with him?"

"No," he stated flatly. "I won't lose."

"And what happens if you win? You know dueling is illegal. If you kill him, you may be forced to flee the country to avoid arrest."

His mouth curled. "Perhaps I won't kill him. Just put a sizable hole in him."

In frustration, Madeline reached out to grip Rayne's arm again. "I will not have blood drawn on my account!"

"It is not your decision to make, sweeting." Deliberately, Rayne pried her clutching fingers away. "My apologies for violating your fierce sense of independence, but that bastard has touched you for the last time."

With that harsh pronouncement, Rayne also turned away and strode rapidly toward the manor house, not giving her a chance to reply.

Madeline stared after him, wanting to curse and scream in the same breath. How had events come to such a sorry pass in so short a time?

She raised a hand to her suddenly aching temple. She couldn't let the duel proceed. Her first priority was to somehow stop it—and then she had to convince her reckless brother to return the baron's property before he was caught red-handed and faced hanging.

Spurred into motion by her conclusions, Madeline

abandoned her basket of flowers and hurried toward the house, a sense of urgency driving her on.

To her mind, persuading Ackerby to call off the duel was likely to be easier than convincing Rayne, who was too stubborn and too ruthlessly determined to champion her in place of her late father. Rayne was clearly a throwback to the feudal era, when wealthy powerful overlords protected the weak and defenseless. But while part of Madeline appreciated his gallantry, *she* was not weak or defenseless. Nor could she bear to see him suffer for her sake.

She could not, however, simply follow Lord Ackerby to London to plead with him, since she had to teach her class at the academy at eleven and she still had significant preparations to make beforehand.

Therefore, Madeline settled on writing to the baron at his home in Portman Square, swearing faithfully to see that his property was returned to him if he would forgo the duel. Meanwhile, she promised, she would speak to Lord Haviland and make him understand how mistaken he had been to issue the challenge in the first place.

And she fully intended to keep her word on that score. She would call on Rayne at Riverwood directly after her class, rationalizing that he might be more amenable to persuasion if she allowed time for his temper to cool. She would claim that she'd given Baron Ackerby permission to kiss her—without revealing the exact reason, since learning of the baron's disgusting proposition would only increase Rayne's wrath.

Madeline winced at the thought of lying to him and pretending that she'd willingly kissed a repellent libertine who normally made her shudder. But Rayne would never withdraw his challenge unless she convinced him that he'd misconstrued Ackerby's embrace.

The second letter Madeline wrote to her brother, demanding to know if he'd stolen the precious heirloom, and if so, that he come to his senses and return the necklace immediately, adding that Ackerby had threatened dire consequences otherwise.

Tucked into the sealed letter, she included the draft for the reward money she had earned. A hundred pounds would give Gerard and Lynette a significant financial start to their married life together, or in the alternative, allow him to afford to buy a wedding gift of jewelry for his new bride that didn't have the taint of being stolen.

She addressed Gerard's letter to Lynette's cousin in Maidstone, Kent. If her written plea brought no response, Madeline was resolved to travel there in person to confront her brother directly. But she disliked leaving Chiswick just now unless truly necessary, since abandoning a post she had barely begun would likely mean the end of her new teaching career.

Her fear for Gerard was tempered by the knowledge that she could possibly apply to Rayne for help in saving her brother from Ackerby's retribution. But then she would have to confess the theft, which might only make Rayne think less of *her*.

Madeline bit her lip as she acknowledged her own selfish motives at keeping the whole sordid matter a secret from him. Just now Rayne thought her qualified to be his wife, but she doubted he would want to wed the sister of a thief who faced prison or hanging. And if she mired his grandmother and sisters in a cloud of scandal, it would be just one more reason he might never love her.

Maman, is it wrong to hold out hope that I might someday win his heart? Madeline wondered wistfully as she sanded and sealed both letters.

Shrugging off her foolish thoughts, she put away her writing implements and went in search of Simpkin.

She found the elderly butler in the Danvers Hall ballroom, supervising the wax removal and cleaning of the chandeliers and replacing burned-out candles with fresh ones.

When she asked him to post the letters for her in Chiswick at once, he readily agreed.

"However, Miss Ellis," Simpkin suggested, "Lord Haviland will surely frank these for you."

Giving a faint smile, Madeline shook her head. It would spare the recipients the cost of postage if her mail bore a peer's stamp, but naturally she didn't want Rayne knowing about either letter.

"Perhaps so, but I don't wish to be any more indebted to his lordship than I already am," Madeline hedged. "And there may not be time to request his frank. I truly need these letters to go out immediately."

Simpkin pulled his watch from his coat pocket to check the hour. "I will see to it myself. If I leave now, I will reach the posting inn in time to catch the mail coach."

"Thank you, Simpkin. I greatly appreciate your kindness," Madeline said earnestly before turning away and heading upstairs to change her gown for her class.

Yet with the threat of the duel hanging over her head like a sword, she knew she would be unable to keep her mind on her lesson or her pupils.

As she reached her bedchamber, Madeline shook her

head again, this time in disbelief. It strained credulity, having two noblemen fighting over her after years of being utterly ignored by the male sex. The irony would even have made her laugh if the situation weren't so perilous.

But instead of laughing, Madeline knew she would be struggling to calm her gnawing fear and counting down the hours until she could visit Rayne and do her utmost to convince him to call off the duel.

Rayne could scarcely believe he'd acted so impulsively in challenging the baron to pistols at dawn. Normally he was not only even-tempered, he was particularly cool-headed where women were concerned. He *never* allowed his emotions to become involved over a woman, not after the heartache Camille's betrayal had caused him a decade ago.

Calling Ackerby out had been decidedly irrational, Rayne knew. And he would be hard-pressed to explain the rage that had overcome him upon seeing that bastard assaulting Madeline Ellis. If it were any other man but himself, he would ascribe his actions to sheer male jealousy.

Yet it couldn't be jealousy driving him, his conscience argued. For jealousy, his feelings would have to be engaged, and whatever tender feelings he held for Madeline derived from his friendship and admiration for her late father, not ardor for her as a lover.

No, more likely his fierce response stemmed from simple protectiveness of the gentler sex, in addition to possessiveness because he'd asked her to be his wife. Those, and the knowledge that he was morally responsible for

Madeline's welfare, made him determined to save her from the baron's lecherous attentions.

To Rayne's surprise, however, Madeline hadn't appreciated his intervention in the least. In fact, she had turned on him, taking him to task for daring to come to her rescue.

Yet he had no regrets, Rayne reflected grimly as he set in motion the steps required of dueling, beginning with writing to the man he would ask to be his second and sending a footman to London to deliver the missive. Ackerby needed to clearly understand that Madeline had a protector and champion now, and if he refused to make a suitable apology, he would be taught restraint at the point of a gun muzzle.

Therefore, it gave Rayne a measure of concern when barely an hour later Simpkin was announced at Riverwood. He had told the aging butler to look out for Madeline and to alert him if the baron dared to show his face again at Danvers Hall.

"Ackerby did not return to harass Miss Ellis, did he?" Rayne demanded as Simpkin entered his study and offered a brief bow.

The butler's brow creased in a troubled frown. "No, my lord. And yet I thought you might wish to know . . . shortly after you left, Miss Ellis directed me to post a letter to Baron Ackerby."

"Did she now?" Rayne asked sharply, troubled himself by the revelation.

"Yes, my lord. And it seemed urgent to her that her correspondence be sent at once. I posted a second letter for her, as well. That one was addressed to a Mr. Gerard Ellis."

"Her brother," Rayne murmured, deep in thought.

"I dislike betraying her confidence," Simpkin explained, "but you asked me to look out after Miss Ellis and to inform you if Lord Ackerby posed a threat to her in any way. And after what you revealed to me about him, I confess it worries me that she felt compelled to write to him."

"You did well to tell me, Simpkin," Rayne assured him. "I will take the matter from here."

He thanked the butler and dismissed him, then stood frowning as he gazed out over the grounds of Riverwood in the direction of Danvers Hall. The news that Madeline had written Ackerby was inexplicably disturbing and caused a myriad of long-buried feelings to surge through Rayne. Suspicion and doubt were foremost, along with uneasiness.

He couldn't help but question Madeline's motives in writing to Ackerby. Why would she send an urgent communication to a nobleman she claimed to despise?

Something else struck Rayne just then as he recalled Madeline's expression when he'd struck down her assaulter: Her eyes were dark with outrage. At the time, he'd thought her wrath directed at the baron for forcing her against her will.

But had he misinterpreted her response? Rayne wondered. Was it possible she was furious at *him* because he had challenged her lover?

Rayne ran a hand raggedly through his hair as he fought his conflicting emotions. He'd trusted Madeline because she was her father's daughter, but he didn't really *know* her. Had he been too gullible in taking her word about her predicament?

Something was wrong, he could sense it. Ferreting out

traitors was his business after all. And for a moment there, Madeline had looked . . . *guilty*. As if she were hiding secrets from him.

Rayne muttered a low curse under his breath. He'd been down this same path once before—a woman hiding secrets from him. And just now all his instincts were screaming out in silent warning that he was about to repeat history.

Questions flowed rapidly in his mind, particularly the chief one: *Was there more to Madeline's relationship with the baron than she claimed?*

He'd been determined to protect her from a libertine, but perhaps she had not actually needed protecting. Perhaps he'd even interrupted a lover's tiff at the inn several days ago, the first time he saw her with the baron.

And in the garden a short while ago, Madeline could have been embracing Ackerby willingly. Perhaps when he'd fondled her breast, her muted cry had been a groan of pleasure. Some women liked rough treatment, even welcomed it.

Rayne's jaw muscles went taut. Surely he was overreacting. Simply because he'd had one bitter experience with a woman's betrayal was no reason to be suspicious of Madeline.

Yet she was hiding something from him, that much was certain. And it wasn't beyond the realm of possibility that she was writing secret letters to her lover. *Just as in your past, when the deceptive woman you loved already had a lover who owned her heart.*

There was no reason to think Madeline was as devious as Camille Juzet. According to Freddie, Madeline intended to send her reward money to her brother Gerard because he needed the funds more than she did. Camille had wanted to help her own brother and other family members flee the local authorities, yet that didn't mean the similarities between the two women extended any further.

He wouldn't leap to conclusions, Rayne decided. There might be a logical explanation for why Madeline had written to both the baron and her brother at the same time, and for now, he would give her the benefit of the doubt.

Meanwhile, however, he would take care to crush any tenderness he was beginning to feel for Madeline. And he would give Ackerby a lesson in honor and manners that he would not soon forget.

Keeping a pretense of composure throughout her class was nearly impossible for Madeline. Her anxiety over the impending duel was simply too great. Hence, the moment she was able to take her leave from the academy, she drove the Danvers gig, which Arabella had graciously loaned her, to Riverwood.

To her dismay, Rayne was not at home, or so his majordomo claimed. Worse, Bramsley refused to say where Lord Haviland could be found, although Madeline suspected he knew very well.

Thankfully, Freddie was still at Riverwood. And yet that gentleman did not look particularly overjoyed to see her when she was shown into the billiard parlor where he was playing a solitary game.

"Can you tell me where I might find Haviland?" Madeline asked him at once. "All Bramsley would say was that he is not here."

"He left for London an hour ago," Freddie replied rather reluctantly.

"Blast it," Madeline muttered, gnawing her lower lip. "I hoped to speak to him and convince him to call off this absurd duel."

"He cannot call it off," Freddie asserted, looking somewhat startled.

"Why not?"

"Because it is a matter of honor. Ackerby went too far this time. You cannot expect Rayne to sit idly by while that rake besmirched you."

"But he did not besmirch me," Madeline replied, raising her eyes to the ceiling. "The entire situation was misconstrued."

Freddie frowned. "Well, it is too late now."

"No, it is *not*. I will just have to go to London myself to speak with Rayne."

"Miss Ellis," he said hurriedly, "you cannot interfere in his business. It simply isn't done. And even if you were to speak with Rayne until you were blue, you won't succeed. I know him. He won't change his mind if he believes he is in the right."

She ignored Freddie's exasperated protest. "I presume he means to spend the night at his house in town?"

Freddie grimaced at her stubborn persistence. "That was where he was headed. He had to collect his dueling pistols and meet with his second. And he knew he would have to rise early tomorrow morning."

It was Madeline's turn to frown. "He didn't ask you to stand as second for him?"

"No." Freddie gave her sheepish look. "I am not the best of shots, and Rayne didn't want me to get hurt in the event I had to step in for him."

"At least he was concerned for your welfare if not his own," Madeline said sardonically. "So who will be his second?"

"He intended to ask Will Stokes."

"Who is Will Stokes?"

"A longtime friend. They knew each other as lads and served together in the Foreign Office."

Stokes must be Rayne's childhood bread thief, Madeline realized, but it was of little importance. What mattered was that she stop the duel before someone got hurt.

But perhaps Freddie was right. Talking to Rayne would likely have little impact. She might have to take more drastic measures to make him see reason.

"Do you know where the duel will be held?" she asked. "Ackerby said they would meet at the 'usual place,' and Rayne seemed to know what he meant."

Freddie's brow furrowed. "Why do you want to know?"

"I just do." When he hesitated, Madeline snapped impatiently, "You might as well tell me, Freddie. I can discover the location on my own, but you will save me the trouble of having to search all of London. Either way, I mean to find out."

His protest grew more vocal. "Miss Ellis . . . Madeline, you cannot interfere in a matter of gentleman's honor!"

"Since I am not a gentleman, I am not bound by your codes of honor."

She meant to prevent the duel somehow, even if she had to persuade the duelers at gunpoint. She still had her pistol with her, Madeline remembered, and she was not about to risk letting Rayne get shot or suffer for killing Ackerby on her behalf.

When she kept her level stare fixed on Freddie, he finally gave a sigh of disgust. "I suppose they mean Rudley Commons. It is a field on the outskirts of London where duels often are held."

"Thank you," Madeline said, relieved that he had given in so she didn't have to spend interminable hours trying to discover the information on her own. "Then will you be kind enough to escort me there tomorrow morning before the duel begins at dawn?"

The strangled sound Freddie made was practically a yelp. "I most certainly will not escort you there! Rayne would slay me if I dared do any such thing."

"I will slay you if you don't."

Regrettably, Madeline could see her threat held little weight, so she tried a different tack, softening her tone to sound more imploring. "You said if I ever needed you to repay the favor I did for you that all I had to do was ask. Well, I am asking now."

"I say, Madeline, that isn't fair!"

"Do you mean to go back on your word?" she pressed. "After all your fine talk about gentleman's honor?"

Freddie glared at her. "You know I cannot."

"Then you will take me tomorrow morning?"

"Yes, blast you, I will take you. But *you* will have to explain to Rayne how you coerced me, or you will have my death on your hands."

"I promise to tell him and absolve you of all responsibility," Madeline agreed, practically faint with relief. At least she now stood a chance of stopping the duel.

Yet the knots in her stomach were still stretched taut

with worry. The danger to Rayne hadn't passed yet. Nor had the danger to herself, Madeline realized with fresh dismay. For the threat to his welfare had confirmed what she already feared: By allowing herself to become so involved with Rayne during the past several days, she'd fallen into deep trouble.

She'd fallen hopelessly in love.

Chapter Nine

I have done it, Maman. I have sealed my fate for better or for worse.

"I still say this is a dreadful mistake, Madeline," Freddie complained as his curricle forged unevenly toward London in the dark of early morning.

Clinging to the vehicle's side rail as they plunged through a thick fog, lurching over potholes and slithering in four treacherous inches of mud, Madeline was more than a little distracted when she answered.

"I clearly understand your feelings, Freddie. You have told me so above a dozen times."

Despite the impropriety, they had quickly come to a first-name basis, since danger tended to make intimate bedfellows.

Just now the danger was in being thrown from the curricle if it slid off the road—a fate that seemed entirely too possible as Freddie's pair of grays labored valiantly to maintain their footing on the perilous surface, their hooves churning up clumps of muck and mire onto the passengers behind.

But while Freddie might be a trifle scatterbrained, he

was an excellent whip, and Madeline trusted him to deliver her to Rudley Commons in time for the duel.

They had left Chiswick well before dawn in the midst of a drizzle, which had since abated. By now her bonnet and cloak were soaked through and covered with mud, and so was the veil she wore to conceal her identity.

Yet Madeline ignored her misery and kept her focus on the road ahead, straining to see through the swirling mists.

She could not as easily ignore Freddie, however. She'd begun to think of him almost like a brother, and regrettably, he was just as stubbornly persistent as her real brother when Gerard wanted his way.

"Truly, you shouldn't worry about Rayne," Freddie repeated for the third time in five minutes. "He is not in much danger since he is a deadly shot."

"Given his former occupation, that doesn't surprise me in the least. I would expect him to be lethal with a pistol. But Ackerby is accounted a fair shot himself. And if either of them were to be hurt or killed this morning. . . ." Madeline shuddered. "I couldn't live with their blood on my conscience."

She drew her cloak more tightly around her, trying to ward off the cold. But the chill in her heart was due to more than the damp fog blanketing the countryside. It was fear, pure and simple.

"I wish we could go faster," she muttered, feeling the urgency anew.

Freddie gave a snort of protest in response. "If we go any faster, I'll land us in a ditch, and I value my horses too much to cripple them. Besides, we have ample time. The duel won't start before full light. You must be able to see your opponent, you know."

His sardonic drawl made Madeline suspect that she had wounded his sensibilities.

"Thank you for driving me, Freddie," she murmured contritely in an effort to soothe his ruffled feathers, adding a low muttered oath, "Devil take it, I cannot believe this is actually happening."

"Nor can I," Freddie agreed. "Rayne is the most sensible man of my acquaintance, even if he *is* prone to excess gallantry. For the life of me, I cannot understand what has come over him."

Madeline could not understand Rayne's adamancy either. "I know. Even if he escapes unscathed, he could face a scandal if he merely wounds Lord Ackerby."

Freddie digested her comment for a moment, then shook his head. "I should have thought of that. Rayne will want to handle the duel discreetly, of course—for his grandmother's sake if nothing else. Lady Haviland will be livid if he stains the family name more than he already has."

"That is scarcely any consolation," Madeline replied darkly.

"Perhaps not. But pray don't distract me any further if you want us to reach London in one piece."

She didn't bother pointing out that Freddie was the one who had been arguing with her nonstop ever since arriving at Danvers Hall to collect her.

Instead, Madeline held her tongue and concentrated on trying to quell the acid rising in her stomach from anxiety in addition to her nausea from the sway and jolt of the curricle.

At least the fog had dissipated a small measure by the time Freddie finally drew his pair to a halt at the edge of a verdant meadow.

Madeline's stomach clenched again as she stared through the dripping mist. There was just enough light for her to see that several carriages had arrived before them, and that a small knot of men had gathered near the center of the field.

"I thought you said they would not begin before full dawn," she exclaimed in dismay.

Not waiting for Freddie to reply or assist her in dismounting, she leapt down from the curricle and charged across the meadow. The hem of her skirts instantly became sodden in the wet grass, impeding her progress further, but iron chains could not have held her back.

Much as she expected, when she marched out onto the dueling field, astonished silence greeted her arrival. She appeared to be a widow in mourning, Madeline knew, with her drab cloak and black bonnet and veil, but Rayne clearly recognized her, judging by his scowl, as did Lord Ackerby.

Not giving them time to react, she pressed her advantage of surprise. "Good morning, gentlemen. I fear you rose early for naught, for I must insist that you call off this illegal enterprise."

The men had been examining two cases containing exquisitely crafted pistols, no doubt inspecting the priming and trigger mechanisms. Standing closest to Rayne was a wiry, sharp-faced man garbed in plain dark clothing whom she assumed was Rayne's second, while the fancy older gentleman beside Ackerby must be acting for the baron.

Rayne's lips thinned in disapproval, while his second's eyebrows rose in unabashed curiosity and amusement.

Madeline, however, could find nothing amusing about grown men putting bullets in one another, and she intended to stop it, even if she had to put herself in the path of the duelers.

But first she had to contend with Rayne, who looked none too happy to see her.

"What the devil are you doing here?" he asked in a grim tone. "You know you don't belong here."

"I beg to differ," Madeline said calmly, trying to keep the quiver out of her voice. "You were fighting over me, so I believe that gives me some say in the matter."

His voice was as stern as she had ever heard it. "You have no say whatsoever."

"Indeed I do," she retorted. "I have no desire to be the cause of a scandal. If you kill each other, it will get out that I was the center of your quarrel, and my good name will be utterly ruined. Well, I will not allow it."

Ignoring her declaration, Rayne glanced beyond her at Freddie, who had traipsed across the meadow more slowly and was now hanging his head. "Lunsford, take her away immediately, if you please."

"He does *not* please, Lord Haviland," Madeline answered for Freddie. "And I am not leaving until you end this ridiculous challenge." She moved between the two opposing camps. "I warn you, if you mean to continue, you will have to fire through me."

Rayne's jaw hardened even further. "I will have you forcibly removed, sweeting."

"You may try." She drew out her own loaded pistol from the reticule she wore looped around her wrist. "Your servants do not want to challenge me, my lord." She waved her pistol toward the middle of the field. "Go ahead and pace off the distance, gentlemen. I promise you, I will shoot the first one of you who fires."

The resulting silence was deafening, as Madeline expected. No doubt they were each judging whether or not her word could be credited.

Feeling slightly hopeful, she spoke again, but this time she turned and addressed the baron. "You and I both know, Lord Ackerby, that the contretemps yesterday was a simple misunderstanding. I am certain you did not mean to become quite so . . . forceful. But now that you have had time for calm reflection absent the heat of the moment, I wonder if you would be willing to proffer the apology Haviland wished for?"

It was evident that Ackerby was no longer in the high dudgeon he'd been in yesterday morning in the Danvers Hall gardens, and Madeline hoped she had given him enough excuse to withdraw gracefully.

Holding her breath, she waited anxiously while Ackerby glanced at Rayne, then cleared his throat. "Perhaps I *was* too forceful yesterday. If so, I beg your pardon, my dear."

"There," Freddie broke in hastily. "Honor is served."

Relief edged his voice, but Madeline could not yet feel the same sanguinity.

Lifting her veil just enough that Ackerby could see the lower part of her face, she silently mouthed the words, *Thank you—you won't regret this,* before saying brightly out loud, "Of course I forgive you, my lord. I am very grateful that we have cleared up this little dispute."

Madeline dropped her veil as she turned back to Rayne. "You will have to be satisfied with that, Lord Haviland—although if your affronted masculine pride insists, you may always delope. Isn't that how it is done if a conflict is to be settled to the satisfaction of both parties?"

She spoke of the practice of firing harmlessly into the air, the safe way of ending duels so that neither opponent suffered physical damage.

Rayne remained grimly silent, his scrutiny of her so intense it seemed to pierce her veil. Madeline's heart was thudding by the time he finally responded in a sardonic tone. "Why waste a good bullet?"

Relief flooded her so strongly that her knees felt weak. But then Rayne spoiled the moment by issuing another threat. "Mark my words, Ackerby, there will be no deloping the next time you dare approach her."

When the baron took a belligerent step forward, Madeline quickly intervened and laid a soothing hand on Ackerby's sleeve. "Thank you for your consideration, my lord. Now perhaps you would like to return home and forsake these miserable elements."

Ackerby visibly gritted his teeth before muttering a summons to his second. "Come, Richardson, we are done here." Spinning on his heel, then, he stalked away toward his carriage, leaving his colleague to hurry after him.

Once the baron was out of earshot, Rayne's friend spoke for the first time, his tone slightly amused. "I am most comforted that you didn't need me after all, Rayne, thanks to this dauntless lady. Would it be too forward of me to beg an introduction?"

"I would be happy to oblige, Will," Rayne replied dryly, "but as you heard, the dauntless lady wishes to keep her name concealed. Perhaps under more auspicious circumstances. . . ."

The man Madeline presumed was Will Stokes accepted Rayne's refusal with good grace. "Well then, I will take my leave of you. Naturally, if you require my services in any other endeavor, you have only to ask."

"My thanks to you for coming today."

With a slight bow, Rayne's second retreated to his own carriage, leaving Madeline alone with Rayne and Freddie.

"Mr. Lunsford and I should be leaving as well," she murmured, not liking the piercing way Rayne was still looking at her. "He rose much earlier than customary for his constitution, and he needs his rest."

Rayne did not appear to buy her argument, however. "Not so fast, darling," he drawled in warning.

Madeline took a defensive step backward. "Freddie will see me home."

"No, he will not. You and I need to have a little discussion just now. Freddie won't interfere if he knows what is good for him," Rayne added, shooting his cousin a scalding look.

So saying, he took her firmly by the elbow and ushered her toward his coach.

"I won't drive home alone with you, Rayne," Madeline said in protest. "I don't trust you after you employed your arts of seduction the last time."

"You needn't worry on that score. I merely want a measure of privacy while I wring your neck."

Understandably, his threat somewhat relieved Madeline. She had feared giving Rayne the chance to repeat his sensual assault of two nights ago, but clearly his mood just now was not the least amorous. Which was fortunate for her, Madeline reflected. Rayne looked distinctly dangerous at present, but she could deal with his anger much more easily than she could resist his seduction.

"Your servants will know if you murder me," she pointed out meekly. "And so will Freddie."

"I intend to deal with Freddie later."

The baron's coach had pulled away by the time they reached the edge of the meadow, and Will Stokes's gig was doing the same.

Rayne, however, was not heading toward his coach, Madeline realized. Instead, he guided her beyond the field's edge into a copse of elms, out of sight of his coach and servants.

Only then did he release her arm and turn on her, flinging her veil up over the rim of her bonnet so he could see her face.

"What in hell's name do you mean showing up on a dueling field?" he said through gritted teeth.

"What in hell's name do you mean dueling in the first place?" she retorted, determined to hold her own in any verbal battle with Rayne.

His eyes only darkened as he glowered at her. "You were worried I would shoot Ackerby, weren't you." It was not a question.

"Certainly I was worried! I didn't want you to suffer the consequences if you succeeded in killing a peer."

If she hoped to soothe his anger with a rational argument, Rayne wasn't listening. "Why are you so damned determined to champion Ackerby?" he demanded.

"I am *not* championing him!" Madeline exclaimed, before forcing herself to take a calming breath. Shouting at Rayne was getting her nowhere, so she tried a milder approach.

"Instead of railing at me, my lord, you should be thanking me for saving you from scandal. And from your grandmother's wrath as well. What would Lady

Haviland say if you broke your promise to marry because you were languishing in prison or worse?"

"My grandmother has nothing to do with this!"

"Well, I think you should have considered her sensibilities before you went haring off challenging Ackerby to pistols at dawn!"

Rayne was still scrutinizing her, his eyes furiously intent on her. "I want to know why you are so set on protecting Ackerby," he repeated.

"I am not, I assure you."

"Then why did you write to him yesterday?"

Startled by the abrupt question, Madeline stared at Rayne, wondering how he had possibly found out about her letter. A moment later it struck her.

"Did you commission Simpkin to *spy* on me?" she asked, her tone incredulous. "I cannot believe it!"

"I asked him to watch out for you in case Ackerby returned, and he thought your communication worrisome enough to report to me."

Madeline clenched her teeth, fuming now herself. Of course Simpkin would be more loyal to Rayne than to her—a fact she would do well to remember in future. But it would be folly to reveal Ackerby's scheme to blackmail her into becoming his mistress. There was no telling what Rayne would do.

Therefore she shaded her answer when she muttered, "I wrote Ackerby to beg him to withdraw from the duel, since I doubted you would withdraw your challenge."

That part was absolutely true, and her lie of omission was justified, to Madeline's mind.

"And your brother? Why did you write to him at the same time?"

Madeline hesitated only an instant before remembering that she had a perfectly good excuse for writing her brother. "I wanted to send him the money Freddie gave me as a reward. Gerard needs the funds just now." Another justifiable omission, she told herself.

When Rayne's fierceness didn't abate, Madeline forcibly swallowed her ire and said in a more earnest voice, "I was afraid for *you*, Rayne, not Ackerby—although I could cheerfully contemplate your demise just now."

She held her breath, hoping her reply would mollify him enough to make him see reason. When his taut expression seemed to relax the slightest degree, relief surged through Madeline. She did not like lying to Rayne, and she would have been hard-pressed to hedge further if he had grilled her about either letter.

"You are without a doubt the most stubborn female I have ever encountered," he finally remarked, yet much of the heat had gone out of his tone.

Madeline smiled faintly. "And you are the most stubborn man. I *told* you yesterday I did not need rescuing, but you would not heed a word I said."

She could swear that Rayne's lips twitched. "*You* have refused to heed me a dozen times over, sweetheart, need I remind you? It is difficult to protect you when you purposely put yourself in danger."

Madeline allowed her smile to widen a little. "You protected me quite well yesterday, knocking Ackerby down into the rosebushes, but there was certainly no need to call him out."

"I beg to differ."

She gave an exasperated sigh at Rayne's intractability. "I am finding it extremely tiresome, my lord, your treating me like a fragile female because of your outsized sense of chivalry. You cannot help playing the hero, but I do not require coddling."

"No, I suppose you don't." Thankfully, his gaze had lightened with a slight glimmer of amusement. "But how am I to restore my sense of manhood after allowing an interfering wench to intervene in an affair of honor?"

"I doubt your manhood is grievously wounded," Madeline said dryly.

"Oh, but it is. And it is up to you to make amends."

Her wariness suddenly returned full force, considering the way he was looking at her. "What do you mean?"

"I want an answer to my marriage proposal."

"This is hardly the time to discuss your proposal," she replied, taking a step backward.

"I don't see it that way, darling. This is the perfect time to resume our negotiations, especially since you owe me for calling off the duel."

Rayne's silky tone put all her nerves on edge, as did the fact that he was slowly advancing on her. Madeline retreated until he had backed her against the trunk of an elm. Her heart began thudding as he stood there gazing down at her.

"It should be abundantly clear by now," he admonished, "that Ackerby's pursuit of you is a compelling reason for you to wed me. He wouldn't dare touch you if you were my countess."

"He won't dare touch me *now* after you threatened to shoot him."

Raising his hand, Rayne put a finger under her chin, trapping her gaze and making her mouth go dry. "You can't be certain of that. I intend to give you the protection of my name and title, Madeline."

"I don't want your protection," she said unevenly. "And I know you don't truly want to wed me."

"You know nothing of the kind. If anything, this incident only confirmed my instincts about you. You're intrepid and brave and a force to be reckoned with. And you are the woman I want for the mother of my heir."

Madeline felt her heart turn over as his blue eyes delved into hers. She recalled Rayne questioning her earlier about her desire for children, his intense expression as he'd waited for her answer, as if her reply were extremely important to him. And perhaps it was. He wanted children more than he wanted a wife.

She had little doubt that Rayne would be a good father to their children. Indeed, he would likely love them far more readily than he would love her. Which was the chief trouble. He wanted her for a broodmare and she wanted love—

He cut off that dismaying thought with a simple comment. "When I was in London on Monday, I procured a special license for us to marry."

Startled, Madeline stared up at him. "That is outrageously presumptuous of you."

"Not at all. I told you, I don't mean to take no for an answer."

An obvious understatement, Madeline thought with exasperated worry as he moved even closer. Rayne was the most relentless man she had ever known, even more so than Ackerby. But at least Rayne's intentions were honorable.

Her thoughts were so preoccupied that she almost missed his next declaration. ". . . the ceremony can take place this afternoon."

"This afternoon! You must be joking."

"You know me better than that by now."

Madeline's chin jutted out defiantly. "Simply because you have decided you will wed me, I must comply?"

The corner of his mouth twisted in a hint of a smile. "No. You will comply because marriage to me is the best future for you. On Monday I also spoke with my solicitors and ordered them to arrange a sizable marriage settlement for you."

His admission gave her pause, since she was reminded of the practical reasons for accepting Rayne's offer. As his wife she would have significant financial security. And she could possibly use his marriage settlement to help her brother get out of the predicament he was in—

No, it was absurd to consider marrying Rayne for his money. She was not a fortune hunter.

On the other hand, Rayne's protection might be very welcome. Her quandary just now—Ackerby holding her brother's theft over her head—had driven home again to Madeline just how powerless she was against someone of the baron's wealth and stature. She wouldn't be nearly so helpless in standing up to him if she were a countess. Admittedly, Ackerby frightened her, not for her sake but for Gerard's.

The prospect of a solitary future frightened her nearly as much, Madeline conceded. She dreaded the dreariness of life lived in chaste spinsterhood. She didn't want to wind up a sad old woman, regretting the emptiness and loneliness of her existence. She wanted the joy of having children, a family, a beloved husband. . . .

While she stood debating, Rayne's hand shifted to cradle her jaw. Her gaze fixed on his mouth as his thumb stroked her lower lip. Then before she could gather her scattered thoughts enough to prevent him, Rayne bent his head to kiss her.

Her breath strangled in her throat at the first contact. Devil take him, this kiss was just as overwhelming as all the preceding ones, full of heat and seduction, power and tenderness.

His lips claimed her possessively, his tongue reaching deep into the heat of her mouth, reminding Madeline just how much she craved his taste, his touch. Even knowing he was bent on gaining her capitulation by exploiting her weakness for him, she couldn't pull away.

His magical kiss went on and on, weakening her will. Madeline silently swore at Rayne, yet the husky moan that came from her throat was more pleasure-sound than protest as she argued halfheartedly with herself. There was no question that his kisses were thrilling, that his seduction was devastatingly effective. But he was relying on physical skill. His heart wasn't engaged and likely never would be.

Even so, her resistance was withering. The truth was, she wanted desperately to be Rayne's wife. . . .

Realizing what she had just admitted to herself, Madeline groaned in disbelief. Was she actually considering agreeing to his proposal of marriage?

His kiss softening, he drew back enough to murmur against her lips, "What did you say?"

"Nothing. I was merely cursing you."

She felt his smile against her mouth. "You have been doing that frequently of late."

"You have given me ample cause." Pressing her hands against his chest, she sucked in a breath. "You *have* to stop kissing me, Rayne. I cannot think when you are assaulting my senses this way."

"That is the whole point, sweetheart." When Madeline failed to be amused, Rayne seemed to capitulate. "As you wish."

He didn't release her, however. He merely stood there, holding her in a light embrace, his forehead pressed against hers while he cajoled her in a soft, persuasive voice. "Come now, love, you've delayed long enough. Say 'yes.' "

Madeline closed her eyes, breathing in the scent of him. The yearning inside her was more powerful than anything she had ever felt in her life. No matter how fiercely she fought it, or how sternly she warned herself about the risk, she wanted to marry Rayne.

Did she dare surrender to the yearning of her heart? She would likely be giving up her dream of a loving marriage—a true love match. Yet being Rayne's wife and risking heartache would be better than watching him marry some other woman. And perhaps—just perhaps—he might someday come to feel a little of the love she had already come to feel for him.

Madeline shook herself mentally. It was idiotic to pin her hopes on foolish fantasies. But still, the lure of what might be possible if she were willing to chance marriage with him was too tempting to ignore.

"If I were to wed you," she said slowly, "I would not give up my new teaching position at the academy."

Rayne went still, as if he hadn't expected her answer. She hadn't either, for that matter. *Am I completely mad, Maman?*

Surprisingly, he only nodded. "I have no objections, although it will be novel, a countess employed as a teacher."

"Arabella still teaches there, as do her sisters, and I mean to earn my keep."

"There is no reason for you to continue, love. You weren't cut out to lead a life of docile servitude."

"There *is* reason. I don't want to sponge off you."

"You would not be sponging. You will be giving me an heir in exchange for marriage."

Madeline winced at the sudden ache in her heart. She would be marrying for love, but for Rayne it would be strictly a business transaction. "I remember. You said a marriage of convenience is all you want," she murmured, wishing he would deny it.

"You understand the advantages of a convenient match, Madeline. You are practical and sensible—when you are not putting yourself in danger. And you know I am not of a romantic turn of mind."

She did indeed know. Love would be no part of their bargain, Rayne had made that perfectly clear to her. She caught her lower lip between her teeth, knowing that if she agreed to his terms, she could never let him know that she had already lost her heart to him. Could she keep such a secret from Rayne?

Madeline took a shaky breath, coming to a conclusion. "Very well," she said unevenly.

"Very well, what?"

"I will marry you."

He looked only marginally surprised, and more than a little satisfied. "Good. I will make the arrangements for this afternoon."

Her brow furrowed as a twinge of panic ran through her. "This afternoon is much too soon."

"Why? A special license allows us to wed anywhere, at any time. And the vicar in Chiswick has already agreed to perform the ceremony whenever I request it of him."

Madeline grimaced. "You were very sure of yourself, weren't you, Lord Haviland."

His mouth curved slightly. "Of course. It was you I was unsure about."

"Won't your grandmother wish to be present at your wedding?" Madeline asked.

Rayne brushed off her concern. "My grandmother is in Brighton at the moment. I don't want to wait for her to return to London, or to spoil her enjoyment of her friend's house party."

"Lady Haviland won't be happy to learn that you have wed me."

"Allow me to handle her."

"What about your sisters?"

"Both my sisters are in Kent, too far away to arrive in time."

Madeline wondered if Rayne meant to exclude his sisters for the same reason he wasn't inviting his grandmother—because they would not approve of his marrying her.

Then he hesitated as if a thought had occurred to him. "Perhaps you would rather have your brother present at your wedding."

She would certainly rather, but she had not been present for Gerard's marriage in Scotland, and just now he was not available to attend hers. Furthermore, if she tried to explain why, his theft would come out.

"I don't require my brother's presence," Madeline replied. "But what is the hurry?"

"I don't intend to give you time to change your mind."

"I won't change my mind," she vowed, even though she was already having alarming second thoughts.

"Then we will hold the ceremony at five o'clock at Riverwood. I'll speak to the vicar about officiating as soon as I return to Chiswick."

Madeline suddenly recalled her own obligations. "I had best return there now. I have a class at ten this morning, and I have a wedding to prepare for. . . ."

The realization struck her with renewed force. She pressed her gloved hand to her temple, feeling dazed by the speed of events. She had come here intending to stop a duel and wound up agreeing to wed Rayne. *Dear heaven, I am mad, Maman.*

"Come," Rayne urged, smoothing her veil into place before taking her elbow. "I will let Freddie drive you home since I must stop at my house here."

She allowed Rayne to escort her to Freddie's curricle, where he was waiting in the seat, holding the reins.

As Rayne handed her up, he must have sensed her wavering resolution, for he said bracingly, "I will see you at five o'clock, love. I'll send a carriage for you at Danvers Hall at a quarter till, and if you are not ready, I will come for you myself."

Madeline had no doubt Rayne would make good on his promise, and so made no reply as she arranged her skirts on the seat. She ignored Freddie's quizzical glance also, and asked him to take her home at once, saying she would explain during the drive.

Just now she was too occupied wondering if she had made a dreadful mistake.

Rayne left the dueling field feeling a strong sense of satisfaction. He'd been seriously displeased to see Madeline this morning, but the end result made up for her maddening interference.

By this evening she would be wedded to him, and by tonight she would be bedded.

The prospect filled him with triumph and anticipation as his carriage negotiated the foggy streets of Mayfair. And when Rayne recalled Madeline's irate responses to his interrogation, he felt an undeniable measure of relief.

She'd had a reasonable explanation for writing to Ackerby, enough to allay his worst suspicions about her. Her concern was for *him*, not the baron.

He had overreacted, Rayne admitted, thinking they might be lovers. And her correspondence with her brother was only the support of a loving sister, not some sinister plot to betray him.

Marriage to Madeline was indeed the right course, Rayne reaffirmed to himself. He could repay his debt to her late father, as well as give her the protection of his name and save her from Ackerby's pursuit.

As for his grandmother, well . . . Rayne knew he might have a fight on his hands. He had little doubt that the imperious dowager Lady Haviland would object to his choice of brides. Thus he'd deemed it better to inform her after the fact rather than risk a disagreeable scene. Grandmother would simply have to be satisfied with the prospect of someday having a grandson to carry on the family title. In any event, he wouldn't let his relative sway him from his course.

Granted, Madeline was vastly different from the vapid debutante he had expected to marry. Yet despite his exasperation with her, he'd never admired her more than when she'd come marching out on the dueling field and pushed her way between two adversaries, threatening to shoot both of them if they refused to withdraw. Even now, the remembrance made Rayne smile.

His opinion of Madeline's mettle had risen another several notches with her stand against him this morning. And despite looking so bedraggled and dowdy in her mud-splattered cloak and dripping bonnet, she had shown the makings of a magnificent countess.

He had spoken the truth to her earlier, Rayne acknowledged. He wanted a woman as feisty and brave as Madeline for the mother of his children.

Yet at the same time, he'd made certain she held no illusions about the basis for their marriage. He wanted her to have no expectation of love between them. Short of that, however, he was willing to predict they would have a highly compatible union.

Unexpectedly, Rayne's feeling of anticipation was interrupted moments later when he arrived at his town house on Bedford Avenue, since the carriage standing at the curb bore the crest of Drew Moncrief, the Duke of Arden. And Arden himself was descending the front steps of Rayne's mansion, evidently having paid an extremely early morning call only to find him away from home.

His curiosity aroused, Rayne strode up the walk in time to meet the tall, elegant, fair-haired duke halfway.

"I would like a private word with you, if I may, Haviland," Arden said in greeting.

His tone was pleasant enough, giving no indication for the purpose of his visit, and Rayne agreed readily and led him inside. Once he'd turned his wet greatcoat and hat over to Walters and seen his visitor's outer garments likewise disposed of, Rayne invited the duke into his study, where they settled on comfortable leather couches.

"My recent involvement with government affairs," Arden began, "has made me aware of your past efforts to defeat Napoleon, protecting national interests from numerous threats over the years. I realize that the Foreign Office no longer funds a department for gathering intelligence, but I suspect your skills could prove invaluable in a domestic matter, Haviland. You are aware that Prinny survived an assassination attempt this past January?"

"I had heard of it, yes," Rayne said.

George, Britain's Prince Regent, had nearly been shot, while his unpopularity was still causing riots now.

"How may I be of service?" Rayne asked Arden.

"Some disturbing rumors have been circulating about a fresh plot to assassinate the Regent. I would like to commission you to investigate. Should you find any credence to the tales, then I want you to foil the plot, if possible."

Rayne bit back a smile, feeling a renewed wave of satisfaction along with a sharp twinge of amusement. Just last week he'd been lamenting the dullness of his life and wishing for more excitement. Thwarting blackmail attempts, fighting duels, arranging marriage to a spirited spinster, and uncovering political intrigues with the prospect of foiling an assassination plot against the Prince Regent were sure to cure his restlessness and boredom.

How fortuitous that Arden's request had come at precisely this moment, Rayne decided. He would relish the chance to pit his wits against a new foe using the skills he'd developed in his former vocation.

But first he had to get past his wedding and wedding night. Not that bedding Madeline would be a hardship. He was greatly anticipating initiating her in the carnal delights of the nuptial bed . . . and sating the powerful sexual desire that had been building inside him ever since their first titillating meeting at the inn when he'd kissed her and tasted a hint of the passionate woman trapped inside that drab exterior.

Still, he was glad for the diversion. A new occupation for his time would give him an excellent reason to keep his distance from Madeline while they settled into married life together.

"I would be pleased to help if I can," Rayne replied easily to Arden. "Why don't you begin by telling me everything you know and have heard so I can judge what may best be done?"

Chapter Ten

*Spellbinding, magical, beautiful, incredible . . . there
really are no words to describe it, Maman.*

How drastically her life had changed in the span of a
single week, Madeline reflected as she stood reciting her
vows in the elegant drawing room at Riverwood.

She'd been in danger of declining into permanent
spinsterhood, yet now she was joining in holy matrimony with a ruggedly handsome nobleman and entering a world of privilege and wealth she could only
imagine.

The small but illustrious list of wedding guests was
just one indication of her altered circumstances. In addition to the vicar and her two new friends from the academy, Jane Caruthers and Penelope Melford, Arabella
and her husband, Marcus, Lord Danvers, were in attendance. So were Arabella's sister Roslyn and *her* husband, the Duke of Arden, as well as the Honorable
Freddie Lunsford.

Madeline felt a trifle dazed by her startling turn of
fortune. Her nuptials were not precisely what she'd expected, either. She wore a pale-green silk gown borrowed from Arabella, with the bust and waist seams let

out and the hem pinned up to accommodate her fuller figure and shorter height.

But most critically, Madeline acknowledged, she had abandoned her dreams and romantic ideals for marriage. She and Rayne were two near strangers who were marrying simply for convenience.

Or at least, *his* motivation was convenience. Hers went much deeper.

Keenly aware of her compelling bridegroom standing beside her, Madeline couldn't help noting the frantic way her heart was drumming warnings about her future prospects. Rayne had frequently taken her to task for risking physical danger, but she had put herself in real peril by wedding him with little hope of mutual affection.

She was in love with a man who had no interest in her other than the heir she could give him.

Madeline was very aware, also, that she was not Rayne's first choice of brides. The beautiful Roslyn might have been standing here instead had she not married her duke.

Madeline swallowed as a pang of sadness twisted inside her. Her father had fairly worshiped her mother, and she'd wanted that kind of profound devotion for herself. Yet now she was prepared to settle for much less. She wanted Rayne to be, if not happy in their marriage, then unassailed by regrets at the irrevocable step he was taking today.

The ceremony was over swiftly, practically before Madeline realized it. Rayne favored her with a brief kiss to seal the union. Then together they accepted felicitations from the various guests.

Madeline responded to the good wishes with a forced

smile, until Freddie's bluntness roused her genuine amusement.

"I confess myself disappointed that Rayne actually got himself leg-shackled," Freddie said, shaking his head sorrowfully. "But if he had to do it, you are likely the best choice he could have made, Madeline."

"Thank you for the compliment, I think," she murmured with a strangled laugh.

"Oh, my admiration of you is utterly sincere," Freddie protested. "You and *I* would never suit, but you and Rayne . . . well, you just might. He needs a wife who can hold her own, and you certainly have no fear of standing up to him."

Under most circumstances, that was true, Madeline agreed silently, except that now her wedding night loomed ahead of her—a fact that Freddie was quick to remind her of.

"I plan to take myself home this evening directly after dinner," he announced, "so that you and Rayne may have Riverwood to yourselves. I have doubtless overstayed my welcome as it is."

The ceremony was to be followed immediately by a small dinner celebration, but Madeline wanted to implore Freddie to stay afterward so she could postpone the inevitable as long as possible.

She scarcely ate a bite during dinner, although she fortified herself with a significant quantity of wine. Despite her intention to pretend nonchalance, she stole frequent glances at her new husband where he was seated at the head of the table on her left. She couldn't stop thinking about the consummation that lay in store for her or calm the butterflies that were rioting inside her at the prospect.

The physical aspects did not really worry her overmuch. Thankfully, Arabella had told her something of what to expect—that she might feel pain and discomfort her first time, but that a considerate lover would make the experience as pleasurable as possible. And she had no doubt that Rayne would be considerate of her virginal state.

What worried Madeline was that giving him her body would leave her even more vulnerable to him than she was now.

Fortunately for the sake of their dinner guests, Rayne carried on the bulk of the conversation with their company. Not that the two happily married couples at the table paid much regard to her near silence.

Madeline couldn't help but notice how contented Arabella seemed with her earl and Roslyn with her duke. Judging by their conversation and their mutually tender glances, it was perfectly clear that both ladies were very much in love—and that their love was returned wholeheartedly.

Which in itself was a little disheartening to Madeline, since *her* marriage fell far short in comparison. And all too soon she stood with her husband in the entrance hall, saying farewell to their guests.

When after their departure, Rayne took up a brace of lit candles to lead her upstairs, Madeline accompanied him reluctantly.

"Are you suffering an illness, love?" he asked as they reached the second floor where his bedchamber was no doubt located. "You scarcely spoke a word at dinner. It is not like you to be so mute."

"I am perfectly fine," she lied, walking beside him down the long corridor.

Nerves clustered in her stomach as he ushered her inside a luxurious chamber.

"This suite will be yours," Rayne informed her. "You'll find your trunk and bandbox in the adjacent dressing room. And your sitting room is to your right."

It was clearly a lady's bedchamber, done in shades of pale blue and rose, Madeline saw with some surprise while wondering why he hadn't directed her to the master's suite. But perhaps he meant to spend the night here with her.

She watched silently as Rayne shut and locked the bedchamber door behind them. Then he set the candles down on a table and went to the hearth to stir the flames.

"I asked that the fire be built up," he added casually. "I mean to keep you warm tonight, but until then, I don't want you to grow chilled."

Madeline swallowed at the implication that they would be naked together.

When she made no reply, he asked in that same easy voice, "Are you worried that I might ravish you?"

To be truthful, she was worried that he would *not*. He would be doing his duty, attempting to beget an heir, but dutifully servicing her was a far cry from being an ardent lover.

"No," she answered unevenly, "I am not worried about ravishment."

Rayne set aside the poker and turned to face her, his intense gaze leveled at her. "You have nothing to fear from me, Madeline."

"That is easy for you to say, since you have done this countless times before."

A smile claimed his mouth. "Not countless. You give

me too much credit for amorous experiences. And I have never once made love to my bride."

While she was considering his comment, Rayne crossed the room to her and reached up to lightly stoke her bare throat. "It's time we undressed, darling."

Madeline stiffened involuntarily. "Must we?" she asked rather breathlessly at the seductive feel of his fingers on her skin.

"I suppose not, but lovemaking is more pleasurable without clothing."

Perhaps so, but he would see her entire body with all its imperfections.

"Your shyness is quite endearing," Rayne observed when she didn't respond.

She gave him a sharp glance. "I don't mean to be endearing."

"I know," he replied with hidden laughter, his warm blue eyes amused and beguiling.

His teasing was calculated to set her at ease, she knew. Yet her misgivings were very real. How a man as beautiful as Rayne could want a plain woman like her, she couldn't fathom.

"I am not your ideal bride," Madeline murmured, "and I never will be."

Rayne's features seemed to soften. "You are entirely too critical of yourself, love. I have told you before how appealing I find you . . . and I mean to prove it to you tonight."

"I would be perfectly happy if you chose to postpone the consummation."

He slanted his head. "But I would not be. Come now, where is your vaunted courage? This morning you were threatening to shoot me. Surely you haven't turned missish all of a sudden," he said with that same glimmer of amusement.

He was deliberately provoking her, Madeline realized. And then he gently gathered her face in his hands and kissed her nose, of all things.

Her heartbeat tripped over itself. Despite her nerves, she was charmed.

"Madeline, sweetheart," Rayne said in a soothing voice, "I have every intention of ensuring your pleasure in our marriage bed. And I will do my utmost to help you over your wedding night jitters. In truth, I am rather unnerved myself."

She frowned at him. "I don't believe it."

"It's true, I swear it. Matrimony will take some time to become accustomed to—for both of us, I expect."

She searched Rayne's gaze for what he was feeling, but she couldn't tell much from his expression. There was tenderness there, and friendly sympathy, perhaps even affection. Yet she didn't dare trust her senses just now. More likely, she was merely seeing what she desperately hoped to see.

She let him undress her, though. It was foolish to keep protesting when she was sure he meant to have his way in the end anyway.

He unfastened the hooks at the back of her gown, then helped raise it over her head. As he took the garment from her, however, he jerked his hand reflexively and winced.

Madeline made a small sound of dismay. "I am sorry—I should have warned you about the pins. Arabella insisted I wear one of her lovely gowns, but I could not let her destroy it permanently by cutting, so the seams are only pinned."

Surprisingly, Rayne responded with a rich chuckle as he laid the gown over the back of a chair. "I always knew you were prickly, love, and now I have proof. You should be wearing a sign around your neck, 'beware the dangerous bride.' "

At the absurdity of the image he engendered, Madeline couldn't help but smile. She hardly noticed when Rayne knelt at her feet to remove her slippers and stockings, but when he glanced up at her, she found herself relishing the laugh lines around his blue eyes.

Then he stood and proceeded to remove her corset, and her breath caught.

"I shall have to ask Arabella to help you choose some suitable bride clothes," he remarked as he next relieved her of her chemise. "I won't have it said that my countess dresses as a governess."

She suspected he distrusted her taste in fashion, but it was hard to think about such mundane subjects as her wardrobe with her heart in her throat.

By now Rayne had tossed her chemise aside, and she stood completely naked before him. For an endless moment, he remained utterly silent as he drank his fill of her.

She felt exposed, uncertain. . . . Yet his bold, seductive gaze seared her wherever it touched. From his expression, she could almost believe he wanted her.

"I knew your body was incredibly lovely," he murmured.

Then he stepped closer and reached up to lightly clasp her bare shoulders. Further surprising her, he guided her to the cheval glass in one corner of the bedchamber and turned her to face her reflection.

Rayne stood behind her, watching her in the mirror. "As I said, incredibly lovely."

Madeline wished she could believe him. She wanted to be lovely and feminine and all the things she was not.

Without waiting for her contradiction, Rayne reached up to her hair and pulled out the pins from the tight knot she wore at her nape, then smoothed out the tresses so that they fell loose and shining around her shoulders.

"I have wanted to do this since the first time I met you," Rayne asserted, his voice a deep, husky sound. "You should wear your hair down more often, sweeting. This style softens your features."

Madeline had to agree with him. The luminous light in the bedchamber helped as well. The play of firelight caught the lighter strands of gold amid the brown of her hair and danced over her pale skin, giving it a rosy cast.

"You forget," she replied her own voice a husky rasp, "that companions are in no position to indulge their vanity, nor are teachers for that matter. Nor can they risk being taken for lightskirts."

"True. But countesses may do as they please in the privacy of their own bedchambers . . . and they *should* do as their husbands please."

At his provocative declaration, Madeline arched an eyebrow. "Is pleasing you a requirement for being your wife?"

The slight gust of his laughter stirred the hair at her temple. "My first inclination is to say 'yes,' but I know better than to make any demands of you, sweet Madeline. And I have no doubt you will please me willingly all on your own."

She felt Rayne's hot gaze on her bare breasts at the same time he wrapped his arms around her from behind. When he cupped her fullness in his hands, her lips parted wordlessly.

As she watched, his knowing fingers fanned over the swelling mounds, then closed to tease the tight peaks, coaxing a response low in her belly and making her shiver with delight.

Yet it was Rayne's look that left her unable to breathe. Under his intense gaze, she actually felt beautiful for the first time in her life.

Her pulse was pounding wildly by now. Even so, Madeline strove to school her own features, afraid all her emotions would be painfully obvious to Rayne. It was difficult to conceal that constant heart-in-the-throat feeling when she looked at him. But it was impossible to hide the desire that was written clearly on her face. Her body was already aching for his touch. She yearned to feel Rayne holding her in his strong arms, kissing her, taking her. . . .

As if sensing her need, Rayne left off fondling her breasts. Instead of gratifying her silent wish, however, he seemed intent on merely tantalizing her further. Lifting her hair, he kissed her nape, then trailed his lips over every inch of her bare shoulders.

Languorous heat was flooding Madeline's veins and suffusing her limbs with liquid heaviness by the time he brushed one last brief kiss on her shoulder. When he stepped back, she didn't know whether she was more disappointed that he was no longer bent on arousing her, or excited that he was proceeding to the next step of the consummation.

Both, perhaps, she thought as he removed his coat. Yet excitement won out as Rayne locked gazes with her.

"You should help me undress, wife. I want you to become intimately familiar with my body."

He never took his eyes off her as she obliged. With trembling fingers, Madeline helped him remove his waistcoat and cravat and shirt. Rayne sat in a chair to remove his pumps and breeches and stockings, but when he stood and turned to face her in all his naked splendor, Madeline could barely do more than breathe.

"You have beautiful eyes," he murmured, breaking the rapt silence.

"So do you," she replied truthfully if distractedly.

Indeed, Rayne was beautiful everywhere. Wantonly, irresistibly so. He was six feet and several inches of masculine perfection.

She was almost startled by his sheer maleness . . . the width of his shoulders, the breadth of his chest, the power and thickness of his thighs, the novelty of his bare loins. Madeline stared hungrily at Rayne as flames and shadows played upon his magnificent body, painfully aware of the urge to reach out and touch him.

With an indulgent smile, Rayne took the decision from her.

"Come to bed with me, love," he urged, skimming his fingers down her arm to capture her hand.

Leading her to the high, canopied bed, he turned down the covers, then lay back among the pillows, holding out his hand in an invitation for her to join him. Madeline hesitated, though, admiring the lithe grace of his large body yet assaulted by a fresh attack of nerves.

Rayne's expression was one of amused patience. He

grasped her hand again and tugged her up onto the bed with him, so that she was kneeling beside him. "No miss-ishness allowed, remember?"

Reminding herself that he had promised her connubial bliss, Madeline found her voice. "What should I do?" she asked more steadily.

"Run your hands over my body. Let your fingers wan-der over my skin."

It was a command she urgently wanted to obey. Lean-ing closer, she reached down and began with his power-ful torso.

He was so very male, she thought, splaying her fingers over the sculpted ridges of his chest, feeling the flex-ing sinews beneath the satin skin. Her own chest felt too small to contain the swell of her fast-beating heart as she allowed her touch to roam farther at will. The heat and steel beneath his smooth bare flesh was kindling to her senses, as was his scent. He smelled of musk and warm skin, Madeline realized, reveling in her explo-ration.

More brazenly, she shifted her hand lower, over his taut abdomen, and then lower still. Bypassing his loins and the swollen column of male flesh that jutted up from a nest of curling black hair, she tentatively rested her hand on his thigh.

When she went no farther, Rayne took her hand again and wrapped her fingers around his thick, straining arousal. Madeline nearly gasped at how big and hard he felt against her palm, but he pressed harder, encouraging her to continue.

"Go ahead . . . you won't hurt me."

To her surprise, the turgid length was velvety soft at

the tip and sleekly rigid elsewhere. And below that, the swollen sacs felt like ripe melons.

Madeline looked up, her cheeks flushing as she met Rayne's gaze. He was watching her, clearly enjoying the look of fascination on her face.

"You are much larger than I expected," she admitted.

"What did you expect?" he asked curiously.

She gave a helpless shrug. "I don't know exactly . . . something significantly smaller. My only basis for comparison has been classical statues. I don't quite see how you will fit."

His eyes alight with teasing laughter, he reached up and slid a hand behind her nape. "I promise you, sweetheart, I will fit perfectly—although first I must make you ready for me."

His fingers spreading deliciously through her hair, he brought her face down to his and kissed her, his mouth brushing against hers in a tender, erotic caress. And when she responded eagerly, Rayne drew her down fully against him, pulling her into the hard strength of his body.

The warmth of his naked flesh beneath hers was another exquisite shock of sensation, as was the taste of his lips. Madeline shut her eyes, cherishing the feelings that were racing through her . . . at the same time acknowledging the danger. This mad rush of emotions Rayne was stirring in—all the heat and want and yearning—would only make him harder to resist.

Yet she didn't have the will to fight it, not when he tenderly eased her onto her back and took complete control of her seduction.

He began by kissing the hollow of her throat, then nuzzling his face in the valley between her breasts. Next he suckled each of her nipples in turn, gently nipping and rasping.

His mouth was hot and sweet and demanding as he attended to the rest of her body. Eventually his stroking hands joined in her arousal, caressing her with the probing eroticism of an expert lover, lingering and taking his time, as if her pleasure was his only pleasure.

Her thighs were trembling when at last his thumb found the curls of her woman's mound and glided downward to her slick, sensitive folds. And when he penetrated her throbbing sex with a slow finger, Madeline arched her back wildly.

"Easy, now," Rayne murmured.

She couldn't be easy, though. She ached with the way he touched her. His lovemaking felt excruciatingly right—a drawn-out seduction by a man determined to shatter every part of her.

Yet he wasn't entirely satisfied by his progress, it seemed.

"Give me your mouth, love."

His roughly sensual voice came to her through her daze, merging with the pleasure vibrating through her body in heated waves.

Wishing desperately that Rayne would take away the ache he'd created in her, Madeline obeyed, raising her face to his. His kiss was hot and bold and thrilling, a spellbinding connection of lips and tongues. When she whimpered with need, his mouth turned even more forceful, yet still remained tender beneath the urgency.

Madeline welcomed his ardor. For this wonderful moment, she was living her most secret fantasy—that Rayne wanted her, loved her.

The scent of him was all around her, and so was his

enveloping tenderness as he eased his thighs between hers and covered her body. The heavy, strange-but-familiar weight warmed her . . . but then his hard flesh slowly, slowly sank inside her.

With his caressing mouth, he drank her gasp of surprise at the burgeoning pressure, soothing her open lips with featherlight kisses. But when he was seated fully in the cradle of her thighs, irrevocably joined to her, Rayne held himself still.

Her breath came in soft pants while her body grew accustomed to the alien hardness impaling her.

Long moments later he broke off his comforting kisses and lifted his head to scrutinize her face. "Are you all right?"

"Yes. . . ." she answered truthfully, feeling the pressure ease as her feminine flesh began to soften and melt around him. "You didn't hurt me."

Something protective and fierce flashed deep in his eyes. "Good. It will only get better from now on, I promise."

I believe you, she thought, gazing up into the dark beauty of his face.

The hushed quiet was broken by the crackle of the fire and the erratic thud of her own heartbeat as Rayne carefully began to move inside her. Holding her captive with the intensity of his blue gaze, he slowly withdrew, only to thrust again even more slowly . . . rising and sinking into her heated wetness with a mesmerizing rhythm, guiding her response with his hand on her hip.

Madeline felt a sob rise up in her throat as too many emotions welled inside her. She had never felt this treasured, this desired. She had never yearned this much.

Rayne made her want him more than she wanted to breathe.

This sort of wanting shouldn't be possible, this burning need to be one with him.

And then the firelight blurred as she trembled uncontrollably. She was only aware of Rayne, of his heat, of his masculine scent, of the way he filled her aching emptiness.

When the cresting wave of passion broke over her, her hips rocked violently in cadence with her cries of ecstasy.

Rayne felt the same violent explosion of pleasure moments later. His body clenched, then shuddered as he came, intense tremors of sensation flooding every part of him.

When finally he quieted, Madeline was still pulsating around him, her breasts rising and falling unevenly with her ragged breaths. Struggling harshly for air himself, Rayne lowered himself weakly to his elbows, sheltering her in a possessive embrace while burying his face in the fragrant silk of her hair.

It was several long moments more before he could find the energy to raise his head—and he suspected Madeline felt a similar blissful lethargy. When he pressed a tender kiss to her damp forehead, she slowly opened her eyes.

Her expression held warmth now, not wariness, and the soft, sated look in her luminous eyes was enchanting.

"I must say," she whispered hoarsely, "that you kept your promise. No wonder you are so fond of lovemaking."

Delight shivered through him, part laughter, part desire. "I was happy to oblige, love."

Carefully withdrawing from the sweet haven of her body, Rayne eased onto his side, then rolled onto his back, drawing Madeline against him so that her head rested on his shoulder.

Her feminine curves aligned perfectly with his harder ones, he noted, breathing her in. When she gave a contented sigh, Rayne acknowledged his own momentary contentment. How right it felt to hold her like this.

Admittedly, he ought to be worried. He had never savored a lover's pleasure so much before. And of all the women he'd bedded, none of them had moved him as much as Madeline had tonight.

A dangerous sentiment, Rayne thought, as his fingers absently stroked the slender stem of her neck beneath her hair.

It wasn't surprising that he felt a fierce protectiveness for Madeline. Or that he'd wanted to banish her insecurities about her desirability. Or that he was keenly, painfully aroused by her potent sensuality. He had been right about her passionate nature. Her alluring, utterly feminine body was pure temptation, a man's private fantasy. The desire to make love to her again was still stinging him.

Shifting his head slightly, Rayne gazed down at her face. By any conventional standards, Madeline was not beautiful or even particularly pretty. But the golden firelight made her so just now. In the rosy aftermath of passion, she looked well and thoroughly bedded . . . her skin flushed and soft, her smooth hair gleaming in the light cast by the dancing flames.

Something primal tugged again deep in the pit of his belly—and that was before her eyelids fluttered open and she met his gaze, her big, gray eyes drowsy and replete.

Indeed, she was glowing.

Rayne frowned at the realization, remembering Madeline's stated desire to find love in marriage. If he wasn't careful, she might grow too enamored of him. He didn't want to raise her expectations or allow her to think he would ever feel anything deeper for her than friendly affection.

He had not given anyone access to his heart for a very long time, and he would never do so again.

At the shy, tender smile Madeline gave him, however, Rayne felt the rare clutch of his heart. His unconscious response should be a warning to him, he reminded himself. It was a mistake to encourage any more intimacy between them. Even now he might already have let it grow too strong.

He couldn't deny, either, that during the enchanting moments when he'd claimed Madeline as his wife, long-dormant emotions and desires had swelled and surged to life within him. Joining with her tonight in their marriage bed was like filling a space in him that had been empty for too long.

Yet he intended to rely on his new professional challenges to fill the void in his life. He'd already begun calculating his first steps and written to Will Stokes to gain his collaboration. In fact, he planned to meet with his former fellow spy early tomorrow morning. If anyone could help him infiltrate a ring bent on assassinating the Regent, it was Will, Rayne reflected.

He wouldn't share the details of his plans with Madeline, though, other than to tell her he had business that needed his attention. Knowing her, she would ask to help him, and he didn't want her interfering, or worse, coming to harm.

Rayne quelled a faint smile at the thought. No, Madeline was not the dutiful wife he had once sought. Moreover, he had a strong suspicion that she would prove much more than he'd bargained for.

Still, he was glad to have chosen her. As for the future of their marriage, he would promise her fidelity, certainly. Since meeting her, he hadn't wanted any other woman and doubted he would anytime soon. But he intended for them to have separate bedchambers and separate beds. And except for conjugal visits, he meant to keep his hands off his new wife. He was determined to curb his lust for her, for he wanted no repeat of his disastrous love affair with Camille Juzet.

Madeline was a hidden treasure, with her innocence and wit and spirited warmth, but he needed to crush any excess tenderness he felt for her.

Just then she surprised him. Reaching for his hand, she placed her mouth against the heart of his palm, making his actual heart lurch again.

It was time to leave, Rayne decided. He had meant to stay until dawn, until he had satiated himself with her body and brought out all the hidden sensuality he knew was waiting to break free inside Madeline. There was also the matter of siring an heir. But there would be opportunities later to work on fulfilling his promise to his grandmother.

Easing his shoulder from beneath Madeline's head,

Rayne sat up and swung his legs over the side of the bed. Rising, he went to the washstand and cleaned himself with a wet cloth, then returned to Madeline and did the same for her.

Her flush revealed her shyness, so for both their sakes, he kept his movements brief and un-loverlike.

Carrying the cloth back to the washstand, Rayne proceeded to pull on his breeches, remarking casually as he did so, "I have business in London first thing tomorrow morning, so I will take my leave of you now."

Madeline had been watching him dress, but at his pronouncement, her head snapped up.

"You won't stay with me tonight?" she asked, her voice hesitant and faintly bewildered.

"I don't want to disturb your sleep when I must rise so early."

Her eyes were huge and bright as she regarded him steadily. She looked almost . . . wounded.

Yet it couldn't be helped, Rayne knew, hardening his resolve. It was best to begin as he meant to go on. There would be less pain for both of them this way.

"You shouldn't worry if you don't hear from me for several days," he added. "Bramsley will keep a close eye on you and see to your protection. And you may apply to him for anything you need in my absence."

His majordomo could be counted on to safeguard Madeline and to watch for Baron Ackerby, Rayne reflected. Yet she didn't seem to appreciate his concern for her welfare.

When she remained mute, merely watching him with those enormous hurt eyes, he collected the remainder of his clothes and went to her bedside.

Bending, he captured her hot, sweet mouth with his

one last time, offering silent reassurance in a brief kiss. Then drawing up the covers to conceal her lovely bare body before he was tempted to rejoin her there, Rayne turned and quietly left her bedchamber, aware of Madeline's wounded gaze following him all the while.

Chapter Eleven

It is extremely disheartening, Maman, when I cannot even keep my husband in my nuptial bed on my wedding night.

When she awoke the next morning after a mostly sleepless night, Madeline lay there a moment taking stock. The strange bed. The unfamiliar delicacy of her body. The heightened sensitivity between her thighs and across her skin. The hurt in her heart.

The memory of Rayne's wonderful lovemaking made her chest ache. Her wedding night was as perfect as nothing else in her life had ever been . . . until he had abruptly left her.

A renewed surge of misery struck Madeline as she clutched a pillow to her middle and squeezed her eyes shut. It was not uncommon for spouses of the noble class to have separate bedchambers, but it was rather mortifying that her new husband had retreated to his own rooms immediately after the consummation. Rayne's abrupt departure for London directly after their wedding night, with scarcely a farewell, did not bode well for their marriage, either.

Yet she was to blame for her current misery, Madeline scolded herself, trying to drum up a trace of her former spirit. It was her own fault for building air castles. The impossible dreams she had woven in her mind of Rayne loving her, of Rayne wanting a real marriage with her, were just that—*impossible.*

She should never have set her hopes so high. She'd known how painful it would be when reality intruded.

You should have heeded Rayne when he warned you of his dispassion. It serves you right for acting so hastily and accepting his proposal.

Throwing off the covers, Madeline sprang from the bed so she could wash and dress. She was highly annoyed at herself for falling in love with Rayne. And she was determined to crush the painful combination of need and longing she'd felt in his arms last night.

Even so, as she found her undergarments that Rayne had removed so seductively last night, she had never been more conscious of a deep, abiding sense of loneliness. After his magical lovemaking, she found it even harder to deny her deep-rooted need not to be alone, to matter to someone.

"But that someone will not be Rayne," Madeline reminded herself sternly. If she expected him to suddenly offer his heart in addition to his hand, she was doomed to disappointment.

She was winding her hair into its customary knot when she recalled Rayne's suggestion that she wear it down to soften her plain features. Her sinking feeling of despair returned full-force, as did her misgivings about her appearance.

Yet there was no point in lamenting her lack of appeal, especially if she had no husband here to try and please. Besides, she was not one to wail about her fate.

She intended to put on a game face and to keep her

day full, Madeline swore, setting her jaw. Immediately after breakfast she would write her brother again. The duel and her abrupt wedding had almost made her forget the danger Gerard was in, and she was supremely anxious to hear from him.

Afterward she would ask Bramsley, Riverwood's majordomo, to show her around the house and make her known to the servant staff.

And she would put in an appearance at the academy this afternoon, Madeline decided, even though both Jane and Arabella didn't expect her to teach any classes today because of her wedding.

She wanted to keep busy so she wouldn't dwell on the disaster she had made of her life by marrying Rayne when she should have known better.

At the start, Madeline's day went precisely as planned. She dined alone in the breakfast room, and afterward Bramsley introduced her to the many servants at Riverwood and took her on an extensive tour of her new home.

Madeline half expected Bramsley to resent her presence, but his demeanor was entirely respectful, if not eager to please. There was no pity in his eyes, either, because she'd been abandoned so shortly after the marriage ceremony. Instead, he acted as if the lord's absence was a common occurrence.

What was *not* a common occurrence was hearing Bramsley address her as "my lady." The first time he did so—greeting Madeline when she left her bedchamber and descended the grand staircase to the ground floor—she gave a start. Remembering that she was now Lady

Haviland, however, she summoned a smile. "Good morning to you also, Bramsley."

"I do beg your pardon, my lady," he intoned solemnly. "I would have sent a maid to you had I known you would rise so early."

Madeline heard no criticism in his tone because of her unexpected habits, merely chagrin that he had not anticipated her needs better.

"To be truthful, I never noticed the absence of a maid, since I am not in the habit of being waited upon. It will be one more thing that I must grow accustomed to."

Looking relieved by her admission, Bramsley responded with alacrity when she asked to see the house after breakfast. "Certainly, my lady. Lord Haviland bade me ensure your every comfort, and I will be pleased to serve you in any way possible."

Madeline would have been happier if Rayne himself were here to perform that particular service—but then she chided herself for the thought. How pathetic it would be if she were to become the possessive, clinging bride.

The tour actually took most of her morning. Riverwood was significantly larger than the estate where Madeline had spent the past five years of her life employed as a companion, and there were many, many rooms.

Her favorite, beyond a doubt, was on the second floor.

"This is the bathing chamber, my lady," Bramsley informed her. "His lordship designed the arrangement and oversaw the construction himself. Hot water is piped here to the tub from the boiler room below, so a regular temperature can be maintained and there is no need to carry cans of water to and fro from the kitchens."

"Very impressive," Madeline replied, eyeing the enormous copper bathing tub with its plethora of pipes. What a delicious luxury to have all the hot bathwater one could want. "Did Lord Haviland design any more of the house?"

"Yes, my lady. The kitchens and fireplaces were modernized as well. But his lordship left furnishing the main rooms to me. He purchased the estate last year from an elderly gentleman who wished to reside with his son, and most rooms were in sore need of refurbishing."

She supposed Rayne had bought Riverwood when he inherited his new title, but she wondered why he would need another country estate when he already had the Haviland family seat in Kent.

"You have excellent taste, Bramsley," Madeline murmured.

"Thank you, my lady."

The furnishings, she had noted, were much like Rayne's town house in London, elegant but comfortable. Madeline thought she would have felt quite at home here if she truly were Rayne's wife instead of one party in a matrimonial contract.

The most masculine room in the house was his study. Here, gleaming wood paneling and plush leather couches and chairs added elegance to the large desk dominating the room.

"His lordship spends much of his time in this chamber when he is at Riverwood," Bramsley said, answering her unspoken question.

Madeline suspected she might not be welcome in this male bastion but decided not to put it to the test. Instead she would use the pretty writing desk in the drawing room for her own correspondence needs.

At the conclusion of the tour, Bramsley again indicated his willingness to accept her as mistress. "I am certain there are changes you would like to make, my lady, and I will do my utmost to see that you are satisfied."

Madeline smiled and shook her head. "I don't mean to change anything as yet. You have clearly done a splendid job thus far at running the household, Bramsley, and I would be obliged if you continue."

The majordomo unbent enough to return her smile and then asked how he might be of service. In short order, he sent a maid up to help Madeline unpack her meager wardrobe and assist her in changing her gown, as befitted a countess. Bramsley also had a footman standing ready to drive her to the academy when she came down again.

She would grow quite spoiled with such luxury, Madeline reflected, deciding that tomorrow she would reassert her independence. For now, however, she would let herself be pampered a little.

When she reached the academy, Jane Caruthers was surprised to see her, but nodded in understanding when Madeline explained that Haviland had gone to London on business. She was gratified when her pupils seemed delighted by her visit and amused by their awe at her becoming a countess overnight.

It was when Madeline returned to her new home that she received a surprise herself. According to Bramsley, Rayne's elderly grandmother, the dowager Countess Haviland, awaited her in the drawing room.

Upon learning of her noble visitor, Madeline shed her bonnet and pelisse and gloves and made her way quickly down the corridor to the drawing room. Entering, she saw the silver-haired aristocrat seated in a wing chair beside a roaring hearth fire.

Lady Haviland, who still wore her own outer garments, was older than expected but there was nothing fragile about her. Her posture was rigid with anger as she turned a piercing perusal upon Madeline, her aura of disapproval unmistakable.

She did not rise or speak a word of greeting. Instead, with no effort at courtesy or even good manners, Lady Haviland demanded icily, "What is this I hear about my grandson marrying you yesterday, Miss Ellis?"

Taken aback by the noblewoman's fierceness, Madeline inhaled a steadying breath and moved into the room. Evidently her ladyship had a spine of steel and a hauteur to match, but as Rayne's elderly relation she deserved respect.

Before Madeline could even offer a polite introduction, however, Lady Haviland gave a shudder of revulsion. "My friend, Lady Perry, who lives very near here, wrote to warn me of your nuptials, but I could not credit such an outrage, despite the reliability of the source. Yet Bramsley says it is true."

Madeline hesitated to reply while debating her approach. Usually with her crotchety former employer, humor served best to deflect wrath. But Lady Haviland was clearly in no mood to be diverted with humor.

"Yes, it is true," Madeline said evenly. "I regret that you had to learn of our marriage secondhand, Lady Haviland. I suspected you might not be pleased."

"*Pleased?* Indeed I am *not*! It is beyond appalling that Haviland would marry a penniless nobody without even informing me."

"Perhaps that is why he waited to tell you—because he anticipated your response."

"The lapse is unforgivable," the lady declared savagely. "I was attending a house party near Brighton, but I came here posthaste the moment I heard. At my age, and with the poor condition of my heart, such grueling travel could very likely mean my death. And now I find my worst fears realized."

Madeline was willing to make allowances for the dowager's rudeness. It was only natural that she would be shocked, even horrified. And if she held her grandson in affection, she would want what was best for him. Certainly she would want to protect the family name and title. But Rayne had chosen a bride who contrasted starkly with the debutantes his grandmother had expected him to wed.

"Such a marriage is not to be borne," the dowager insisted, her tone adamant. "You are nothing more than a lowbred servant."

Madeline felt herself stiffen. "I beg to differ. I am a gentleman's daughter."

Lady Haviland sent her a scathing look. "Your father was a common soldier."

"My father was an officer who served on the Duke of Wellington's staff."

"Pah, that is hardly a qualification to become a Countess of Haviland—the offspring of Army riffraff."

At the spurious denigration, Madeline's fingers curled reflexively into fists. She could have pointed out the sacrifices her heroic father had made for his country— living away from his family for years, coming home for brief furloughs before packing his gear and striding off to war again, facing perils that the Lady Havilands of the world could only imagine, giving his very life for his noble cause. But she suspected a defense of her father would do nothing to change the dowager's low opinion of her.

"Your bloodlines are unsavory in other respects," her ladyship continued in that same derisive tone. "Your mother was *French*." She said the word as if it were dirty.

Having reached her limit of forbearance, Madeline responded with sugary sweetness. "Yes, my mother was French, Lady Haviland. But she could claim aristocratic ancestors on both sides of her family dating back before the Norman Conquest, when your ancestors were likely peasants tilling the fields."

"Impertinent girl! You will keep a civil tongue in your head!"

Her tongue had been known to land her in trouble, Madeline reflected, but she struggled to bite it now in the face of the dowager's fury. She did not want to alienate Rayne's grandmother entirely.

Instead, she forced a pleasant smile. "Clearly you consider me unworthy to assume your title, Lady Haviland, but I was not born into penury or service, and your grandson deemed my bloodlines adequate enough for his purposes."

The dowager subjected her to another searing inspection. "It is not only your bloodlines at issue. Look at you. You are practically dressed in rags."

She wore a serviceable day gown that admittedly had seen better days, but Madeline remained silent, knowing she would lose any argument about her wardrobe.

"Even worse, you are a mere country rustic. Do you

have any notion of the expectations of Haviland's rank? The decorum required of his position in society?"

With effort, Madeline kept her reply calm. "Haviland himself does not seem bothered by my lack of decorum. If he has no objections, my lady, how can you?"

Rayne's grandmother stood abruptly. "Obviously there is no point in continuing this discussion since you are set on thwarting me. But you should know that without my support, you will be utterly shunned in society."

"That is severe punishment indeed," Madeline murmured.

The dowager's expression turned livid. "It is beyond me, what arts you used to ensnare a gentleman so far above your station, but you have obviously blinded Haviland to what he owes his family name. Have you no shame, girl?"

"I am hardly a girl anymore."

"True. You are nothing but a spinster fortune hunter. Well, I have news for you, Miss Ellis. You will never see a penny of my fortune. My grandson was to inherit my vast holdings, but I intend to withhold every cent until he comes to his senses."

Madeline quelled a frown, not liking the threat—although her consternation was for Rayne's sake, not her own. She didn't want him to be deprived of his inheritance because he had stooped to wed her.

Lady Haviland, however, forestalled any reply with an abrupt question. "Has a notice of your nuptials appeared in the papers?"

"Not to my knowledge."

The dowager looked relieved. "Then it is not too late."

"Too late for what?"

"For an annulment, naturally."

A strange prick of fear struck Madeline. Would Rayne's grandmother succeed where she herself had failed? She had tried repeatedly to convince him of the unsuitability of their marriage, but he might actually listen to his beloved relative when he hadn't listened to her. If Rayne were to seek an annulment now—

She refused to let her thoughts dwell on such an alarming possibility. Instead, Madeline lifted her chin defiantly, her own tone frosty as she responded. "If you are so opposed to our union, Lady Haviland, I suggest you take up the matter with your grandson."

"I intend to, I promise you!"

Clenching her jaw, Madeline crossed to the bellpull. "Now that you have insulted me in every possible way, I will ask Bramsley to show you to your carriage."

Quivering with rage at her dismissal, Lady Haviland straightened to her full imperious height, staring at Madeline as if she were a particularly repulsive form of insect. Without another word, the dowager stalked from the room, leaving Madeline vibrating with anger herself at the exceedingly unpleasant interview.

Rayne would not be happy with her for quarreling so openly with his grandmother. Yet she had been given little choice.

Madeline pressed her lips together, trying to calm her anger. Still, she couldn't help recalling one of Lady Haviland's parting shots, accusing her of luring Rayne with her seductive arts. The very thought was laughable. She *had* no arts!

Nor did she have a wardrobe befitting a countess, Madeline remembered.

With a grimace, she glanced down at the gown her noble visitor had found so objectionable. Admittedly her pride had been a little stung by the accusation that she wore rags. And if she was to take her proper place as Rayne's wife, it would behoove her to dress the part. Rayne tended to flout society and all its rules, but she already had numerous strikes against her, many of which his grandmother had so unkindly pointed out just now.

Chewing her lower lip thoughtfully, Madeline crossed to the writing desk at one side of the drawing room, intending to pen a note to Arabella. She hesitated to ask her neighbor for advice the very day after her nuptials, not wanting to confess that her husband had pointedly abandoned her during their wedding night.

Yet Rayne had said he wanted Arabella to help her choose some suitable bride clothes, no doubt because he feared *she* didn't have good enough taste—and also, perhaps, because she would deem his expenditures "charity" and refuse to accept.

But Madeline was prideful enough to want to dress properly so that she could hold her head up the next time she faced his scornful grandmother or any of her other detractors. Therefore she would commission Arabella's dressmaker to fashion her a new gown or two.

She might have married for convenience, Madeline thought defiantly as she searched the desk for writing implements, but so had countless other women. She would simply have to make the best of her situation. Although her dreams of a loving marriage might never be fulfilled, she had made her current bed and had to lie in it now, even if her new husband would not be there to share it with her.

* * *

" 'Tis no surprise you took on this mission," Will Stokes said to Rayne with a grin. "I told you a life of leisure would never suit you. And you never could sit idly by when a life is at stake, even if that life happens to belong to our sorry excuse for a Regent."

"I'll give you no argument on either account," Rayne replied. This past year he'd been bored beyond tears by the indolent life of a nobleman. And Prinny had indeed made a poor Regent, earning the wrath of his subjects for squandering outrageous sums on his own pleasure— although his dissipation didn't make him deserving of assassination.

Rayne had spent much of the day setting his investigative plans in motion. Currently he sat in the small parlor of Will's home, wrapping up the final details of the operation and sharing an excellent port, which he'd recently given Will as a gift to celebrate his promotion to senior Bow Street Runner.

Their deliberations today had gone much as those in the past, except that this was a case of domestic espionage rather than one on foreign soil. They'd worked together for so many years, they could practically read each other's thoughts. Will was particularly good at disguises, while Rayne's sheer size and height rendered him too noticeable to fade easily into the background. Therefore he usually supplied the brains and strategy.

Espionage was a game of intrigue and lies, and Rayne had proved particularly adept at it. He'd speedily moved up the ranks of the diplomatic service until he was assigned the most important missions. Then five years ago, at the instigation of Foreign Secretary Viscount Castlereagh, Rayne had formed an elite cadre of agents under his direct command.

He ran the operations himself, directing a score of men and three women at ferreting out French secrets, cultivating informants, supplying bribes to buy intelligence, breaking codes, translating missives from various languages, intercepting couriers, seizing diplomatic dispatches, and tracking enemy spies across the continent, among other objectives.

Now, however, his task was to foil a potential plot against the Prince Regent. The first attempt on Prinny's life had occurred nearly nine months ago, when two bullets were fired through his carriage window on his way home from opening Parliament. But the shooter had never been apprehended. According to Arden's information, a secret political association had been formed in the South Midlands with the goal of disrupting the British monarchy. Two men—brothers, actually—were rumored to be the ringleaders of the revolutionaries and were now fomenting discord here in London.

Rayne had once had a vast network of agents to call upon, but those numbers were greatly diminished now, since like Will, many of his former cohorts had found other employment. To carry out this operation, he'd employed Will—temporarily on loan from Bow Street— along with several other men he trusted. For the next fortnight at least, they would keep the suspects under surveillance and look for opportunities to infiltrate their ranks.

"So how are you liking your marriage shackles?" Will asked in an abrupt change of subject. "I confess you gave me a facer when you decided to wed so suddenly."

Rayne shrugged, surprised only that his friend had waited until now to comment on his impetuous marriage. "Well enough," he answered. "It's too soon to tell, since it has been less than a day."

"I thought you had set your sights on a very different sort of wife," Will prodded. "Your new lady hardly seems like a biddable female."

Rayne couldn't help but chuckle. "Biddable she is not."

"Then why did you wed her? Because your grandmama wants you to set up your nursery?"

"That, and because I owed it to Madeline's father to look after her. You knew David Ellis. She is his daughter."

"Ah," Will said with a tone of understanding. Will knew his history with Captain Ellis and so had no trouble grasping his prime rationale for choosing her.

Taking a sip of port, Will cocked his head at Rayne. "Shouldn't you be with your new bride, then? When Sal and I jumped the broom, we spent our first week in bed. 'Tis how we made our little Harry, in fact."

Rayne would actually like nothing more than to return to Riverwood and spend the next week in bed with Madeline, but he wouldn't let himself. He was better off keeping his distance from her for the next several days or more. "I mean to remain here in London for a time to see if we make any progress exposing our plotters."

Will shook his head good-humoredly. "You always did put duty before pleasure."

Pleasure was indeed the word that came to mind when he thought of his marriage bed, Rayne reflected, assaulted by a sudden memory of Madeline—the warm silk of her body pressed against his, her flesh soft and yielding under his searching hands and mouth.

His body's primal reaction to their lovemaking had

been unexpectedly powerful—which was precisely why he would be very wise to stay away from her for a time.

"She must be unlike Mademoiselle Juzet for you to have risked wedding her," Will remarked.

Reminded uncomfortably of his former love, Rayne felt his jaw tighten involuntarily. Will was one of the few people who knew about his painful brush with betrayal.

Rayne understood why Camille had acted as she did all those years ago. She'd loved her family dearly and her lover even more—and her loyalty to them overshadowed any feelings she'd developed for *him*. When her father had run afoul of Fouché's deadly secret police and her entire family's lives were threatened, she'd had no qualms about seducing Rayne so he would bring them safely to England. He would have saved her family anyway had she simply told him the truth. But Camille had made him love her before he'd caught on to her deception.

Afterward, Rayne had redoubled his efforts at his spy career, determined to wipe away the memory of his foolish weakness. He'd sought out the most dangerous missions, taken more personal risks.

He'd never seen Camille again, although he knew that she and her family had returned to France at the war's end. Yet the experience had changed him significantly. Even though he was no longer bitter now, or even cynical about love, merely guarded, he had no intention of repeating his disastrous mistake.

The comparisons between his first love and his new wife were unavoidable, however. Camille had wanted him for his connections and wealth, which was a chief reason Madeline had appealed to him so strongly. She was very much the opposite of Camille in many respects.

She was not a seductress like Camille either, Rayne thought. He doubted he would have to worry about Madeline taking a lover behind his back. For that reason he was glad for her relative plainness.

And like Camille, Madeline wanted to help her younger brother. Yet she didn't harbor any devious ulterior motives, plotting and scheming against him all the while.

He'd been too quick to judge Madeline, Rayne again admitted to himself. His suspicions about her relationship with Ackerby were likely unfounded.

Interrupting his musings just then, Will raised his glass in a toast. "I trust you will enjoy wedded bliss as I have, my friend."

In reply, Rayne took a long swallow of port to finish off his glass. By his own design, wedded bliss was not in his future. But he expected to be fairly content with the bargain he and his new bride had made.

His sanguinity was short-lived, for when he arrived at his house on Bedford Avenue, Rayne found a terse note from his grandmother summoning him for a command appearance at the Haviland family mansion in Berkeley Square. His mouth curved sardonically as he read her missive. It should not have surprised him to learn Lady Haviland was in town, since her network of social spies was as efficient as his own international one had been.

Anticipating her disapproval of his marriage, Rayne was in no hurry to comply with his summons. Thus, he first took the time to change into evening attire in preparation for dining at Brooks's Club afterward. When he did call upon his grandmother, he was required to cool his heels for a quarter of an hour before being admitted upstairs to her bedchamber.

Lady Haviland was lying in her bed in the darkened room, her eyes closed, a damp cloth pressed to her brow. Her color was good, however, with none of the paleness expected of an invalid, so Rayne was easily able to suppress his twinge of guilt. His grandmother's heart always weakened considerably whenever she wanted leverage over him, as no doubt she did now.

When she finally deigned to open her eyes, he took her hand and carried it gently to his lips. "I regret you are feeling ill enough to take to your bed, Grandmother," he murmured.

She appraised him with considerable disfavor, and her voice held the same condemnation when she responded. "You know very well that *you* caused this latest heart spell, my boy."

"If you are suffering renewed palpitations, love, then you should not have made the journey from Brighton alone, particularly since I planned to come and fetch you at week's end to convey you to Haviland Court."

"I could not wait till week's end to confirm the awful truth. How *could* you, Rayne? Marrying that little upstart? I will never be able to hold my head up among the ton again."

With effort, Rayne refrained from replying as forcefully as he wanted. "I doubt my marriage will diminish your enormous consequence in the least, Grandmother."

She snatched her hand from his grasp. "How little you know. But the humiliation I face is only a fraction of the reason I am so dismayed. When I met your Miss Ellis this afternoon, she was even worse that I imagined."

"You called at Riverwood?"

"Certainly I called there. I had to see her for myself. She was unforgivably rude and impertinent."

Rayne hid an amused grimace. That was one battle he would have enjoyed seeing. Although wishing he'd been there to spare Madeline the confrontation, he imagined she had held her own well enough, even against his indomitable grandmother. Yet it was precisely why he hadn't told his family about his plans to wed beforehand, fearing they would subject Madeline to their censure.

"Why did you choose her, of all people?" Lady Haviland demanded.

He had a ready answer. "Because I realized that any of the simpering misses I've interviewed to date would drive me mad within a week of marriage."

"You have clearly made a wretched mistake, Rayne. How well do you even know that woman?"

"Well enough. Her father was a good friend of mine."

He wouldn't reveal his obligations to David Ellis to his grandmother. He would prefer she think he'd chosen Madeline for her own sake rather than give his relative more ammunition to use against her.

"Madeline is a good match for me, Grandmother. I am proud to call her my wife, and I expect that one day you will be also. But even if not, I trust you will welcome her into the family."

In response, Lady Haviland raised her hand to her forehead and pressed on the cloth adorning her brow, as if to remind him of her frail condition. "I simply cannot welcome her, Rayne. I doubt I can ever forgive you, either. The only thing I ever asked of you was to marry well, and now you have ruined *everything*."

"I agreed to wed a genteel young lady so I could sire

an heir, which is exactly what I have done. I have ful-filled my pledge to you, love."

"You have done nothing of the kind!"

Rayne kept his gaze steady in the face of the dowager's savage glare. "Have you forgotten why you wanted me to wed in the first place? Your concern was that the Haviland title and fortune not go to my Uncle Clarence."

"Certainly that concerned me. Clarence is a gamester and a scapegrace, undeserving of the title. But that is not the sole reason I wished you to marry. I was worried for your future, Rayne. And now I worry for your children's future. You may care little for the nobility of our family bloodline, but I don't wish my great-grandchildren to be tainted by French blood."

Rayne felt a muscle tighten in his jaw. "Your objection is duly noted, Grandmother, but I expect this to be the last I hear of it."

"You do not care at all what I think?"

"Yes, I care. But we have had this discussion before. I agreed to follow your wishes up to a point, but you will not run my life, or dictate whom I will or will not marry."

Her expression hardened even further. "I suppose I should have expected a disaster of this sort. You always were a stubborn rebel. To think that I was so elated when you promised to give up your wild adventures and settle down."

Rayne didn't intend to tell her that he was still pursu-ing some of the wild adventures she found so objection-able. Nor would he press her to accept Madeline just now. His grandmother needed a little time to adjust to her dashed expectations, and he would give it to her.

Lady Haviland, however, was not ready to abandon her aims, it seemed. Struggling to sit up in bed, she tossed the cloth aside and placed an imploring hand on his arm. "It is not too late for an annulment, Rayne. We can say that you belatedly came to your senses and realized your mistake."

He eyed her narrowly, wondering if she meant to declare warfare on his new bride. If so, she would quickly have to revise her perspective.

"There will be no annulment, Grandmother," he replied, his tone final. "You will just have to be satisfied with my choice."

The flash of fury in her eyes was unmistakable. "I will never be satisfied," she insisted.

"Then we will forever be at odds."

Lady Haviland continued to regard him with extreme displeasure before removing her hand from his arm with a derisive sniff. "Until just this moment I never realized how heartless you are, Rayne. The gossips are already sharpening their spiteful tongues, but I will bear the brunt of their venom, not you."

"You should pay the gossips no mind."

Her look held scorn. "As if I could. The least you can do is refrain from formally proclaiming your marriage in the *Morning Post* and *Chronicle*. I have no desire to become an object of ridicule in stark black and white."

He could agree to that, Rayne decided, since he didn't want Madeline subjected to the savagery of intense public scrutiny. The quieter he kept his marriage, the easier it would be for her to find her bearings as his countess. "Very well, I won't submit any announcements to the newspapers."

His grandmother breathed a pained sigh. "Undoubtedly, word of your union has already spread. One cannot keep a scandal of this magnitude quiet for long."

"It is hardly a scandal," Rayne said dryly.

"It most certainly is," she muttered in derision. "And you will likely be the death of me."

He bowed respectfully. "That would be extremely unfortunate, love, but I have high hopes you will outlive all your grandchildren. And to help ensure it, I will summon all your various doctors to attend to you immediately."

She hesitated, then waved her hand in dismissal. "That will not be necessary. I will suffer in silence, as I always do. Now take yourself off, sir, since you are so vexingly determined to disoblige me."

Rayne knew he had called her bluff, for she disliked being poked and prodded by her physicians. "As you wish, Grandmother."

Aware that he hadn't ended her objections to his marriage, though, he crossed to the door and let himself from the room, feeling her irate gaze boring into his back, as intense as any enemy surveillance.

Chapter Twelve

I have decided to take fate into my own hands, Maman.

To post her latest letter to Gerard, Madeline drove herself into Chiswick alone. After what had happened with her first correspondence, she didn't want Rayne's servants alerted to her attempt to contact her brother.

When she returned home to Riverwood, a note from Arabella was waiting for her, suggesting that they drive to London tomorrow and spend the day visiting her dressmaker and various other shops. She also suggested that Madeline make a list of items she needed.

The writing desk in the drawing room was out of paper, however, since she'd used the last sheets to write Arabella and Gerard. Not wishing to take Bramsley from his duties to fetch more paper for her, Madeline decided to search for it herself, starting in the most logical place—Rayne's study.

Most of the drawers in his massive desk were locked, she discovered, but the lower left one was accessible. Inside, she found a thin sheaf of papers containing what looked to be a list of names, scrawled in a bold handwriting that she assumed was Rayne's.

Madeline was about to return his papers to the drawer when an underlined name leapt out at her: *Roslyn Loring*. Curious, she let her gaze skim down the entire list. There were some three dozen female names in total, and Rayne had made notations beside each one.

It seemed to be a list of candidates he had considered for matrimony.

Startled by her deduction, Madeline perused all the pages in detail. Rayne had made three more columns to accompany the names. The first heading was *"Feat.,"* which she took to mean distinguishing physical features, including hair color—perhaps so he could remember the individual ladies or tell them apart.

The two other columns appeared to be descriptions of intelligence and personality and character. Under *"Intelligence"* he had assigned each lady a numerical rating 0 to 9. But under *"Pers/Char"* were words:

Lively. Timid. Charming. Talks too much. Dull. Deadly dull. At least half of the candidates were rated "dull" or some variation thereof, but there were also some even less flattering terms such as *Simpers, Fawns, Vain,* and *Greedy*.

A pang of jealousy struck Madeline when she saw that Roslyn Loring had received a 9 for intelligence and a description of "intriguing" for personality—clearly the highest rating for anyone on Rayne's list. And yet, she noted, "beautiful" did not appear anywhere on the pages.

Madeline chewed her lower lip thoughtfully. If this was Rayne's tally of the advantages and disadvantages of the bridal candidates he'd considered and rejected thus far, she supposed she could take heart, since he seemed to value brains and spirit over beauty.

"May I assist you, my lady?"

With a start Madeline looked up to find Bramsley standing in the study doorway, frowning at her in disapproval.

"I was searching for writing paper," she explained hastily.

"Forgive me, my lady, I should have mentioned it before. Lord Haviland does not allow anyone to touch his desk. Indeed, I am the only staff permitted to enter his study."

Feeling somewhat guilty, Madeline shoved Rayne's lists back in the drawer and stood. "I am sorry. I wasn't aware that his study was off limits to me. But of course I will respect his wishes."

It wasn't surprising that Rayne would be protective of his privacy since his entire profession had been built on secrets, but she felt very much like Bluebeard's wife at being caught here, even though she had certainly *not* been snooping.

Bramsley pointedly interrupted her musings. "I will be happy to bring you the writing paper you require, my lady."

"Thank you," Madeline said rather meekly.

Preceding the majordomo from the study, she watched as he shut the door carefully behind them. Then, desiring to change the subject, she added casually, "I am planning a drive with Lady Danvers to London tomorrow to visit her dressmaker, if you need me to perform any errands for you while I am there."

Bramsley stared at her a moment, making Madeline keenly aware that she had just committed a solecism.

She sent him a rueful smile. "I suppose my habits as a former companion are too ingrained. My offer is vastly out of place, isn't it? Of course you have a large staff to call upon to run errands for you."

His expression softened several degrees. "Indeed we do, my lady."

"It will doubtless take me awhile to learn what is expected of me in my new position, so I hope you will bear with me."

"Certainly, my lady," the majordomo said with genuine warmth this time. "But if you mean to visit London . . . I should also have mentioned earlier, his lordship bade me instruct you on the financial arrangements he made on your behalf. Any bills you incur should be sent to his London residence, but he also established an allowance for smaller personal necessities. As for the estate, I generally manage the household accounts and landholdings, but he directed me to make the books available to you as well. If you wish, my lady, I will present them for your review when I bring the writing paper."

Madeline felt strangely gratified; Rayne had remembered that she'd handled all the accounts of her family's farm for years. "I should like that, Bramsley. Will you bring them to me in the drawing room?"

"As you wish, Lady Haviland."

The majordomo bowed deferentially and then took himself off to fulfill her request. As Madeline made her way slowly back to the drawing room, however, the account books were not foremost on her mind. Rather, she was remembering Rayne's list of marital prospects.

Her name had not appeared among the candidates, yet she couldn't help wondering how he would rate her. She had worried that she couldn't possibly compete with all the beauties who had thrown themselves at Rayne's head, but perhaps her plainness was not such an enormous drawback after all.

Even so, she would be wise to improve her appearance and make herself more attractive to him if possible. A new wardrobe would help, but more drastic action was obviously needed.

Besides, she'd had enough of wallowing in self-pity, Madeline decided. She would not be a helpless victim of circumstances, passively bemoaning her fate. She might have foolishly fallen in love with Rayne, but since she couldn't change her feelings for him, her best course was to try and change his feelings for *her*—or at least make him want her enough to share her bed for more than mere conjugal duty.

Madeline frowned in thought. A good soldier's daughter would marshal her defenses and call in reinforcements, but whom could she rely upon? She'd never had sisters or close women friends to discuss female matters with, and her conversations with her late mother were strictly one-sided. Therefore, she was at a severe loss in dealing with a husband who wanted her only for the children she could give him.

Yet Arabella had agreed to help her shop for clothing. Now Madeline wondered if she should also ask her neighbor for advice on how to appeal to a man of Rayne's stamp. She would never be as captivating as Roslyn Loring in his eyes, of course, but perhaps with assistance, she might become enticing enough to keep him in her bed.

And she did have the advantage of being married to Rayne, after all, Madeline reflected, setting her jaw with determination. Even if she wasn't able to inspire his passion at present, she would have opportunities to rouse his desire that none of his other bridal candidates had had.

Madeline gave serious consideration to developing a new strategy for her marriage so that by the time Arabella called for her the next morning as arranged, she was prepared to swallow her pride and ask for her neighbor's help in a much more intimate arena than fashion.

Arabella's first words, however, gave her pause.

"I am more than happy to advise you on purchasing new gowns, but my sister Roslyn has a better eye for styles and colors than I do. I hope you don't mind that I took the liberty of inviting her to accompany us this morning."

Madeline was a little taken aback. She was coming to know Arabella fairly well, whereas Roslyn was nearly a stranger. Yet she could hardly protest her employer's generosity.

"I hate to impose on her grace," she settled on saying.

"It is no imposition, truly. Roslyn is eager to help you. And in a way, she will be fulfilling her pledge to Haviland. We attempted to find him a suitable bride, but since he made an unexpected match on his own, it is only fitting that we endeavor to make your introduction to society successful."

"Well, if you are certain she won't mind . . ."

"I am certain," Arabella assured her. "The ton will be agog to see Haviland's new countess, and as a duchess, Roslyn can foster your acceptance even better than I can. As for me," she added with a smile, "I want to smooth your path for my own selfish reasons. I'm exceedingly grateful that you plan to continue teaching at the academy, Madeline. Not only have you spared me the trouble of searching for your replacement, our pupils adore you and would be heartbroken if you had to resign simply because you married a nobleman."

At the praise, Madeline felt her cheeks flush. "It has been a pleasure to teach them."

"I hope it will continue to be so for a long time to come. But I collect you would rather discuss our shopping expedition just now." Arabella's glance took in Madeline's outdated pelisse. "Do you have a sum in mind for how much you wish to spend on a new wardrobe?"

"Cost does not seem to be a concern," Madeline replied dryly, still bemused by her sudden wealth.

In addition to arranging an account for her gowns and other large purchases, Rayne had given her a shockingly generous allowance for fripperies. In fact, she had two hundred pounds of pin money burning a hole in her reticule right now.

But her bride clothes were not her chief worry. Taking a breath, Madeline plunged ahead and told Arabella of her dilemma—confessing that she had made a marriage of convenience but had little notion how to proceed with her new husband.

Nodding in understanding, Arabella gave a soft, wry laugh. "Marriage is unnerving under any circumstances, but I would find it petrifying to wed as you did. So you would like my opinion on how to manage a husband?"

"Yes, but even more . . ." Madeline faltered, striving for the right words. "The thing is, Arabella, I hold little feminine appeal for a man such as Haviland, and I thought . . . perhaps you could advise me on how to change his perception of me. You see, I hope to make him want me as his true wife, but I suspect I will need to improve more than just my attire in order to accomplish it. Lord Danvers is clearly enamored of you, so I wondered if . . . if you would mind telling me some of your secrets."

Arabella pursed her lips thoughtfully. "Of course I will, but I know an even better person to ask. Her name is Fanny Irwin . . . although I hesitate to introduce you since you might be offended."

"Why would I be offended?"

"Because my friend is a renowned courtesan. Fanny had a genteel upbringing but left home when she was sixteen to seek her fortune. We have known each other since we were in leading strings, though. In fact, we were neighbors and bosom friends in Hampshire and played together as children." Arabella wrinkled her nose in amusement. "My sisters and I refused to repudiate our friendship with Fanny, much to the chagrin of the ton, but you might not care to be associated with her."

Madeline was a little surprised at the sisters' relationship with a famous courtesan, but she had no objection. "I don't mind in the least. I would be grateful for any help she could give me."

"Trust me, her help will be substantial. She was instrumental in aiding both me and my sisters in our understanding of men and husbands. But we should keep your consultations confidential so you don't invite scandal unnecessarily."

When an image of Rayne's imperious grandmother flashed through her mind, Madeline murmured her agreement. "That would probably be wise, given Haviland's illustrious relations."

"Didn't you say that he is away on business?" Arabella asked. "How much time do we have before he returns home?"

"I am not certain," she admitted. "That is part of the problem—I am not really a part of his life so he didn't feel the need to keep me informed of his plans."

"Well, we will soon change that," her neighbor said with conviction. "But we had best spend the entire day in London. While Madame Rousseau is fitting you, I will send word to Fanny and ask her to receive us this afternoon if she can manage to break free. And in between, we can visit the shops. You needn't worry, Madeline. Roslyn and I will ensure that you have the perfect wardrobe, and Fanny will oversee the rest. Between the three of us, we will turn you into a bride that Haviland cannot fail to notice."

Madeline smiled tentatively, feeling optimistic for the first time since speaking her wedding vows. She'd been crushingly disheartened when Rayne had left her bed so unceremoniously, but now she saw the silver lining in his abrupt departure. She could make use of his absence to turn herself from a caterpillar into a butterfly. No doubt it would take quite some time and effort.

They called for Roslyn on the way to the dressmaker's salon, and Arabella spent the short drive to Madame Rousseau's explaining to her sister what was needed. Madeline soon learned how fortunate she was to be taken under their wing.

Their attempt to turn her into a fashionable lady began with making countless decisions from an overwhelming number of options. Together they pored over sketches of various garment styles and designs and debated a dizzying array of fabrics and colors before winnowing down selections. The choices the sisters made in conjunction with Madame Rousseau were exquisite—beautifully cut apparel that shouted taste and refinement and that slimmed and flattered Madeline's buxom figure.

She felt awed by the result, and more than once had to fight a lump in her throat. She had never owned many pretty gowns—had refused to let herself yearn for them, in fact—so suddenly experiencing such riches was like awakening in a fairy tale.

The entire morning was devoted to gowns and outer garments. After partaking of a light luncheon supplied by the modiste, the ladies set out to visit other shops that were the next-highest priority . . . milliners for hats and bonnets and cobblers for shoes and slippers. Since time was growing short until their appointment with Fanny at three o'clock, Arabella suggested they return to London later in the week for such accessories as chemises and petticoats and corsets, silk stockings and garters, gloves, fans, and jewelry.

Madeline's confidence in their plan grew as the day wore on, in large part because Arabella and Roslyn were so certain it would work. Roslyn's graciousness and warmth was particularly infectious. She was every bit as approachable and understanding as Arabella, and she heartily approved of the proposal to involve their notorious friend Fanny Irwin, responding with a private disclosure of her own when Madeline admitted her hopes about her marriage.

"This past summer," Roslyn confessed, her tone one

of sympathy and kindness, "I sought Fanny's advice about making a gentleman fall in love with me. If you wish to make Haviland love you, you could not find a better champion than Fanny."

If you wish to make Haviland love you. Madeline felt her breath catch at the simple phrase. She had set her sights on making Rayne *desire* her, thinking that would be a daunting enough task. But now she let herself wonder if it would be possible to win his heart.

No, you would be a fool to raise your hopes so high, Madeline scolded herself. It would be enough to have Rayne want her. Besides, she added, striving to dampen her rash optimism, to achieve even that much, the courtesan would have to be an utter miracle worker.

It took very little time later that afternoon, however, for Madeline to decide Fanny Irwin indeed might be able to work miracles.

Shortly after arriving at the courtesan's private residence in a quiet, surprisingly elegant neighborhood north of Hyde Park, the sisters left her in Fanny's capable hands, with Arabella promising to call back for her in two hours.

"Give us three hours," Fanny said briskly, acknowledging the difficulty of the challenge ahead of her.

Shepherding her guest up the staircase to the second floor, Fanny led the way through her bedchamber and into a well-lit dressing room, then got right down to business by ordering Madeline to remove her pelisse and gown and corset.

Madeline felt extremely self-conscious when she had stripped down to her shift, but Fanny appeared oblivious to any discomfiture. Frowning, the courtesan walked in a slow circle around Madeline, studying her closely while analyzing her physical assets and drawbacks.

"Your eyes are definitely your best feature," she finally proclaimed.

Madeline couldn't disagree. Only her eyes had any real claim to beauty.

"But you also have a very pleasing figure, lithe and curvaceous. The kind of body men dream of. Surely your husband has noticed."

When Madeline felt herself flushing, Fanny smiled dismissively. "If I am to advise you, Lady Haviland, you must overcome your modesty at once, for I intend to go into much more intimate detail with you before we are done. As I was saying, you have the lush sort of body that appeals greatly to men."

Her gaze left Madeline's lavish breasts and returned to her face. "Your lips are unfashionably full, but that again is fortunate, since men will tend to think of you as kissable. Has no gentleman ever attempted to steal a kiss from you?"

"Once or twice," Madeline conceded. Actually Baron Ackerby had attempted it more frequently, but an arrogant roué did not count as a gentleman, despite his noble rank.

Fanny made another slow circle, then seated Madeline at a dressing table before a large mirror and turned her attention to her client's mass of ordinary brown hair.

"The color is acceptable but the style . . . Do you always wear your hair scraped back so severely?"

"Yes." She normally coiled her hair into a knot at her nape or plaited it up neatly.

Fanny shook her head in disapproval as she pulled the pins from Madeline's tresses. "Men usually relish long hair, so we shan't shorten the length, but we must do something to soften your face . . . some curled tendrils over your forehead and at your temples."

Since it was similar advice to what Rayne had given her, Madeline didn't dissent.

"I will have my hairdresser cut and style your hair later, but meanwhile . . . I expect the most immediate impact we can have will be to pluck your eyebrows somewhat. They are far too heavy for your face and make you appear more masculine than you should. Can you see what I mean?"

"Yes," Madeline answered again, observing her dark, slashing eyebrows in the mirror while Fanny's inspection continued.

"Your complexion is fine enough, but the hue is too sallow. You would benefit from the judicious use of cosmetics. A little rouge on your cheeks and kohl about the eyes will allow you to make the most of your features. And I can teach you several other tricks to whiten your skin . . . barley water, lemon juice, milk baths. Even so. . . ."

Fanny resumed frowning. "You can take more pains with your appearance and enhance your physical attributes to increase your husband's attraction for you, but when it comes to winning his devotion for the long term, it is your manner and actions that will serve you best."

Madeline stared at her in surprise. It seemed strange to hear a woman as strikingly beautiful as Fanny suggest that demeanor was more important than beauty. "What exactly do you mean by manners and actions?"

"Wait here, my lady. . . ."

Behind her, Fanny turned away and left the dressing room. When she returned, she was carrying a slim leather-bound volume that she handed to Madeline.

The book was entitled *Advice to Young Ladies on Capturing a Husband* by an Anonymous Lady. Looking up, Madeline saw that Fanny wore a secretive smile rather than a frown.

"Very few people know that I penned this," Fanny commented.

"*You* are the anonymous lady author?"

"Yes. This was actually my first attempt at earning an income outside my current profession, and it has sold quite well. But I have since tried my hand at writing a Gothic novel, since that genre can be much more lucrative. I would like to leave the demimonde, you see, so that I might marry a respectable gentleman I have my sights on, and I calculate that my best chance is to develop a successful career as a novelist."

Madeline surveyed the courtesan with genuine admiration and relief. It was not only flattering that Fanny would trust her enough to reveal her secret hopes, her confession put Madeline at ease for the first time since arriving.

"I should dearly love to hear *that* story, Miss Irwin," she said with a hint of amusement. "Without a doubt, you are one of the most fascinating people I have ever met."

Fanny laughed. "I will gladly tell you my tale, my lady, but for now, we should focus our efforts on you. Why don't you read my book later and then we can discuss it in depth next time we meet?"

"I certainly will," Madeline said, thumbing through the pages.

"It contains a great deal of general information about relationships between the sexes, but I suspect I will need to be much more explicit with you. You are fairly inexperienced in the arts of seduction, aren't you?"

Madeline sent her a rueful smile. "I am afraid so."

"Well, we will change that very shortly. Perhaps you should tell me how you and Lord Haviland came to be married."

And so it was that Madeline found herself confessing some of her own most private secrets—how she and Rayne had met, how he felt obligated to protect her because of her late father, how Rayne had proposed to her and then pursued her until she agreed, how he had left her bed abruptly on their wedding night.

"I admit it was mortifying," Madeline finished in a small voice, "and painfully disappointing."

Fanny nodded in understanding. "Clearly you surrendered too easily by accepting his offer of marriage so soon. Trust me, men like your husband want a challenge, which leads me to another point. You cannot let him discover that you have fallen in love with him. Wearing your heart on your sleeve is almost certain to frighten off a man."

Madeline's smile was wry. "You mean I shouldn't let on that I think my husband the most wonderful man I have ever known?"

"Not quite," Fanny said with surprising seriousness. "Overtly admiring a man is an excellent way to increase his ardor. I meant that you shouldn't appear so enamored of him that he knows he has the upper hand. You must keep him guessing. He should be striving to win *you*. Since Haviland obviously considers his courtship of you over, you will have to court him instead."

"Court him?"

"Yes, but very subtly, of course. You cannot let him know you are pursuing him. You must become a seductress without him divining your real intentions."

"A seductress?" Madeline repeated, her voice rising even higher.

"Don't worry, I will teach you how." Fanny's brow furrowed thoughtfully. "What do you know about your husband's personal affairs? I have not heard of Haviland engaging in any amorous liaisons here in London. If he keeps a mistress here in town, he has been very discreet about it."

Madeline froze. Rayne had said he needed to be in London for what he termed "business." She hoped that was indeed the case. The possibility that he might have a mistress was too depressing to consider. "I wouldn't know," she conceded.

"Well, no matter. If he does have an inamorata now, you will just have to tempt him away from her, so that you are the only woman he wishes to have in his bed. But by the time I have finished instructing you, you will be able to make him half-crazed with desire for you— and passion is only a few steps away from making a man love you beyond reason. Now let me call my dresser so we may get started."

Two hours later, Madeline stared at herself in the mirror with disbelief. Her entire appearance was altered. The slender wings of her brows, the delicate rose tinge of her cheekbones, the curled wisps framing her face, the touch of kohl highlighting and emphasizing her large

gray eyes, all contributed to making her appear a different woman than the plain, dowdy spinster who had
walked into Fanny's private quarters.

She looked almost . . . Pretty was too tame a word.
And she was not precisely beautiful. Compelling, perhaps. Definitely intriguing.

And even more crucial than Fanny improving her
looks, she had spent more than an hour giving Madeline
a frank, explicit, eye-opening tutelage on the art of making love to her husband, so that she could eventually
win Rayne's elusive heart.

"I am amazed," Madeline said simply. "How can I
ever thank you, Fanny?"

The courtesan smiled modestly. "You needn't thank
me. Arabella and Roslyn and Lily have supported me
unerringly all these many years, despite the threat to
their good name. It is only right that I repay their loyalty
by performing a favor for one of their friends."

"Even so, I am overwhelmingly grateful for all you
have done."

"We are not finished yet," Fanny said with a smile.
"We still have much more to discuss if you are to become comfortable playing the temptress. If necessary, I
can come to Chiswick and meet you at Danvers Hall.
You will want to keep your plans secret from your husband. But although this is just the first step in your campaign to win his affections, I would say you are well on
your way to becoming the object of Haviland's dreams."

"So would I," Madeline murmured, marveling at her
new self. The reflection staring back at her in the mirror
looked like the very kind of woman who could capture
and hold a man like Rayne. And she had every intention

of putting her newly learned arts of allurement to the test.

Rayne seemed to admire boldness, so she would give him boldness. And if she had her way, she would turn their union into a love match by becoming a seductress in their marriage bed.

Chapter Thirteen

*I sincerely hope Fanny's techniques prove successful,
Maman.*

Judging that enough time had passed for him to safely
return home, Rayne penned his new wife a note, saying
to expect him early Tuesday afternoon, nearly a week
after taking their nuptial vows.

When he arrived at Riverwood, however, he was informed by Bramsley that Lady Haviland had just left for
the Freemantle Academy and planned to be there the remainder of the day.

Rayne stifled his odd twinge of disappointment, since
going their separate ways as husband and wife was precisely what he wanted from his marriage. Repairing to
his study, he turned his attention to the estate business
that had accumulated during his absence.

When Madeline finally did appear, she halted in the
doorway and eyed Rayne where he sat behind his desk.

"Welcome home, my lord," she said pleasantly as she
proceeded to remove her gloves and bonnet. "I trust
your business dealings in London were successful."

Rayne recognized the stab of pleasure he felt at hearing Madeline's voice and seeing her for the first time

since their wedding night. Upon realizing how much he had missed her during their separation, however, he frowned at himself. Then his gaze arrested as he took in her appearance.

Madeline looked different somehow. She wore a royal blue, short-waisted spencer over a pale blue kerseymere gown that was the height of elegance.

"Is that one of your new gowns?" he asked, trying to pinpoint the difference in her as he rose to his feet.

"Yes. Arabella recently took me shopping in London."

"I know. Bramsley informed me."

Madeline stiffened slightly although her tone remained bland when she asked, "Oh, is Bramsley giving you daily reports on my activities?"

"He gives me regular reports on everything having to do with the estate."

"I see. Then I had best watch myself," she replied, dimpling, "since you have so many spies in your household."

Rayne couldn't tell if she was jesting—but then she changed the subject by turning slowly in a circle to show off her gown. "I am grateful for Arabella's attempt to bring me into fashion, but you may regret your generosity when you see the bills. I made a large dent in the dress allowance you arranged for me."

"I have already seen some of the bills, but I don't regret the expense in the least," he assured her.

"To be truthful, neither do I. Your grandmother seemed to think the rags I wore were not befitting a countess."

Rayne winced. "Did she demean your attire?"

"Among other things," Madeline answered lightly.

Realizing that she hadn't crossed the threshold into his study, Rayne came out from behind his desk and moved toward her. "I am sorry you had to endure her reproach, sweetheart. I imagine it was exceedingly unpleasant."

"It was a little uncomfortable," Madeline acknowledged. "But then it was to be expected. I knew she would never approve of me. In fact, I warned you, you will remember."

"So you did, but my grandmother's opinion has no bearing on our marriage."

"Still, I truly am sorry for coming between you," Madeline murmured, her tone holding genuine regret.

Rayne shook his head as he came to a halt before her. "You are not to blame whatsoever. . . ."

His voice trailed off. Her hairstyle was different, he realized, and so was her face.

Yet before he could comment, she interrupted his thoughts. "Have you had tea yet?"

"Not yet. I was waiting for you." He had supposed they would sit down together over tea so that he could catch up on her past week.

Madeline flashed him a rueful smile, however. "I am sorry for inconveniencing you, my lord, but I partook of an ample tea with our pupils at the academy. I will ask Bramsley to serve you at once. Meanwhile, I hope you will excuse me. I mean to go upstairs and take a bath. I have become quite fond of your marvelous bathing chamber. It is a luxury I never dreamed of."

Rayne meant to take Madeline to task for addressing him as "my lord" a second time, but the image of her bathing her luscious body hit him hard in the loins and totally distracted him. And her next casual comment struck him even more forcefully:

"You are welcome to share my bathwater. It seems a shame to waste so much hot water, even if you can well afford it. I should be finished by the time you have your tea."

Turning away from the doorway, she strolled down the corridor toward the front entrance hall.

Rayne watched her leave, his brows furrowed as he followed the gentle sway of her hips. Had Madeline just asked him to join her bath? Or was she merely being frugal in wanting to conserve hot water and thus proposing he bathe after her?

Either way, Rayne couldn't get her suggestion out of his mind as he returned to work. A half hour later he gave up all pretense of concentration.

No doubt it would be folly to join his new wife in the bathing chamber, yet he couldn't stay away.

Madeline reclined against the sloping back of the large copper hip bath, counting the passing minutes along with the rapid beats of her heart. Ordinarily she relished luxuriating in the silken heat of so much water, but anticipation was twisting knots in her belly while she waited to see if Rayne would join her.

She had surprised him, that much was evident. His eyes had darkened as he'd stared at her, trying to divine her intent—which was precisely what Fanny Irwin had predicted he would do.

Thus far Fanny's plan seemed to be working. Madeline had deliberately delayed at the academy long after Rayne was expected home so as not to appear at his beck and call. A woman who was too available was much less of a prize for a man, according to Fanny, so it was wise to keep him guessing.

Madeline wasn't certain she had the confidence required to carry out her campaign, even after all of Fanny's expert counsel. She had never been a seducer or siren. But she'd prepared as carefully as she could for this moment, laying out linen towels and scented soaps before undressing and sinking into the bathwater up to her shoulders.

Her heart thundered in her chest when at last she heard a swift rap on the door, followed by Rayne softly calling her name.

"You may enter," she replied, sitting up.

As the door opened to admit him, Madeline modestly reached for a linen towel she'd left lying on the stool beside the tub and held it up to shield her naked torso from his view. Rayne was unaware of the assault she intended to launch against him, and she intended to play the innocent as long as possible.

"I am sorry for my tardiness," she apologized as he shut the chamber door behind him, "but I am not quite finished with my bath. The hot water was just too alluring. Do you mind waiting a few more minutes?"

She kept her look guileless, even though the giddy rush of nerves was making her light-headed. Rayne's expression, on the other hand, was more piercing than usual.

"No, I don't mind," he said, settling onto the adjacent stool.

Madeline gazed up at him beneath her lashes, hoping she looked properly flustered at having an audience. "Do you mean to watch me?"

"You needn't be shy. I have seen all your lovely charms before, remember?" When she hesitated, Rayne added in an amused tone, "You cannot very well bathe holding a towel."

"True." Nervous laughter escaped her throat. She would have to do better than this, Madeline scolded herself. Fanny had schooled her over countless hours, and so she had the necessary knowledge to become a *femme fatale*. She just needed to apply it.

"Very well," Madeline murmured, tossing the towel aside.

If her goal just now was to tempt Rayne while letting him think he was the pursuer, her ploy seemed to be working. She felt his hot gaze rivet on her bare, glistening breasts.

Madeline permitted herself a faint inward smile. Now that she had his undivided attention, it was time to ratchet up the stakes.

Shifting her position, she rose to her knees and reached over the high side of the tub, into the basket resting on the floor. Retrieving a cake of fine soap, Madeline sank back down, but only enough so that the water level was above her waist. With slow deliberation she drew the bar over her naked shoulders, then down her throat and between her wet breasts.

"This soap is sinfully lavish, softer on my skin than any I have ever known. It is French, is it not?"

"I wouldn't know," Rayne said slowly. "Bramsley is in charge of household purchases."

Was it her imagination or had his voice suddenly grown thick? She couldn't tell when he asked in an amiable way, "Do you need my help washing? Would you like me to scrub your back?"

Not wanting to seem too eager, Madeline declined his

offer with a knowing smile. "Thank you, but I can manage."

Rayne continued to watch her intently as she soaped herself, but only a short while later he broke the silence with an observation.

"There is something different about you. It is more than just your new gown."

"I took your advice and styled my hair in a modish way."

She had gathered the length of brown hair and twisted it into a loose knot on the top of her head, leaving numerous damp tendrils to curl around her face.

"It's very becoming."

Madeline let herself blush at his compliment, deepening the rose hue of her skin which was already flushed from the moist steam in the room. "I admit it is gratifying to look well. You wouldn't understand because you have always been beautiful."

"Beautiful?" Rayne protested with an edge of humor.

"For a man, you are strikingly beautiful."

She saw the tug of an appreciative smile at her flattery. "And you always have been too self-conscious about your appearance, sweetheart."

That wasn't quite true, Madeline knew. Until meeting Rayne, she had never been particularly sensitive about her looks, for there was no man she'd wanted to captivate. "It is easy for you to dismiss the issue of appearance. You never had to deal with the affliction of being plain."

"You are not plain any longer."

"Thank you," she replied, somehow managing to keep her tone light and to hide the warm glow his praise engendered. "But I collect you benefit as well. If you find me more attractive, it will be easier for you to achieve your goal."

"My goal?"

"Of begetting an heir. Isn't that why you wed me?"

"In part."

"Perhaps we should take this opportunity then. You proved that one can make love in a coach. Can it be accomplished in a bathtub?"

The heavy fringe of his lashes lowered over his breathtaking blue eyes. Rayne was considering her, judging her, trying to determine her intent. "What are you implying, Madeline?" he finally asked. "Do you want me to make love to you here and now?"

She gave a shrug of her bare shoulders. "It is merely a suggestion. I suspect it will take longer to sire a child if we keep separate bedchambers and you only share my bed during conjugal visits. But I want to fulfill my part of our bargain, Rayne."

Madeline could hear her heart beating as she waited for his answer. She truly wanted to give Rayne a child, but just this moment she would settle for arousing his passion.

"Indeed," she added, dropping her own voice so that it was low and husky, "I consider it my duty to make love to you."

"Your duty," he repeated dispassionately.

She let her eyes tease him. "A very pleasant duty, of course."

Her throaty voice seemed to affect him, for he smiled a slow, sensual smile. "I am at your command, wife."

"Why don't you undress then?"

Standing, Rayne complied, shedding his clothing without further comment.

The memory of his naked body danced across her mind, but a memory couldn't compare to Rayne in the flesh. Madeline caught her breath at the raw power of his tall, sinewed male form.

There was something untamed about him, an intense edge that didn't fit the conventional boundaries of a nobleman of leisure. That magnificent chest, for instance, was solid with muscle, while his thighs were those of an athletic horseman who had spent long hours in the saddle.

She could scarcely believe this glorious man was her husband. It was even harder to credit that she could arouse his lust so strongly, even though Rayne had told her from the first that he wanted her. Yet his desire for her was evident, she realized, following the line of dark hair trailing down his belly to his loins where the thick length of his arousal jutted out.

Madeline bit her lip, remembering the feel of him moving inside her, the incredible pleasure he had given her. This time, however, *his* pleasure was her primary aim. A shiver stole through her at the prospect.

His movements were lithe and graceful as he climbed into the bath with her. Madeline moved to the foot to allow him room, causing water to lap at the edges of the tub, while Rayne positioned his back against the higher end.

"Now what did you have in mind?" he asked, the sound rich and very male.

When she felt a rush of heat at the husk in his voice, Madeline murmured a silent oath, vexed at herself for reacting that way. She was supposed to remain in control, ravishing Rayne while letting him think it was his idea entirely.

"You are the expert lover," she replied. "I will leave it to you."

"Come here then," he commanded. "You are too far away."

Still kneeling, Madeline moved between his spread thighs. Rayne was close enough that she could smell the musky scent of his skin mixed with the fresh fragrance of soap. Yet apparently it was not near enough for him, for he slid a possessive arm around her waist. Madeline found herself drawn against the hard planes of his body, the heavy fullness of him pressing against her belly.

"I shaved this morning," he told her, "but I fear my jaw may be too rough for your tender skin."

She regarded his handsome features, seeing the shadow of stubble on the lower part of his face, but shook her head. "I don't mind."

"Good, because I want to kiss you."

He ran his thumb over her lower lip with a sensuous stroke, then lowered his head to hers. His mouth was a wicked warmth, his lips gliding over hers with seductive pressure. Understandably, Madeline fell headlong into his kiss, drinking him in, relishing the dance of their mating tongues. When finally Rayne set her mouth free, she drew back, dazed by the piercing arousal he'd stirred in her.

She swallowed hard, trying to remember her plan to seduce him rather than be seduced. "You should let me scrub your back," she murmured. "Isn't that a wifely duty?"

"Later. For the moment, I have something else in mind."

Taking the cake of soap from her, he lathered his hands and spread them over her shoulders, then directed his attentions higher. Her throat arched as he pressed his palm to the slender column, holding his hand there against her erratic pulse, molding it to fit before slowly sliding down again.

When his fingertips skimmed the undersides of her breasts, her nipples instantly turned into two demanding peaks of arousal, which Rayne then circled with his thumb.

A moan of pleasure slipped from Madeline's throat at the primal pleasure he was giving her, but Rayne stopped her from closing her eyes. "No, watch me."

"Why? What do you plan to do?"

His slow, lazy smile was absolutely devastating. "You'll see."

Dropping the soap over the tub's side into the basket, he returned both hands to her breasts, letting his slick palms glide over the ripe mounds. Her rose-hued nipples were already pebbled and hard, and Rayne's plucking with his fingers only made them more keenly sensitive, while watching him arouse her heightened the feeling even further. Madeline sucked in a sharp breath as his erotic caresses speared a hot ache through her.

Then he slid one hand downward into the water, reaching for the dark thatch of curls crowning her thighs. Her entire body flushed a welcome, but she grasped his arm to stop him from touching her there. "Rayne, darling, I have a favor to ask of you."

Curiosity lifted one of his brows. "What favor?"

"Ours may be a marriage of convenience, but there is no reason we cannot enjoy it, isn't that right?"

"Yes. I've told you so."

"Yet as it stands now, our relationship is highly unequal. You have all the experience while I have almost none."

"So?"

Madeline took a breath. "So I want to learn how to please you. Will you teach me?"

His half-lidded gaze was assessing. "You already please me, sweeting."

"But there is much more I could learn. You are a legendary lover, and I want to be worthy of you. Please, will you show me the secrets of being an ideal lover?"

A spark kindled in his eyes. "You are serious?" Rayne asked.

"Utterly."

When he locked gazes with her, something primitive, powerful arced between them. In response, Madeline felt another hard ache flare between her thighs.

"How do I pleasure you, Rayne?" she asked with more insistence.

"There are numerous ways to arouse a man."

"Name one."

"You can begin by touching me."

Reaching into the water, she let her fingers trail down over his flat, hard abdomen. She could feel the muscles bunch beneath her touch, even before she reached the underside of his loins and cupped the firm, velvety pouch below his swollen manhood. "Like this?"

He gave a soft murmur of assent as his male member jerked. "That can drive a man wild."

"What about this?" When her fingers curled around him, the thick, erect length surged in her hand.

"That is highly pleasurable, also," Rayne admitted in a strangled voice. "Stroking me would be even more effective."

She did as he suggested, lightly fondling his rigid, straining arousal. It quivered in her hand, and in response, something deep within her body shivered in purely sensual reaction. Then Rayne reached down to assist her. Curving his fingers around hers, he stroked his sex within their joined grip.

To her delight, his face darkened with a sensual flush, while his breath started to come more rapidly.

"I'm certain there is more."

"Use your imagination, sweeting."

She gave him a considering look. "I think I should explore your body with my lips."

From the hot gleam in his eyes, she could tell he approved of the idea. "Pray, go ahead."

Still holding his shaft, Madeline leaned forward and kissed the wide expanse of bare chest, her tongue licking the moisture from his skin, but the simple caress wasn't satisfying enough to her. "If you stood up, I could reach more of you."

"I imagine you could."

Obligingly, Rayne rose to his feet and reclined against the high sloping back of the tub, his buttocks resting against the smooth metal, his loins directly in front of her face. He looked perfectly at ease, yet she sensed he was not nearly so relaxed as he appeared.

Indeed, his body tensed when she cupped water with her hands and let it dribble over his pulsing erection. Since she couldn't recall precisely what Fanny had told her, however, Madeline simply followed her instincts. Running her palms upward along his powerful thighs, she leaned closer and touched his arousal with her lips.

She heard his sharp intake of breath as she lapped at the sparkling drops of water beading on his manhood.

Madeline glanced up at him, her smile provocative, slightly challenging. "I want to drive you insane with lust, Rayne. How do I do that?"

"I'd say you are well on your way."

The teasing light in his eyes had disappeared completely, to be replaced by a sensual intensity that seared her.

"What do I do now?"

"Why don't you put that luscious mouth of yours to use?"

He remained still, his hands braced on the rim on either side of the tub, giving her complete control of his seduction. Excitement shot through her, flooding her veins with shuddering heat.

Her hands were shaking a little when she threaded her fingers through the curling hair at his groin. Then, craving the warmth and taste and feel of him, she bent forward and suckled him.

His body went rigid at the first touch of her mouth, and remained that way for the delicate searching of her tongue. When she glanced up again to gauge his response, his mouth curled in a tight smile that seemed half pleasure, half pain. "That isn't bad for a novice."

Feeling challenged, Madeline returned her full attention to arousing him, letting her tongue and lips roam at will, her caresses inviting, teasing, promising.

Rayne gave a growl of approval and gripped the side of the tub more tightly. An answering sound rasped from Madeline's throat. She was fascinated by his response, warmed by the pleasure she felt at pleasing him.

"God," he muttered as she suckled him more strongly. "And you said you didn't know how to arouse me."

"You are an excellent tutor."

He was no longer so nonchalant, she thought triumphantly as his hips thrust forward. She slipped her hands behind him, glorying in the way his masculine buttocks hardened in her hands.

"Does this hurt?" she murmured, her question slightly taunting as her lips enveloped him more fully.

"Yes, I am in excruciating pain. I'm ready to burst. . . ."

As if to prove his words, his hips arched again.

With greater assurance, Madeline drew his rigid flesh even deeper into her mouth, continuing her carnal ministrations, until his hand suddenly reached up to clutch in her hair, stilling her. "That is enough torment."

She glanced up, wondering if he really meant for her to stop.

There was nothing casual now about the glitter in his sapphire eyes, Madeline saw. His hot gaze scorched her, and she stared at him in turn, thrilling at the sight. She saw need in his eyes, sexual need for her.

She felt beautiful in that moment. Beautiful and omnipotent. Madeline savored her first feelings of power as a woman as she let herself get lost in his incredible eyes. Heat poured through her, making her weak and shaky.

She must have had the same effect on Rayne, for he suddenly lowered himself into the tub. Water sloshed over the rim as he hauled her into his arms. They were both trembling now, with poignant desire and sharp need pulsing between them.

Taking control, Rayne parted her thighs and tugged her onto his lap, so that she straddled him, her cleft nestled against the swollen ridge of his manhood. The contact was a delicious shock.

"I've wondered how it would feel to have you ride me."

The image of his erotic words made her feel even more faint. She caught her breath as Rayne guided her down slowly so that she was sitting astride him. It was like riding a powerful stallion, except that she was impaled on his rigid shaft. Her body was molten, raw with wanting him.

When he was finally sheathed in her body, Madeline whimpered at the exquisite sensations. The fullness was blissful—yet Rayne seemed determined to increase her ecstasy. His lips came down hard on hers as he began to move inside her, his mouth feverishly eating hers.

His kiss was a lover's demand, a little fierce, a lot possessive, but she met each questing stroke of his tongue with her own urgency, her mouth locked with his, seeking, searching, aching.

The tempo quickened rapidly. Her thighs locked around his hips as he plunged inside her over and over again, the friction of their wet, slippery bodies compounding her desire with searing intensity. In only moments Madeline was gasping for breath, but still the sensual explosion inside her took her by surprise. Rayne captured her scream of pleasure as she bucked and shook in his arms. Her sheath contracted powerfully about him while liquid fire poured through her.

Rayne found his own powerful climax an instant later while her body still vibrated around him, the echo of her raw throaty cries mingling with his groans.

When they both finally stilled, Madeline collapsed upon his chest, her heart hammering, her breath coming in pants. She felt liquid and sensuous and too weak to move. The heat of their passion had melted every bone in her body.

Rayne seemed just as spent. His rasping breath harsh

and uneven, he lay there with his head back against the tub, his arms held loosely around her as she floated in the water.

It seemed a long while later when he gave a hoarse chuckle. "This was not exactly the welcome I expected. Unquestionably, I have never enjoyed a bath more."

The warm glow in her body expanded at his soft laughter. Madeline still couldn't bring herself to move, however. In truth, she wasn't sure her limbs would ever function again. Joined to Rayne, she'd experienced that startling sense of fullness again, not just of her body but of her heart.

At the same time she felt an almost euphoric sense of exhilaration. Rayne's wild, physical response to her lovemaking had sent her hopes soaring, had made her believe in possibilities. After such incredible passion, she found it far easier to see a glimmer of promise for their future together.

Even though love was no part of their bargain, Rayne's love was what she wanted, what she dreamed of. Her happiness depended on winning his heart.

Of course she didn't dare tell him so for fear of driving him away. Yet she had begun to hope that Rayne would come to want her someday, not just for the pleasure she could bring him, not for the children she longed to give him, but for herself.

Reminded of her campaign, Madeline stirred in his arms and weakly pressed a kiss against his bare shoulder. "That was a most enlightening lesson in lovemaking," she murmured.

"You make a splendid pupil," he replied languidly.

When she lifted her head to gaze at Rayne, his eyes

were still shut, but the tender smile that curved his mouth made her want to crawl inside of him.

The quivery feelings in her chest intensified—a warning sign, Madeline knew. She would have to end this intimate interlude before she gave away her feelings.

Only a moment more, she promised herself, resting her cheek in the curve of his shoulder with a contented sigh.

Rayne was feeling the same languor, experiencing the same swell of bone-deep satisfaction. He had found Madeline's wicked innocence completely entrancing.

Strange how he had once thought her plain. She was nothing like the drab spinster he'd thought her at their first meeting. Her innate sensuality not only had stirred and excited him, it had more than proved a match for his own libidinous nature. He could still feel the fever her passion had left on his skin, even though the water was cooling.

His new wife was indeed much more than he bargained for, Rayne acknowledged.

No sooner had he silently voiced the thought, however, than Madeline eased away from him. Untangling their limbs, she pulled herself up by the rim.

With effort Rayne opened his eyes, watching as she climbed from the tub, his gaze fixed on her lithe, lush body. To his disappointment she wrapped a length of linen towel around her dripping form, concealing her delectable curves from his view.

"You are not leaving, are you?"

In response she glanced over her shoulder and sent him a tantalizing smile. "Surely you can bathe without me."

If he didn't know better, he would call that look flirtatious, provocative even. He was sorely tempted to rise up from the tub and drag Madeline back into the water with him.

Rayne felt himself frown. Between her improved looks and changed demeanor, he almost didn't recognize his new bride. In truth, he wasn't certain he liked this seductive side of Madeline. He could see no artifice in her wide gray eyes just now, yet all his instincts were suddenly on edge.

"You needn't go," he said without inflection.

"I'm afraid I must. I have to dress and prepare for this evening."

"This evening?"

Her own tone remained casual as she explained. "I forgot to mention . . . Arabella is holding a dinner at Danvers Hall for some of the neighboring families, with cards afterward. I mean to attend, but you needn't bother if you don't wish to. I know you don't care for dull social occasions."

Rayne frowned again, realizing that Madeline had made plans of her own and was set on living her life without him. But wasn't that exactly what he wanted from her?

"I want to attend," he replied. "My presence can only help your introduction to society."

"Then I will send her a note, saying to expect you."

After drying off, Madeline pulled on a highly feminine dressing gown of jade green silk, leaving it partially open as she sauntered over to him and bent to place a light kiss on his lips. Searing heat shot through Rayne again before she closed the wrapper and hid her womanly charms once more. Then, gathering up her clothing, she left the bathing chamber, shutting the door softly behind her.

Rayne found himself staring at the door, admittedly taken aback by the alluring change in Madeline. He was pleased by her newfound sensuality and her bold advances, yet he was accountably wary at the same time. In his experience, a woman bent on seduction could be deceptive and dangerous. Camille had used his seduction for her own ends—

Perhaps he was overreacting again, Rayne realized, just as he'd done when he'd misjudged Madeline's relationship with Baron Ackerby. He was keenly aware of the depth of his mistrust after experiencing Camille's betrayal. Unconsciously, he had started looking for signs that his wife intended to betray him, too.

Yet even if her motives were totally pure, Rayne had to acknowledge that he was becoming too attracted to his enchanting new bride.

From now on he would have to keep up his guard better, he reflected as he set his jaw and reached for the soap once more.

Chapter Fourteen

Rayne makes a woman desperately yearn for his kisses, Maman, but I hope to make him yearn for mine. Regrettably, he seems stubbornly resistant to all my efforts.

The change in Madeline was clearly noticeable to Rayne. When they dined at Danvers Hall that evening, she wore a stunning evening gown of white Brussels lace over a slip of pale green sarcenet. Her hair was dressed in a much softer style than before, her shimmering tresses threaded with seed pearls and emerald green ribbons.

Madeline's features seemed softer as well, more delicate and refined somehow. In truth, Rayne decided, his new wife looked almost beautiful with her sophisticated, fashionable veneer. From watching her interact with the other dinner guests, it was obvious she was ready to take her place at his side as his countess.

Understandably, Rayne spent the entire evening fighting his attraction. There was no question that the new Madeline was lovelier than the plain spinster he had wed the previous week. And although her outer appearance was not as important to him as her spirit and her intelligence and her lively wit, he couldn't help being affected by the change in her. To his chagrin, Rayne felt an unwanted softening inside him, a weakening of his resolve to keep his distance from Madeline.

His weakness only intensified once they returned home to Riverwood and retired for bed. Madeline had also acquired more confidence in her feminine appeal, apparently, in addition to her newfound sensuality, for when Rayne escorted her upstairs to her bedchamber door, she paused to look up at him.

When she met his gaze with her luminous gray eyes, her glance both inviting and questioning, Rayne couldn't help remembering how hot and eager she'd been in his arms just a few hours earlier. He could still feel her tight sheath clenching around his cock in a violent climax.

Recollecting her taste, her texture, her warmth, Rayne felt a powerful surge of lust ripple through him—which might have been exactly her intent. From her expression he could tell she knew he was thinking of their bath. Her lips curved with that same tantalizing smile she had flashed him this afternoon during their passionate encounter in the bathing chamber.

His gaze fixed on her full, ripe mouth for a dozen heartbeats . . . but then Rayne forced himself to take a step back. He longed to follow Madeline into her bedchamber and spend the entire night ravishing her. He wanted to be inside her again in the most desperate way. Yet he left her at her door, determined to limit his connubial demands, despite his professed desire to sire an heir.

He already felt too much need for Madeline. Until he discovered a way to be with her, to be inside her without allowing her to slip any deeper inside *him,* he intended to stay away.

Not surprisingly, Rayne had difficulty sleeping that night, finding it all but impossible to drive away the memory of making love to Madeline. He woke the next morning, feeling restless and irritated. It was understandable that he wanted her so badly, but why he was having such trouble maintaining his emotional defenses—when he'd vowed to feel nothing more for her than carnal desire—was much harder to fathom.

He had a similar problem when Madeline joined him at breakfast, looking fresh and lovely in a cream-colored muslin morning gown. He longed to pull her into his arms so he could kiss that alluring mouth and that even more alluring body.

Doubtless that explained why he was thankful for the minor incident that put him on his guard once more. They were engaging in polite conversation at the breakfast table, discussing the guests Madeline had met the previous evening, when she accidently let slip a revelation. Rayne had just complimented her on her success in winning over their neighbors.

Madeline gave a small laugh while wrinkling her nose. "To be truthful, I am attempting to become more like Roslyn Moncrief. I know you admire her immensely. How did you describe her? 'Intriguing'? And you rated her very high on intelligence."

Rayne's gaze sharpened at her observation. There was only one way Madeline could have learned how he'd evaluated Roslyn: from rummaging in his study desk.

"How did you learn of my admiration for her?" he asked mildly.

Madeline suddenly gave a start. When she sent him a guilty look, Rayne wondered if she would confess or try to bluff her way out of her self-induced trap with a lie.

After a hesitation, she evidently decided to come clean about her transgression. "I happened to see your list of bridal candidates the other day."

When he gave her a long, level look, Madeline added earnestly, "I was not snooping precisely. I was looking in your desk for writing paper. One of the drawers was unlocked, and when I came across your list of ladies' names, I was curious enough to want to read your comments."

When he remained silent, she placed an imploring hand on his arm. "I am sorry, Rayne. I didn't mean to pry. It won't happen again, I promise you."

Her look was innocent enough, but then he had been fooled before by an imploring expression on a pretty face. He let the matter drop, yet the knowledge that Madeline had searched through his private papers to ferret out his personal secrets was enough to make him again question whether her word could be trusted.

Two days later, another more serious incident occurred that raised Rayne's suspicions even further. It was late in the afternoon when he caught Madeline attempting to eavesdrop on his conversation.

Since returning to Riverwood, Rayne had received several reports from London regarding the progress in breaking up the assassination ring. As he dismissed the latest courier with some final instructions, he opened his study door to find his wife loitering in the corridor outside.

Madeline gave him an amiable smile as she offered an apology of sorts. "I was just debating whether to knock, my lord. I didn't wish to intrude on your privacy."

Rayne wasn't sure if he believed her excuse for not making herself known, but he had no desire to discuss the matter before an audience. Thus, he nodded at the courier in dismissal.

When they were alone, Madeline slanted a glance up at Rayne from beneath her eyelashes. "You missed tea again. I came to invite you to have it with me."

Since he could think of no good reason to deny her invitation, Rayne followed her from his study and accompanied her to the drawing room, where his staff had already laid out an appetizing tea.

As she poured for him, Madeline commented in a casual tone, "I did not realize that you were still involved in your former spy activities."

"What makes you think I am still involved?" Rayne hedged.

She gave him an arch look. "When I see shadowy figures coming and going from your study at all hours of the night and day, it is not hard to guess."

"And you assume my visitors have something to do with spying."

"Yes. There is an urgency about them . . . a seriousness that would be lacking if they were simply interested in business matters. They don't seem to be supplicants, either—hangers-on demanding favors of you—which you doubtless have in great abundance, given your illustrious title and wealth."

"Why all the concern about my endeavors just now, sweeting?" Rayne responded evasively.

Madeline raised a quizzical eyebrow. "Why not? Should I not wonder what is occupying my new husband's time? Is it unreasonable that I would be curious about your affairs now that we are wed, even if we do have a mere union of convenience?"

Perhaps it wasn't unreasonable, Rayne decided, but

her pointed interest made him uneasy. He wanted to fob her off, but Madeline persisted with her observations.

"I thought you had given up your career in intelligence, but it wouldn't surprise me if you decided to continue in some fashion. You thrive on challenges. I can't imagine you being content with the tame life of a nobleman."

When Rayne didn't reply to her prodding, she added with a provocative smile, "I suspect men of your profession do not simply fade into the woodwork, especially someone of your caliber."

If she was attempting to flatter him for her own purposes, she would realize he was immune to such tactics.

"I haven't decided yet what to do about my future," he finally answered.

Which was true. After Napoleon's first defeat in 1814, his friend Will Stokes had turned to catching thieves and criminals and had recently suggested Rayne join him as a Runner. Yet working for Bow Street as a thief-taker didn't hold quite the same allure as pitting his wits and skills against deadly French agents.

Still, this latest enterprise had given Rayne a glimmer of an idea for what he might do with his life. Foiling civilian plots might cure his ennui and restlessness and fill the hole that losing a career in British foreign intelligence had left.

Madeline continued to study him as she sipped her tea. "When you do decide about your future, I should like to know."

"Of course."

She didn't seem satisfied. "Pray, just answer me this. If you are involved in any dangerous enterprises, should I be worried for your safety?"

"No, there is no need for you to worry about me at all."

His answer seemed to frustrate her, judging from the annoyance and disappointment that swept fleetingly across her features. But Rayne wasn't about to discuss the threat to the Prince Regent's life. Even setting aside the question of Madeline's motives, he didn't want her prying into his business. Interference from an amateur could jeopardize the best of plans. Besides, Madeline would almost certainly ask to help.

Rayne shook his head at the irony. If he had wanted a meek, biddable wife who wouldn't meddle in his affairs, he should not have chosen her. Perhaps he'd made a mistake in settling on Madeline. She had a clever, keen mind. If she wanted to uncover his secrets, she was in the perfect position to do so, living in his house with him. The past few days, however, had left Rayne wondering if she had crossed the line from simple wifely curiosity into something more sinister.

Either way, he could sense something was wrong, off-kilter somehow. Madeline obviously wanted something from him; he just wasn't sure what it was.

Perhaps he was simply looking for reasons to push her away, Rayne reflected, yet he knew from hard-earned experience to listen to his instincts, a wisdom honed over many years dealing with secrets and lies and betrayals.

And even if his instincts were off the mark this time, eavesdropping on his visitors was certainly not the way to persuade him to trust her, nor was asking him probing questions about his future in the intelligence business.

* * *

From her perspective, Madeline was not the least surprised that Rayne wished to keep part of his life secret from her, even though she was now his wife. Old habits died hard, notwithstanding the fact that she had her own secrets to hide from *him*.

She'd seen the way Rayne had looked her over, measuring her, when she merely questioned his future ambitions. His suspicious nature was perhaps one reason he was so determined to resist her advances.

She wasn't prying into his affairs, though. Fanny had counseled her to show an avid interest in her husband, and it was no pretense. Naturally she was interested in every detail of Rayne's life and his expectations for his future. And of course she would worry about his safety if he had returned to the spy business.

But chiefly Madeline wanted to know what was keeping him from paying attention to her just now, so she could adjust her campaign for his seduction.

She knew that winning Rayne wouldn't happen overnight. Even so, she was annoyed and frustrated at the slow pace of her progress. How was it possible that she felt so much while he was left totally unaffected? Just being near Rayne tested the limits of her willpower. She yearned for him with a physical ache. More important, she wanted to be inside his heart.

Fanny had been so certain that her methods would break through the defenses even of a man like Rayne, yet Madeline worried that they didn't seem to be working.

She was also beginning to grow more worried about her brother, since she'd heard nothing from Gerard and received no response to her two letters. She didn't even know if he and his new bride had arrived safely in Maidstone, Kent, at the cottage belonging to Lynette's Dubonet cousin Claude.

At least Freddie Lunsford's dilemma was apparently solved. Madeline received a brief, scrawled note from Freddie, reporting that Madame Sauville was seething but that he was free of her blackmail and still in his father's good graces.

In another fortunate turn of events, Madeline managed to gain another friend and ally. Tess Blanchard, the other part-time teacher at the Freemantle Academy, returned home to Chiswick, having spent the past fortnight in Brighton at a house party.

Tess was a stunning beauty with luxurious sable hair and a carriage that boasted unmistakable gentility. She appeared to be slightly younger than Madeline, about Roslyn's age of two and twenty. Tess's flawless complexion and figure, too, lit an irrepressible spark of envy in Madeline's breast. Yet her smile was kindness itself when Madeline first met her at the academy between classes.

"Please let me know if I may help you in any way, Lady Haviland," Tess said at once. "I am in your debt, since you assumed my teaching responsibilities while I was away."

"I was glad for the opportunity," Madeline responded, drawn in by the beauty's warmth, "but I wish you would call me Madeline. I am not at all accustomed to being addressed by formal titles."

"I will," she agreed readily, "if you will call me Tess. As I was saying, I am grateful to you, since your arrival allowed me to spend time with my cousin Damon, Lord Wrexham. Damon recently wed Lord Danvers's younger sister Eleanor, and I am his only remaining close family."

"So I heard. Actually, Arabella and Jane have told me a great deal about you." Madeline had heard most about the charities that Tess had devoted herself to since losing her beloved betrothed in the Battle of Waterloo two years ago. "Your charitable endeavors are so very admirable."

Tess flashed another warm smile. "Your husband has contributed generously in the past, but now that you are here, perhaps I might persuade you to become involved and utilize your role as Countess of Haviland. It is amazing how influential an aristocratic title can be when soliciting charitable donations."

"Yes, indeed. I would like that very much."

Tess paused, giving her a considering look. "Arabella mentioned that Fanny Irwin has been advising you. Pray don't be alarmed," she said when Madeline looked taken aback. "Belle didn't betray your confidences. It is just that she has been pressing me to ask Fanny for help with my own situation."

"Your situation?" Madeline asked curiously.

"My unmarried state." Tess uttered a rueful laugh. "Arabella is so enamored of her own wedded bliss that she wants me to find the same happiness. I have known Fanny for several years now, but I never thought to enlist her help in plotting affairs of the heart. It was clever of you, Madeline."

"It was Arabella's idea," she admitted.

Tess lowered her voice to a confidential undertone. "If it is not too forward of me to ask, have any of Fanny's method's worked?"

"It is too early to tell just yet," Madeline answered truthfully, "but I still have high hopes. And there is no doubt that Fanny improved my confidence immeasurably— which was no small feat, given how impossibly naïve I was when it came to dealing with the male sex."

"Thank you," Tess said earnestly. "I am out of mourning now and determined to move on with my life, so employing Fanny's expertise seems a wise plan."

Since Jane Caruthers joined them, Madeline had no more chance for conversation with Tess just then, but she was greatly looking forward to becoming better acquainted with her intriguing fellow teacher.

On another front entirely, Madeline had to deal with two other members of Rayne's family. It came as a bit of a surprise when his two sisters called at Riverwood the following afternoon without any advance warning.

They were there to inspect her and take her measure, Madeline suspected, regretting that once again Rayne was absent, having left for London that morning.

As she made her way to the drawing room where Bramsley had ushered the ladies to wait for her, Madeline tried to recall what she'd learned about them in the past week of her marriage. Penelope was older than Rayne by two years, Daphne younger by about the same. The sisters had each married baronets, which made Penelope, Lady Tewksbury, and Daphne, Lady Livermore.

They were both handsome women, Madeline saw upon entering, with raven hair and blue eyes like their brother, although not nearly as tall. Both were perched stiffly on their chairs, as if reluctant to settle in for too long. And at first glance they looked as haughty and imperious as their grandmother, the dowager Countess of Haviland.

They also appeared unwilling to welcome Madeline with any more enthusiasm than had their noble relative. Judging from their chill greetings, their grandmother had not relented in her opposition to her, Madeline realized with a sinking heart; she simply was not considered good enough to be admitted into the family.

She smiled politely, however, and kept her own tone amiable as she welcomed the sisters to Riverwood and expressed pleasure in meeting them.

When she asked if they would care for refreshments, Penelope responded tersely. "Thank you, no. We will not be staying. We merely wished to see what sort of female our brother chose to wed." After a moment's hesitation, she added, "I confess you are a surprise."

"Oh, how so?"

"You are significantly older, for one thing."

Madeline kept her lips closed to keep herself from retorting.

"We supposed Haviland knew what was due his family name, but unfortunately we were mistaken."

Daphne spoke up then. "It is also because Rayne is not the marrying kind, and we didn't think he would ever succumb, despite our grandmother's most persuasive efforts. Penelope and I both wed shortly after our comeouts, as expected of young ladies, but Rayne has resisted matrimony all these years."

"I did not have a comeout," Madeline admitted pointedly, "so I had little opportunity to meet eligible gentlemen."

Penelope's expression was close to a sneer. "So we heard. We understand you were employed as a companion."

"I was indeed."

"At least it is a relief to discover you are not quite beyond the pale. We feared you would prove an utter embarrassment." Penelope eyed Madeline's fashionable round gown. "Grandmama led us to believe you had regrettable taste in attire. But that gown you are wearing is unexceptionable."

"Lady Danvers has been advising me on purchasing my bride clothes," Madeline said, persuaded that a little name-dropping would not hurt with her two judges.

Penelope ignored her mention of her noble neighbor. "You made a serious error challenging our grandmother. You have made an enemy of her."

"It certainly was not my intent."

"She means to cut you dead."

"A fate worse than death," Madeline murmured mostly under her breath.

Penelope's gaze sharpened. "I don't believe you comprehend what is in store for you. You will be shunned by society. You will not be received in any of the best homes. Tell me, have you received any cards of invitation since your marriage, other than those from your provincial neighbors?"

Madeline felt her hackles rising but schooled her features to blandness so as not to appear defensive. "I would hardly call the Countess of Danvers and the Duchess of Arden provincial," she answered sweetly. "I am gratified to name both ladies as friends."

Daphne broke in. "She has a point, Penny."

"Hush, Daphne." The elder sister turned her attention back to Madeline. "If you are garnering attention, it is because you are a novelty for people who want to view Haviland's new countess."

"Perhaps so," she agreed. "But truthfully, it doesn't

concern me much. Moreover, Rayne has handled our correspondence thus far, so I am unfamiliar with what cards we may have received."

Penelope's sneer deepened. "I would not put it past Rayne to toss them away. He never has paid proper attention to correct manners."

Madeline flashed a cool smile at her. "No, he was more concerned with lowbrow affairs such as ridding the world of a tyrant."

Daphne was eyeing her with growing wonder. "You are as blunt and outspoken as Grandmama described you."

Her smile turned wry. "I imagine Lady Haviland had stronger words than *that* to describe me."

"Don't you care at all that you have earned her wrath?" Daphne asked curiously.

Madeline sobered. "I care that my husband not suffer because of me. I never wanted to come between him and his family. But I cannot change my birth or breeding." She slanted a glance at Penelope. "Just so you know, I received a genteel education, and I am aware of the correct way to use a knife and fork, among other things."

Penelope responded to her provocation. "But can you host a dinner to honor a diplomat or give a ball for four hundred guests?"

"Not at present, but I am a quick study, and I have friends who are generous enough to teach me what I need to know."

She didn't point out that Rayne's sisters should rightfully be helping her make her way through the treacherous waters of the ton.

"I think you might do for Rayne after all," Daphne said slowly.

Madeline felt a measure of surprise. Perhaps Rayne's younger sister was prepared to be a bit more forgiving than the elder. "Why do you say so?"

"Because you don't back down from confrontation. Rayne is exactly that way, too, so you must be well-matched." The smile Daphne offered her was full of charm with a hint of devilry. "Rayne was named by our father, after the Norse word, Raynor—did you know?"

"No, I didn't know."

"It means 'warrior from the gods,' actually. Papa fancied himself a Greek scholar, but in between his Greek phases, he studied the Norsemen."

"Daphne, pray don't let your tongue run on," her sister commanded.

Daphne, however, refused to comply with the order. "Penny and I gave our children plain, old-fashioned English names, though. Hers are named Michael and Peter, mine are Francis and Henry."

"That is quite *enough,* Daphne," Penelope said more insistently.

"Rayne told me his oldest nephew is twelve and the youngest is four," Madeline observed, disregarding the tension between the two sisters.

"Yes," was Penelope's brusque answer, but Daphne unbent even further, going so far as to laugh. "Trust me, Lady Haviland, you don't want to encourage me to discuss my children unless you have all day. I can sing their praises endlessly."

"You sound very fond of them."

"I am indeed, and so is Penny, to be truthful—"

Cutting her sister off abruptly, Penelope focused her haughty gaze on Madeline. "Mention of our sons brings us to the point of our visit."

"And what is that?" Madeline asked more politely.

"Shall we deal in plain speaking?"

"By all means."

"It is our hope," Penelope said, looking uncomfortable for the first time, "that you will not cause a rift in our family that can never be mended."

"Yes," Daphne chimed in. "It would not be fair to Rayne if Grandmama disowned him, but it would be even more unfair to our sons. Although we might be pleased if she were to leave her immense fortune to us, our sons would not be permitted to see their Uncle Rayne then, and they are excessively fond of him."

Madeline's brow furrowed. "You allow your grandmother to rule all your lives?"

Daphne wrinkled her nose. "I fear so. Grandmama controls the purse strings, you see, and we don't want to deprive our sons of their rightful inheritance, so we dance to her tune."

Madeline paused a long moment before replying. "So what is it you wish from me?"

"Well . . ." Daphne grimaced. "I am not certain there is anything to be done at this point, even if you could bring yourself to beg Grandmama's forgiveness for standing up to her. I doubt that even an abject apology would work."

"Did your grandmother sanction your coming here?"

"No, she doesn't know. But Rayne is our brother after all, and we are concerned for his welfare, as well as that of our sons. Besides, we wanted to see what manner of bride Rayne had chosen."

"I am surprised Lady Haviland did not forbid you outright."

"Oh, she *did*. She was extremely upset to learn of his

marriage—livid is the word. She positively raged about the way you spoke to her."

"I suppose I did not show her proper obeisance," Madeline remarked lightly.

"You most certainly did not," Penelope interjected as she rose to her feet. "Come, Daphne, this visit is at an end."

"I suppose we should go," Daphne agreed rather irreverently, "since we have stayed longer than the requisite fifteen minutes."

It seemed irrational that they had traveled all the way from London only to stay for such a short time, Madeline mused, but then they had never intended their visit to be an offer of friendship, even though they were her sisters by marriage now.

"Good day," Penelope said in that same cold tone, confirming Madeline's assumption.

Penelope was striding purposefully toward the drawing room door when Daphne lowered her voice to a stage whisper. "To be honest, Penny refused to call on you until I convinced her I was coming with or without her. She dislikes it immensely when I can lord it over her."

Daphne started to follow her sister when she suddenly paused. "By the by, has Rayne given you the Haviland jewels yet?"

The question caught Madeline off guard, since she wasn't aware of such a thing. "Not yet, no."

"You should ask him for the jewels. It hardly seems fair that they will go to you," she added good-naturedly, "since Pen and I have more right to them. But they are entailed along with the title. That is another reason

Grandmama is so furious at you. She will be loath to give them up."

"She may keep them as far as I am concerned."

Daphne stared at her. "You are far more generous than I could be in your shoes."

A thought struck Madeline just then. "Do you know where the jewels are kept? In a bank vault? Or a safe here or in Rayne's London house?"

"In a bank, I think." She smiled apologetically. "I had best go. Penny becomes extremely cross when her wishes are thwarted, just like Grandmama."

"Well, thank you for coming. It was a pleasure to meet you."

"You as well, even though I wouldn't dare acknowledge it if we were to encounter one another again. I am quite sorry."

"So am I," Madeline said sincerely. Daphne had a large measure of Rayne's charm, while Penelope was much more like their grandmother. Madeline doubted they would become bosom friends, at least not as long as Lady Haviland commanded their slavish obedience, but she would very much have liked to know Daphne better. And she hated to think of causing a breach between Rayne and his sisters.

When Rayne returned home late that afternoon and went straight to his study, Madeline knocked on his door as soon as she learned of his arrival.

"Your sisters called here today," she remarked upon gaining admittance.

Rayne's gaze seemed sympathetic as he invited her to take a seat on the sofa. "I trust they treated you with more consideration than my grandmother did?"

"Slightly more so. Daphne actually became quite congenial as time passed."

"What did they want?"

"To judge me, I suspect. At least they approved of my gown," Madeline said humorously.

Rayne's gaze swept over her stylish attire. "You should fit in their lofty circles quite well, dressed like that."

For some reason she suspected his observation was not a compliment. Frowning, Madeline directed the conversation down a different path. "You seem to be on good terms with your sisters. Are you very close?"

Rayne shrugged. "I am fond of them, but I wouldn't say we are particularly close. Penelope is the managing sort and henpecks her husband relentlessly. She takes after my grandmother, in fact. There is more hope for Daphne. She's given to theatrics, but her wit can be amusing. Both are society creatures, which you know I don't care for. At least they revert back into rational beings in the company of their sons—although they coddle the boys more than I would like. A pity they didn't bring my nephews here with them."

"Yes, I would have liked to meet them," Madeline agreed. She paused before adding, "Daphne said Lady Haviland may leave her enormous fortune to your sisters because you wed me."

Rayne regarded her without expression. "My grandmother is free to distribute her fortune as she sees fit."

"Of course she is. But I would not like you to suffer because of me, Rayne."

The look he gave her was penetrating. "That is considerate of you, sweetheart."

"I wish there was something I could do to allay your

grandmother's concerns about me," she said with true remorse.

"Don't dwell on it."

Madeline smiled faintly. "I cannot help but worry about it. Daphne also mentioned that the family jewelry is normally passed down to all the Haviland countesses."

For a fleeting moment Rayne's features seemed to take on a hard edge. "Is that a rebuke because I have been negligent? Do you want me to send for the Haviland jewels so you may wear them?"

"No, on the contrary. I don't wish to increase your grandmother's enmity by depriving her of what she considers to be her rightful property."

"Since the jewels are entailed, you have valid claim to them now."

It was Madeline's turn to shrug. "I have never worn expensive jewelry, and I feel no need to begin now. I won't miss what I have never had."

Rayne studied her for a long moment, as if trying to determine her veracity. Madeline felt suddenly discomfited by his scrutiny.

"If you must send for the jewels, does that mean they are kept in London?" she asked to redirect his attention.

"Yes," he replied after a brief hesitation.

"But you do have a safe here in your study?"

"Why do you ask?"

Actually, she was interested to know how difficult it would have been for Gerard to have stolen Baron Ackerby's heirloom necklace from his safe, yet she couldn't tell Rayne that.

"I was merely curious. You must have a place to keep your important documents."

"Yes, I have a safe here."

"How does it work? With a built-in lock? Or a pad-lock?"

He was regarding her again with his unsettlingly candid gaze. "The lock is an integral part of the safe. I keep the key in a secure location. Why all the interest, love? Do you have something you want to protect?"

"No, I just wondered." Madeline decided she would be wise to change the subject. "Well, I will leave you to your business. Before I go, however . . . I thought we might dine together tonight."

"I intended to dine with you," Rayne replied in a rather cool tone.

"No, I mean . . . in my rooms."

He leveled another piercing look at her. "What did you have in mind?"

Madeline felt her cheeks warming. It was uncomfortable to boldly proposition Rayne, especially since he wasn't giving her any encouragement. Yet if he was set on ignoring her, she would have to persuade him differently somehow. "I would like to dine with you in my sitting room tonight. Will you please indulge me?"

His gaze dropped to her breasts for an instant, then returned to her face. "Very well," he replied with no inflection in his voice at all.

His lack of enthusiasm did not bode well for her scheme, Madeline realized. She would just have to hope that what she had planned for this evening would please him.

By the time Madeline left his study, Rayne's unease about his new wife had grown fivefold. Her concern over his grandmother's fortune and the Haviland jewels had triggered a churning sensation deep in his gut. And her pointed interest in his safe had only compounded his disquiet.

His mind filling with chaotic, half-formed thoughts, Rayne strode over to his study window and stared broodingly out at the estate grounds. Perhaps he wasn't overreacting after all by harboring suspicions about Madeline. He'd trusted her because of his close friendship with her late father, but he didn't really *know* her. Unequivocally, his doubts about her were rising daily.

Mentally, Rayne went down the list of her suspect actions. The first strike against Madeline was the most damning: She seemed to be trying to seduce him in much the same way his former love had. Yet her motives eluded him.

Was financial trouble driving Madeline? Rayne wondered. She claimed that she didn't covet the Haviland jewels for herself, but could he believe her? She certainly hadn't objected to spending enormous sums on her new wardrobe—even if her purchases had been made at his own urging.

And then there was her guilty expression when he'd caught her out the other day. When he'd forced her to admit that she'd sneaked into his desk, she claimed to be searching for writing paper. But what had she really been looking for? The key to his safe? Why? Because she believed he kept valuables there?

Rayne locked his jaw, unable to quell the alarms that were sounding loudly in his head, and more painfully, in his chest. And as he stewed over the answer, a supposition struck him that felt right: Madeline's brother Gerard could be the reason for her machinations.

By her own admission, she had sent the monetary reward for retrieving Freddie's love letters to her brother, so Gerard evidently still needed funds.

Indeed, if Madeline wanted to save her brother from financial catastrophe, Rayne realized, her sudden acceptance of his marriage proposal made eminent sense.

Had she wed him solely for his wealth? If so, it was his own bloody fault. He had rushed her into marriage, not relenting until he had his way.

Rayne ran a hand raggedly through his hair. Perhaps Madeline had even played him for a fool from the beginning. She'd claimed to have no interest in his fortune, yet in reality she could be as grasping as Camille had ever been.

At the oppressive thought, Rayne stared unseeingly out the window, assaulted by dreaded feelings of déjà vu. Camille had desperately needed funds to help her family escape from France and so had pretended to welcome his love. The similarities between the two women were inescapable. In using him to fulfill her own objectives, Madeline could well put family loyalty over him, just as his former love had. She might possibly even betray him in order to help her brother.

Was she needy enough to be hatching some mercenary scheme against him? Could she even be in league with Baron Ackerby in some way? She'd clandestinely written to Ackerby and then claimed she was only imploring him to call off the duel. But was there more to her story?

Whatever her purpose, the evidence against Madeline was steadily mounting. What seemed to have innocent explanations at the time now seemed ominous.

It shouldn't disturb him this much, Rayne told himself, yet the peculiar ache tugging at his chest wouldn't go away.

At the admission, he muttered a savage oath under his breath. He'd vowed never to travel that path again, but apparently it was already too late. Madeline meant far more to him than she should.

So what ought his course be now? He needed to expose her motives first, of course. He could set a trap for her in order to test her loyalties. If she was after the contents of his safe, he could tell her where to find the key and then see if she took the bait. He could even lure her to expose her motivations by employing outright lies. There was no reason for him to feel guilt when Madeline herself was so evasive. He would have to think more on the best approach.

As for tonight, it was clear she planned to devote this evening to his seduction. He'd intended to abstain from claiming his husbandly rights, but the rush of primal lust he'd felt at her invitation had been so sharp and undeniable, he'd given in to his hunger for her and accepted her offer to dine in her chambers.

The muscles in Rayne's jaw tightened as he ground his teeth. He was about to let Madeline entice him into her bed again, but the more she attempted to captivate him, the more distrustful it would make him.

And if she thought to achieve her mysterious aims by making him fall under her spell, she would discover that she was playing with fire.

Chapter Fifteen

*My campaign to win Rayne's heart does not appear
to be succeeding, Maman, despite my best efforts.*

Madeline exerted great care in staging another seduction scene, this one in the sitting room adjoining her bedchamber. She had the servants place a table and two chairs before the hearth, along with a decanter of wine and two goblets on a side table. She asked for dinner to be delayed, however, since she intended to take her plan for seducing Rayne to passionate new heights.

For this one night, her most ardent wish was to be the lover he wanted. She wore a jade green dressing gown of shimmering silk, courtesy of Fanny Irwin—the same one she'd worn to entice Rayne in the bathing chamber. The garment was soft, feminine, romantic, and made her feel pretty and powerful, as if she might truly conquer a man like her husband. Yet butterflies were still rioting in her stomach when a quiet knock sounded on the sitting room door.

She went to answer it herself, admitting Rayne, then shutting the door again behind him. He had dressed informally, Madeline saw, in a burgundy brocade dressing gown with pantaloons and slippers beneath.

She also noted a barely visible tension across his shoulders as he scanned the result of her efforts—not a good sign when she had expected to please him. Outside, it was dark and rainy, but inside, the crackling fire had taken the October chill from the air. The flames and one low-burning lamp cast a cozy, intimate glow throughout the sitting room.

When Rayne turned to face her, though, Madeline could detect almost no emotion in his expression.

"I trust you are not too hungry," she ventured to murmur. "I told Bramsley I would ring for dinner to be served later. I thought we might enjoy a glass of wine first."

"As you please."

Hiding her disappointment at Rayne's dispassion, Madeline moved past him and poured him some wine. When she brought the goblet to him, he studied the ruby liquid without drinking, his beautiful eyes hiding behind that dark fringe of lashes as he voiced a question.

"What is going on in that clever head of yours, sweeting?"

"What do you mean?" she asked innocently.

"Just what are you planning?"

"Why, nothing more than an intimate dinner. But if you want to seduce me, I won't put up any resistance."

Rayne's dark-lashed eyes lifted negligently to lock with hers. "What if I don't wish to seduce you?"

Madeline swallowed hard, determined to persevere. "Then I shall have to take the initiative."

His gaze narrowed in speculation. "You don't think seduction is best left to the experts?"

She could detect no teasing in his question, but she resolutely kept her own tone light when she replied.

"Perhaps so, but I am attempting to increase my expertise. You said you would teach me how to arouse you."

"Oh, no," Rayne responded firmly. "This time you are on your own, love. I want to see how good a pupil you have become."

Hiding how unnerved she was, Madeline raised her chin and resorted to bravado. "I am an excellent pupil, and I will prove it to you."

Taking a deep breath, she unfastened the hooks at the front of her dressing gown, then slipped out of it. The garment fell to the floor in a delicate pool, leaving her completely naked.

Rayne's features arrested as he took in her form, and several heartbeats passed before he spoke. "Words fail me."

Madeline smiled in relief at the admiration in his tone. "Truly? I have never known you to be speechless."

"I am now."

"You will be more so when I ravish you."

His boldly familiar gaze raked over her bare body. "Behold me in transports of delight."

He did not appear to be overwhelmed by delight, yet there was no doubt he was affected by her. Undeniable attraction sizzled between them as he stepped closer.

Without warning then, Rayne reached out to flick her left nipple with his thumb. Blood rushed to every part of Madeline's body that he had taught to feel pleasure.

Rayne suddenly seemed amused. "So you mean to play the temptress again? Very well, then tempt me."

Madeline bit her lower lip at the unmistakable challenge in his tone. This was *not* the response she had hoped for. There was interest in his eyes just now, perhaps even heat, yet there was no passion and certainly

no overwhelming love. Instead, Rayne seemed emotionally distant, determined to hold himself apart from her.

Madeline felt a twist of longing so strong her stomach
hurt. She might be chasing a dream, using seduction to
make Rayne love her, but she wouldn't give up just yet.

Confiscating his glass of wine, Madeline took a deep
swallow for courage, which drew a surprisingly sharp
look from Rayne. Then taking his hand, she led him
over to the hearth, where the table and chairs had been
arranged for her purpose.

Setting the goblet down on the table, Madeline
reached up and pulled the pins from her hair. Thankfully, Rayne's gaze riveted on her as the silken mass fell
down to curl around her breasts.

"You have on far too many clothes," she said in a low,
husky voice. "I intend to take them off."

"Do as you wish."

His studied nonchalance was beginning to annoy her.
Lifting her face to his, Madeline kissed him flirtatiously,
letting her warm mouth linger against Rayne's as she un-
tied the sash of his dressing gown and pushed the lapels
apart, then slid the brocade off his magnificent shoulders to expose his broad bare chest.

Leaning even closer, she raised herself up on her tip-
toes and outlined the shell of his ear with her tongue
while pressing her belly against his loins. Beneath his
pantaloons she could feel Rayne's erection swell instantly at the erotic sensation.

At least his physical lust seemed real. His gaze was hot
on her now, and the air had grown sharp with expectation even before she finished undressing him.

Dropping to her knees before him, Madeline removed
his bedroom slippers, then unbuttoned his pantaloons

and drawers and drew them down his powerful legs. Upon standing once more, Madeline caught her breath at the splendor of his superb body rippling with supple muscle, the mysterious allure of his rampant male flesh rising from his loins.

Rayne was aroused and made no secret of it.

She felt a rush of damp heat between her thighs. She had incited his arousal, and the knowledge excited her.

"What now?" he asked.

The words were faintly taunting, and Madeline could not let his challenge go unanswered.

"Now I demonstrate the skills I have learned," she promised.

Pressing her hand against his bare chest, she guided him backward toward the chair facing her. When Rayne sat at her urging, she knelt between his parted thighs. His naked masculine beauty made her yearn to caress him with her hands and her mouth, and she intended to fulfill her desire without delay.

Rayne leaned back lazily—until she surprised him by dipping two fingers in the wine glass and painting his chest with the cool liquid.

"It seems you have a hidden wicked streak after all," he commented in a huskier tone than before.

Madeline smiled a soft, sinful smile. "I am only trying to prove your match, darling. Your wicked streak has been evident since the first moment I met you."

Wetting her fingers in the wine again, she artfully trailed a path down the muscles of his abdomen. Rayne's eyes gleamed with a different light now; the spark of heat in the blue depths had changed to hunger.

Determined to rattle his composure even further, Madeline traced the heavy sacs below his tumescence, slowly brushing the soft skin. Then reaching higher, she curled her fingers around his thrusting erection, molding her palm to his hardness. The thick length surged in her hand, while Rayne tensed visibly.

"You need to keep still," she ordered with a provocative smile. She dipped her fingers once more and held his gaze, looking directly into his eyes as she painted the thick head of his shaft with wine.

A muscle jumped in his jaw that was suddenly tight, Madeline saw with satisfaction. He wasn't the only one affected, either. She was certain Rayne could see the flush of her own arousal, the rapid flutter of her pulse in her throat.

She bent to his groin then, letting her tongue lick the sweet wine from his rigid flesh, making his breath hiss. His taste was hot and heady and highly arousing all by itself.

Holding his swollen member in a light grasp, she let her mouth close around him fully. When he groaned at the pleasure of it, she suckled harder, relishing her feeling of power at the way Rayne was responding to her touch.

His hips arching against the torment she was inflicting, he started to slide himself slowly between her lips, his hips rising reflexively off the chair, but Madeline would have none of it.

"Be still," she commanded in a husky voice, "or I will stop."

He obeyed, yet she suspected it required a great effort for him to maintain control as she explored him. His fingers pressed into the chair's seat as she went on arousing him, her hands a continuation of her mouth, stroking, squeezing, taunting, while her tongue stimulated him relentlessly.

Finally he let out a soft curse and caught her hair to make her lift her head. "Enough, witch."

He was staring down at her, his eyes dark with need. Knowing the expression in her own eyes was one of hunger, of craving, Madeline gazed steadily back at him, this beautiful man who made her heart and soul ache.

Desire throbbed thick and heavy between them as Rayne's gaze traveled from her wet lips to her bare breasts, to the taut nipples that were already straining for his touch.

"Come here," he demanded.

Not giving her time to refuse, he grasped her shoulders and drew her up, pulling her astride his thighs. Madeline, however, had no intention of denying the deep, powerful longing inside her. Her body burned for the completing fullness of before, the bliss of being joined to Rayne in the most intimate way possible. She was dizzy with wanting him.

Pleasure, desire, need, all driving her on, Madeline eased herself over him, preparing to mount him, but to her surprise, Rayne stopped her.

"No," he warned at her eagerness. "Slowly. Hover over the tip of my cock . . . tease me first. Then without warning plunge onto me."

Holding his gaze, she lowered herself slightly, rubbing her slick, swollen sex against the hard, thick ridge of his member. It gratified her to see the flames that sparked in his eyes.

Vowing to outlast his control, she held herself there, just hovering over the tip of his throbbing erection, barely touching, teasing the sensitive crown with her sleek heat. Taunting him further, Madeline arched her back, her breasts thrusting out to graze his mouth, the nipples pebbled and hard.

The difficulty, however, was that her brazen movements were arousing her as much as they were him.

Rayne must have seen the feverish desire in her eyes, for he reached down between their bodies and cupped his hand against her cleft, stroking her provocatively.

Her nerves shook.

"Want me?" he ground out.

Yes, she wanted him. She wanted desperately to feel him silky and hot inside her. She was already wet and aching for him.

"So what do you intend to do about it?"

Needing no further invitation, she sank down to envelop his shaft, impaling herself. The tight, glorious fit of his hard flesh in the slick softness of hers sent a fierce rush of renewed pleasure spiraling through Madeline— and evidently Rayne as well. He swore beneath his breath as her feminine sheath enveloped him.

She felt the shudder that went through him, wracking his body, and her sense of power swelled further, along with her own arousal.

His jaw clenched with need as his hands closed over her buttocks. He held her there for a moment, then lifted her and brought her back down so that he could thrust even more deeply inside her.

Then, to her bewilderment, he suddenly inhaled a ragged breath and gripped her hips to hold her still.

"You have too much control," Rayne muttered hoarsely under his breath.

Reaching for the wine, he repositioned the goblet to clear a space on the table's surface. Even more surprisingly, he slid his hands beneath her buttocks for support and stood up with her, then turned and set her on the edge of the table beside the wineglass.

Madeline clung to him, scarcely believing he meant to withdraw from her when her body was so primed for him.

Thankfully, he didn't; Rayne kept his thick shaft planted firmly inside her.

"Lie back," he instructed.

He meant to take her on the table, she realized in gratitude. Madeline obeyed, although she was trembling enough that he had to help her.

When she was splayed before him, his pulsing hardness holding her pressed wide open, he continued watching her. His glance seared her skin, just as if he was caressing her with his lips, with his warm breath. Then raising her hand, he drew her forefinger into his mouth, suckling, all the while making no effort to disguise his blatant appraisal of her body.

Madeline gasped as he made love to each of her fingers one by one. The erotic caresses, combined with his sensual scrutiny and the feel of his rigid heat deep inside her, made her loins throb even more fiercely. The sensations were feverishly intense, with all that barely leashed vitality focused on her.

A moment later, however, Rayne changed tactics. Releasing her hand, he reached for her rib cage and slid his thumbs upward to brush the underside of her breasts, shooting fiery sparks through Madeline.

When he pinched one nipple into an obedient pout, she clenched her teeth. "Do you mean to torment me?" she rasped.

His slow smile was part wolfish, wholly enticing. "Oh, yes. Exactly as you are tormenting me."

Dismayingly, he eased his manhood from her body, although he remained standing between her parted thighs. Madeline almost cried aloud in disappointment, yet Rayne wasn't finished with her. He dipped a forefinger in the wine and rubbed it over her lips and down her throat. She drew another sharp breath at the cool, sweet feel of the liquid. Then rewetting his fingers, he shifted to her stomach, drawing swirling patterns on her skin before moving back up to her jutting, naked breasts.

"Rayne, please. . . ."

"Hush, darling. Begging me won't do any good."

As he spoke he coated her tight nipples with wine, his slick fingers plied the aching buds, pulling and caressing the engorged tips.

Dangerous. Oh, this man is dangerous, Madeline thought dazedly, closing her eyes.

Then he suddenly left off, drawing back his caressing hands. Madeline's eyes flew open in confusion.

"You need to offer your breasts to me so I can suck them."

"Rayne . . ." she started to protest.

"Now, love, or I'll stop at once."

She couldn't bear for him to stop. She wanted his mouth on her naked skin, her fever-hot breasts. She wanted his mouth . . . everywhere.

Biting her lower lip, Madeline lifted her hands brazenly to the wine-scented mounds of her breasts.

"Now play with those lovely nipples. Pretend your hands are mine."

Her fingers plucked at the crests, just as Rayne had done.

"A wanton woman," he said approvingly. "How provocative."

She was indeed a wanton woman. She felt primitive, carnal, exquisitely female.

Yet Rayne didn't suck her nipples as he'd promised. Instead his gaze raked down her body, his eyes hot, touching her everywhere. Then his head lowered slowly to her belly to lick at the wine he had traced on her skin.

He took his time, as if he intended to savor her at his leisure. His tongue teased her with maddening delicacy, playing her masterfully with taunting spirals and erotic touches designed to devastate. Madeline shivered with pure wanton pleasure. Then finally, finally, he moved up to her breasts.

She gave a muted cry when his hot mouth closed over her budded nipple, sucking it sharply. For long moments he lavished attention there before attending the other breast with as much ruthless tenderness, making Madeline whimper and arch involuntarily against the exquisite pressure.

"Hungry?" he demanded in a taunting whisper. "I am, but not for food. It's your pleasure I'm starving for."

Placing one last kiss on each of her aching nipples, he raised his head. Using both hands then, he spread her legs even wider, positioning her silky body open for his pleasure, and smoothed his hands up her inner thighs.

At the feel of those sensuous fingers gliding upward, Madeline tried not to squirm. Yet her hips stirred and shifted, lust making her feel restless to the point of screaming. From the sensual glint in Rayne's eyes, she could tell what was to come.

"Don't move," he ordered. "Your body is impatient, but you aren't allowed to move."

How could she remain still when he knew precisely what to do to make her wild?

Coating his fingers in wine once more, he painted the dusky triangle of curls between her thighs, then the lips of her sex, dewing the hardening, aching flesh with glossy moisture.

With fierce effort Madeline forced herself to lie still as she watched her own seduction, arousal searing through her, dark and thick, as his hand cupped the rise of her silky mound, molding her.

Then Rayne stopped once more. Dragging his brilliant gaze over her in a lazy caress, he smiled devilishly.

"Touch yourself for me, darling, between your thighs."

Responding willingly, she let her legs fall open further and slid her fingers into the moisture between her folds.

"Are you ready for me?" he asked, his voice very low and intimate.

"*Yes,*" Madeline rasped. "More than ready."

She felt on fire as liquid heat poured into her center; she burned there. When his fingers cupped her again, it was all she could do to keep from moaning.

Holding his hand still, Rayne captured her gaze with his. The air around them shimmered with sexual arousal as he leaned closer.

"I want to taste you everywhere. . . ."

He bent down to her, breathing in the heat and wet scent of her body, then pressed his mouth against her mound, kissing her cleft. "You're so sweet and tempting."

Madeline moaned aloud as ravenous hunger swept through her.

"Good, you're hot for me," he observed, his voice

deep and resonant and sexual. "That is exactly how I want you."

His hands were on her buttocks now, his tongue lapping the wine from her feminine folds, suckling the throbbing bud of her sex. She shuddered as he feasted on her but nearly came up off the table when his tongue thrust into the hot, quivering core of her.

At her helpless response, Rayne applied himself to the task of really making her moan. He tortured her with exquisitely slow thrusts, using his tongue with devastating thoroughness. In only moments Madeline was panting, her body arching wantonly for him, her fingers clutching in his hair.

"That's it . . . I want you writhing and hungry."

"Rayne, merciful heaven, please. . . ."

She was dimly appalled to realize she was begging. But he only held her surging body down, his mouth pressed hard to her, clearly savoring the soft cries she made, the breathless moans.

At last he relented. "Why don't I let you come now?" he murmured before giving her one final, fierce caress with his mouth.

Madeline climaxed with a scream, her teeth bared in fierce, primitive surrender as a powerful firestorm rocked her.

For a full score of heartbeats afterward, she lay there sprawled senseless while Rayne continued to kiss her softly between her legs, absorbing the rippling aftershocks with his mouth.

"You look like a woman who has just been thoroughly pleasured," Rayne observed finally, his tone satisfied.

"You are a fiend," Madeline muttered, opening her eyes.

The slight curve of his lips radiated male arrogance. "No, merely a skilled sensualist." He took her hand and brought it to his naked loins, stroking her fingers with the velvet-sheathed hardness of his arousal. "But I'm weary of exerting all the effort. It is your turn now."

Requiring no further urging, Madeline reached for him. Her need to feel possessed by Rayne was as fierce as her desire to please him. Parting her thighs in eager welcome, she keened a soft moan as he sank his rigid shaft into the hot haven of her body. When he began to move inside her, she wrapped her legs tightly around his hips. His movements were sensual and powerfully controlled, the intensity of his expression spellbinding, his eyes hard with desire.

Yet his restraint fractured eventually, as did hers. Her blood pumping wildly, she began to jerk her hips, her whimpers turning to sobs.

"Madeline. . . ." Rayne grated her name between his teeth, his voice harsh with the same urgency that was now knifing through her, his beautiful face taut with pleasure.

His answering growl inflamed her. She was on fire again, burning for him, and knew she couldn't hold back much longer. She was in agony, sweet tumultuous agony. And so apparently was Rayne. . . .

All his muscles quivered, straining with hunger, as he fought for control. When she clawed at his back, his control shattered with enough force to make his body convulse.

He exploded inside her, frantically groaning his release against her mouth. Moving with the thrusts of his body, Madeline felt every pulse beat of his hot, shuddering climax before she erupted in her own, her inner muscles spasming again and again and again.

When it was over, he collapsed against her, his face buried in the silk of her shoulder, his breath ragged in her ear.

He held her pulsating body until the glorious waves of ecstasy finally faded. Then, weakly, Rayne eased himself off Madeline and helped her to sit up.

"I suggest we have Bramsley serve dinner," he murmured. "I for one am famished. Lovemaking always gives me an appetite."

Still in a love daze, Madeline felt stunned by his callous words. How could he be so cold?

When Rayne lifted her from the table so she could stand, she clutched his shoulders for support, since her limp knees wanted to buckle. Yet as she stared into his eyes, Madeline realized she hadn't been mistaken about his detachment; Rayne was deliberately pushing her away.

It was clear she hadn't touched any of his emotions with her attempts at seduction. If anything he was even more distant now than on their wedding night. There was passion in his touch, yet the tenderness he'd once shown her was entirely missing.

A hollow ache tightened Madeline's chest. Rayne was an amazing lover, generous with his body but not his heart, and the way he had of holding back while giving to her carnally only underscored the vast canyon yawning between them.

Another wave of shocking longing swept over Madeline. She was desperately hungry for more than carnal pleasure with Rayne; she frightened herself with the strength of her want. Yet she couldn't tell him of her love, for it might drive him even further away.

Feeling unaccountably wounded, Madeline moved unsteadily over to where her dressing gown lay pooled on the floor. Picking up the garment, she drew it on to shield her nakedness—and her vulnerability.

Then she forced herself to smile at Rayne, determined to pretend that his coldness hadn't caused her such intense pain.

"Perhaps we should dine downstairs after all," she said lightly. "We don't want your servants to suspect we have been making inappropriate use of this table. I will dress and meet you in the dining room in half an hour, if that is agreeable?"

"Yes, that is agreeable."

Vowing not to show her hurt at his cool indifference, Madeline turned away and headed toward her bedchamber.

Rayne watched her leave, torn between guilt and relief. It had taken all his willpower to resist Madeline's endearing attempts at seduction. Then she'd smiled that enchanting smile again and he was lost. When he'd made love to her, he felt her warmth, her wetness pulling him deeper and deeper. He wanted to impale her until he drowned in her.

Clenching his teeth, Rayne swiftly began to dress. He was losing the battle with himself, despite the memory of his past betrayal. He would have to gird his loins much more forcefully, so to speak.

He pulled on his pantaloons with a jerk, reminding himself of all the reasons he had to be wary of Madeline. She hadn't drugged his wine as another female spy had once done, yet she had ratcheted up her seduction with an aggressiveness that even Camille had never dared use.

Throwing on his dressing gown, Rayne stalked from the sitting room. Madeline held him trapped in a web of raw need, but it was time to break free. Tonight he would begin laying his own trap for her in order to uncover her true intentions.

Chapter Sixteen

It is doubly painful, Maman, to see my cherished hopes endangered by my own brother.

Throughout dinner Madeline managed to pretend a nonchalance she didn't feel. Rayne maintained the same cool detachment as earlier, with no intimacy or tenderness or humor or the provocative banter that had marked their relationship before their marriage.

When he announced his intention to spend the next few days in London, Madeline was not certain whether to be disappointed or relieved. At least during his absence she could take stock of her failing campaign and perhaps consult with Fanny and the Loring sisters to revise her strategy.

Surprisingly, Rayne mentioned where in his study his safe was located—hidden in the wall behind a George Stubbs painting of a Thoroughbred racehorse—and where he usually kept the key—in a jar in his bedchamber wardrobe. His good-night kiss was a bare brush of her lips, though, so Madeline retired to bed despondent.

Rayne was gone from Riverwood when she awoke the following morning. Depressed and bleary-eyed, she had to hurry to make her class at the academy on time. And when she arrived home shortly after noon, a letter was waiting for her.

Madeline's heart leapt when she recognized the scrawled handwriting. Gerard had finally responded to her appeals for a reply.

After handing her pelisse and bonnet to Bramsley, she went upstairs to read the missive in the privacy of her own bedchamber.

The handwriting was particularly bad, Madeline saw upon breaking the wax seal, as if her brother had scribbled in some urgency.

Maman, we taught Gerard to write better than this was her distracted thought as she struggled to make out some of the initial words. Her heart sank with each succeeding revelation.

My dearest sister,

I must confess, you were correct in your allegation. Before eloping, I did indeed take the de Vasse necklace from Lord Ackerby, but only in order to return it to Lynette's parents, who are the rightful owners. The vicomte and vicomtesse's jewels were stolen shortly after they fled for their lives during their country's ghastly Revolution. The necklace illicitly wound up in the possession of the previous Baron Ackerby, who passed it down to the current one. I have no intention of giving it back to this Ackerby.

The difficulty is that he visited the farm two days ago with three of his henchmen and tore the house apart, looking for the necklace. When they couldn't find it, they had the dastardly gall to beat Mrs. Dobson to force her to give up my location. She refused, loyal soul that she is, but I think it is only a matter of time before Ackerby finds me.

Madeline gave a soft cry at the thought of their dear, sweet, elderly housekeeper being tyrannized by the baron's ruffians. Clapping her hand over her mouth, she read on.

My beloved's parents know we took refuge at her cousin Claude's cottage in Maidstone. Lynette wrote to them last week to tell them she was safe and happy. But since she has received no word in reply, she fears they have disowned her for wedding me, just as we expected. I can only fear what they will reveal to Ackerby if he questions them.

Madeline shook her head in growing alarm, imagining the uproar at the de Vasse house if Ackerby had descended upon them with his henchmen. Lynette's parents would have been extremely upset that their only daughter had absconded with an English farmer, gentleman or not. They might even be angry enough to disclose Gerard's location to Ackerby.

I only heard just this morning from Mrs. Dobson, who wished to warn me. I don't dare let Ackerby find us, so we have left Claude's cottage and gone into hiding nearby.

Utterly dismayed, Madeline sank down in a chair. *Gerard, you foolish boy, what have you done?* Ackerby would not give up trying to regain his property, even by violent means.

I have one last favor to ask of you, dearest sister. In addition to the draft you recently sent me, I need another two hundred pounds to leave the country. I plan to take Lynette to France where Ackerby will have no legal authority, even should he pursue us.

I am gratified that you are now married—felicitations on your good fortune, by the by. But since you are a countess, surely you can persuade your new husband to advance you the funds. I am certain Haviland can afford it—his grandmother's wealth puts Croesus to shame. I will repay you eventually, I swear to you.

Madeline's hand went to her aching temple. Did Gerard actually expect her to implore Rayne for money so he could whisk the jewels out of the country? Evidently so, judging by the next paragraph.

Since I cannot come to you for fear of being seen, I need you to forward a bank draft for the funds to me at the Blue Boar Inn in Maidstone, in care of the proprietor, Ben Pilling. I will visit the inn on Wednesday at one o'clock in the afternoon to collect the draft. If your letter is not there, then I will return again each day for a week. But the longer you delay, the greater the danger we will be in. I know you will not fail me, though, dearest Madeline.

Your loving brother, Gerard

Fear and frustration warring inside her, Madeline clenched the letter in her hand. If her brother was caught with the priceless heirloom, he could face prison or transportation or even hanging, not to mention bodily harm if the baron's henchmen found him. Of course

Ackerby would want retribution. At this point, even if she could persuade Gerard to return the necklace immediately, it might make no difference.

"How could he, *Maman*?" Madeline murmured to herself, fighting down a wave of panic. "It is beyond belief that Gerard would endanger himself and his new wife this stupid way. It is awful enough that Mrs. Dobson was beaten for concealing his whereabouts."

I know, dearest, Madeline's mother answered in her mind. *But Gerard was always the romantic sort. Perhaps this is his way of meting out justice.*

"Or perhaps he only wants to curry favor with his new bride's parents," Madeline retorted under her breath.

Trying to quell the swell of dread inside her, she muttered an imprecation that was half oath, half plea for Gerard's salvation. Yet imploring Heaven for help would likely have little effect. She wanted to throw herself upon her bed and wail also, but crying would not solve her dilemma or extricate her brother from his reckless idiocy, either. She couldn't give in to panic as she wished to.

"So what should I do, Maman?"

Her mother's voice was frustratingly silent, however.

"I must rescue Gerard from his own folly. I promised you solemnly to look after him and I mean to keep my word."

Yes, certainly you must, my darling. You cannot allow him to be harmed.

Springing to her feet, Madeline began to pace her bedchamber. For much of her life she'd championed her younger brother, loved him, nurtured him. She had supported Gerard's recent elopement because she wanted him to have a chance for happiness. Lynette's parents would never have permitted their daughter to marry him otherwise. No doubt Gerard believed that by returning the necklace to the vicomte and vicomtesse, he could win their support. But if he was dead or imprisoned, it wouldn't matter that he had won over his bride's parents.

Therefore, Madeline concluded, she would have to go to Maidstone herself and physically take the necklace from Gerard and hand it over to Ackerby. If it was found in *her* possession rather than her brother's, her new title would help protect her. And surely Rayne would step in if—

Madeline halted abruptly in her tracks.

Oh, dear heaven, Rayne.

What if he found out about her brother's crime? What if the world learned of it? If the dowager Countess Haviland already deplored her grandson's choice of brides, what would she say to Madeline having a criminal for a brother?

No, Madeline thought, feeling a fresh surge of panic. She couldn't drag Rayne into a scandal that could stain his family name and alienate his grandmother even further. She had to rectify matters on her own while keeping her brother's shameful misdeed secret.

Moreover, she didn't have the right to take Rayne away from his current endeavors. If he *had* immersed himself in his former profession once more, no doubt he was doing important business.

But most crucially of all, she feared Rayne would be even less likely to love her if her family caused him ignominy.

As the tightness in her chest intensified, Madeline

murmured another imprecation. This disaster was coming at the worst possible time in her marriage.

Yet what choice did she have? Gerard was her brother, her flesh and blood. She couldn't abandon him to his folly simply because she wanted a chance at her own happiness.

Stiffening her spine, Madeline forced herself to take a deep, steadying breath. "Forgive me, *Maman*," she muttered aloud, "but when I see Gerard, I plan to throttle him."

Meanwhile she had to quickly decide her best course of action. Somehow she had to make her brother behave responsibly and give the necklace into her care and then prevent Lord Ackerby from taking any retribution for the theft.

As for the additional funds Gerard needed to flee the country, Madeline reflected, she would certainly not ask her husband for more money. She didn't want to be any further burden to Rayne, not after costing him so much already. He had already spent a fortune on her clothing.

What was left of her quarterly pin money would have to do for now. Combined with the hundred pounds she had already given him, it would be enough to fund Gerard and Lynette's passage to France and get them temporarily settled. Afterward she could send Gerard her salary from her academy employment. . . .

Yes, Madeline vowed, she would handle this problem herself, without asking Rayne for help, without causing him embarrassment or disgrace. She loathed the thought of sneaking around behind his back, but there was no help for it.

She would leave at once for Maidstone. From her recollection, the town was southeast of London in Kent, on a main route to the coast—perhaps fifty miles from here, at least a half day's drive. She would call at Claude Dubonet's cottage first, to see if he could tell her where Gerard and Lynette had hidden themselves. If not, she would wait for Gerard at the Blue Boar Inn and confront him when he arrived tomorrow afternoon to collect his bank draft. Perhaps she could even return home by late tomorrow night.

She had to think up a story to explain her absence from Riverwood, of course. Rayne had gone to London again for several days, so she had a little time before he missed her.

She would have to watch herself with Rayne's servants, though, given their staunch loyalty to him. Which meant she couldn't use his coachman or footmen or grooms. Therefore, she would have to borrow or hire a carriage.

But how? Arabella was in London just now. . . . She could say she was going to visit with Arabella, but instead she would make directly for a posting inn as soon as she arrived in London, so she could hire a traveling chaise to take her to Maidstone. Arabella would likely go along with her plan if she revealed that she had an urgent family matter to attend to.

And Bramsley would likely not question her intentions, either, since she'd spent quite some time in London with Arabella this past week. He was unlikely to deny her the remainder of her pocket allowance when she asked him for it—

A knock on her bedchamber door startled Madeline out of her fretful ruminations. When she answered it, she discovered Bramsley standing there as if she had conjured him.

"Miss Blanchard has called for you, my lady," the majordomo informed her.

Madeline stared blankly at Bramsley for a moment—until she recalled having invited Tess over for luncheon only a short while ago when they'd crossed paths at the academy. She'd thought it a good opportunity to become better acquainted. Regrettably, though, she had no time for friendly cozies just now, Madeline decided, or the emotional fortitude, either. On the other hand . . . she froze as a thought struck her. Tess might be the perfect person to help her.

"Would you escort Miss Blanchard here to my bedchamber, Bramsley?"

It was an odd request, but the majordomo did not seem overly disconcerted. "Certainly, my lady, as you wish."

When he was gone, Madeline headed directly for her dressing room to fetch her bandbox. If she intended to travel to Maidstone, she needed to pack for a stay of at least one night, perhaps more.

When Tess arrived, Madeline was nearly finished filling the bandbox.

"I am so very sorry, Tess," she apologized at once, "but I must cancel our luncheon. I have just learned of a minor family matter that I must straighten out."

Tess was instantly concerned. "I hope it is not too serious?"

I hope so, too, Madeline muttered to herself. Aloud, she managed to sound reassuring. "I don't believe so, but it requires me to be away for a day or two. I dislike imposing on you, but I don't feel I can leave Arabella shorthanded with no notice. Would you mind very much taking my class at the academy tomorrow and perhaps Thursday as well?"

"Certainly, I will be happy to do so. You handled mine when I was away."

"Thank you," Madeline said in gratitude.

"Is there anything else I can do for you?" Tess asked. "You seem upset." When Madeline didn't immediately reply, Tess pressed in a low voice. "I have seen that look on the faces of countless women in difficulty, Madeline. If you are in trouble of some kind, I would like to help."

She remained silent as she met Tess's perceptive gaze. The beauty's expression was full of sympathy. Perhaps Tess was so compassionate because of her past experiences in dealing with victims of misery and misfortune.

At Madeline's hesitation, Tess hastened to add, "You can count on me for complete discretion, if that concerns you."

Discretion wasn't the sole issue. Tess was nearly a stranger, yet she could be trusted, Madeline felt sure of it. The question was, why would Tess trust *her*?

"Are you certain you wish to involve yourself with my problems, Tess? You scarcely know me."

Tess smiled faintly. "Arabella has vouched for you, and that is good enough for me. Moreover, I have seen how cruel the world can be to women with little family or resources. We ladies must stick together, I believe."

Giving a pained laugh, Madeline inhaled a steadying breath. She disliked dragging anyone into her potentially scandalous affairs, but she would be supremely grateful for an ally. Deciding to accept Tess's offer of help, she nodded.

"Very well . . . I need to go to London at once so I can hire a post chaise, but I would rather my husband not know of this particular endeavor. Would you mind if I borrowed your carriage and coachmen to take me into town?"

"I will do even better. I will drive you to London myself."

Madeline searched the other woman's kind eyes. "Doubtless you are wondering why I wish to keep secrets from Haviland—"

Tess held up a forestalling hand. "I don't require an explanation unless you wish to tell me. You need a friend just now, and I am available."

Madeline wanted to hug Tess for her trust and unquestioning support. But she settled for murmuring another heartfelt thank-you.

"Do you wish to leave now?" Tess asked, eyeing the bandbox on Madeline's bed.

"Yes, if you don't mind. But will you give me a few minutes first? I must speak to Bramsley and make some financial arrangements."

"Of course."

"And I should order a meal packed for us since I deprived you of the luncheon I promised you," Madeline said as an afterthought.

Responding with a light laugh, Tess professed herself capable of going without lunch this once. But in truth, Madeline was glad for the mundane distraction of providing sustenance for their journey.

It would help her to take her mind off her fears for her reckless brother and her attempt to save him from destroying his life with his quixotic but criminal undertaking.

* * *

"Mr. Bramsley is awaiting you in your study, my lord," Walters informed Rayne as he entered his London manor late that night.

Nodding at his chief aide, Rayne felt his chest tighten. If Bramsley had personally traveled all the way from Chiswick, the news could not be good. The hour was advanced, nearly midnight. Rayne had just returned from his club, where he'd spent the evening trying to distract himself, for even though his plans to thwart a ring of assassins were reaching a critical point, the possible drama playing out at his country estate in Chiswick disturbed him far more.

With effort, he kept his expression neutral as he greeted his majordomo in his study.

"What information do you have for me, Bramsley?" Rayne asked, pretending a dispassion he wasn't feeling.

"You directed me to investigate anything out of the ordinary regarding Lady Haviland, my lord," Bramsley responded with reluctance, not questioning why the earl was spying on his wife yet obviously not eager to bear bad tidings, either.

"And you noted something unusual about her behavior," Rayne prodded.

"Yes, my lord. Her ladyship departed Riverwood suddenly this afternoon."

"Did she attempt to open my safe first?"

"Not as far as I could tell. But she requested the remainder of her pocket allowance before she went with Miss Blanchard to London."

"She has gone to London before during my absence from Riverwood," Rayne observed.

"Yes, but this time she said she planned to stay at the London home of Lady Danvers this evening, and I know for a fact that her ladyship left London yesterday for the Danvers family seat."

Hoping there was a simple explanation for his wife's actions, Rayne set his jaw muscles and forced himself to remain silent as Bramsley continued.

"I thought it best to err on the side of caution, so I had John James follow Lady Haviland as you instructed. I received word from James only an hour ago, so I came directly here to report to you."

John James was a former agent for British Intelligence who had remained in Rayne's service after Napoleon's defeat. He'd been sent to Riverwood only this morning for just such an event, since he had extensive experience in following suspects without being detected. By posing as a footman on Bramsley's staff, James would have ample opportunity to watch Madeline.

"He must have discovered a serious transgression," Rayne said, fighting the hollow sensation in his gut.

"I fear so, my lord. Miss Blanchard set Lady Haviland down at The Swan, where she hired a post chaise and set out to the east, toward Canterbury."

Rayne frowned at the revelation. The Swan was a major coaching station on the outskirts of London, so it made sense that Madeline would go there if she needed an unmarked traveling carriage. But he would have expected her to head for home in Chelmsford in Essex, not Canterbury in Kent. The road to Canterbury continued on to Dover, a seaport on the coast, which offered swift passage to France, Rayne thought absently.

"And did James follow her from The Swan?"

"Yes, on horseback. When Lady Haviland reached Maidstone early this evening, she stopped first at an inn for a short while, then called at a nearby cottage, where no one seemed to be at home. Then she returned to the inn—The Blue Boar—and took rooms. Evidently she is waylaying there overnight."

Maidstone was also in Kent, not too far distant from the Haviland family seat, Haviland Park, but it was even more puzzling that Madeline had chosen to stay there overnight—unless, of course, she had a prearranged meeting. The sinking sensation sharpened in Rayne's stomach as Bramsley concluded his report.

"James intends to keep on Lady Haviland's trail and will send word directly here if she continues on her journey."

"Thank you, Bramsley. You've done well. Tell Walters to have my carriage waiting at first light," Rayne added dismissively, "and take yourself off to bed."

"If you please, my lord, I would rather return to Riverwood tonight. I have other duties there."

"As you wish. I will take over from here."

Bramsley bowed and exited the study, leaving Rayne alone with his tumultuous thoughts.

He had every intention of following his errant wife's trail to discover what machinations she was involved in. But he would wait until morning. He could depart tonight, but he wanted to delay the moment of truth a little longer.

Rayne uttered a caustic, self-deprecating laugh upon acknowledging his weakness. Perhaps it was craven of him, but he was loath to confirm that Madeline had betrayed him. More crucially, he had no desire to arrive in the middle of the night only to discover his wife in bed with her lover.

Before he could wrench his mind away, the image of Madeline giving her lush, beautiful body to another man flashed in Rayne's head. A sensation somewhere between fury and anguish rose up within him, yet he fiercely quelled it, determined to consider the situation with ice-cold logic rather than raw emotion.

With unsteady hands, Rayne poured himself a stiff brandy, then sank onto the sofa and stared unseeingly at the fire. Even so, he knew that neither the potent liquor nor the crackling flames could take away the sudden chill he felt inside.

Be careful what you wish for, he thought bleakly. He had wanted proof that Madeline was keeping something from him, and now he had it. She'd set out on a clandestine journey and lied about her destination. A journey he would never have known about if not for being alerted by the servants he'd set to spy on her.

Madeline's furtiveness proclaimed her guilt louder than words—but guilt for what?

Why hadn't she come to him? If she needed financial help for her brother, as Rayne had earlier surmised, she should have known he would give it, even if it meant funding Gerard's peccadilloes.

But perhaps the problem was not her brother. Perhaps Madeline had gone to meet not Gerard but Ackerby.

The sick, clammy chill of dread seeped from Rayne's gut into his heart. Had she gone to meet her lover, just as Camille had done? Was history repeating itself? Ten years ago he had followed Camille to a rendezvous with her lover. It was how he'd learned of her betrayal.

The two cases were eerily similar, Rayne reminded himself grimly. Madeline might not be only out for herself, but it was looking more and more likely that she had sacrificed herself to him in marriage in order to help her brother or even her lover.

Rayne gulped a long, burning swallow of brandy, no longer able to crush the storm of emotions roiling inside him . . . hurt, anger, bitter disappointment, jealousy, even a twinge of panic.

Even when Camille had broken his youthful heart, he hadn't felt this kind of pain. Even during his worst missions, when he'd faced danger, treachery, and death, he hadn't felt this emptiness, this hopelessness. What a fool he'd been to think Madeline an ideal match for him.

He cursed fervently at himself. He had let Madeline inside him. He'd made himself dangerously vulnerable to her, misjudging the very real threat of what she could do to him.

And now he would have to pay for it.

Squeezing his eyes shut, Rayne laid his head back on the sofa. It was going to be a long night, one where he doubted he would get much sleep.

Chapter Seventeen

Love should not hurt this much, Maman.

Hearing a carriage arrive in the stableyard of The Blue Boar Inn, Madeline paused in her fretful pacing to glance out the window of her hired room. Upon recognizing the Haviland crest on the coach's door panel, she gave a start of disbelief.

Merciful heaven, Rayne! What was he doing here?

Madeline watched in dismay as her tall, powerful husband stepped from the vehicle and glanced upward, his piercing gaze scanning the floors above the inn's front entrance.

Her heart leaping in panic, she drew back from the window to avoid being seen. Yet Rayne must know she was here. Why else would he have stopped at the very inn where she was waiting for her wayward brother to make an appearance?

How had he even found her? Madeline wondered. And what the devil should she do about it? The proprietor, Ben Pilling, would surely admit to her presence and direct Rayne to her chamber.

Madeline squared her shoulders. She wouldn't remain

here cowering. It would be far better if she went downstairs to face Rayne before he came in search of her.

Taking a steadying breath, she gathered her reticule and left her room, then negotiated a short stretch of corridor and descended the front staircase to the entrance hall.

As expected, she found Rayne engaged in conversation, but not with the innkeep. Instead, he stood near the open door to the tavern, speaking in low tones with a brown-haired man who looked oddly familiar. Unable to place him, she turned her attention to her husband. Rayne still wore his caped greatcoat but had removed his stylish beaver hat and gloves.

Just then he glanced around and spied Madeline where she had paused on the final stairstep. Rayne didn't smile or speak. He merely gave her a measuring stare.

For a fleeting moment Madeline could see anger there in his eyes, along with several other indefinable emotions. But then his gaze turned inscrutable again as he crossed the entry hall to her.

"My lord, what brings you here?" she murmured, trying to keep the telltale nervousness from her voice.

"I could ask the same of you, my love." His own tone was mild, almost silken in fact, but the underlying edge made Madeline swallow. She was loath to tell him about her brother's theft. And yet she knew she would have no choice but to explain.

When she remained silent, Rayne's features hardened discernibly. "We had best hold this discussion in private, wouldn't you say?"

"Yes . . . of course. I have bespoken a chamber upstairs, if you care to join me."

After giving a slight nod at the brown-haired man, Rayne took her arm and urged Madeline back up the stairs and down the corridor. When they reached her room, he released his grasp and let her precede him inside.

After a few steps, Madeline turned to face him, but Rayne hesitated on the threshold, filling the doorway, tall, dark, intense. His gaze searched the room, fixing on the neatly made bed for a long heartbeat. Finally, though, he entered and shut the door behind him.

"Well?" Rayne asked in that same silken tone that made her want to shiver. "Would you care to explain what brought you fifty miles from home to sojourn at a strange inn?"

"It is a long story," Madeline began in a tentative voice.

"I have ample time. I am not going anywhere at the moment."

She fought the urge to twist the strings of her reticule between her fingers. "How did you know where to find me?"

"I had you followed, sweeting."

Her eyes widened in bewilderment, then narrowed again as comprehension struck her. The brown-haired man. . . . Only now did Madeline remember where she'd seen him before. He was Riverwood's newest footman—John James was his name.

"You set James to spy on me," she said in disbelief.

"I'd say your clandestine behavior warranted it," Rayne retorted coldly.

Madeline parted her lips to defend herself, yet she could think of no appropriate reply. Her behavior had indeed warranted Rayne's suspicions. Yet it still hurt to know he had trusted her so little that he'd actually ordered his servants to follow her.

Her speechlessness, apparently, resulted in Rayne losing patience. "Whom are you protecting?" he suddenly demanded. "Your brother? Or your lover?"

Madeline gave a start. "My lover?"

His blue eyes pierced her. "It appears as if you have arranged a lovers' tryst here. Do you dare deny it?"

"Of course I deny it! I have no lover."

The air between them vibrated with suppressed tension. "You aren't here to meet Ackerby?" Rayne asked.

That line of attack took Madeline aback even more. "Why on earth would you think I was meeting Ackerby?" she replied in dismay.

"The first time I encountered you, you claimed to be fleeing from him. You were sleeping at an inn, garbed only in your nightdress. Who is to say you weren't having a lovers' quarrel then?"

Madeline gazed at Rayne with incredulity. "Are you *mad*? How could you possibly think I would want Ackerby? He makes my skin crawl."

Rayne stared back at her, all emotion concealed behind his dark-fringed blue eyes.

"He most *certainly* is not my lover!" Madeline insisted.

"Then what was he was doing at Danvers Hall kissing you in the garden?"

At her husband's harsh tone, she raised her chin defensively. "He came to blackmail me."

Ire sprang into Rayne's eyes, then faded as if he'd exerted savage control over all his emotions. Crossing the room, he tossed his hat and gloves on a table. "I think you had best explain," he said grimly.

"I will gladly do so if you would give me a chance," Madeline retorted.

When their glances clashed, Rayne visibly clenched his jaw. "Pray continue." He settled in a chair at the table. "I am waiting."

Madeline inhaled a deep breath. "The truth is . . . I am trying to save my brother from being hanged."

She couldn't tell from Rayne's expression if her revelation elicited any sympathy from him, but at least he hesitated before prodding in a slightly less wintry voice, "Go on."

Madeline did fumble with her purse strings then, slipping them off her wrist as she moved closer to Rayne so she could set her reticule on the table. "Well . . . you see . . . Gerard eloped with his childhood sweetheart some three weeks ago, but before he left for Scotland, he stole a priceless heirloom from Lord Ackerby."

In a halting narrative, Madeline confessed the whole story, including Gerard's motive for stealing the necklace and his desire to hand it over to his new bride's parents, who reportedly were the original owners.

She went on to relate the complications of Ackerby's wrath—that Gerard and Lynette had spent the first week of their married life a short distance from The Blue Boar Inn, at a cottage belonging to Lynette's cousin, Claude Dubonet; how Gerard had learned about the assault on their housekeeper; and Gerard's subsequent fears that Ackerby and his henchmen were on his trail, which had scared him into leaving the cottage with his wife and going into hiding.

"Gerard decided to flee to France to avoid Ackerby's retribution," Madeline concluded in a small voice, "and so asked me to advance him the funds by letter. But I came here myself instead, to convince him to return the necklace to Ackerby."

"You intend to return it?" Rayne asked tersely.

"Of course. It is the only honorable thing to do. The necklace does not belong to Gerard, and he has no right to give it away. And by returning it, I hope to persuade Ackerby to spare my brother a prison sentence or worse."

Rayne did not appear entirely convinced that she was telling the truth. Did he think her complicit in her brother's crime? Madeline wondered, watching his face.

His tone held a distinct coldness when he spoke again. "So you lied to me and concealed your whereabouts, professing your destination to be Lady Danvers's home in London?"

"I did not actually lie to you," she protested. "I merely did not tell you I was coming here."

"You lied to Bramsley, which is nearly the same thing."

"It is not at all the same! I didn't want your servants or any of your other connections knowing that my brother is a criminal."

Rayne's hard gaze searched her face. "So why didn't you come to me and request my help?"

"Any number of reasons. I didn't want to burden you with my problems, for one thing. And I needed to act quickly if I hoped to save my brother from his own folly—and to avoid a scandal as well. Your family is already appalled enough by your marriage to me. How would your grandmother react if she learned that Gerard had stolen from a peer? Or if he were thrown in prison or hanged?"

Not replying, Rayne regarded her intently, as if trying to judge her veracity.

Madeline bit her lower lip. She couldn't tell him the chief reason preventing a scandal was so crucial to her—because she was desperately in love with Rayne and feared losing any chance of winning his love—for then he might pity her and that would be insupportable.

"How was Ackerby blackmailing you?" he finally asked.

"He had just learned about the theft when he came to Danvers Hall," she answered honestly. "He suggested that if I became his mistress, he would not press charges but allow Gerard to keep the necklace."

Something dark and dangerous flashed in Rayne's eyes. "So what did you tell him?"

"I refused, of course. But I promised to make Gerard return his property if indeed he had stolen it. Ackerby said he would allow me time to get the necklace back in exchange for a kiss, and he assaulted me before I had the chance to object. *That* is why you found us kissing in the garden. But then you struck him and knocked him down and goaded him into a duel. He was so furious I feared he would take immediate action against my brother. So I wrote to Ackerby to beg him to hold off until I could speak to Gerard myself and convince him to give up the necklace."

"Was your concern for Gerard the reason you demanded we call off the duel?"

"In part. I also worried that you might be hurt. Ackerby is accounted an excellent shot."

Rayne continued to scrutinize her. "Why should I believe any of this?"

"Why shouldn't you believe me?" Madeline countered. "I am telling the truth."

"That remains to be proven. You could just as easily be in league with your brother."

She winced at his reply but strove to quell her rising despair. "I can understand why you would consider some of my actions suspect, Rayne, but not why you could think I would betray marriage vows by taking a lover—and with Ackerby, of all men."

"What reason have you given me to think otherwise?" he rejoined. "You claimed you were shopping with Lady Danvers during your frequent jaunts to London last week, but yesterday you lied about being with her. It's conceivable that you used her as cover for a secret affair with a lover."

The accusation both distressed and stung Madeline. "*You* spend much of your time in London without telling me what you are doing. How do I know you are not engaged in an affair? Perhaps you have a mistress in keeping there."

"Perhaps I do."

The words cut straight into her heart. Madeline found it hard to swallow for the tightness in her throat. It seemed small consolation that Rayne compressed his lips as if regretting his biting reply.

After a moment, he changed the subject, using a softer tone. "So what is your plan, Madeline? You say you are waiting here for Gerard to collect his funds."

"Yes. According to his letter, he plans to arrive today at one o'clock."

"An hour from now."

"Yes," she answered, keenly aware of how slowly the hours had crawled by.

"You don't know where Gerard might be at the moment?"

"I haven't a clue. I went to Claude Dubonet's cottage last evening and again this morning, but no one was at home. And the innkeep does not know where Claude has gone, or where Gerard is hiding."

A long silence ensued. Madeline held her tongue, waiting for Rayne's next questions, yet she was beginning to feel sick inside at his damning allegations. Even though his face remained stark and expressionless, she suspected he didn't fully believe her, that his angry suspicions were still simmering.

With his former profession making him justifiably mistrustful, Rayne was predisposed to think the worst of her, especially when the evidence pointed to her guilt. But still it greatly upset her that he considered her capable of such nefarious deeds—being in league with her brother's theft, and worse, betraying her holy vows by taking a lover. Her head might understand his logic but her heart did not.

"So you intend to confront Gerard when he arrives," Rayne continued.

"Yes."

"What if he is right—that Ackerby's henchmen are on his trail? You realize you could be putting yourself in danger."

Dully, Madeline glanced down at her reticule. "I have my pistol with me."

"What good will a single shot do against determined thugs?"

"I will make do somehow."

Rayne muttered a low oath. "A foolish tactic if I have ever heard one. You should not even be here."

"What choice did I have?" she asked. "Gerard is my brother. I could not simply abandon him."

"You could have come to me," Rayne reminded her rather fiercely.

"I thought I could handle the situation on my own. Besides, I wasn't sure you would see Gerard's side of the matter."

"What side is that? That he is not only a thief but a reckless idiot as well?"

Madeline bit her lip, although Rayne's charges were nothing more than she had made herself. "Until now Gerard has never violated the law, but he is in love, Rayne. Sometimes love makes people do idiotic things."

"And treacherous things as well."

She opened her mouth to speak but paused because her throat suddenly hurt with the need to cry. To her great shame, hot tears burned at the back of her eyes.

Not wanting Rayne to see, she turned and moved blindly to the window.

Behind her, he observed, "If you are watching for your brother, you shouldn't bother. He is unlikely to enter by the front door."

"I know," Madeline murmured. "I asked the innkeep to inform me when Gerard arrives."

"And you trust him to oblige?"

Unwillingly, she glanced over her shoulder at Rayne. "I paid him a generous sum."

"Yet he may double-cross you and warn Gerard."

Rayne abruptly stood and went to the door.

"Where are you going?" she was startled into asking.

"To have a word with John James. He can keep watch on the innkeep so we will know at once when your brother approaches him."

With that, Rayne let himself from the room.

Madeline felt a hopeless laugh well up inside her. Rayne was completely taking charge as usual. He was a warrior, a modern-day white knight. Even if he thought her guilty of treachery and betrayal, he would try to protect her from harm, and perhaps her brother as well. Yet she couldn't help the bleak sensation of despair spreading through her chest.

Letting her head drop, Madeline wrapped her arms around herself, fighting desolation. Her body was trembling with emotion while helpless tears seeped from the corners of her eyes.

How could Rayne possibly ever come to love her if he mistrusted her so profoundly? If he thought she might be guilty of thievery and even infidelity? If his suspicions ran so deep that he had set his spies to watch her every move?

She had scant hope of winning his love if he trusted her so little.

Yet she had only herself to blame, Madeline thought, struggling against a sob. She had been seduced by her own fantasies, the ones deep in her heart.

Weakly, she let the tears fall during the interval Rayne was away. As soon as she heard footsteps in the corridor, though, she dabbed at her wet eyes and cheeks. She hated crying in front of him. She couldn't, wouldn't, let him know her heart was breaking.

Thankfully, she was almost able to regain a semblance of control by the time Rayne entered. She was surprised, however, when the innkeep's wife bustled in behind him, bearing a tray laden with ale and meats and cheeses.

"I ordered a meal," Rayne said in explanation.

With a cautious smile at Madeline, Mrs. Pilling deposited the tray on the table, then curtsied and left. When they were alone again, Rayne held out a chair at the table for her.

"Come, sit down," he ordered.

She risked a direct glance at him. His eyes had lost that fierce, hot intensity and instead merely looked moody and dark.

"You should eat something," he urged.

"I am not hungry."

He hesitated, looking as if he would press her, but then he murmured, "Very well," before settling at the table and helping his own plate. He had also found some newspapers from somewhere, Madeline realized when he opened the pages and began to read. No doubt he had long experience waiting for his operations to result in some sort of action.

She couldn't eat a bite, though, not when she felt cold and hot and sick to her stomach. In addition to her despair over Rayne, she was half out of her mind with worry for Gerard.

Mentally, Madeline shook her head. She was admittedly resentful that Rayne appeared so calm, but then he was no ordinary man. With his vast experience in intelligence, he was likely inured to danger, impervious to fear. The baron's henchmen would not frighten him—

She froze as she suddenly had a horrifying thought. "What if Ackerby's ruffians have already found Gerard?" she asked in alarm.

"It's possible," Rayne said, looking up. "If your brother doesn't arrive by two, we will search the area until we find him." His gaze sharpened again. "But you will let *me* deal with Ackerby's thugs, Madeline. I've had a great deal more experience with their sort than you have."

Madeline remained silent. Rayne was treating her like a fragile flower again, and yet she didn't intend to object. In this instance he was right; she was far out of her depth. Indeed, she was actually relieved he was there to help her face this crisis. Even if his lack of trust made her heart ache, she was glad not to be alone.

Still, she couldn't help remembering two nights ago when there had at least been a pretense of passion between them. This heavy, tense silence was even worse than his detachment had been.

Feeling her despairing ache intensify, she turned back to the window to watch and wait.

By her calculation, it was a full, interminable hour later before anything happened. In the interval, Madeline saw a great deal of activity in the inn yard below, but as Rayne had predicted, there was no sign of her brother.

Her first indication that something was wrong came when Rayne threw down his newspaper. As he surged to his feet and sprang for the door, Madeline heard shouts coming vaguely from somewhere in the inn.

The commotion grew louder when Rayne flung open the door.

"Stay here!" he threw over his shoulder before sprinting from the room.

It sounded very much as if a fight was ensuing on the floor below, Madeline realized, her heart suddenly pounding in her chest. Quickly snatching up her reticule, she fumbled inside for her pistol as she disobeyed Rayne's order and ran after him.

He had already reached the bottom of the staircase by the time she came to the head. Madeline's heart leapt to her throat and lodged there as she took stock of the struggle in the entrance hall. Three rough-looking men were conducting a savage assault on her brother and James.

One had Gerard pinioned by the throat while attempting to drag him out the front door. Across the way, James was struggling valiantly to keep the other two brutes at bay with his fists. The innkeep, however, was standing by, watching impotently, while a small crowd of customers had gathered to gawk in the open tavern door.

Just as James was felled hard to the floor, Rayne gave a shout and plunged into the fray, blows flying.

Gerard must have sneaked in another entrance, Madeline concluded, and so had the louts attacking him. Thank God, James had been watching for him, or they might have succeeded in seizing her brother and hauling him off.

As it was now, James was knocked out cold and Rayne had his hands full dealing with the two thugs, so there was no one to help Gerard. Outweighed by several stone, he was struggling futilely against the bruiser's choking grip.

Madeline couldn't shoot for fear of hitting Gerard, so she did the only thing she could think of. She scrambled down the stairs and flung herself at his attacker, pounding the brute's shoulder and head with one fist and kicking his brawny legs with both her feet.

The man was so startled, he almost released his hold, but he abruptly recovered and began fending off her blows with a meaty fist. One swing contacted her right cheek, making her see stars as she stumbled backward.

Madeline gave a cry of pain but surged forward again at Gerard's assailant, more determined than ever. She had no notion of time, merely the panicked, fiercely protective instinct to save her brother from harm, yet at least several moments passed before adamant hands gripped her and pulled her away.

Madeline gave another cry, this one of protest, as she felt her pistol being usurped from her grasp. The next instant Rayne was standing protectively in front of her, holding the gun's muzzle to the brute's temple, saying in a lethal voice, "If you are fond of living, you will release him."

The ruffian froze at the threat, then quickly freed his captive and held up his hands.

Madeline also halted at the sight of her armed husband looking so deadly dangerous. Rayne had laid the other two assailants out on the floor, she saw, while Gerard had dropped to his knees and was doubled over at the waist, holding his throat and hacking as he gasped for breath.

Panting hard herself, Madeline sank down beside her brother. Rage and fear were flaring wildly through her blood, but relief was beginning to hold sway.

"Dear God, Gerard," she implored, placing a careful hand on his shoulder, "are you all right?"

In addition to a reddening throat, his nose was dripping blood and his damaged left eye had begun to swell. Despite his injuries, though, her brother nodded unsteadily and croaked, "I will be . . . in a moment. . . ."

Gerard coughed again, then peered up at Rayne. "I say . . ." he rasped, "that was a smashing right . . . you gave that blighter. You must have . . . sparred at Gentleman Jackson's club."

Madeline felt a twinge of exasperation. It was just like her brother to ignore a brush with death in favor of admiring the skilled fighting form Rayne had displayed in demolishing his opponents.

"You must be Haviland," Gerard added in a hoarse voice. "Thank you—you came at a very good time."

"Don't thank me, thank your sister," Rayne replied grimly.

Gerard threw Madeline a feeble grin. "Thank you, dearest sister. You have my utmost gratitude."

Rayne, on the other hand, cast a dark glance down at her. "I believe I told you to remain upstairs."

She didn't dignify his criticism with a response. He should have known that iron chains could not have kept her away when Gerard's life was in danger.

As she helped her brother to stand, though, Rayne's gaze fixed on her face, on the ripening bruise on her cheek.

"This bastard *struck* you," he muttered as his free hand reached out to gently touch her cheek.

Rayne's face was so dark with anger that Madeline flinched and drew back from him. "It doesn't signify. Gerard is safe and that is all that matters."

At her faint recoil, a different emotion flickered in Rayne's blue eyes, something much like remorse. Dragging his gaze back to the miscreant, he tightened his grip on the pistol and pressed the muzzle harder against the man's skull.

"Who sent you to apprehend Ellis?" he demanded in that same quietly lethal tone.

" 'is lordship . . . Baron H'ackerby," the fellow answered quickly, obviously not wanting to tangle with so formidable a nobleman.

Just then John James came awake with a groan. When the erstwhile footman abruptly pushed himself up on his elbow, prepared to rejoin the fight that had already ended, the innkeep at last involved himself in the contretemps and hurried over to help James to his feet.

Upon noting the gawking crowd gathered at the tavern door, Rayne brusquely told them to go about their business, then sent the innkeep a glance. "Have you a room where you can hold these louts, Mr. Pilling?"

"Aye, m'lord," Pilling said, pointing at a doorway behind the high counter where the inn ledger lay. "Beyond my office is a storeroom with a sturdy lock."

"Good. I will want to speak to them in a moment, before they are taken to the roundhouse to be charged with assault."

He handed Madeline's pistol to James, who promptly assumed custody of the one conscious prisoner. Then Rayne gestured at the two unconscious thugs before addressing the proprietor.

"Take care of those other two, if you please," he directed Pilling. "I suggest you bind them securely. And fetch damp cloths for her ladyship and her brother as soon as you are done."

"Certainly, m'lord, right away."

"Meanwhile, I intend to commandeer your office for a short time, unless you object?"

"No, no, m'lord, no objection a'tall. Whatever you wish."

Rayne lent a shoulder to the injured Gerard and helped him limp behind the counter and into the inn's small office. Madeline followed reluctantly, aware that

Rayne wanted privacy in order to question her brother about his alleged criminal activities.

There was only one chair behind the desk, and Gerard sank into it gratefully before accepting Rayne's handkerchief to stanch his nosebleed.

Rayne, however, gave him no time to relax. "I suggest you start explaining, Ellis," he commanded the moment Madeline had shut the door behind them.

"Explain?" the younger man hedged.

When a muscle in Rayne's jaw hardened, Madeline quickly broke in. "He already knows everything, Gerard, so you may as well be completely honest."

Rayne's glance connected with hers briefly before he returned his piercing attention to her brother. "I have heard your sister's version of the tale. Now I want to hear yours."

Gerard eyed Rayne cautiously, as if determining how much he could leave out. He must have concluded that prevaricating would be perilous to his welfare, for he grudgingly launched into a narrative that confirmed Madeline's entire story, acknowledging his theft of the priceless necklace and the subsequent events that had led to his being assaulted by three of Ackerby's henchmen.

When he concluded, Madeline couldn't help voicing her distress. "Gerard, how could you *steal* like that?" she murmured in dismay.

Shifting his glance to her, Gerard hardened his jaw. "If you mean to read me a lecture, Maddie, you needn't bother. I would do it all over again."

"But the necklace does not belong to you."

"No, the Vicomte and Vicomtesse de Vasse are the rightful owners," he said fiercely. "There is a miniature of Madame la Vicomtesse wearing the necklace for her betrothal portrait. It was her prize possession, and she intended for her daughter to inherit it one day. Moreover, I only took the necklace, not any of the other jewels that were stolen from them."

"What other jewels?" Rayne interjected.

"The vicomte owned an invaluable collection of family heirlooms. The third baron—the current Lord Ackerby's father—stole it all."

"That is a serious accusation, Ellis," Rayne observed.

"Yes, but it is true," Gerard insisted. "Like many other aristos, the de Vasses were forced to pay exorbitant sums to be smuggled out of France at the height of the Revolution, but they still had a fortune in jewels remaining when they arrived in England. Shortly after they settled in Chelmsford, their home was robbed and all the jewels disappeared. Then several years later the collection resurfaced in the possession of Ackerby's father. It could never be proved that he orchestrated the theft, but he clearly obtained the jewels through illicit means and profited immeasurably from the crime. When confronted by the de Vasses, though, the baron refused to honor their claim and merely chided them for leaving their valuables unattended."

"That still does not entitle you to take the necklace," Madeline said tersely.

"I was only standing up for justice, Maddie," Gerard argued. "With *Maman*'s history, you know all too well about the plight of the émigrés. Those who were not guillotined by the revolutionary government or murdered by the rabble were left homeless and penniless, including Lynette's parents. After watching most of their family and friends beheaded and losing nearly everything they possessed, they came to England in hopes of beginning a new life—only to have their future shattered when their sole means of support was stolen from them. It's not right that Ackerby should be allowed to keep their only legacy."

"So you decided to rectify matters by taking the law into your own hands?" Madeline demanded. "By stealing from the late baron's son? How can you justify such self-serving logic? Even if his father *was* guilty as you say, this Lord Ackerby had nothing to do with a crime that happened many years ago."

Gerard scowled. "I cannot believe you are taking Ackerby's side!"

"I am not! I only want to keep you out of prison, or worse."

Her brother's features lost some of their fierce belligerence. "It is not merely that I want to inveigle my way into the good graces of my new bride's parents, Maddie. It is that I can't bear seeing Lynette so desolate. She has cried herself to sleep every night since we eloped, knowing she is estranged from her family. Whatever love she has for me will swiftly die if I cannot win their forgiveness and reunite them."

Madeline hesitated, sympathizing yet not wanting to accept Gerard's claim that his theft was justified. "If Lynette truly loves you, she will put your life over her parents' material gratification. You could have been *killed* today. She is unlikely to be any happier if you are hanged—or if you both must spend the rest of your lives hiding out in France as fugitives."

"No, Lynette agrees with me. She wants her parents to have the necklace, even if we must live in France." Gerard's expression turned imploring. "Please, Maddie, you have to help me."

Feeling a welling impotence, Madeline gazed back at her brother in dismay and frustration.

"What would *Maman* say about your stealing?" she finally muttered.

"It is unfair to bring her into this," Gerard objected more quietly. "*Maman* is long gone. And in any case, I believe she would want to see justice done."

Perhaps he was right about that, but still. . . . Madeline raised a hand to her temple. Not only was her bruised cheek throbbing, her head was aching with the futility of making her brother see reason. "Don't you realize that you are destroying your entire future, Gerard? Not to mention that I may never see you again. You have to give the necklace back to Ackerby."

"I cannot, Madeline. I *will* not."

A tense silence ensued. Rayne, who had been watching their altercation without commenting, broke their impasse.

"There is a simple solution to your dilemma," he said slowly.

When she turned to eye him, Rayne expounded. "I will purchase the necklace from Ackerby and gain his agreement not to press charges against your brother."

"I say, that would be 'capital' of you!" Gerard exclaimed.

Madeline stared at Rayne, however, torn between distress and hope. With his chivalrous streak, he was determined to defend the weak and vulnerable and fight for justice. Gerard's lamenting the plight of émigrés had been a far better way to gain Rayne's sympathy than expressing fear at losing his wife's love. But she couldn't let

Rayne make the financial sacrifice that trying to purchase the necklace would entail.

Nor could she understand why he would even want to help her brother out of his self-inflicted dilemma. A brief while ago, Rayne had grimly accused her of betrayal and adultery. His features were enigmatic now, devoid of emotion, giving no clue as to what he was thinking or feeling.

"It would not be 'capital,' " Madeline replied before addressing Rayne. "Even if Ackerby is willing to part with the necklace—which is gravely doubtful—it would cost you a fortune, and I can't allow you to throw your money away in support of my witless brother's felony."

The barest of smiles flickered at the corner of Rayne's mouth. "Stubbornness is clearly a family trait," he observed in a dry tone.

Madeline stiffened. "I have told you before, my lord, I do not want or need your charity."

Gerard hastened to break in. "Well, I am not too proud to accept his charity. I cannot thank you enough, Lord Haviland. I swear I will repay every penny somehow, although it may take years."

"Years?" Madeline repeated in a scoffing tone. "You will be in his debt for centuries."

"That is still better than being exiled to France."

Aware she was losing the argument, she rephrased her protest to Rayne. "Just how will you convince Ackerby to part with the necklace and overlook Gerard's theft?"

"It should not be too difficult," he replied, "considering that he set his henchmen after your brother and assaulted your housekeeper. Ackerby will not want his savagery to become known, or allegations about his father's complicity in the original theft to come out."

Madeline shook her head, her feeling of helplessness growing.

"Come now, Maddie," Gerard pleaded. "You don't want me to have to flee the country, do you? This is the perfect solution."

Knowing she was beaten, she let out a heavy sigh. "Oh, very well. But you don't deserve to get off this easily."

Her scamp of a brother beamed a grin. "Of course not. I know how fortunate I am, best of sisters."

She bit back a retort, restraining the desire to shake him, but then Rayne interrupted.

"Where is the necklace now?" he asked her brother.

Gerard answered willingly. "With my wife, Lynette. We took refuge at a farmhouse a few miles from here." His expression sobered. "I should get back to Lynette as soon as possible. She will worry if I don't return shortly."

"Did you ride here?"

"No, I walked."

"Then I will drive you there in my carriage. I first want to question Ackerby's minions to discover where he can be found. Meanwhile, you should clean up your appearance. Your bride will be alarmed to see you looking so battered."

Hesitating as if he might say something further, Rayne cast a glance at Madeline. Anger flickered in his eyes again when his gaze fixed on her bruised cheek. He even raised his hand as if he might touch her to offer her comfort . . . but then he drew back.

Without another word, Rayne let himself from the office—ruthlessly reminding Madeline of the vast chasm that still remained between them.

A moment later Mrs. Pilling arrived, carrying cloths and a basin of warm water along with a jar of unguent, which she deposited on the desk. Desperately needing the distraction, Madeline automatically reached for the cloth to administer to her brother's injuries as she'd done countless times in the years since their mother's passing.

When she gently dabbed at the vicious cut above his eye, Gerard winced in pain, yet Madeline knew the pain filling her heart went much deeper.

Her brother would likely come out of this debacle with his love and his future assured, but she had no such hopes for her own love and future, considering the shambles she had made of her marriage.

Chapter Eighteen

I should have guarded my heart much better, Maman. Now I must pay the price.

Rayne avoided reflecting on the future of his marriage for the time being, since there were more immediate matters to settle—namely reuniting Gerard Ellis with his young bride and convincing Ackerby not to pursue criminal charges against him. Yet Rayne's conscience was smiting him ruthlessly.

Not only had Madeline told him the truth, not only had her motives been entirely innocent, but far from betraying him, she had actually been attempting to *protect* him. To shield him and his family from scandal by preventing her brother from carrying out his idealistic, love-struck schemes.

How could he have been so blind to her true nature? Rayne wondered as his coach trundled along a country road toward the farmhouse where Ellis's wife was concealed. How could he have misjudged Madeline so egregiously? So willfully?

Rayne watched her now as she sat on the opposite seat, beside her brother, listening as Ellis recounted the details of his recent elopement and effused about newly married life. Her brother's spirits were understandably high since the end of his ordeal was in sight.

Madeline, however, was unusually quiet—and Rayne well knew *he* was the cause.

He voiced a silent invective at himself as he stared grimly at her bruised cheek. He was profoundly relieved that his suspicions about her were unfounded, yet his relief warred with even more profound feelings of guilt and remorse.

At least dealing with Ackerby should be simpler than resolving his self-imposed problems with his marriage. Once their prisoners had regained consciousness, Rayne had quickly elicited the information he sought, beginning with how they had picked up Ellis's trail:

When the housekeeper refused to reveal her employer's location even under physical duress, Ackerby had questioned the Vicomte and Vicomtesse de Vasse about where to find their daughter. Upon hearing their new son-by-marriage branded a thief, they were eager to confess so as to save Lynette from prosecution.

As a result, yesterday Ackerby had sent four men ahead to Maidstone to apprehend Ellis at Claude Dubonet's cottage. Upon arriving late last evening, however, they found no one at home. They watched the cottage through the night and into this morning, until hunger drove three of them to the inn in search of a meal, where they spied their quarry by mere chance. Their plan had been to carry Ellis to the cottage to await the baron's further instructions, since "Lord H'ackerby" was expected to arrive there this afternoon.

To maintain the element of surprise, Rayne intended to head to the cottage himself and confront Ackerby there, as soon as they collected Lynette.

Meanwhile, James would deliver the three ruffians to the Maidstone jail using Madeline's hired vehicle—which left her no means of transportation and necessitated her riding in Rayne's coach.

Yet she clearly had no desire to be alone with him. When the carriage eventually came to a halt in a farmyard and her brother jumped out, Madeline did likewise.

"I shall help Lynette gather their belongings," she murmured before hurriedly following after Ellis.

Rayne watched as brother and sister entered the farmhouse together. Then, too restless to wait passively, he descended from the carriage and strode a dozen paces away, where a break in the farm buildings offered a view of the rolling Kentish countryside.

A nip of fall scented the brisk wind that buffeted him, while gray clouds scudded ominously across the sky overhead. With his mind assaulted by such troubling thoughts, however, Rayne scarcely noticed the threatening weather. Instead, he kept remembering the bruise marring Madeline's lovely cheek.

The image of her battered face heaped hot coals upon his already guilty conscience.

There was no question that he would pay whatever price was necessary to purchase the necklace. The cost didn't concern him, even though Madeline chaffed at having to accept his "charity." For only when her brother was out of danger would she rest easy. He owed her that much, Rayne acknowledged, after the baseless accusations he'd made against her.

True, Madeline should have come to him at the first sign of trouble. Doubtless, her outsized pride and fierce independence had contributed to her determination to handle the brewing scandal herself. But Rayne knew he was solely to blame for imagining her betrayal.

Upon learning of Madeline's clandestine journey, he'd let his suspicions reach a boiling point. The thought of her indulging in adultery roused something dark and dangerous inside him.

Yet it was no excuse that his past had made him distrustful of seductive women. He was wrong to let his obsession with a previous broken love affair cloud his judgment so badly.

He'd realized the sheer idiocy of his mistake while confronting Madeline today—upon seeing the utter honesty and vulnerability in her face as she confessed her reasons for tearing off to Maidstone.

When he accused her of being involved with a secret lover, she looked distraught and dismayed that he had questioned her integrity and honor so baldly. And when he implied that he might have a mistress in keeping, she reacted as if he'd struck her.

A short while later, when he returned to her room upstairs after conferring with James, Rayne had known she was weeping, even before he heard the telltale hitch in her breathing.

He couldn't forget that despairing look in her eyes. He'd hated seeing her so upset, hated that he was the cause, her eyes hot and bright with unshed tears.

Then directly after the fight, when he'd spied her bruise and reached out to comfort her, Madeline had flinched from him.

Rayne had wanted to brutalize himself then.

He'd also vowed at that moment to help her rescue her brother from his folly. But in truth, he'd never met a woman less in need of aid than Madeline. Rayne had little doubt she would have found a way to defeat Ackerby's henchmen on her own if need be. Madeline had remarkable nerve, undeniable courage, and ingenuity.

And he perfectly understood her fear at watching her brother being assaulted. Even so, he'd felt a chilling fear himself, seeing her battle a brute more than twice her size.

At the same time, he'd felt a fierce protectiveness unlike anything he'd ever experienced before. That, and admiration. Madeline had fought Gerard's attacker with the fierceness of a mother tiger.

Indeed, the entire time, her actions had been motivated by love of her brother. She had championed Gerard, fought for him with an unshakable loyalty.

Rayne stared darkly out at the distant countryside. He wanted that precious loyalty from Madeline for himself. Yet he knew he would have to earn it.

He could perhaps begin by establishing more honesty in their marriage. Madeline was right—he'd been keeping countless secrets from her. A situation he intended to rectify as soon as he could arrange some privacy.

He wanted to take her home to Riverwood, Rayne reflected, not only to begin repairing the damage he'd wrought, but to care for Madeline after the difficult time she'd had. Just now, however, his pressing duties to the Crown had to take precedence over his personal affairs. Besides, sharing his secrets alone would hardly make amends for his own unforgivable conduct.

Furthermore, he had little chance of improving his relationship with Madeline unless he was totally honest with himself. Unless he acknowledged the turmoil of emotions that had governed all his responses since wedding her:

The savage jealousy that gripped you at the possibility of her having a lover.

The searing wash of anger you felt upon learning Ackerby had attempted to blackmail her.

The killing rage that ripped through you when she was struck by a brute.

And your most bewildering reaction of all. . . .

Why had the prospect of Madeline's betrayal been so much more painful than Camille's? Granted, he'd been a callow youth then; now he was a mature man, with a man's needs and perspective.

Yet that still didn't explain the ferocity of his responses.

He could only draw one conclusion, Rayne conceded. He'd been deceiving himself for days now about his feelings for his convenient bride.

He had labored determinedly to hold himself apart from Madeline, to maintain a cool detachment. He'd tried to convince himself that none of his feelings for her went very deep. Yet she had obviously touched emotions he'd buried long ago.

He'd known Madeline for only a short time, but she had burrowed beneath his skin.

And now whenever she looked at him, her lovely eyes were dark with hurt.

So what the hell do you do now?

He wanted to ease her pain, pain that he had caused. But even more, he wanted . . .

He wanted . . . what?

* * *

Sitting beside Rayne on the way to Claude Dubonet's cottage, Madeline did her best to push her marital woes to the back of her mind, yet they remained simmering beneath the surface, along with a profusion of dismal emotions. At the moment, however, trepidation was her foremost feeling, since Gerard's fate was still uncertain.

Had Baron Ackerby arrived yet from Essex? And if so, would they find him at the cottage? Most crucially, would Ackerby agree to sell the necklace and renounce his threat of retribution?

Gerard maintained that Claude Dubonet would not be at home to receive them, since he was employed as a French tutor for the local gentry and had reported to his daily job this morning. Recently Claude had spent his nights at the same farmhouse as Gerard and Lynette—which belonged to a friend—for fear that Ackerby's men might assault him as they had the Ellis housekeeper.

Apparently Gerard was not quite as worried about his future as Madeline was, judging from his hopeful smile as he held his blushing bride's hand. Lynette was pretty, petite, and shy, but she fairly worshiped Gerard—which was likely a large part of her appeal, Madeline suspected. After years of being raised by an older sister, Gerard was happy to have someone to look up to *him*.

On the other hand, her brother might merely be putting on an optimistic face or making a show of bravado. Or he might simply be placing all his faith in Rayne.

For herself, Madeline was very, *very* glad Rayne had decided to take the lead in confronting Ackerby, even if it put her further in his debt and bolstered her growing certainty that he would never come to love her.

A few moments later, Gerard suddenly spoke as he peered from the coach window.

"There, that is Claude's cottage up ahead—the one with the green shutters. And that," he added more grimly, "is Ackerby's carriage standing out in front."

Madeline's stomach tightened when she spied the vehicle. The baron was indeed lying in wait for her brother.

Rayne took command then, addressing Madeline first. "It would be best if you remained here with Lynette for the time being. Ellis, you will come with me."

"Yes," Gerard agreed, visibly girding himself for the impending confrontation.

Madeline wanted to accompany them, but Lynette looked frightened enough to need consoling. Moreover, as the two gentlemen descended, the cottage door was flung open and the Vicomte de Vasse came striding out, with his vicomtesse directly behind him.

"Papa! *Maman!*" Lynette exclaimed in a bewildered tone, clearly surprised to see her parents this long distance from home.

Madeline was also taken aback by their unexpected appearance, even more so when the vicomte headed directly for Gerard, fury written on his features. As the French aristocrat forcibly grasped her brother by his coat lapels, Madeline scrambled from the coach, hoping to prevent more violence. Lynette was obviously of the same mind and followed directly on her heels.

Fortunately Rayne intervened and pulled the two men apart. At the same time, Lynette was noticed by her mother, who gave a glad cry and hurried forward to embrace her wayward daughter.

But Lynette seemed more concerned about her new

husband. De Vasse stood cursing Gerard in French, calling him a devilish cur, among other aspersions.

"Papa, no!" the girl cried, extricating herself from her mother's attentions to rush to Gerard's side. "You cannot say those awful things."

Her father turned his anger on her. "*Ma petite,* how could you wound your *maman* that way? This man is a thief!"

"No, you don't comprehend—"

"I comprehend perfectly. He not only stole my only daughter and sullied her name but endangered her very life!"

"That is not true, Papa!"

"Indeed, it is, Lynette! As Ellis's accomplice, you will be locked in prison with him."

Madeline hurried to speak up. "It will not come to that, monsieur."

De Vasse hesitated while eyeing her, but then shook his head angrily. "I will not risk it. We have come to bring our daughter home."

Gerard's jaw hardened with similar determination. "Lynette is my wife now, sir. You have no right to dictate to her."

"You keep out of this, you *canaille*!"

"Please, Lynette," the vicomtesse pleaded, weeping openly now. "Lord Ackerby has given us the opportunity to make you see reason. We traveled here with him in his carriage. But his patience will not last long. For your own safety, you must return home with us."

"I would strongly advise that you heed your parents, Mademoiselle Lynette," a new male voice suggested.

Baron Ackerby, Madeline realized, had emerged from

the cottage, flanked by a burly man whom she guessed was his fourth lackey.

"I intend to have Ellis arrested for theft," Ackerby announced to the group at large.

In protest, Madeline took a protective step toward her brother, but Rayne's hand came down on her shoulder, heavy and reassuring while he again intervened.

"I believe you will have to rethink your position, Ackerby, given the new circumstances."

The baron did not look at all pleased by Rayne's presence. "What the devil are you doing here, Haviland?"

"I've come to resolve the issue of your missing heirloom. Your other minions had an unfortunate setback when they assaulted Ellis earlier today, but I trust you and I may resolve this dispute in a more civilized fashion than fisticuffs."

Ackerby's features froze, then tightened as he digested Rayne's disclosure. "I have no notion what you are talking about."

"No, but you will. If we may have a word in private, I have a proposition for you, one that will be worth your while to consider."

At Rayne's urging, they moved aside, out of earshot. Madeline knew he was informing Ackerby about the assault on her brother and using it as leverage to purchase the necklace, for she could see the baron's face first flush with anger, then grow ever more furious.

The Vicomte de Vasse, however, was clearly frustrated at being uninformed. "What are they saying, Lynette? What is happening?"

"You will see, Papa," she answered with rising confidence.

Yet Madeline held her breath as she watched the tense exchange between the two noblemen.

Finally, though, Rayne seemed to prevail. Glancing back at the group, he called to Gerard. "We have reached an agreement, Ellis. May we trouble your friend Dubonet for writing implements?"

"Certainly, of course, my lord," Gerard responded eagerly.

All three men disappeared inside the cottage, leaving Madeline alone with Lynette and her parents. When they came out again several minutes later, Ackerby stalked directly to his carriage and barked a terse order to his coachman, demanding to be conveyed to London at once. When he hastily settled inside, the fourth bruiser barely had time to jump on the rear footman's perch before the vehicle lurched into motion.

When Ackerby had departed, Rayne nodded at Gerard, who gave a faint smile of gratitude and withdrew a velvet pouch from his coat pocket. Taking Lynette by the hand, he went to stand before the vicomtesse.

"I believe this belongs to you, madame."

With a wary glance at her husband, the noblewoman took the pouch, but her expression turned to shock when she opened it and peered inside.

"*Mon dieu,*" she breathed. Her hands shook as she withdrew a magnificent ruby necklace accented with smaller diamonds and gold filigree. "I never thought to see this again."

"The necklace is rightfully yours, madame," Gerard said gently, "since it was stolen from you many years ago."

"Yes, *Maman,*" Lynette seconded. "Gerard risked his life to recover it for you. You should be grateful to him."

Lynette was shading events in favor of her beloved, leaving out Rayne's part in the repossession entirely, but Madeline knew this was not the moment to quibble.

"I know not what to say," the vicomtesse murmured, tears of astonishment and awe pouring down her cheeks.

The vicomte's scowl had faded as he studied Gerard's battered face, but now his voice turned suspiciously husky when he added with evident gratitude, "This necklace is our only legacy from our former life."

Madeline understood why it was an emotional moment for both aristocrats. At least she'd had a home and a country to belong to, since her English father had wed her French mother and spared Jacqueline the destitute life of an émigré. But Lynette's noble parents had endured a much harder existence.

The vicomtesse finally regained enough composure to reach up and embrace Gerard and kiss both his cheeks. "My dear boy, this was good of you—exceedingly."

"It was my pleasure, madame," Gerard replied with appropriate humbleness. "I wished to repay you in some small measure for the honor of wedding your beautiful daughter."

At the allusion to their elopement, the vicomte's dark frown returned. But rather than growling out fresh invectives, he gritted his teeth and cleared his throat in an obvious struggle for forbearance.

Rayne moved to Madeline's side then and spoke quietly. "I suggest we leave these good people to resolve their differences. Ellis, you have transportation to convey your bride and her parents home to Chelmsford?"

"Yes, my lord. My carriage is stabled nearby. I cannot

thank you enough, Lord Haviland," Gerard added gratefully.

"As I said before, you should thank your sister."

Gerard dropped his young wife's hand and stepped closer to Madeline, pulling her to him in a fierce embrace. "My eternal thanks, Maddie," he whispered in her ear. "You truly are the best of sisters."

Feeling the ache of tears in her own throat, Madeline returned his embrace warmly. "Just promise me you will keep out of trouble for a while at least."

Releasing her, Gerard stepped back, grinning. "I will do my best, I swear it."

Leaving her brother beaming with relief and happiness, Madeline allowed Rayne to hand her into his coach. As she settled next to him, she felt hopeful that Lynette's parents might come to forgive Gerard for stealing their daughter from them.

As the coach pulled away from the cottage, she turned to Rayne at once. "I gather Ackerby agreed to sell you the necklace?"

"Yes. You needn't worry about him any further, Madeline. He means to drop the entire matter."

"He did not appear too happy about it."

"He was not," Rayne replied dryly. "Particularly since I warned him that if he dared to threaten you or your brother again, I wouldn't hesitate to put a bullet through him. But I gave him a signed vowel, which he will redeem as soon as he returns to London."

"How much did you offer him?"

Rayne hesitated a moment. "Ten thousand pounds."

Swallowing a gasp, Madeline gazed at him with regret. He had paid an outrageously exorbitant price so that Gerard could gain approval for his marriage. "I wish it had not cost you so very much."

"It was worth it to free your brother from his difficulties. And before you protest your increased debt to me, you should know that I consider the necklace our wedding present to Gerard."

She felt a rush of gratitude toward Rayne. She had wanted to give her brother a chance for happiness, but Rayne had made it possible. If she hadn't fallen in love with him before, his generosity would have won her heart irrevocably.

Still, she knew her own chance for happiness had grown depressingly more dim. At the moment she couldn't read a single emotion on Rayne's face, but she couldn't forget his ugly suspicions about her. Without even basic trust between them, she doubted he would ever return her love.

His tone, however, was rather quiet when he spoke again. "I suggest we return to the inn to pay your shot and collect your clothing. And I need a word with James before we return to London."

Madeline looked a question at him. "We?"

"Yes," Rayne replied. "I'll discharge your hired carriage so that you may travel with me. I have urgent business to attend to in London, so I must be on my way as soon as possible."

She felt uneasy at his plan. With their marriage on such precarious ground, she didn't know if she could bear so many hours in a closed coach with Rayne. Yet after all he had done for her, she had no right to argue.

When they arrived at The Blue Boar, Madeline dutifully went upstairs to collect her valise. Then, while

Rayne attended to the other matters he had spoken of, she returned to his coach to wait for him.

She was deep in her morose thoughts when Mrs. Pilling came hurrying out to the yard, carrying a large basket, which she handed inside to Madeline. "His lordship ordered victuals for you, my lady. And some hot bricks for your feet."

It was considerate of Rayne to think of her comfort, Madeline admitted, even though his thoughtfulness was likely driven more by mere courtesy and his particular brand of chivalry toward the fair sex than by his desire to succor her specifically.

The bricks were very welcome, considering how chilled she was. But that, too, was a measure of her despondency, since she suspected her shivers were not solely caused by the brisk weather.

When eventually Rayne settled beside her on the velvet squabs, the feminine places in her body reacted as they always did to his nearness, with heat and longing. Yet other parts of her—her stomach especially—responded by tightening. This was the moment she had been dreading. She couldn't face any more of Rayne's damning accusations just now, not when her defenses were so frail.

As the coach began to move, they stared at each other for a long drawn-out beat, the tension rife between them.

Then Rayne surprised her by handing over her pistol. "James professes his thanks for its use."

To her further surprise, Rayne's mouth quirked with a semblance of his former humor as she tucked the weapon safely in her reticule. "Isn't this how we first met? At an inn, with me returning your pistol after you brandished it at me?"

Madeline, however, could not bring herself to smile at the memory, or argue that she had never actually brandished the weapon at him. Just now she could only regret that first unexpected meeting with Rayne. If not for that, she would never have fallen headlong in love with him and made herself so pathetically vulnerable to crushing heartache.

When she remained silent, Rayne indicated the basket on the floor. "Why don't you see what Mrs. Pilling supplied? You need to eat."

She was not particularly hungry, despite the fact that the danger to her brother had passed. But eating offered a distraction from her conflict with Rayne, so she inspected the contents of the basket, finding bread and cheese and cold meats, a bottle of wine, and a flask of hot tea.

Madeline partook of the food without enthusiasm, while Rayne settled for a glass of wine. Eventually he broke the silence.

"I am fully aware that I owe you an apology, Madeline. Several in fact."

At his quiet admission, she went still, scarcely believing she had heard correctly. Her gaze flew to his face and remained there while he continued.

"You should have come to me when you first realized your brother was in trouble, but I should have been more accepting of your reasons. I regret the accusations I made, sweetheart. I should have known you would not be trysting with a lover."

Madeline bit her lower lip. Was Rayne saying that she was the kind of woman who wouldn't attract a lover? Or that he believed her claims of innocence?

He seemed sincere, perhaps even contrite—or was that merely wishful thinking on her part?

"You were right," he added in the same solemn tone. "I *have* been keeping secrets from you."

Her searching gaze locked on his blue eyes, while her stomach clenched in a knot. At his mention of secrets, she was suddenly certain Rayne meant to confess to having his own adulterous affair.

Yet his next words dispelled her worst fear. "My absence from Riverwood this past week had nothing to do with having a mistress, Madeline. I am not keeping one. Rather, I was commissioned by the Home Secretary to investigate a plot to assassinate the Prince Regent."

"A plot?" she repeated after a moment, afraid to let herself feel relief.

"Yes. You recall meeting my friend, Will Stokes? He assumed my duties during my absence today, but events are coming to a head, which is why I must return to London at once."

"Of course," Madeline murmured, her sinking despair reappearing with a vengeance. Rayne had left important matters of state at a crucial stage in order to rush off to Maidstone to deal with her problems, and now he was clearly impatient to resume his responsibilities.

"Perhaps it would be best if you returned to Chiswick tonight," he suggested. "Just now my staff there can better care for you than I can. As can your new friends."

Madeline flinched inside, even though understanding why Rayne wanted to be rid of her. She would only be a distraction when he needed to concentrate on foiling the plot. Rayne would find it hard to forgive himself—or her—if the Regent was killed while he was away.

"Yes," she agreed, latching on to the first excuse that occurred to her, "it would be best. I am scheduled to teach at the academy tomorrow, and I have neglected my classes long enough."

Judging from his expression, it was not the reply he wanted. Yet he didn't press her. "Very well. My carriage will take you on to Riverwood after depositing me in London."

Nodding, Madeline returned the remains of her meal to the basket. Then folding her arms protectively over her middle, she averted her gaze to stare out the coach window. The emptiness inside her yawned wide, while countless self-recriminations pummeled her.

She had been such a fool, Madeline reflected. She'd tried to become a *femme fatale,* allowing Rayne to take over her heart so completely that she had become a different creature, one she barely recognized.

She should have known that seducing him would never work, that winning his love would be impossible. She blamed herself most, but Rayne was at fault as well, because of all the things he'd made her hope for, yearn for.

She wished now that she had guarded herself better against hope. If she had, she wouldn't be feeling this desperate hurt in her heart.

She had to do better at protecting herself, Madeline vowed.

Acting on her new resolve, she eased away from Rayne, from the warmth of his big, muscular body.

"I think I would like to try and rest now," she said in a dull voice. "I had little sleep last night."

He hesitated for a moment, as if he might say more, but again he didn't press. "As you wish."

Something dark and heavy pressed down upon Madeline's chest as she curled up in the far corner, facing away from Rayne.

Even though she pretended to sleep, however, she remained awake the entire time, her eyes dry and burning. The rhythmic jolt and sway of the coach was broken at regular intervals when they changed teams.

It was several hours later, after darkness had fallen, when she thought she felt Rayne's light touch against her nape.

"We are here."

Madeline sat up as the coach came to a halt.

A footman opened the vehicle's door, and Rayne gave her a long, silent look before stepping down.

Then he turned back to say quietly, "I meant my apology, Madeline. But we will discuss it when this is all over."

Only then did she realize that what Rayne was doing could be highly dangerous.

"Please take care," she urged in a small voice.

"I will, love."

Love. He didn't mean the endearment, of course, she knew as he shut the door. It was merely a figure of speech for Rayne, one he used frequently.

The coach moved on, leaving her feeling excruciatingly lonely and alone. There was a great, deep emptiness inside her that she feared would never go away.

How does one survive heartache, Maman? Madeline thought bleakly . . . although she was unsurprised when her mother failed to answer.

Chapter Nineteen

The emptiness is unbearable, Maman.

Faith, but she was miserable, Madeline thought as she drove herself home from the Freemantle Academy the following afternoon. Not even the lively enthusiasm of her pupils during a French grammar lesson had been able to dispel the gloom that covered her like a shroud.

Her heart was a leaden weight in her chest—a weight that only increased when she glanced over her shoulder and recognized the barouche bowling down the drive behind her gig.

Apparently the dowager Countess of Haviland had come to call again at Riverwood.

"Wonderful," Madeline muttered, inwardly wincing. "Her visit will doubtless cap my misery to perfection, *Maman.*"

She drove the gig around the manor to the stables, where she turned the vehicle over to a groom. Then, reluctantly, she entered the house and found Bramsley at the front door, admitting the dowager to the entrance hall.

The elderly noblewoman's lips pinched when she caught sight of Madeline.

Madeline, however, forced herself to curtsy politely upon reaching her visitor. "My lady, welcome to Riverwood."

Lady Haviland's expression only darkened. "I wish to speak to you in private, Miss Ellis."

Madeline winced again at the mistaken form of address. Evidently Rayne's grandmother refused to acknowledge the legitimacy of her marriage. "May Bramsley take your bonnet first? Or offer you refreshment?"

"No, he may not. I shan't be staying. Please conduct me to a parlor at once."

After shedding her own bonnet and pelisse and turning them over to Bramsley, Madeline obeyed Lady Haviland's command, all the while gritting her teeth.

As expected, her ladyship refused a seat when it was offered. Instead, she launched into speech as soon as the door was shut behind them.

"I shall come directly to the point, Miss Ellis. What sum would convince you to leave England for good?"

Madeline stared. She had braced herself for some form of attack, but not this utterly unexpected question.

Lady Haviland continued brusquely. "I am prepared to offer you a small fortune if you will relocate to the Continent or any other country outside of Britain."

"Why would you make me such an offer?" she asked in bewilderment.

"So that my grandson's unacceptable marriage can be annulled and he can begin anew with a more suitable choice of brides."

Madeline felt her heart jolt. When she remained speechless with dismay, her visitor expounded.

"Haviland regrets wedding you and wishes to dissolve your union, but he is too honorable to seek an annulment."

"But you are not?" Madeline retorted reflexively.

The countess's mouth tightened. "I want what is best for my grandson. He has come to realize his mistake in marrying you, and I have the wherewithal to resolve his problem. I will give you fifty thousand pounds if you agree to disappear from his life, Miss Ellis. After a proper interval, Haviland can have the marriage annulled and find a countess who befits his noble station."

He has come to realize his mistake in marrying you. The words tore through Madeline.

Shaken, she moved over to the settee and sank down. Rayne's grandmother was bribing her to leave his life for good?

Her hand stole to her heart as she stared blindly down at the Aubusson carpet. She only vaguely heard the dowager speaking again.

"I warn you, Miss Ellis," her ladyship was saying, "if you refuse, Haviland will not see a penny of my fortune, and neither will you." Receiving no reply, the noblewoman sniffed. "I suppose I cannot blame you for wishing to improve your lot in life by snaring my grandson, but this is your chance to do even better. It should prove little hardship for you to move on to more vulnerable prey, since you only married Haviland for the lure of my wealth."

Madeline raised her gaze in protest. "I did *not* wed him in anticipation of his inheriting your fortune."

Lady Haviland gave her a haughty glance. "I beg to

differ. I know your kind, girl. You are nothing but a greedy, social-climbing upstart."

Stiffening, she shook her head. "You know nothing about me, my lady. I wed Rayne because I came to love him."

The dowager made a derisive sound. "That is a bald-faced lie if I have ever heard one. You could not possibly fall in love in so short a time."

But I did, Madeline thought despairingly. *To my great regret.*

She didn't want to give Rayne's grandmother the satisfaction of seeing her pain, however, so aloud she said dismissively, "I will consider your offer, Lady Haviland. Now I will thank you to leave."

Not accepting so easy a victory, the dowager eyed her with a dubious scowl. "I wish to have your answer now."

"I am sure you do, but I am not prepared to give it just yet."

"Fifty thousand pounds is an enormous sum, Miss Ellis."

"A hundred times that amount would not elicit my decision any sooner."

Thankfully, Lady Haviland backed down, albeit grudgingly. "Very well. But I expect to hear from you shortly." Turning abruptly, she regally whisked herself from the parlor.

The encounter left Madeline reeling. She couldn't breathe for the crushing weight in her chest. Her world was crashing down around her. Rayne wanted to annul their marriage and was willing to pay her for the chance to do so.

The thought of ending their marriage, of uprooting

her entire life and abandoning all that remained of her dreams, of leaving Rayne so that he could wed some other socially acceptable lady. . . . Dear God.

She could believe that Rayne regretted marrying her, especially after their clashes during the past few days. But understanding his perspective didn't make it any less excruciating.

She felt raw inside, stricken with a horrible emptiness.

Oh, why had she ever succumbed to Rayne's seductive proposals? Enduring a lonely spinster existence would have been far better than this anguish.

She couldn't bear to leave him. How could she when she was so desperately in love with him? Yet perhaps, Madeline thought bleakly, it would be best for Rayne if she accepted his grandmother's offer.

Should she give him his freedom? Could she make such a sacrifice for his sake?

Just then Bramsley tapped gingerly on the parlor door. When Madeline looked up blindly, concern wreathed the majordomo's features. "Are you unwell, my lady?"

Madeline swallowed. Her throat ached from the force of her refusal to give in to weeping, yet she temporarily won the struggle. "No, I am not unwell. What is it, Bramsley?"

"Mr. Lunsford has called and wishes to know if you are at home to him."

"Pray tell him that Lord Haviland is in London."

"Mr. Lunsford specifically asked for *you*, my lady."

Before Madeline could answer, Freddie came sauntering into the parlor. She shut her eyes momentarily, wishing she didn't have to deal with him just now.

"That will be all for the moment, Bramsley, thank

you," she said as her latest visitor flung himself into a chair without ceremony.

"I say," Freddie greeted her, "was that Lady Haviland's carriage I passed?"

"Yes," Madeline answered dully, feeling hopelessly dismal.

"What did she want?"

It was just like Freddie to be so ragmannered, but Madeline barely registered the infraction. "It doesn't matter. Why are you here, Freddie?"

"I've come to beg a favor of you."

She frowned at him. "Are you in another fix? If so, you should apply to Rayne—but he is not here at present. He is in London."

"Don't I know it," Freddie said peevishly. "Some sort of hush-hush spy business, I collect. But no, I am *not* in a fix this time . . . for once. I learned my lesson with the last debacle. I am keeping well away from scheming widows."

"Then what do you want?"

"I hoped you might put in a good word for me with a young lady I have my eye on."

Madeline's eyebrow rose. "You are interested in a young lady?"

"Yes, but it is all quite proper. Miss Merrywether is the sort of female whom even my stickler father would approve of. And she has the loveliest smile—enough to make a chap go dizzy. But she says her mama would not allow her to further our association, since I have developed a rakish reputation. Me, a rake! It is quite unfair, since I don't hold a candle to the true rakes of the Beau Monde. Besides, I have become rehabilitated. I've given up any thoughts of debauchery and fun under pain of being disinherited."

Madeline was growing dizzy herself with Freddie's meandering commentary. "So how can I help you?"

"You could improve my suit if you would sing my praises to Miss Merrywether and her mama. They will take special note of your opinion, you being a countess and all."

"But I may not be a countess for much longer," Madeline said morosely.

His expression arresting, Freddie sat up. "What the devil do you mean?"

Madeline shuddered as she recalled the dark dilemma she was facing. "Never mind. But I am afraid I cannot help you just now."

"Why not?"

"Freddie, please—just leave me alone."

"My, you are viperish today."

Raising a hand to her temple, Madeline grimaced at his complaint, knowing she had no right to take her despairing mood out on him.

"What is it, Madeline?" he pressed. "Do you have the megrims?"

She sighed. "No, it is nothing like that. I beg your pardon, Freddie. I am just poor company today."

His gaze turned somber. "Why don't you tell me what has you so blue-deviled?"

"It would not make any difference."

"How do you know unless you try? I can be a good listener if I truly put my mind to it. And you look as if you could use a friend just now."

Madeline debated a long moment before deciding that

Freddie was right. She badly needed a friend, given her current emotional state—her mind spinning with turmoil, her chest aching with grief and anger.

"Very well, I will tell you," she murmured before spilling out the truth in a rush. "Lady Haviland offered me fifty thousand pounds if I would leave England and disappear from Rayne's life so he could secure an annulment and marry someone more suitable. And I don't know what to do," she finished miserably.

Freddie's eyes widened with shock. "*Fifty thousand pounds?* Why, that is a king's ransom."

"I know," Madeline agreed.

"But of course you will not accept."

"No? Why should I not? Lady Haviland said that Rayne now realizes his mistake in marrying me. I don't want to remain his wife if he doesn't want me."

Freddie's brow furrowed in thought. "And you trust that old bat's word? Maybe Rayne does *not* want you, but I can't credit that he would send his grandmama to do his dirty deeds for him and buy you off with a bribe. It was likely Lady Haviland's idea entirely."

"Even so, perhaps it is best if I accept her offer."

Shaking his head, Freddie rose and began pacing the floor. "You should not be so hasty, Madeline. You are not nearly as unsuitable as Lady Haviland claims."

She appreciated his indignation on her behalf, but Freddie was hardly a good judge of the ton's standards.

He didn't allow her time to reply, however. "*I* think you make Rayne an admirable countess. I have thought so from the first. In fact, I was the one who encouraged him to propose to you."

"You were?"

"Yes, indeed. I knew he needed a wife in order to sire

an heir, and you seemed a good choice. Even if you are no beauty, a man can be comfortable with you." Freddie paused in his pacing to eye her. "Although you *do* seem to have improved in looks of late."

Madeline flinched at his backhanded compliment. "I hoped Rayne would come to love me someday," she said in a small voice.

He made a dismissive sound. "I don't know if that is possible, considering the way his heart was broken."

She stilled. "What do you mean, his heart was broken?"

Freddie halted altogether to look at her. "I do not really know the details. I only heard that Rayne had a tragic love affair with a Frenchwoman many years ago. Much more tragic than anything *I* ever suffered. But if the rumors of a shattered affair are true, you cannot expect Rayne to recover quickly."

"You said it happened years ago."

"So I heard, but I could be mistaken. Besides, love is not all it is cracked up to be, Madeline. *I* know. I have been in love countless times—and I am almost ready to give it up altogether."

She couldn't help a shaky laugh. "I cannot imagine you giving up on love, Freddie."

He grinned at her. "No, I don't suppose I could, either." Then he sobered. "You should not make any hasty decisions," he repeated, "particularly when you are feeling so low. If you ask me, you should give Rayne a chance to fall in love with you if he can."

"I have tried," Madeline admitted. "But my efforts have had no effect. On the contrary, they seem to have made matters between us even worse."

"Perhaps you just need to give him more time."

"How much more time?"

"How should I know? I am obviously no expert on love. But I cannot believe you would be vanquished so easily. Do you mean to give in to Lady Haviland without a fight? Honestly, I thought better of you, Madeline."

Freddie had a point, she realized, straightening her spine. She at least needed to drum up the courage to confront Rayne, even though she wasn't sure what good it would do her. If he truly wanted to dissolve their marriage, there was likely nothing she could say to change his mind.

Feeling that hollow, crushing ache flood her again, Madeline pressed a hand to her stomach. She hadn't known she was capable of feeling such emptiness.

Still. . . . Despite what his disdainful grandmother thought of her, she was indeed worthy of him, and of being his countess.

Squaring her shoulders, Madeline set her jaw. If Rayne wanted their union annulled, he would have to tell her so to her face.

She stood abruptly.

"What do you mean to do?" Freddie asked.

"I am going to London to speak to Rayne."

"You cannot. He is hip-deep in spy matters, remember?"

Madeline sank back down, frustration and despair warring inside her. Again Freddie was right. At this very moment Rayne was probably attempting to stop the assassination of England's Prince Regent. She at least needed to wait to confront him until he concluded his mission. The future of her marriage might be of vital import to *her*, but it did not quite trump the fate of the country or the Regent's very life.

So why did it feel as if her own life was hanging in the balance? Madeline wondered desolately. And why was it so hard for her to make the noble choice?

Chapter Twenty

Is it possible that he truly loves me, Maman? Dare I believe it?

A warning shout rang out across from the Parliament building, alerting Rayne of the danger to his charge. Acting instantly at the prearranged signal, he shoved England's portly Prince Regent to the pavement and covered the great bulk with his own body, much to the chagrin of His Royal Highness. Yet the pistol shot that immediately followed whistled harmlessly overhead.

Moments later, Rayne glanced across the street to see a cadre of agents led by Will Stokes swarm three armed culprits, who seemed shocked to have their assassination plot foiled.

Meanwhile, Prinny lay beneath Rayne, gasping and cursing. However, upon realizing that only his dignity had suffered, the prince broke into a sheepish grin.

"By God, you were right, Haviland. They were out to kill me."

"Fortunately they missed, Your Highness," Rayne said, helping the corpulent prince to his feet to the tune of creaking corsets.

"My thanks to you, Haviland. How can I ever repay you?"

"There is no need, Highness. But you might recognize the efforts of Runner Will Stokes. Stokes put a great deal of time into vouchsafing your protection this past sennight."

"That I will," the Regent agreed. "And I will also mention your services to your grandmother. Mary raised a formidable grandson, if you ask me."

"Thank you, sire," Rayne said in a drier tone.

He stepped back as the Regent's usual retinue came rushing toward him in alarm. Prinny himself did not seem overly upset, as a man who had just escaped death ought to be. Indeed, he appeared rather cheerful about the thwarted assault. Perhaps because although he was reviled in many quarters for his infamous extravagances, an attempt on his life might actually raise his stock in public opinion. While his subjects might not care for his policies or personal conduct, most did not want him *dead*.

Rayne turned Prinny over to his royal coterie with a bow and extricated himself. Then moving through the gawking crowds, he crossed the street to find Will supervising the arrest of the three main perpetrators. None of them bothered protesting their innocence, since they'd been caught red-handed after being carefully followed for days.

Happily, the extensive surveillance Rayne had arranged was paying off. These three plotters would be put on trial and their fellow conspirators rounded up. Rayne was confident that with the preponderance of evidence against them, they would likely be found guilty.

As the three were being bound and loaded into a

wagon to be taken to the Old Bailey, Rayne reflected on the irony of having to deal with prisoners twice in as many days.

"Excellent job, my friend," he said to Will. "His Highness sends his compliments, by the by."

Will grinned more broadly than Prinny had. "You and I still work well as a team, old chap."

"So we do," Rayne agreed.

"Are you certain I cannot persuade you to join Bow Street?"

"Not at present—although I promise to give your suggestion due consideration. Pray excuse me now, however. I have some urgent personal business to attend to."

"Your new bride," Will commented with a slyly amused glance.

"Just so," Rayne replied, inwardly grimacing.

He was anxious to return to Riverwood. He hadn't liked sending Madeline home when they had so many critical issues to settle between them. And now that he'd done his duty by his country's sovereign, impatience was gnawing at Rayne relentlessly, along with his guilty conscience. He owed Madeline a more abject apology than the unsatisfactory one he'd given her yesterday.

To make amends, Rayne intended to stop by his town house briefly on the way to collect the best pieces of the Haviland jewels. He would also order Walters to oversee his affairs until further notice, since he was planning an extended absence from London. Directly afterward, Rayne would hasten to Riverwood, where he hoped to spend some very private time with Madeline, attempting to resolve the turmoil he'd created in their marriage.

To his surprise, however, when he reached Bedford

Avenue, his younger sister met him at his front door in place of Walters, and she was clearly distressed.

"Thank heavens you are here, Rayne," Daphne declared, dragging him inside. "I must speak to you at once."

"What is it, love?" Rayne asked, noting that Walters was hovering nearby.

Daphne allowed the servant to withdraw a circumspect distance before saying fretfully, "I came straightaway to warn you. I thought you should know what scheme Grandmama is plotting against your new wife."

Rayne felt his stomach muscles clench. "What do you mean, plotting?"

"Grandmama went to Riverwood this afternoon, intending to offer Madeline a huge sum so that your marriage can be dissolved."

"Dissolved?"

"As in annulled," Daphne explained worriedly.

A dozen questions streaked through Rayne's mind, but he settled for a simple one. "How did you learn of her scheme, Daphne?"

"She mentioned it to Penelope, and Pen let it slip to me. Grandmama told her not to worry—that your marriage would not stand."

His muscles coiled even tighter. After the groundless accusations he'd made, Madeline might be eager to find a way out of their marriage, enough to accept a generous offer of independence.

"Walters!" Rayne barked at his aide's retreating form.

"Yes, my lord?"

"Have a swift horse saddled for me at once."

Riding would be much faster than traveling by coach or even curricle. Moreover, it would take precious moments to harness either carriage, moments Rayne feared he didn't have.

"Certainly, my lord," Walters replied before leaving promptly to do his bidding.

"Where are you going?" Daphne asked as Rayne spun on his heel and headed for his study.

"Where do you think? I need to find my wife before it is too late."

When Daphne tried to follow him, Rayne halted long enough to grasp her by the shoulders and plant a swift kiss on her forehead. "You have my utmost gratitude, sweetheart, but you may go home now." Then pointing his sister at the front door, he gave her a gentle push.

As he continued on his way to the study, however, Daphne called after him. "I like Madeline a great deal, Rayne. I don't want Grandmama to interfere with your chance at happiness."

"Trust me, I won't allow her to," he said determinedly. "Now take yourself home and let me deal with our grandmother."

Not waiting to see if Daphne obeyed, Rayne entered his study. After retrieving a key from his desk, he opened his safe and withdrew a large velvet-covered box. Ten minutes later, he was riding toward Chiswick at a gallop, the jewel case strapped to the rear of his saddle.

His fresh mount ate up the miles, yet Rayne still had too much time to dwell on his frantic thoughts. The fear welling inside him was perhaps the closest he'd ever felt to true panic.

His chest was wire-tight, and so was his gut. He couldn't lose Madeline now just when he'd come to realize how much she meant to him. Yet he might very well have driven her away. His grandmother's financial proposition could be the final blow.

Without a doubt he was outraged and furious at his elderly relative's machinations, and he intended to stop the dowager's meddling once and for all. But for now he had to intercept Madeline before she had a chance to leave him.

Even so, Rayne kept a lookout for his grandmother's carriage as he galloped the road toward Riverwood, while self-recriminations went around and around in his head.

He'd accused Madeline of adultery and lies, yet the real deception had been on *his* part—for convincing himself he wanted nothing more than a marriage of convenience with her.

The truth was staring him in the face, though.

He *loved* Madeline. Loved her deeply.

The power of his new emotions really was not so shocking when he considered it, Rayne realized. He had locked the door on his feelings for so long, he hadn't even recognized them when they appeared. But his love had been growing from the first moment of meeting her.

His blindness also made perfect sense. In his fierce determination to protect himself, he'd banished tender sentiments like love from his life, keeping his heart frozen by design. But love had little to do with logic. And despite his fear of betrayal, he'd had no choice but to succumb to Madeline.

In her own uniquely spirited way, she had pierced his armor and burrowed unerringly into his heart.

And now? Rayne wondered broodingly.

He'd originally wed her because he needed a wife to give him heirs. But now he wanted so much more. He wanted Madeline as his friend, his lover, his life's mate, not merely the mother of his children.

And he wanted her love in return.

Yet what did *she* want?

A fresh wave of apprehension struck Rayne. No doubt he could forcibly prevent Madeline from leaving him, but she might never be able to love him after the unforgivable way he'd treated her.

His gut churning to the rhythm of galloping hoofbeats, he spurred his horse harder, urgency driving him to even greater speed.

Rayne was barely a mile outside of Chiswick when he recognized the barouche lumbering toward him as belonging to his grandmother. Deliberately he swung to the right and came to a halt directly in the vehicle's path, where his sweating mount remained prancing and snorting.

At first, Lady Haviland's coachman whipped up the team as if intending to barrel straight through Rayne. But as the distance closed between them, the servant started sawing frantically on the reins, trying to slow the barouche.

"My lord!" the coachman exclaimed as Rayne nudged his horse sideways at the last moment to avoid a collision. "I mistook you for a footpad."

"Be easy, Muller. I want a word with my grandmother."

"Haviland!" an imperious voice demanded. "What on earth is the meaning of this?" The noblewoman had let down the carriage window in order to hail him, Rayne saw.

"I should ask you the same question, Grandmother," he replied in a dangerously silken tone.

Her lack of protest along with her wary expression told him she knew exactly why he was there.

Rapidly dismounting, Rayne ordered Muller to turn her ladyship's carriage around and return to Riverwood. Then tying his horse to the rear of the barouche, he climbed inside to confront his relative.

"Why are you behaving in this havey-cavey fashion?" Lady Haviland sputtered, attempting to bluster her way out.

Rayne returned her haughty gaze with a hard one of his own. "I think you know, Grandmother. We have a grave matter to discuss, wouldn't you agree?"

His worst fear was that Madeline would be gone by the time they reached Riverwood. His second was that she would be packing. According to his grandmother, Madeline had not refused her offer of fifty thousand pounds out of hand, and had even promised to consider it.

Therefore, as soon as the barouche came to a halt in the drive, Rayne bounded out and threw an order at the coachman before taking the front steps three at a time.

When he shoved open the front door and burst into the entrance hall, the first person he spied was his major-domo.

"Bramsley, where is Lady Haviland?" Rayne demanded.

"In the green parlor, my lord."

His racing heartbeat slowed the slightest measure. At least she was still here.

"Have my horse stabled," Rayne ordered as he

brushed past Walters, "and see that the case behind my saddle is brought to my study."

"Certainly, my lord."

When he reached the parlor, he found Madeline seated on a sofa.

"Thank God," Rayne murmured under his breath before realizing her face was buried in her hands.

Then Madeline looked up and noticed him. Her expression held unmistakable pain, Rayne saw, relentlessly flogging himself.

He was vaguely aware that Freddie was present, too, but he only had eyes for his wife.

"Rayne," she gasped, her voice barely audible. "Is something wrong?"

"Yes, something is very wrong, Madeline," he said quietly. "I understand my grandmother made you an outrageous financial offer."

Her eyes were dark and full of despair. "Yes," she whispered.

"I hope you did not consider it."

Before she could reply, Freddie stuck his oar in. "It may not be my place to say so, Rayne, but your grandmother is a perfect witch."

"I completely agree," Rayne said in a terse voice.

"Then what do you mean to do about her?"

Ignoring his cousin, Rayne held out his hand to Madeline. She might not believe any professions of love just now, so he would just have to show her. "Please, will you come with me, love?"

Her wide, questioning eyes seemed too big for her face, but she rose hesitantly.

Without speaking, Rayne escorted her out to his grandmother's barouche. He had ordered Muller to remain there in the drive and was infinitely glad to see he'd been obeyed even though the dowager had very likely threatened her longtime servant with dismissal.

Flinging wide the carriage door, Rayne stepped into the opening. Lady Haviland sat stiffly on the far side of the barouche, her spine rigid as she stared straight ahead, refusing to acknowledge him.

"It is time for you to proffer my wife a sincere apology for your shameless meddling, Grandmother," Rayne prodded.

At his demand, however, the noblewoman visibly bristled. "I refuse to hold this discussion in front of the servants, sir," she declared with an imperious wave of her hand to indicate her coachmen and grooms.

Her staff, however, was not their only audience, Rayne noted, since Freddie had followed him outside, as had two of his own footmen. Yet he was unswayed by her argument. "Do you think I give a damn who hears?"

At his adamant tone, his grandmother's expression changed, while her own voice softened to hold an almost pleading note. "Rayne, do you not see? I only have your best interests at heart. You made a dreadful mistake, marrying as you did. I wanted heirs to the Haviland title, true, but not at this price."

"Grandmother . . ." Rayne said warningly, his anger rising.

In response, Lady Haviland gave a faint cry and clutched her hand to her heart. As she slumped against the corner seat, Rayne ground his teeth. He'd seen this same dramatic performance before, more than once. Suspecting she was feigning a heart seizure yet again, he decided to call her bluff.

"Muller, please take Lady Haviland directly to her

doctors in London. She is too weak to continue this discussion at the moment and needs to be confined to her bed."

His command had the desired effect. As he made to shut the carriage door, Lady Haviland sat up abruptly. "No, wait!"

Rayne drew Madeline forward, holding her tucked against his side, as if sheltering her from attack. And when his grandmother gave his wife a scathing glance, he laid down his gauntlet. "If I must choose between the two of you, Grandmother, it will be Madeline. I love her, and I intend to keep her as my wife. There will be no question of annulment."

He felt Madeline stiffen against him. She had been watching the elderly noblewoman, but at his declaration, her shocked gaze lifted to his.

Her luminous eyes held confusion and doubt as she whispered in disbelief, "You love me?"

Rayne gave her a tender smile. "More than I can say, sweetheart."

Returning his attention to his grandmother, he said in a cutting tone, "You will accept her into the family or I will have nothing more to do with you. Until then, you are not welcome here or at any of my homes."

Lady Haviland had set her jaw stubbornly, but it went slack at his threat. Evidently she believed him, for she finally muttered, "Well then, if you insist. . . . I *apologize*."

"That is not good enough," Rayne snapped. "You should direct your apology to my wife."

The dowager pressed her lips together tightly, her expression sour. But then exhaling a peeved sigh, she gave in. "I beg your forgiveness, Miss Ellis— That is, Lady Haviland. I should not have interfered in your affairs."

Rayne started to remonstrate at her spiteful tone, but Madeline placed a hand on his arm.

"Thank you, my lady," she said softly. "If you agree, we will forget this contretemps entirely and put it down to a misunderstanding."

Lady Haviland looked as if she might refuse the offer of peace, but eventually she gave a brusque nod.

"That will do for now," Rayne said tersely, deciding not to force the issue any further at the moment. Although it was not the concession he wanted, his grandmother had made a significant step with her grudging apology, and Madeline was evidently willing to drop the matter. Rayne felt his heart swell at her generosity.

Signaling to the coachman, Rayne stepped back, drawing Madeline with him. They both watched as the coachman flicked his whip at the team and the barouche pulled away.

Then Rayne turned to Madeline. She was gazing up at him, the look in her eyes one of longing, of hope—her expression exactly mirroring the emotions he felt.

Chapter Twenty-one

So this is what you meant by the joy of true love, Maman. I agree, it truly is magical.

Madeline scarcely dared breathe as she stared up at Rayne. Her heart had begun to slam in slow, painful strokes while her thoughts and emotions rioted.

"Have I rendered you speechless for once?" he asked softly.

She tried to swallow past the dryness in her throat. "I think perhaps you have."

Realizing how her voice quavered with uncertainty, Madeline steeled herself to pose the crucial question that had haunted her since receiving his grandmother's shattering proposition. "Did you mean it? You don't want an annulment?"

"Not only do I not want an annulment," Rayne declared, "I would hunt you down to the ends of the earth if you tried to leave me."

His un-loverlike vow might be based purely on male possessiveness, Madeline thought, dazed, but at least it gave her reason to hope that Rayne wanted to keep her as his wife.

On the other hand, his shocking declaration of love

had been made in the heat of anger at his elderly relative. Could she possibly let herself believe that he truly meant it?

Oddly, the look in Rayne's eyes was a mixture of regret and worry as he regarded her with a searching gaze. "I understand my grandmother offered you fifty thousand pounds to annul our marriage, Madeline."

"Yes," she said, still hoarse.

"I was terrified you would accept."

Rayne was terrified? Not a tenth as terrified as *she* had been, she would wager.

Madeline shook her head adamantly. "I don't want your grandmother's money, Rayne."

"Why then did you tell her you would consider her offer?"

"Because I thought she was making it on your behalf—that you wanted me to agree to an annulment."

A muscle flexed in his jaw. "No, I knew nothing about it. If I had, I would have done my damnedest to spare you her vitriol. I am so very sorry, sweetheart. Her intrusion was outrageous and unforgivable."

Squeezing her eyes shut briefly, Madeline gave a deep shudder of relief. "I thought an annulment would be in your best interests," she whispered. "Lady Haviland believes you deserve a wife who can move in your social circles and enhance your standing in the ton."

Rayne's expression remained solemn. "I don't care what she believes. You know I don't give a damn about the ton. Besides, you are perfectly qualified to move in any circles you choose—mine, hers, the Crown's, anywhere."

Madeline inhaled a shaky breath. Hope filled her chest

along with a faint, burgeoning feeling of joy. Did she dare give in to it?

Aloud, she added haltingly, "The difference in our social stations was not the only reason I thought an annulment might be best for you. Lady Haviland also told me you wouldn't inherit a penny of her fortune if I remained wedded to you."

His gaze narrowed. "So you were trying to protect my inheritance?"

"Well . . . yes."

Rayne looked as if he was striving for patience. "In the first place, I have my own fortune and don't need my grandmother's."

"You do?"

"Yes. I am a very wealthy man. Didn't you realize it?"

"No," Madeline said weakly. "Your sisters were extremely worried that their sons would be cut off from your grandmother's largesse. And Freddie said she was holding her fortune over your head to force you to take a suitable wife."

"That isn't the case at all. Thanks to several wise investments in the East India Company, I am nearly as well off as my grandmother, so you needn't sacrifice our marriage for my sake."

"Oh," she murmured.

"Have you nothing else to say?"

In truth, she did, but she had difficulty gathering her courage, fearing Rayne's response. Finally, though, Madeline forced the words out. "Did . . . did you mean it? You truly love me?"

His features softened. "Absolutely, I meant it. I truly love you, sweet Madeline."

A sharp, fierce joy hit her. She felt shaky, trembling inside.

At her speechlessness, Rayne moved closer. Reaching up, he curved his palm gently against her cheek, taking care to avoid the bruised skin there, and bent his head as if intending to kiss her. . . .

Before his lips met hers, however, Madeline heard the sound of a throat being cleared. A fierce wave of disappointment shot through her at the reminder that they were not alone; Freddie still hovered nearby, although one of Rayne's footmen had disappeared, leading his horse around to the stables, and the other had withdrawn a discreet distance.

"By Jove," Freddie enthused, "now *that* is a romantic vow if I have ever heard one. You should be quite happy now, Madeline. All your fears were for naught."

Flustered by their unwanted audience, Madeline drew back from Rayne, while Freddie continued his cheerful observations. "Rumor has it that Rayne is the ideal lover, but I can clearly see that for myself now. No doubt I could take lessons from him—"

"Freddie, old friend," Rayne interrupted sharply, "will you please make yourself scarce? Whatever your problems, they will have to wait for some future time. At the moment, I require privacy with my wife."

"Certainly," Freddie said, grinning. "I am merely reveling in the chance to crow. It is about time you succumbed to love. I was growing weary of always being the besotted one. And just think, *I* am responsible for your matchmaking—"

"Freddie," Rayne growled.

"Very well, I am leaving! But Madeline, when you are

free, pray remember that I need you to champion me with Miss Merrywether's mama."

"I will, Freddie," she promised, although all her attention was on her husband.

Rayne responded in kind, taking her hand and touching his lips to her fingers. "Shall we continue this conversation inside, love?" he asked. "We have some very private matters to discuss."

When Madeline gave him a shaky smile of agreement, his large, warm hand settled on the small of her back and guided her up the front steps of the manor, leaving Freddie behind to arrange for his curricle to be brought around.

Once inside the house, Rayne led her to his study and shut the door firmly behind them. "Now, where were we?"

Having halted, Madeline turned to face him expectantly. "You were about to kiss me if I recall."

A quick smile flashed across his mouth, then disappeared. "I would like to do much more than kiss you, love, but I believe I must first proffer you an abject apology. For my grandmother, and more important, for myself."

Hiding her regret, Madeline quelled her need to feel Rayne's reassuring embrace and said simply, "I don't need apologies, Rayne. I only need to know you love me."

His eyes were intent and very blue. "I *do* love you, Madeline. And I am not about to let you leave me. But at least allow me to explain why I was so resistant to you."

She did want very much to hear his explanation, so

she accompanied Rayne to the sofa, where he drew her down beside him.

"I admit I tried my damnedest not to fall in love with you," he began. "In fact, I planned never to feel anything resembling love for the rest of my life."

Held transfixed by his gaze, Madeline ventured a guess at what had precipitated his resolution. "Freddie said you once experienced a tragic love affair and never recovered."

Rayne grimaced. "Freddie is a damned rattlepate."

"But is it true?"

"Yes—although my story was not exactly tragic. Some years ago I fell in love with a Frenchwoman who pretended to return my ardor so that I would save her aristocratic family from persecution. But as soon as they were safely in England, she cast me aside to return to her lover."

Madeline felt a protective rush of sympathy at Rayne's confession. "She must have been mad to prefer anyone over you," she declared loyally.

Again his smile was fleeting. "I am honored by the compliment, sweeting—but in all honesty, I could understand her desire to be united with her lover. Yet having my first youthful love betrayed set me on my guard. After the war's end, I returned home to England determined to remain forever unencumbered by emotional attachments." He reached up and stroked her cheek with a fingertip. "But you changed all that for me, Madeline."

"It did not seem so," she said in a small voice. "Since we spoke our vows, you have grown more and more distant by the day."

"I know, and I regret my retreat, sweetheart. My only

excuse is that I needed time to acknowledge my feelings for you."

Capturing her hand in his, Rayne laced their fingers together. "I should have suspected my undoing much earlier. When I was with you, you drove me wild, and when we were apart, I thought about you constantly. The most telling sign, though, was that I flew into a jealous rage every time Ackerby came near you, when normally I am notoriously even-tempered."

Both of Madeline's eyebrows lifted. "You really were jealous?"

"Supremely."

She shook her head, marveling at Rayne's admission. "I have never known any man to feel jealousy on my account."

"I was, fiercely. That was the chief reason I was so enraged when you set off for Maidstone. I thought you intended to meet Ackerby for a tryst."

"I did plan to meet him eventually, but not for the reasons you thought. I was trying to save my brother."

"I realize that now . . . but at the time I was too blinded by my own past. I feared history was repeating itself with you. But it was absurd to link you with my first love. You are nothing like her in numerous respects."

Madeline met his gaze questioningly. "What hurt most was that you mistrusted me enough to think me guilty of infidelity."

The regret in Rayne's eyes was unmistakable. "I am sorry, love. But once my suspicions took root, they fed upon each other. And in my own defense, there were a number of other reasons I began to doubt you. Not the least was because you suddenly became a different woman than the one I wed. You were clearly working your feminine wiles on me—exactly the way my former love had done."

It was Madeline's turn to look guilty. "You weren't mistaken, Rayne. I was purposely acting the seductress."

"Why?

"Because I was madly in love with you, and I wanted you to love me in return."

His gaze fixed on her, fierce and intent. "You love me?"

She nodded. "I have for a while."

The brightness in his blue eyes took on an even deeper glow. "Thank God," he murmured fervently, tightening his hand around hers.

"It was why I agreed to marry you," Madeline added, "and why I tried so hard to seduce you." Her lips twisted in a rueful smile. "How ironic. In my attempt to become more alluring, I only drove you further away."

Rayne laughed softly yet disagreed with her observation. "I wouldn't say you drove me away. The more seductive you were, the harder I fell."

"You fooled me completely."

"I fooled myself as well. It was only when I learned from Daphne what my grandmother planned that the truth hit me about my feelings for you. And then I feared I was too late—that you would accept her offer before I had a chance to dissuade you."

"I would not have made so crucial a decision on Lady Haviland's word alone, Rayne. I intended to go to London to see you first, but I didn't want to interrupt your efforts to save the Regent's life. I still don't. Shouldn't you be in London just now?"

"No. Prinny is safe for the time being."

"So you broke the ring of potential assassins?"

"Barely an hour ago . . . and afterward I rode straight here."

"I never doubted you would succeed in stopping them," Madeline said admiringly. Then she shuddered upon recalling her painful suspicions. "You can't imagine how relieved I was to learn why you were avoiding Riverwood and staying in London so often instead. I feared you were keeping a mistress."

"I am not, Madeline."

"But you implied as much yesterday."

"It was cruel of me to mislead you. Can you ever forgive me?" The flash of tenderness in his eyes was so naked and intense, yet so soft, her heart melted.

"Of course." She could forgive Rayne anything now that she could believe she had captured his heart.

He slid an arm around her shoulders. "I haven't so much as thought of another woman since I met you."

"Truly?"

"Yes, truly."

The expression in Rayne's eyes, so filled with desire and tenderness, set her heart to thudding. He intended to kiss her at last, Madeline thought with joyous anticipation.

He brought his fingers to the thickly beating pulse at her throat, then cupped and tilted the back of her head. His warm breath caressed her mouth before his lips began to play over hers with delectable pressure. Then slowly, his tongue slid into her mouth, tangling in a sensual dance.

Madeline moaned helplessly and raised her hands to his silky, raven hair. His kiss was tender, magical; the sensations he roused were spellbinding. His tongue stroked provocatively against hers, seducing, while his lips molded, tasted, teased.

His exquisite assault stirred a wildness in her blood and reawakened the intense yearning inside Madeline. When he at last broke off, she was breathing heavily. She wanted to protest his cessation, but Rayne pressed his lips into her hair, and drew her close against him.

With a dreamy sigh, Madeline rested her head against his shoulder. "I still find it hard to credit that you fell in love with me," she said after a moment. "How did it happen? I am nothing like the other candidates you were considering for marriage. Certainly I am no beauty."

She felt the tenderness in his touch as he caressed her nape. "I see I will have to cure you of a grave misconception, darling. You are the most beautiful, the most desirable, the most special woman I have ever known. And I love you dearly."

I love you dearly. Madeline closed her eyes to savor the most beautiful words she had ever heard.

"I couldn't help but love you," Rayne continued thoughtfully. "I think it began when you threatened me with your pistol the very first time I met you."

A teasing note of humor had entered his voice, but Madeline still took issue with his claim. "I never actually threatened you that first time, you will remember."

"No, you saved your threats for when I dueled with Ackerby." Rayne chuckled softly. "It's fortunate I like my women strong and feisty."

She pulled back to eye him. "You think me feisty?"

"That, among many other estimable attributes. You're kind, brave, honorable, caring, clever, resourceful. . . .

Your spirit, your wit, your liveliness, your warmth, your sense of adventure, all captured my heart."

Warmed all over by his praise, Madeline smiled with quiet delight. "I confess I have never thought of myself as adventuresome."

"You must be. I've had more adventures in the past fortnight than in the past two years. Come to think of it, I haven't had a tame moment since your advent into my life. But that is just the way I want it."

"Are you certain, Rayne?"

He might have heard a trace of lingering doubt in her question, for he caught her chin and stared at her steadily. "Utterly certain, my love. You are far more than I bargained for in a wife, but *exactly* what I want."

When Madeline remained silent, drinking in his reassuring gaze, Rayne ran his thumb over her lower lip. "I've told you from the first that you have too little faith in your own appeal."

"So you did, but I didn't believe you really meant it."

"I trust you will believe me now."

"Yes—but was it any wonder I didn't think you could ever love me when you would not even remain with me on our wedding night?"

"No, it's no wonder. It was unforgivable of me, I know."

Madeline narrowed her brows at him. "We have yet to spend even one night together, let alone share our nuptial bed."

Looking repentant, Rayne pressed a light kiss on her lips. "I mean to remedy that directly. You are sleeping in my bed from now on. Beginning tonight."

Madeline gave a sigh of satisfaction and approval and rested her head once more on his shoulder.

"You made an accomplished seductress, I must say," Rayne remarked, pressing a kiss on her hair this time.

She smiled again. "I had help. I thought I needed more ammunition to capture a man like you, so I asked Arabella and Roslyn how they had made their husbands love them. They were kind enough to advise me, and one of their courtesan friends taught me some of her arts."

"A courtesan? Indeed? I should like to hear *that* tale."

Madeline's face flushed, but she decided not to mention Fanny Irwin's advice book to young ladies on capturing a husband, or her even more personal instruction on seduction. "I may tell you someday, but for now I mean to keep my techniques to myself. You have too many advantages as it is."

"Very well, but otherwise, I suggest we strive for more openness from now on. We've kept too many secrets between us. No more secrets, love, agreed?"

She lifted her head to look at him again. "What about your spy secrets?"

"Well, some of those may have to remain confidential," Rayne admitted.

"So you mean to continue your spy career?"

"The Foreign Office has little need for diplomatic intelligence at present, but I'm considering working for the Home Office. I haven't decided yet. I may be occupied enough keeping Freddie out of trouble." A fond smile curved Rayne's mouth. "I suppose we do owe our marriage to Freddie after all. If not for him, I never would have encountered you that night at the inn."

The tender laughter in his eyes made her heart swell. "We owe Lord Ackerby as well," Madeline pointed out. "Although I loathe giving him any credit."

Rayne's expression turned pained. "As do I. I still think you should have let me shoot him during our duel. I would have, had I known he was blackmailing you."

Choked laughter stirred in her throat. "Then I am glad you didn't know."

"Actually, I'm surprised he had the nerve to tangle with you. But you should have come to me at once when you found your brother in difficulty."

"I realize that now. I promise I will in the future."

"I trust so. You are too independent for your own good, dearest Madeline." Lifting her hand to his lips, Rayne brushed a caressing kiss on her knuckles. "See, I am not enamored of *everything* about you. You have your faults as well as your good qualities . . . as do I. And then there is my grandmother."

Rayne's amusement suddenly disappeared. "I still must apologize for her abominable proposition. I don't expect you to forgive her."

"It won't be easy, but I mean to try. I don't want to create a permanent rift between the two of you."

"Any rift is of her own making, and she well knows how to mend it. If she won't, I will cut her from our lives."

"She is your family, Rayne. And she is of an age where it is difficult for her to change her ways."

He shook his head at her generosity. "You never cease to amaze me."

It thrilled Madeline to hear Rayne offer her such praise, but he gave her no time to dwell on it.

"Speaking of family . . ." With a hand, he motioned toward his massive desk. "Do you see the case over there? Those are the Haviland jewels, and they are rightfully yours now."

Madeline felt touched by the significance of his gesture; Rayne was fully acknowledging her as his countess. Yet being his countess had negligible importance compared to being his wife. "I never wanted your jewels, Rayne. I only wanted your love."

He brought the back of his hand softly down the side of her face. "That means more to me than you can possibly imagine, sweetheart. And I want your love . . . more than anything in the world. I want your loyalty and your trust, also. I envied your brother for the loyalty you showed him this past week. But I know I must earn those things for myself."

Madeline held his gaze solemnly. "Do you know what else I want, Rayne? I want a real marriage with you, not one of convenience. I know you only wed me to gain an heir, but I want to be a true wife to you."

"I have every intention of having a real marriage. What do you say that we make a fresh start, sweetheart?"

"I would like that above all things."

"Then it is settled. From this moment on, we begin our marriage anew."

"And I will sleep in your bed tonight?" she asked hopefully.

"Absolutely. As you said, I never gave you a proper wedding night. But I warn you, love, I intend to do the seducing tonight."

Reaching up, Madeline wrapped her arms around his neck to invite her husband's enchanting kiss. "I won't give you any argument for now. You know my resistance to you has always been impossibly weak."

With a husky laugh, Rayne bent his head to claim her lips.

* * *

Their second wedding night was blessedly different from their first, Madeline noted thankfully—beginning with an intimate dinner for just the two of them. Then Rayne led her upstairs to the lord's apartments rather than to hers.

His bedchamber was elegant but clearly masculine, done in accents of dark greens and golds, while the massive bed no doubt had been built to accommodate Rayne's large body. True, the quiet hearth fire and candles cast a warm glow similar to the one she'd arranged for their most recent tryst. But this time the desire vibrating between them was rife with affection and love, not suspicion and doubt.

Moreover, Madeline reflected, glancing up at Rayne as he ushered her into the room, she was no longer an innocent, inexperienced virgin as on her wedding night. She knew precisely what ecstasy lay in store for her this evening. And as their gazes touched, she realized her husband was having the same thoughts.

Expectation quivered through her when Rayne shut the door behind them, locking them in together. His eyes were the color of midnight sapphires as he moved toward her. With just one glance from those incredible eyes, Madeline could feel herself growing warm and liquid with arousal. She felt soft and swollen inside, weak with need for him. Her heart fluttering with excitement, she started to undress.

Rayne, however, stopped her by raising an imperious hand as he crossed to her. "I told you, love, it is *my* duty to do the seducing tonight."

"Then why don't you begin?" she asked impatiently.

His slow smile nearly brought her to her knees. Yet he

took his own deliberate time removing her gown and underclothing.

When eventually she was naked, his darkened eyes raked over her, searing her. He was near enough that Madeline could feel the warmth of his splendid body— but still he didn't touch her.

Instead, he began to undress himself, making her wait even longer. He shed his coat and cravat and shirt, then his shoes and stockings and breeches. Finally, at last, he stood nude before her.

In the simmering glow of firelight, Madeline drank in the sight of him—his powerful form, the hard planes, the rippling muscles, all as magnificent as ever. In truth, Rayne seemed to have grown more beautiful since the last time he had made love to her.

So beautiful he took her breath away.

His dark virility was a striking contrast to her pale softness as he stepped closer. She was hungry to touch him, yet he wouldn't allow her to take the initiative. Placing his hands at her waist, he bent his head.

Even then he didn't kiss her as she longed for him to do. His lips merely skimmed her mouth, her cheekbone, her temple, then buried themselves in her hair.

"I want this night to be perfect for you," he whispered.

It *would* be perfect, she knew, savoring the feel of his deep voice vibrating through her. Madeline shivered in anticipation. She ached with wanting Rayne, loving him. She wanted desperately to have his strong arms wrapped around her, wanted to burrow beneath his skin.

Yet he was obviously determined to go slowly, to draw out the moment.

His movements languid, Rayne took the final step toward her, eliminating the distance between them. Feeling his warm, naked skin against her at last, Madeline caught her breath. Then he slowly pulled her even closer, into the hard heat of his body.

The erotic sensation of his embrace—his sinewed muscles, his swollen member caressing her belly—intensified the painful yearning gathering inside her, even before Rayne raised his hands to cradle her breasts provocatively. Her nipples changed in a rush, answering the seductive caress of his palms.

Madeline swallowed a moan but instinctively thrust her breasts into the exploration of his hands.

"So sweet," he murmured, his voice a husky rasp in her ear. "So beautiful."

Her response was a helpless pleasure sound as her head fell back to give his mouth better access.

His thumbs passed in scorching circles over her nipples while he bent again to trail flaming kisses down the arch of her throat. The sharp delight of it stabbed Madeline in her midsection and deep in her loins.

Bracing her hands on his shoulders, she whimpered. Then Rayne's mouth closed wet and hungry on a cresting tip, his velvet-rough tongue laving the peaked nipple.

The sensation streaking though her was so excruciatingly keen, her knees went weak.

He attended her breasts for some time, suckling, arousing, tormenting. Finally he slid both arms around her to embrace her fully, drawing her even closer to his body.

Heat and hunger flooded through her in violent

waves. She needed Rayne to assuage the sweet hurt between her thighs, in her throbbing breasts.

She almost cried in relief when he lifted her up and drew her legs around his hips, locking her to him.

Carrying her to the bed, he lowered her to the silk sheets and followed her down. His eyes smoldered as he pressed his naked body against hers, letting her feel his hot skin, his rampant arousal.

Raising her arms to twine them around his neck, Madeline drew Rayne's head down to her. She gloried in the way her body meshed perfectly with his, yet it was his lips—the taste, the texture, the warmth—that set her heart soaring.

His kiss was an intimate knowing of her mouth that kindled a wonderful, craving weakness in every fiber of her being. When eventually he broke off, she stared at Rayne, gazing deep into his eyes.

He returned her avid regard with a soft smile as his hand rose to trace her lips. "How do I describe all the ways I find you beautiful?" he murmured.

His fingertips brushed across her cheek with unbearable tenderness. "You are exquisitely lovely to me, Madeline, but your beauty comes from within as well as without. You're exciting and intriguing and incredibly stimulating. The pleasure I get in looking at you rivals the joy I feel at simply being with you, in knowing you are my wife."

He was intent on showing her his love, Madeline knew, a poignant ache welling in her throat.

His hand moved down to cover hers and press it over his heart. "No other woman could ever satisfy me more or be a better match for me, sweetheart. You are everything I ever wanted, could ever want. I need you like I need my next breath. . . ."

Those were the last words he spoke for a long while. Madeline's breath fled completely as he set about offering her physical proof of his lover's vow.

Rayne devastated her with his tender touches and caring kisses, until she was trembling violently. Until she was wild with lust and longing. Until her veins were flooded with shuddering heat.

Her body was pulsing, shaking with need for him; her feminine hollows wet with desire, yearning to merge with his hard male flesh.

At last he guided her palm to his naked loins, while his own hand slipped between her legs, pressing against her feminine cleft. Madeline gave a hoarse whimper and arched her back.

Her skin burned against his naked arousal as it probed her slick folds. When he eased the silken head of his shaft into her quivering flesh, Madeline drew a long, shuddering breath at the feel of his thick member gliding deep inside her.

He sank slowly, only to withdraw partway, then thrust inside her again and slide home to the hilt.

Impaled by his hardness, she moaned at the fullness of his penetration.

Yet Rayne was nearly as affected by the exquisite sensations as she was, she suspected. She felt a tension quivering inside him, and knew his passion-hazed eyes mirrored her own.

"Beautiful," he whispered again as he began to move inside her, his voice thick with desire.

Madeline wrapped her legs around him, welcoming him, holding him tightly, striving to take him even deeper into her body as she spoke the words that filled her heart. "I love you, Rayne . . . so very much."

In response, his eyes seemed to blaze with an inner fire. His hand clasping her buttocks, he lifted her hips to meet his, driving his huge, burning shaft into her.

"And I love you, sweet, darling Madeline," he rasped.

She wanted to weep at the beauty of it. She did sob at the spellbinding sensations Rayne created when he continued whispering promises, endearments to her, urging her on.

She could feel his increased urgency now. His breath was harsh and uneven, his touch no longer gentle as he brought his mouth down on hers and intensified the rhythm of their joining.

When another sob of pleasure sounded from her throat, Rayne's kiss grew rougher, fiercer, almost primitive. His caresses were equally as fervent as his arms came fully around her, holding her with crushing tightness. She could taste the desire in him, the emotions, the passion.

The fierceness of his embrace was an avowal of love, Madeline knew with absolute certainty.

Her heart thundering in her chest, she kissed him back as though her soul depended on answering his insistent demand.

A taut, savage need blazed between them now. She welcomed the hard thrusting of Rayne's body as he took her, his tongue plunging in the same relentless cadence as he filled her again and again.

The tension built between them until it was unbearable. When the shattering tumult broke within her, Madeline cried out, a cry that was matched the next instant by the rough groan bursting from Rayne's throat.

They came together in a firestorm of love and pleasure, his lips drinking in her wild moans.

Ecstasy left them clinging together in the aftermath. After a time, Rayne's hand rose to cradle Madeline's throat, soothing her thundering pulse beat, while his mouth feathered kisses over her face.

Then, easing his weight beside her, he pulled her close and enfolded her in his embrace.

Madeline lay there bonelessly with her head on his shoulder, marveling at the joy she was feeling. Her chest literally ached with the fullness of love. The consummation of their second wedding night had not only been a confirmation of their marriage vows but a fierce mating of souls.

She was truly Rayne's wife now. She felt cherished, loved.

And she felt raw with love for him—her possessive, protective, warrior knight; her dangerous lord who had given his heart over to her to protect and keep safe.

With a deep sigh of contentment, Madeline pressed a kiss on his bare skin.

Her display of affection made Rayne stir enough to speak. "I trust," he murmured hoarsely, "that after tonight, you will no longer doubt how special you are to me, or how much I love you."

Madeline couldn't help but smile with renewed joy. She had no doubts any longer about Rayne's feelings for her. "I admit, you did a fair job persuading me just now."

"Merely *fair*?" Shifting his hold, Rayne placed a finger under her chin, compelling Madeline to lift her gaze to his. "Seriously, wife, do you have any notion how much I love you?"

"I am beginning to understand," she replied with complete honesty. She knew Rayne loved her with the same fire and passion that coursed through her soul.

Even so, Madeline pursed her mouth provocatively as she looped her arm around his neck. "But I think I need much more convincing, husband. Why don't you show me again?"

Her seductive challenge made Rayne laugh softly and lower his head to claim her lips. "I will, love, gladly. Just as soon as I recover my strength from our last devastating bout of lovemaking."

Epilogue

I miss you deeply, Maman, but I know you would be happy for me now that I have found the other half of my heart.

London, November 1817

Rayne woke slowly to the mingled sensations of pleasure and contentment. Pleasure, because he had spent much of the rainy afternoon making love to his wife before falling asleep from satiation and exhaustion. Contentment, because they were celebrating the midwife's prediction that Madeline was to have his child.

She lay spooned in his arms now, still dozing peacefully. The rain had stopped, leaving their London bedchamber filled with a hushed peace.

Carefully, Rayne slid his hand over Madeline's naked belly, savoring the feel of her lush, warm body. Marveling at the thought of his seed growing inside her.

Easing away slightly, he raised himself up on one elbow, the better to see her. There was an added glow about her, he noted, admiring how fine and clear her skin was.

How could he have ever thought her plain? Rayne wondered. When had he started to think of her as beautiful? Possibly from the very beginning. Yet her beauty was more than skin deep. Madeline intrigued him, excited him, touched him, stirred him.

And in the past weeks since acknowledging their love for each other, Rayne had made it a point to show her by deeds and not merely pretty words just how lovely she was to him, how much she meant to him.

He was determined to vanquish all her doubts. Madeline was still new to love, though, and so had needed frequent reassurances. In their marriage bed, however, she displayed a flourishing confidence, slipping into the role of enchanting seductress with instinctive mastery.

Her passion was a wondrous gift, yet it was her passionate spirit that had grabbed him by the heart. His need for her was growing more powerful by the day.

Lifting his hand, Rayne brushed an errant tress back from her face, his fingers lingering on her soft, silken skin. He'd found an unexpected treasure in Madeline, without question. She was a vibrant, dynamic woman who took life by the throat. She had lured him into reaching out for love again, warming the cold places inside his heart and filling up the empty places in his soul. He couldn't fathom now how he'd ever thought he could live without her.

He loved her dearly, fiercely.

His tender caress eventually had the desired effect, for Madeline stirred awake. Looking sleep-tousled and warm and oh, so desirable, she turned slowly to gaze up at him.

As if sharing his thoughts, she gave him a languid, sated smile that was pure love.

Rayne felt his heart jolt in his chest. He wanted to see

that beautiful smile every day of his life, wanted her laughter lighting up his days.

"I didn't mean to fall asleep," she murmured huskily. "I hold you to blame, my handsome husband. Your virility devastates mere ordinary females such as I."

Laughing lightly, he touched his fingertips to her lips, loving the joy reflected in her face. "There is nothing whatsoever ordinary about you, darling. And you are even more to blame for us falling asleep. You obliterated my senses this afternoon. I may never recover."

When her smile turned brilliantly sensual, Rayne gave in to his aching hunger and drove his fingers deep into her hair to bring her face close to his. In the instant before he claimed her lips, he saw her lustrous eyes grow smoky and hot.

For a long, pleasurable moment, Madeline yielded to his lush invitation . . . but then she pressed her palms against his naked chest and compelled him to break off his kiss.

"Rayne . . . Will Stokes should be arriving soon, have you forgotten your engagement?"

"No, I haven't forgotten."

"It would be scandalous to be caught lazing abed all afternoon."

"He will understand."

"Seriously, Rayne. . . ."

He capitulated with a final, lingering kiss. "Very well, if you insist."

Rayne helped Madeline rise from the bed then, although her succeeding efforts to wash and dress were interrupted by more frequent kisses and his need to wrap his arms around her.

Clearly she did not mind, however; judging from her delighted sighs, she relished his distractions.

When Rayne assisted with the hooks at the back of her gown, he couldn't resist sliding his hands around her waist to cradle her faintly swelling stomach.

At his gentle touch, Madeline gave another sigh, this one of utter contentment. "It still awes me, how drastically my life has changed," she murmured. "Two months ago I never could have dreamed I would have a wonderful husband to love and cherish, or that I might be expecting your child. I am brimming over with happiness, Rayne."

He rested his chin on the top of her head. "So am I, love."

"Happiness seems to be rife these days. Your grandmother may seriously disapprove of me, but hopefully she will be pleased to learn that your title may soon have an heir. And you should be pleased, knowing you needn't labor at siring a child for a while."

Rayne pressed his smile into her hair. "It was a labor of love, I assure you."

Madeline gave a soft laugh. "And Gerard has found happiness as well, thanks to you. Lynette's parents have accepted him fully as their son. But who would have ever thought that Freddie would bestow his affections on a proper young lady and therefore please his father?"

Rayne's lips curved at the prospect of his impetuous cousin settling down in respectable matrimony. Certainly a great deal had changed in the two months since he'd met Madeline.

"And all three of the Loring sisters are wildly happy in their marriages," Madeline continued her tally. "Perhaps Lily most of all."

The youngest Loring sister had recently returned from her wedding trip with her new husband, the Marquess of Claybourne. Lily had taken to Madeline straight-away, and they were fast becoming friends.

"I will always be grateful," Madeline added sincerely, "to Arabella and Roslyn for helping me capture you, Rayne—and to Fanny, too."

"You give them too much credit, my sweet."

"I don't believe so. Fanny's advice particularly was in-valuable in making you take notice of me."

He hadn't been surprised to discover the name of the courtesan who'd tutored Madeline in the tricks of her trade. What was surprising, however, was learning that Fanny Irwin had set her talents to another career alto-gether—writing Gothic novels. Her first effort had re-cently been published anonymously to vigorous sales if not great literary acclaim.

"Now I only worry about Tess Blanchard," Madeline admitted, her tone turning troubled.

The biggest surprise of all was that Miss Blanchard had found herself compromised by a neighboring duke and had wed him to avoid a full-blown scandal.

"Tess longed to marry for love," Madeline said in con-sternation, "but their union is far from a love match. At least they seem to have a strong physical attraction for one another, judging from the fireworks between them. I hope Fanny can help Tess's marriage the way she did mine."

"Perhaps you should allow them to solve their own problems," Rayne suggested mildly.

Madeline started to disagree, just as she heard the sound of carriage wheels slowing outside in the street. Accompanying Rayne over to the window, she glanced down and recognized the dowager Countess of Haviland's barouche.

A knot formed in the pit of Madeline's stomach at the thought of facing her nemesis again.

"I suppose your grandmother is responding to your message about my condition," she remarked to Rayne. Out of courtesy, he'd sent his elderly relative a brief missive yesterday, informing her of Madeline's likely pregnancy, although he hadn't spoken to Lady Haviland since their heated confrontation at Riverwood many weeks ago.

"I would expect so. We shall see."

Rayne appeared in no hurry to finish dressing, however, and Madeline was even less so. By the time they went downstairs, Lady Haviland was awaiting them in the drawing room.

The dowager rose imperiously when they entered. Yet surprisingly, she wore an uncertain expression on her face, as if she feared her reception. Still, she scrutinized Madeline intently to the point of making her blush.

"I understand felicitations may be in order," Lady Haviland stated coolly, yet with none of the belligerence Madeline expected.

"That depends," Rayne replied, his own voice terse, "on whether you repent your disgraceful conduct. I gave orders for you to be refused admittance until you are willing to treat Madeline properly and welcome her into the family. You must have convinced Walters that you were ready to concede."

The dowager bit her lip. "Yes."

His expression remained cold, giving no quarter, as he put his arm around Madeline's shoulders protectively. "Yes, *what*, Grandmother?"

"I have come . . . to welcome your wife into the family."

Rayne grew impatient at her grudging acquiescence. "My wife's name is *Madeline,* Grandmother. And you may tell her directly to her face, since she is standing right here."

For a moment, a struggle played on the countess's haughty features, but then her inner conflict seemed to collapse. "Very well, then," she said, her tone amazingly contrite as she met Madeline's gaze. "Welcome, Madeline. I was exceedingly wrong to act so abominably toward you, and I humbly beg your forgiveness. It is my fondest hope that we may begin anew."

Taken aback by her ladyship's evident humility, Madeline glanced at Rayne, then again at his grandmother. "Of course, my lady. I would very much like to start anew."

Lady Haviland looked vastly relieved. "Thank you, my dear. And now if you don't mind, I shall sit down. My heart is rather weak, you know."

Madeline saw Rayne's grimness fade, only to be replaced by a hint of exasperated amusement as he went to aid his relative in settling into a comfortable chair.

"Your apology was adequate, Grandmother, even pleasing. But your continued search for sympathy is growing old. According to your doctors, you are quite healthy for a lady of your advanced years. You may even outlast all your grandchildren."

"I seriously doubt that," her ladyship muttered, "when you particularly insist on being so disobliging."

Seeing Rayne's frown, however, she caught his hand. "Forgive me, my boy, I do not mean to quarrel. In all honesty, I am no longer opposed to your marriage. I hoped you would marry well and provide an heir so that your scandalous wretch of an uncle could not claim the title, but I want even more for you to be happy. And Daphne tells me that Madeline has made you very happy and will doubtless be a good mother to your children."

"Extremely happy, Grandmother," Rayne agreed. "But you won't be pleased to learn that I mean to continue working in my previous profession."

Rayne had accepted a position as a special agent reporting to the Home Secretary, Viscount Sidmouth—his task, to keep the country and its citizens safe from domestic threats rather than foreign ones.

Madeline was very glad that Rayne had found a fulfilling new purpose for his special skills, for she understood his driving need to help others. Indeed, his valor and compassion and strong sense of justice were largely what had made her fall in love with him in the first place.

At his announcement, Lady Haviland made a visible effort to bite her tongue. "You have changed my perspective on that front, too, Rayne. Prinny himself praised your valiant service to the Crown, and you know I would never interfere with the Regent's desires. Indeed, you have made me quite proud, my boy."

When Rayne bent down to kiss her cheek, the noblewoman stiffened slightly at his affectionate gesture, then looked pleased. "I must say, Rayne, I am supremely glad you have found happiness in matrimony. Heaven knows, I never did with your grandfather, who wed me only for my fortune."

Pressing her lips together in memory, she returned her attention to Madeline. "You are not as mercenary as I feared, or you would have accepted my offer of a fortune. I think that proves you love my grandson at least a small measure."

"I do love him, Lady Haviland. Immensely."

"If so, then you may be worthy of him after all. And you have drastically improved your appearance with your more fashionable attire. Now if you would only cease teaching at that plebeian school, I could introduce you in my circles with few qualms."

"Grandmother," Rayne said warningly while Madeline only smiled.

Her life would be as fulfilling as Rayne's, teaching and guiding the eager pupils at the Freemantle Academy, forming their young minds and providing them with the aptitude to become young ladies.

But most fulfilling of all would be having her own children. Hers and Rayne's.

"Oh, very well," her ladyship gave in with a huff. "I will do my best to work with what I have."

Just then Walters appeared at the drawing room door and cleared his throat politely. "Mr. Stokes to see you, my lord."

When Rayne raised an eyebrow at Madeline, she knew he was reluctant to abandon her to the mercy of his disapproving relative.

Even so, she voiced encouragement. "Go ahead and see to your business with Mr. Stokes, Rayne. Lady Haviland and I will use the time alone to become better acquainted."

He hesitated, then nodded. "Excuse me, Grandmother, but I have a prior engagement."

Taking Madeline's hand then, Rayne drew her outside, into the corridor.

"Are you certain you can stomach being alone with her?" he asked when he'd shut the door behind them for privacy.

"Yes, I am certain," Madeline replied. "Your grandmother's attempt to reconcile with me is doubtless because she believes your threat to cut her out of your life. But even if she isn't sincere about welcoming me into your family, I have hopes of winning her over someday."

"I still find it remarkable that you are willing to forgive her. You are far more generous than I could ever be."

Madeline smiled. "I can forgive her, Rayne, because deep down she loves you and wants what is best for you. And if you think about it, we also owe her our thanks. She is the one who demanded that you search for a bride. Otherwise, you would never have felt compelled to make a marriage of convenience and wed me."

Rayne grinned slowly, his voice an affectionate tease as he responded, "You are not in the least convenient, love, to my great relief and delight. Fortunately, I relish a challenge."

Madeline laughed. "As do I. I am quite content being wed to a former spy and mastermind. Any other man would have been far too tame and bland for me."

"You have fully tamed me, love. But I believe I deserve greater credit for being astute enough to choose you."

Gazing up at him with amusement, Madeline placed her hand on Rayne's chest, feeling the strong, steady rhythm of his heartbeat. "I am profoundly grateful you chose me, dearest husband. You rescued me from the forlorn life of a spinster."

"And you, sweet Madeline, saved me from a life of

utter boredom and misery. Even more crucially, you saved me from a life without love."

With a soft smile, she shook her head in amazement. "It is a wonder we survived the machinations and follies of our various relatives and acquaintances—my brother, Ackerby, your grandmother, even Freddie."

Rayne slid his arms around her, letting her feel the reassuring warmth of him as his fierce protectiveness surrounded her. "I know. And now, regretfully, duty calls me away."

Lord Sidmouth had requested Rayne's help with a new case, and Rayne had summoned Will Stokes to assist. The two of them were knee-deep in plotting a new operation now.

"Will is waiting for you," Madeline reminded him.

Thankfully, Rayne delayed his departure long enough to share a passionate kiss with her. At the taste of his marvelous lips, she sighed with contentment, feeling loved, feeling treasured and cherished.

And when he finally released her, she let him go willingly. Even though she would miss him while they were apart, she knew a profound joy at the certainty that Rayne would always come home to her.

Her heart swelled at her good fortune as she watched her tall, handsome husband stride away.

With a private smile then, Madeline turned back toward the drawing room in order to rejoin his grandmother. She would win over the imperious Lady Haviland in the end. She'd had ample experience dealing with crotchety old noblewomen, and Rayne's grandmother would be no exception. Particularly if she gave him the heir her ladyship wanted so badly.

Madeline only wished that her own beloved mother could be here to hold her first grandchild in her arms.

Opening the door to the drawing room, Madeline paused, then swallowed the poignant ache in her throat, knowing her mother would be at peace.

"You needn't worry about your children any longer, *Maman*," Madeline murmured. "Gerard and I could not possibly be any happier."

Read on for an exciting taste of

To Desire a Wicked Duke

by Nicole Jordan

Chapter One

I have been off the Marriage Mart for a good while now, but I am quickly learning an indisputable rule of engagement with the opposite sex: When you play with fire, you are likely to be burned....and Rotham is the hottest sort of fire.
— DIARY ENTRY OF MISS TESS BLANCHARD

Richmond, England: October 1817

The kiss was amazingly insipid.

Disappointment surged through Tess Blanchard as Mr. Hennessy drew her more fully into his embrace. She had expected so much more when she acquiesced to his impulsive gesture.

More excitement, more pleasure, more *feeling*. In short, she had secretly longed to be swept away by romantic passion.

Instead she found herself logically analyzing the construction of his love-making. The precise pressure of his lips. The exact angle of his head. The unarousing feel of his arms around her.

There was no spark, no *fire* between them at all, Tess realized sorrowfully. The entire business left her remarkably cold.

Oh, Patrick Hennessy certainly *seemed* skilled in the art of kissing, she mused as his mouth plied hers with increased ardor. But surely a man who counted himself such an expert lover should have elicited a stronger response from her?

Not that she had much basis for comparison. This was only the second man she had ever romantically embraced in her three-and-twenty years.

It had happened purely on a whim. One moment they were laughing together over a line in the comic play Hennessy had written. The next, an arrested expression claimed his features as he gazed down at her. When he stepped closer and bent his head to capture her lips, Tess had no thought of stopping him. For too long she had let herself languish on the shelf in the game of love, refusing to open herself up to renewed heartbreak. But it was past time to reenter the lists.

Admittedly, in Mr. Hennessy she was drawn by both curiosity and the lure of the forbidden. She knew better, of course. A proper lady did not indulge in scandalous experiments with libertine actors behind the stage curtains. Hennessy was known as something of a Lothario among the London theater crowd, in addition to being a brilliant performer, a successful manager of his own troupe, and a budding playwright as well.

Then again, perhaps she was not giving him a fair chance.

Closing her eyes more tightly, Tess made a stronger effort to enter into the spirit of the kiss. In response, Hennessy's hand stole lower down her back, over her derriere, to pull her closer. Despite her own lack of enthusiasm, she had evidently affected *him,* judging by the swelling hardness she felt pressing against her lower abdomen—

"Well, well, are you practicing to play the part of lovers in your production, Miss Blanchard?"

At the sharp-edged drawl, a startled Tess tore her mouth away from Hennessy's—and froze in mortification upon recognizing that sardonic male voice. Obviously she had failed to hear anyone enter the ballroom where their makeshift stage was erected.

Good Lord, what utterly dreadful timing, to have her transgression discovered by the arrogant, infuriating Duke of Rotham, elder cousin of her late betrothed. Rotham had stepped behind the stage curtains to find her locked in a clandestine embrace with the man she had hired to produce her amateur theatrical.

Scalding heat flooded Tess's cheeks as she pulled away from her partner in crime. Hennessy had also reacted to the duke's unexpected appearance by releasing her instantly. Yet the actor looked not only guilty but somewhat alarmed, as if he'd been caught in a hanging offense.

Squaring her shoulders, Tess turned to face Ian Sutherland, the tall, lithe Duke of Rotham. His handsome face was an enigmatic mask in the muted daylight seeping over the stage curtains from the ballroom windows, but his mouth held a tightness that signified displeasure.

He had no right to judge her, she told herself defiantly.

"You are mistaken, your grace," Tess murmured, striving to keep her voice calm as she responded to his mocking tone. "There are no lovers in Mr. Hennessy's play. It is merely a comedy of manners about a mischievous ghost."

"You were testing out a new role then?"

"What may I do for you, Rotham?" Tess asked, ignoring his jibe. "We have only just concluded the dress rehearsal and still have a great deal to accomplish before this evening's performance."

They had constructed a stage at one end of the ballroom of her godmother's country mansion for the theatrical—the crowning entertainment of the charitable benefit Tess had organized. Tess had engaged Hennessy and his troupe to put on the one-act play and direct the houseguests in their respective acting roles.

"I doubt your preparations entail kissing the hired help," Rotham drawled in that annoyingly cynical tone of his.

Tess stiffened. "It is hardly any of your business whom I kiss, your grace."

"I beg to differ."

Renewed ire rose in Tess. She would not allow him to dictate to her, as he was so fond of doing. Indeed, they had had similar arguments before. The Duke of Rotham was head of the family she would have married into had her betrothed not perished two years ago at the Battle of Waterloo. But they had no real blood ties, and Rotham was mistaken in thinking that he had any say over her affairs. Particularly her amorous affairs.

Shifting his attention, Rotham turned his penetrating gaze to Mr. Hennessy, who still seemed wary and on edge. "I expected better of you, Hennessy. You were supposed to be protecting her, not assaulting her. Is this how you fulfill your duties?"

The actor shot the duke a chagrined look of apology.

"I beg your forgiveness, your grace. I fell down in my duties deplorably." Rather sheepishly, he turned to Tess. "A thousand pardons, Miss Blanchard. I was vastly out of line."

Tess started to respond, but Rotham interrupted her. "I'll thank you to leave us, Hennessy. I shall deal with you later."

Her jaw dropped at Rotham's arrogant dismissal, but before she could raise an objection, Hennessy gave her a brief bow, then pivoted with alacrity and disappeared through a part in the curtains.

She remained speechless as she listened to him bound down the stage steps and hurry away across the ball-room. It was hardly chivalrous of him to abandon her to the mercies of the duke, Tess thought resentfully. No doubt he preferred not to challenge a nobleman of Rotham's station and ruthless influence.

However, when she at last gathered her wits enough to protest, Rotham held up an imperious hand, forestalling her. "You should know better than to indulge in trysts with libertines such as Hennessy."

Prickling with indignation, Tess returned a mutinous look. The nerve of him, scolding her for a sin she had not even committed. "I was not indulging in any *tryst,* your grace. It was just a simple kiss."

The corner of Rotham's mouth curled. "It did not look at all *simple* to me. You were participating fully."

He sounded almost angry, although why he would he be angry with her for returning the actor's kiss, she couldn't fathom.

"What if I *was* participating? It is no crime—"

Realizing how high-pitched and flustered her own

voice sounded, Tess took a calming breath and forced a cool smile. "I truly cannot believe your gall, Rotham. How someone of your wicked character can deride another man for rakish behavior—or criticize me for something so innocent as a mere kiss—is the *height* of irony. Do you even recognize your hypocrisy?"

A hint of sardonic amusement tugged at his lips. "I acknowledge your point, Miss Blanchard. But I am not the only one concerned about your relationship with Hennessy. Lady Wingate is worried that you have become overly attached to him. In fact, she sent me to find you."

That gave Tess pause, as doubtless Rotham knew it would. Lady Wingate was not just Tess's godmother but chief patron for her various charities. She could not afford to offend the woman whose generosity impacted so many lives for the better.

"I have not become attached to Hennessy in the least," Tess finally replied. "He is a valued employee, nothing more."

"Do you go around kissing all your employees?" Rotham taunted. Before she could reply, he shook his head in reproach. "Lady Wingate will be severely disappointed in you. She arranged a lavish house party solely for your sake, so you could dun her guests for your various charities. And *this* is how you repay her?"

Unable to refute the charge, Tess regarded Rotham in frustration. Her godmother had long disapproved of her endeavors to promote her charitable organizations and had only recently relented and invited some four dozen wealthy guests to a week-long house party, thereby providing Tess with a captive audience. She'd spent the past week attempting to persuade each one of them to contribute to her causes.

"Do you mean to tattle to her?" she asked Rotham.

His answer, rife with mocking humor, disturbed her. "That depends."

"On what?"

"On whether or not you intend to continue your liaison with Hennessy."

"I tell you, I am *not* having a liaison with him! You have completely misconstrued the matter."

"Who initiated the kiss?"

"What does that matter?"

"If Hennessy took advantage of you, I will have to call him out."

"You cannot be serious!" Tess stared at him, appalled to think he might not be jesting. The last Duke of Rotham, Laurence Sutherland, had ended his licentious career when he was killed in a duel over a married woman by her jealous husband. His son Ian had followed a similar reckless path all through his youth, generating wild tales of gambling and womanizing. Ian Sutherland's scandalous endeavors had earned him the nickname "the devil duke" when he came into the title eight years ago. But surely he would not actually *shoot* Hennessy for the mere act of kissing her.

"You know very well that dueling is illegal," Tess objected, "in addition to being dangerous and possibly even lethal."

Rotham's mouth tightened again, as if he too had recalled his sire's ignominious end. "Indeed."

When he said nothing further, Tess suddenly recalled the confusing remark he'd made before ordering the actor from the ballroom. "What did you mean when you said Mr. Hennessy should have been 'protecting' me?"

Rotham waved a careless hand in dismissal. "It is of no import."

"I should like to know." Tess fixed him with a stubborn gaze, determined not to back down.

He must have sensed her resolve, for he gave a shrug of his broad shoulders. "When you began spending so much time at the Theatre Royal in Covent Garden in preparation for your last charity event, I charged Hennessy with keeping an eye on you. The theater district is a dangerous area, especially for an unescorted young lady."

Her eyebrows lifted in puzzlement. "So you asked him to look after me?"

"Yes. I paid him a significant sum, in fact."

So *that* explained why Hennessy always insisted on escorting her to and from her carriage, Tess realized, and why he had hovered around her whenever she attended rehearsals. She had thought it was because the actor was growing enamored of her company. Irrationally, she couldn't help feeling a prick to her self-esteem.

"My companion usually accompanies me to the theater," she pointed out to Rotham.

"Your companion is an aging spinster with all the substance of a butterfly. She would be no help whatsoever if you were confronted by trouble."

That much was true, Tess conceded. Mrs. Dorothy Croft was tiny and gentle and soft-spoken, as well as being a bit scatterbrained. The impoverished friend of Tess's late mother, Dorothy had needed somewhere to live after being widowed, so Tess had opened her home in Chiswick to her. The relationship had also benefitted Tess. With a genteel, elderly lady to lend her single state respectability, she had much more freedom to conduct her charitable endeavors.

"I have a sturdy coachman and footmen to provide me protection should I require it," Tess argued.

Rotham's gray gaze never faltered. "Even so, I thought it wise to ensure your safety. And you would not readily have accepted any edicts from me."

That was also certainly true. They had long been at odds—which is what made Rotham's current interest in her safety so startling. That he might be seriously concerned for her welfare had never crossed her mind.

"Well, you needn't worry about me, your grace. I am capable of providing for my own protection."

"Then you should refrain from kissing the likes of Hennessy. And he had best keep away from you. If he dares to touch you again, he will answer to me."

At the edge of possessiveness in the duke's tone, Tess's eyebrows narrowed in disbelief. He could not possibly be jealous. No doubt he was merely angry at Hennessy for disobeying a direct order, and at her for daring to contradict him.

"Your transgressions are a thousand times worse, Rotham."

"But I am not an unmarried young lady, as you are."

"I am not so young any more," Tess rejoined.

Instead of replying, Rotham hesitated, as if suddenly aware how sharp his tone had become. Shaking his head, he seemed visibly to repress his emotions, as if distancing himself from their argument.

His succeeding laugh was soft and laced with real amusement. "You are hardly ancient, Miss Blanchard. You only just turned twenty-three today."

Tess eyed him with suspicion. "How did you know it was my birthday?"

"As head of the family, it is my business to know."

"You are not head of *my* family."

"For all practical purposes, I am."

There it was again, that ironic drawl that convinced her he was deliberately attempting to provoke her.

It was infuriating, how Rotham always seemed to get under her skin, Tess reflected. Particularly when she was normally serene and even-tempered.

She had always thought him vexing—and deplorably fascinating. Rotham not only had a wicked reputation, he even *looked* wicked. He had striking gray eyes fringed by dark lashes, with lean, aristocratic features that were handsome as sin. His hair was a rich brown shot with gold threads, several shades lighter than her own sable hue, and held a slight curl. He possessed the muscular build of a sportsman but with a lethal elegance that proclaimed his nobility.

Yet it was Rotham's powerful personality that made him utterly unforgettable.

At the moment his features were mainly in shadow, since it was barely noon on a gray, rainy autumn day and they were shrouded by stage curtains. Yet he still had the strange ability to affect her, Tess acknowledged.

She'd felt that same magnetic allure the first moment of meeting Rotham during her comeout four Seasons ago, when he'd deigned to dance with her. But shortly afterward, she'd fallen in love with his younger cousin Richard.

Ever since, she had felt guilty for her forbidden attraction to the Duke of Rotham. He was every inch the fallen angel. And lamentably even now, she felt his hypnotic pull as his gray gaze bored into her. . . . .